WHEN BUTTERFLIES CRY

NINIE HAMMON

STERLING & STONE

WHEN BUTTERFLIES CRY

Chapter One

On Monday, August 11, 1969,
two events on different sides of the planet
happened at *exactly the same instant.*

One of them was in the
Vale of Amberclewydd, Wales,
where it was 10:33 a.m.

ALASTAIR SHELBOURNE STOPPED in his daily trek up the
mountain to the ridge when he heard voices rising out of
the fog that lay like clotted cream in the valley at his feet.
On the first day of the school year, children in the Gaynor
Junior School were singing *All Things Great And Beautiful* and
their voices, drifting eerily up through the thick white mist
into the bright morning sunshine, were the voices of
angels. The 62-year-old grandfather stood still, listening.
Then he smiled. It was the last time he ever would.

Seconds later, he heard a grinding, rumbling sound.
When he looked up, his final smile melted off his face like
wax from a flickering candle flame. The gigantic pile of

coal slurry on the mountain above the village—above the *school*—was *moving!* The slurry had begun to slide, to flow down into the fog below in great liquefied waves, a thundering black avalanche.

For every moment of Alastair's few remaining hours on earth, he would hear that rumble. Long after the heartbeat of eerie silence that suddenly fell over the village below, long after the screams of the injured and the desperate cries of horrified parents finally stilled, he would hear the roaring, crashing, grinding sound of a million tons of coal waste plunging down the mountainside.

Only one other villager saw the slag heap collapse into the valley below. From a field dotted with grazing milk cows above the puddle of fog near the school, ten-year-old Andy Shelbourne turned from a just-milked Welsh Black, stared in stupefied horror and went instantly numb all over. The bucket slid out of the child's unfeeling fingers and dropped to the ground. Even before the milk splashed out on the grass, the youngster had kicked off the heavy, muddy Wellies and was sprinting barefoot toward the gray stone building where the sound of children singing had begun to falter, drowned out by a great rumbling roar.

Just as the wall of liquefied coal waste slammed into the back of the school, Andy raced through the front door, looked up and saw the roof collapsing. There was only time and breath enough to call out a single word—Baby Girl's name.

With that cry, a sound echoed in the child's head, as if the name were ricocheting off the stone walls in the ancient village church. But the echoing voice was not Andy's. *Someone else* had cried out and the two anguished voices melded to produce an agonized wail so loud and powerful it ripped open the very throne room of heaven itself, and for a frozen moment it drowned out the roar of the black monster hurling down the mountainside.

Only for a moment, though. Then the rumble swallowed the world and the avalanche buried the school and everyone in it beneath more than a million tons of sticky coal slag. No one inside Gaynor Junior School that day got out alive.

The other event was 6,000 miles away,
on the east bank of the Song Dong Nai River, South
Vietnam,
where it was 4:33 p.m.

AT THE INSTANT a little girl's name rang out above the roar of death in a Welsh village, U.S. Army Chaplain Grayson Addington fell to his knees outside another village on the other side of the planet, tilted his head back and called out another little girl's name.

"Saaaadie!"

When the word left his lips, the name reverberated in his head, echoed like it was bouncing around in an oil drum. More than that, he heard another voice cry out a name, too, in perfect unison, and the combined voices produced a great roaring sound.

There followed a moment of such profound silence that surely the universe held its breath, the globe of earth stopped revolving on its axis and ceased spinning around the sun. Something *happened* in that moment. Something fearful and powerful. Grayson sensed it, but didn't know what it was.

Then he slumped and whispered, "Almighty God, *please!* Protect her!"

Life slowly let out the gasp it had sucked in, breathed a tormented sigh of fear, pain and loss, and Grayson felt a hand on his shoulder.

"Padre?"

He opened his eyes and for a moment saw nothing but bright light. Then the reality of steaming jungle, the river stink of black mud and dead fish, the harsh, staccato bark of Vietnamese voices and his pack straps cutting into his shoulders slammed down around him with a clang like the door of a jail cell banging shut.

"You okay, sir? You were yelling."

"Yeah, I'm …" he struggled to his feet and bent to pick up his helmet. The small silver cross on the front was barely visible through the encrusted mud.

Grayson was tall, six feet four, with a rugged, beard-stubbled face where easy smiles once fit comfortably in the folds around his mouth. His hazel eyes, at one time warm and engaging, now peered out of deep, dark hollows beneath thick black brows. When he clamped his helmet back on his head, a lock of dirty hair Piper maintained was "the exact same color as maple syrup" escaped to fall in a widow's peak on his forehead.

Beside Grayson was one of the replacements, the new guy, Washington. They called him Dollar Bill, or sometimes just Dollar. The soldier looked at him with obvious concern in his eyes. Young eyes. Nineteen, maybe. Greenhorn. It didn't take long here to learn how to stifle your give-a-damn and when that happened, Dollar Bill wouldn't allow himself to care about *anything*—about the guy next to him getting his arm shot off—let along worrying about Grayson's momentary brain burp.

That's what it'd been. A brief black-out. It wasn't the

first. A kind of flashback, though it wasn't like all the others. They had been re-enactments of his ever-growing repertoire of horrible experiences. What he could remember of this one—it was fading blessedly fast—was utter darkness. Then the darkness moved, writhed, rumbled and he realized it was a thing, a living thing with dumb, evil intent—rushing toward Sadie! The toddler lay sleeping peacefully in her "big girl" bed in her grandmother's house in the mountains of West Virginia and the huge monster was after her, its mouth open, ready to—

Head injury. Combat fatigue. Exhaustion. Shell shock. Take your pick.

"Father, I—"

"Do I look like your father, soldier?" Grayson growled. He pointed to his neck. "You see a white collar?"

"No, sir. It's … I understand why you..." He glanced back over his shoulder at the village where a little girl stood beside the last hut.

Grayson turned then and his eyes met hers.

"Go on," he told Dollar Bill and shrugged the young soldier's hand off his shoulder. "Give me a minute."

Grayson was nailed to the spot by Nguyen's gaze. He could only look, though. He couldn't do anything to help her. He couldn't protect her when the Cong slipped into the village tonight or tomorrow or the next day. Flushing out collaborators, summarily executing anyone who'd gotten chummy with the Americans.

Had Nguyen been careful to throw away all the candy wrappers, the ones she folded and put in her pocket? Had she—?

"Gotta go *now*, Padre," KFC, the radio man, called out. The squirrelly little chicken farmer was as jumpy as spit on a griddle.

"All the APCs are gone but ours," Haystack put in. "We don't hurry, we're gonna be flyin' solo."

Dollar Bill put his hand on Gray's shoulder again and this time Gray reluctantly allowed Dollar's grip to urge him toward the armored personnel carrier. But he kept looking back. His gaze was hooked to Nguyen's until she lowered her head, turned and walked slowly into the village. As he stumbled toward the waiting APC, he frantically tried to banish Nguyen's face, tried to replace it with the face of his own little girl. He hadn't held Sadie, touched her soft skin and golden hair since she was eighteen months old, had watched her grow into an adorable toddler in pictures. But he couldn't find those images, those frozen slices of reality, anywhere in his head. He only saw Nguyen, imagined her face a mask of terror if somebody in the village ratted her out to the Cong.

Two days later
Wednesday, August 13,1969
Vale of Amberclewydd, Wales
Noon.

It was the fog. Maybe if it hadn't been foggy that morning down in the valley … Maybe …

"Maybes'll drive ye daft," Alastair Shelburne said aloud in Welsh, but nobody heard him and most wouldn't have understood him if they had. Only the old in Gaynor still spoke their native language.

If the fog hadn't … He didn't speak the words, but he couldn't keep them out of his mind as he stood in the tiny vestibule of the small Welsh chapel, the cold of the ancient stone floor seeping up through the holes in his shoes, the smell of wet dirt mixed with the cloying aroma of death in his nostrils.

Stretched out on the hand-carved oak pews in the sanctuary were one hundred nine bodies from the school, laid feet to head, four to a pew some of them because they were so small. The cemetery would soon be full of fresh-cut headstones, white teeth among the centuries-old gray stones so pitted and weathered the names had long since worn away.

There'd be one hundred thirty-one new graves once they recovered all the bodies. They'd dug out Baby Girl. She lay in there beyond the wooden doors, her face waxen, only 6 years old! His older grandchild had been home with the cows that day and should have been safe! But Andy'd rushed into the school to save Baby Girl. Alastair let out a shuddering sigh. Now Andy was gone, too, still entombed with more than a dozen other children and two teachers in the rubble of a school buried under a pile of coal slag fifty feet deep! They wouldn't dig down to the bottom of it, wouldn't dig out the nearby cottages or the post office or …

If they'd seen it coming, they could have got out, got away!

He didn't believe that, of course. He *had* seen it coming and there'd been no time to get the children out. But there had to be someone, something to blame. One hundred and twenty-two children—6, 7 and 8 years old—half the children in the village!—had been crushed to death at their desks as their sweet voices carried up to him through the mist.

Alastair strangled back a sob. Wasn't seemly to cry in public, though he was alone in the vestibule with no one there to see. Both his grandchildren, his only kin in all the world, were gone.

The thick white fog had hidden death from the children's tender eyes but not from their ears. They'd heard the rumble. That sound had been growling non-stop in Alastair's head day and night since it happened two days ago. He couldn't sleep for the roar of it. Couldn't think with it booming in there between his ears. It was the last sound the precious little ones ever heard.

It would be the last sound Alastair Shelbourne ever heard, too.

The old man turned and stepped out of the church into air so wet it left moisture on every surface it touched. He lifted his shotgun. A small man with short arms, he could still reach the length of the barrel with the end of it in his mouth. Alastair Shelbourne was the first villager who crumbled under the staggering weight of grief. He wouldn't be the last.

The rifle barrel felt cold on his lips, cold as death. Then he squeezed the trigger.

Wednesday, August 13, 1969
North of Long Binh, South Vietnam
where it was late afternoon.

THE SOUND of a single gunshot startled Grayson Addington awake. He didn't pass through any of the intermediate stages, didn't go from groggy or fuzzy to bleary-eyed alert. He simply went from sound, dreamless sleep to hyper awareness in an instant.

Well, there was a moment of confused disorientation until he figured out that he had, indeed, fallen sound asleep standing up. He dug at his swollen red eyes with knuckles cracked and oozing pus from jungle rot. Shook his head. He had only blinked—or so he thought—as he

8

leaned against a post that supported a piece of roof and the last remaining wall of a hut in … Nope, it was gone. The name of this particular village was nowhere in his memory banks. It looked, smelled, sounded and felt exactly the same as the previous half dozen villages they'd passed through in the two days since he'd climbed into the last APC in a convoy and driven away from a dark-eyed little girl. He hadn't slept more than a few hours snatched here and there since then, couldn't close his eyes without seeing her face.

At least Grayson hadn't dropped his rifle when he nodded off, still clutched the M16. Well, technically it wasn't *his* rifle, of course. Grayson was a chaplain; chaplains were non-combatants.

"They're pulling out," he whispered to Haystack, incredulous.

One shot meant they were leaving, didn't it? Full scale frontal attacks came at dawn and dusk when it was hard to see movement in the undergrowth. Sneak attacks came at night, when you sometimes didn't find out Charlie was there until you felt the cold steel of a bayonet.

Haystack was crouched in the bushes in front of a tree a few feet away, a gangly farm kid with hay-colored hair that went every which way—even wet. He'd said the only time in his life he hadn't had to slick it down with Vitalis was when they'd shaved his head in boot camp. But it had grown out long now.

Haystack'd gone boots-down out of the same gunship as Gray, the first chopper carrying Charlie Company of the 151st Infantry Kentucky National Guard, and now his short-timer's stick was so short he kept it in his pocket! A short-timer's stick was a tree limb, a branch, whatever a soldier could get his hands on to mark every day so he could keep track of his time in-country. Gray had left his

… somewhere. But Haystack had sat down that first night and carefully carved on four small sticks *every day he had left*—deep groves evenly spaced from one end to the other. Then every morning after that, he cut off the end of a stick at the last mark. Now, he was down to one stick and it was the size of a harmonica.

Which meant, of course, that Haystack, Gray and the remaining members of Charlie Company were 30-days-and-out so they weren't even supposed to be on this patrol. Short-timers like that were unreliable. Once you'd made it through 11 months here and the end was in sight, you got to acting funny. The fatalism that kept the terror at bay began to evaporate as soon as you could see daylight at the other end, could actually consider life and people and a world beyond. Some short-timers would start wearing two flack jackets, would sleep in their helmets or keep their faces ash-blackened even when they weren't on patrol. Haystack had stopped brushing his teeth because he said he didn't want them shining, making a target. Had completely stopped smiling, too.

"Haystack, you reckon they're gone?" Gray whispered.

Haystack still didn't answer. Gray turned to look at him, saw the bullet hole in the center of his forehead right below the lip of his helmet and the gray slime of his lique-fied brains on the tree trunk that held him upright, like he was just sitting there staring at the sky.

Well, that explained the one gunshot. Sniper.

Gray quickly looked away, sucked in a breath, tensed for the agonizing blow of grief. But it didn't come. He felt nothing at all. And that scared him almost as bad as the gooks still hiding out there in the trees. He couldn't muster so much as a wisp of sorrow, let alone shed a tear for a poor kid who still had a trace of adolescent acne and had admitted shamefacedly that he was still a virgin at nineteen.

Setting aside emotion—terror, grief—to do what had to be done was what soldiers called "Doin' the necessary." Gray had gotten way too good at it.

Then the edges of the world around him began to soften, darken. Long shadows stretched out toward him, sound dialed slowly down until he could hear nothing at all. He shook his head furiously to clear it. Battle fatigue. Exhaustion. Like what had hammered him outside Nguyen's village. No, *not* like that. Not at all. Something had *happened* then. Some great force, some pulsing energy had—

He froze, stared at the road with wide, unbelieving eyes. Then Grayson Addington forgot all about the power he'd felt two days ago that was destined to change the course of every day of the rest of his life. The power that was, in fact, at work at that very moment on a West Virginia mountainside. He forgot about everything, his attention riveted to the apparition that had materialized on the other side of the road.

Nguyen!

At first, Grayson thought he really had blacked out, that he was dreaming or hallucinating. But then KFC hollered, "Look, it's Nguyen!"

It couldn't be, but it was. The little girl he'd abandoned two days ago in Yan Ling, at the mercy of the other villagers to protect her from the murderous wrath of the Viet Cong—that little girl had just stepped out of the jungle. She merely stood there, looking at Grayson.

"How'd she get here?" Dollar Bill called out. He was crouched beside an overturned cart, next to the bloated carcass of a dead pig. "We left her thirty klicks back."

A klick was a little over half a mile.

"She couldn't have walked this far," Beanie said from the other side of the cart. "*Somebody* brought her ..."

"...and it wasn't *us*," Bagpipes finished for him from his spot a few feet back, hunkered down behind a stack of firewood.

Grayson's heart began to hammer in his chest and every explosive pump shook him. As he watched, hypnotized, Nguyen took a couple of steps in their direction, then stopped.

"Hi, Grape!" she called out. Her lips parted in a huge smile, so wide it seemed to split open the whole bottom portion of her face. Belying its presence were twin streams of tears running down her cheeks.

Grayson felt a hole open up beneath him, felt himself begin to topple down into it.

"I find you," she said cheerily, paused, then continued just as cheerily, "Now you un-ray."

Un-ray. Pig Latin. *Run!*

Chapter Two

Sadler Hollow, West Virginia
Wednesday, August 13, 1969
where it was morning.

Piper Addington knelt on the shiny hardwood floor, tucked a strand of black hair behind her ear and took the crying toddler into her arms.

"Shhh, Sadie," she crooned, hugged the little girl tight to her chest and rocked slowly back and forth. "It's okay, Honey, Mommy's gotcha. Shhhh."

The little girl continued to cry, great heaving sobs of terror, and clutched her mother's neck so tight Piper could barely catch her breath. She looked out over the child's shoulder at Marian, who shook her head sadly.

"It was the m-m-mailman, that new young fella, one of Charley Bishop's boys, come to the door 'cause the catalogue wouldn't fit in the mailbox," Marian said, indicating the thick book marked "Sears" on the kitchen table. "P-p-pore little thing. Never did see a child feared of strangers as she is."

Piper could feel the toddler trembling, almost vibrating against her chest. "Did he say something to her? Startle her?"

"He was only bein' friendly, leaned over and said 'hidy' through the screen and she commenced to squallin'."

Sadie was frightened of everybody and *terrified* of men. And that was a significant problem because Sadie was … what was it Carter'd called her … a fairy child, so strikingly beautiful she could literally take a total stranger's breath away. Her eyes were extraordinary. Piper had read somewhere that Elizabeth Taylor had violet eyes. Sadie's were darker than violet, a shade of blue that was almost purple, huge, wide and sparkling, cradled in lashes so long and thick they lay like twin fans on her rosy cheeks. Her oval face was flawless, with a heart-shaped mouth, full, bright-red lips and dimples in each cheek so deep you could eat pudding out of them. At not quite two-and-a-half years old, her hair was a thick cascade of shiny, honey-colored natural curls that hung down past her waist. Sadie's was an enchanted, ethereal, other-worldly beauty that everyone who saw her gawked at or gushed over— which never failed to send Sadie into hysterics.

Piper pried the child's arms away from her neck, set her down on the floor and leaned back.

"You're fine." She reached out and wiped a tear off the child's left cheek with her thumb. "Nobody's going to hurt you." She made her voice sound relaxed and confident. "Now, go on and play."

Sadie's breathing still hitched in and out in the aftermath of the crying jag and when Piper stood, the toddler lifted her arms and wailed, "Hold you!"

"I'm not going to hold you," Piper said firmly, whereupon Sadie grabbed her mother's leg with her left arm and popped her right thumb into her mouth.

"And get that thumb out of your mouth," Piper said out of habit, knowing the child would keep the thump right where it was, snug as a cork in a bottle of white lightning, until she calmed down, and nothing short of an amputation could remove it. "Let go of my leg and scat. Go on now, shoo."

Grudgingly, Sadie released her grip on Piper's leg and wandered over to a metal stove and miniature refrigerator Carter'd brought to her a couple of weeks ago. She removed the thumb from her mouth only long enough to tell her mother, "I make fri chicklin for Rasmus" then popped it back in. A small smile skittered so fast across the lips wrapped around her thumb it was hard to tell if it'd ever really been there at all. She picked up a small plastic frying pan and placed it on the fake burner and began to stir make-believe food with her left hand.

Piper watched her for a moment, studied the child. Thought again as she had countless times before that the little girl bore little resemblance to either of her parents. Both she and Grayson were dark. Her own hair was, in fact, as black as the coal they dug out of the mountain, her eyes twin chocolate drops. But Sadie was as fair as her Uncle Carter.

Which likely didn't please Grayson.

Piper sighed.

She suspected there might be quite a few things that didn't please her husband when he got home in October. The last time Piper and Grayson had been together had been in April—a week to the day before the deadly ambush at Fire Base Eagle's Nest—and even then he'd been somebody she didn't know. It had been just the two of them in Hawaii for a week of R & R and it'd been R & R alright. Ranting and Raving. No, that wasn't fair. Most of the time it'd been Restrained and Reserved. They'd hardly talked at all. *He* had hardly talked at all—which had made his shouting tirade after she accidentally slammed a door so dramatic. And what would he be like now, after he'd had to send thirty-nine of the boys he'd ministered to for four years to hospitals in the U.S. and eighteen more back home to Kentucky in body bags?

"Y-y-you alright?" Marian asked. Her voice, soft and airless, shook in rhythm with the random tremor. The intermittent palsy that gripped her whole body in an involuntary vibration sometimes rocked her so violently she sounded like a little kid who'd just come in the house with teeth chattering after playing outside in the snow. "I heard you up last night with the l-l-little un. You gonna g-g-get big ole dark circles underneath your eyes."

Marian Addington leaned against the frame of the door leading into the kitchen, tried to make it look casual, not like she'd have fallen down if the jam hadn't been there to hold her up. Her thick, coarse hair, the dark gray of a ten-penny nail was pulled back into a tight bun at the base of her neck with a spider-web hairnet to corral any stragglers. In the loose-fitting green print dress cinched with her ever-present apron, her bones stuck out at harsh angles. Flesh hung loose on her face and her cornflower blue eyes were sunk in deep hollows. But the eyes were alive! Sharp and quick as they had ever been. Constant agony hadn't dulled them. Yet.

"I'm fine," Piper said, "but you're not! You go sit down and let me bring you—"

"Don't you be fussin'—"

"I'll make you a cup of tea."

"I can get tea my own self. I'm not—"

There was a knock at the front door.

Sadie let out a startled little cry, dropped the plastic bowl full of blocks she was stirring with a big wooden spoon and raced toward the closest adult, Marian, and tried to bury herself in her grandmother's aproned skirt. If the old woman hadn't held fast to the door frame, the toddler would have knocked her off her feet like a tackle diving for a receiver below the knees.

Piper turned toward the door. Her heart began to knock so hard her vision pulsed with every beat. She hadn't noticed that Marian had pushed the door closed after Sadie'd come unglued over the mailman. Piper always kept the door *open*, only the screen shut, so she could see if a black car pulled up out front, see if two unsmiling soldiers in dress uniforms got out. So she'd know before they even stepped up on the porch. For some reason, that didn't seem as horrible as opening the door and finding them there, eyes full of the nightmare truth their words had not yet spoken.

Piper's mouth went as dry as a dust bunny. She'd dreamed it again last night, awakened in the midnight dark in sweat-tangled sheets. Maybe she'd cried out and that's what Marian had heard.

The dream never varied. Instead of a black car and soldiers walking slowly, solemnly up the walk to the porch, it is Grayson himself. In the evening shadows, the gray half-light of dusk, Grayson walks silently up the road, dressed in his combat uniform, a duffel bag slung over one shoulder. His face is unsmiling, his skin bleached the kind of white moonlight imparts to fair skin, bloodless skin. And there's no moon. His clunky boots don't disturb the dust in the road and in that perfectly normal way of dreams, she can see him, but she can also see through him, can see the trees behind him as if he were a glass holding dirty water. The whole front part of his shirt is black in the dim light, but she knows its real color is red. His shirt is soaked in black-red blood. He doesn't speak, just stands there, staring at her with dead eyes. That's when she starts to scream, a wail as haunting as the lonely cry of children lost in the dark. It is that cry that always awakens her.

She could hear a faint echo of it now.

"It's only Stella, bringing over some squash out of her garden," she told Sadie, but her voice wavered. "Or Digger with that chain he borrowed."

She crossed to the door and stood in front of it, willing herself to reach out. But her trembling hand refused to obey.

Chapter Three

THE SUDDEN THUNK of a bullet sent splinters into Grayson's hair out of the wall he was leaning against and he cringed back, hunkered down lower, jerked his gaze away from the little girl in the road and followed the line of fire to the trees where the sniper was hidden. When the gooks pulled back, they always left snipers behind to pick off as many as they could to keep you from following them.

Haystack wouldn't be following. He wouldn't be going home to that girl he said had eyes the blue-green of Kentucky bluegrass. The gawky blond farm boy would never again sound that braying laugh, either, like he'd done from the doorway of the hut that day after Nguyen saved Grayson's life.

A flare catapults Grayson from an uneasy sleep. Advancing gooks have tripped a wire that sent the torch high into the black sky and the whole world instantly turns an odd florescent white.

Whap!

The bullet flies by so close to Gray's right cheek he can actually feel the air rearrange itself in its wake. Grayson had hunkered down the best he could in his hole, tried to fold his lanky frame in tight enough to completely fit under his poncho in the drenching rain, and now he has to struggle to sit up.

Still he manages to level his rifle a full second before his mind tells him to, and the rest of what happens lags behind, too. Like when the lips of the people on the black-and-white screen of the Magnavox television in the PX at Ft. Bragg moved but were out of sync with the sound, the words delayed by a beat or two. Reality is like that now. Gunshots slam into their targets a beat behind the splat sound. Men fall, their death screams a full second after blood spews out of their mouths in their final breath.

Claymores rip through the gooks' ranks, mowing them down like a scythe, but more spring up to take their place. Again and again he fires, each retort a beat behind the recoil.

Then he pulls the trigger and there is no recoil. Even the silence of an empty magazine is delayed a second.

The gook he is trying to shoot is forty feet away. And then he is right in front of Grayson. One, two. With no time that Grayson is aware of in between.

It seems to take a hundred years to leap to his feet and slam the butt of his rifle into the gook's weapon, knocking it aside. Then Gray jumps out of the hole, bends low and starts to run toward the only available cover—bushes next to the latrines.

He's almost there when something slams into his side—a boot— and all the air explodes out of his lungs. He sees a flash of brown coming at his face, like the gook has swung the butt of his own rifle around at Grayson. Then the world goes black.

The stench awakens him. The overpowering, putrid smell of excrement—human, not animal—is so strong it burns his nostrils when he inhales. Grayson opens his eyes, sees a green blur and closes them again. But he can't breathe. He starts to cough and feels a small hand clamp firmly over his mouth. Lips next to his ear whisper soft but harsh, "Shhhh."

He manages to choke off the cough but is certain he will not be able to hold onto the vomit that is rising in his throat at the stench. He opens his eyes, tries to focus, to hold on.

All he can see is dirt in front of his face. He is jammed into some tight space with a weight on top of him and he can barely move his diaphragm to get a breath. And the stink!

Involuntary heaving starts in his gut. The hand clamps tighter over his mouth. Whoever is on top of him can feel the spasms. Gray can't move, and with that hand over his face, when he starts to vomit, he'll choke. All at once, he feels horrifically claustrophobic.

Penned in. Can't breathe. About to—

"Swallow it or die!" The whisper is so soft it is like he thought it instead of heard it. And so harsh it is like a slap in the face.

The accent is unmistakable. Vietnamese.

One of the AVRN—South Vietnamese Army soldiers who followed along behind the GIs, watching what they did and nodding their heads up and down as if they understood what was going on? No, whoever is draped over his back is as small as a child.

Grayson summons every ounce of strength he possesses. One beat. Two. The reflexive heaving batters against his rigid diaphragm like waves in a storm hammering the rocks on the shore. Again and again.

He clamps his jaws together so tight pain shoots up the muscles in the side of his face and into his ears.

He holds his breath … and then the world begins to go dim and is no more.

GRAYSON HELD HIS BREATH NOW, too. His heart hammered in the big vein in his neck as he swept his gaze in a wide arc across the trees, searching for a deeper shadow in the shade, a length of limb too straight. He examined every leaf, every twig. Life and death dangled by a bright, slender thread—the glint of sunlight on metal.

He saw nothing, though, scanned the mottled, shadowy

jungle a second time, then slowly sighed out his breath and allowed he gaze to settle on Nguyen.

Marian Addington felt Sadie crash into her legs and the jarring impact set the soup of razor blades, nails and shards of broken glass—that's how she pictured it—in her belly to sloshing around, slicing her open in half a dozen different places.

The sudden agony in her gut didn't hurt near as bad as the sudden terror in her heart, though. She knew just like Piper did who might well be standing on the porch, understood why she raised her hand so slowly to open the door. That mutual dread was part of the bond the two women shared, which was much deeper than standard mother-in-law/daughter-in-law fare. Marian often thought of Ruth and Naomi from Scripture. "Whether thou goest, I will go, whether thou dwellest, I will dwell. Your people shall be my people and your God my God."

Please, Lord, don't let it be no soldiers out there. Don't take my Grayson ... our Grayson.

The only woman *either* of her sons—Grayson or Carter—had ever taken a shine to still hesitated, her hand frozen in the air inches from the knob. Another beat, then Piper reached out and pulled the door open. Marian tensed, wanted to look away but couldn't.

Piper blocked her view, and the old woman's vision had got so bad lately that of a night when she read her Bible, she had to use a flashlight, squeeze up her eyes all squinty like and get down so close the pages fluttered when she breathed. Didn't mind that, of course. A body had ought to get up close to the word of God and breathe it down deep into their soul.

Right now though, Marian wanted to see clear! Almost as bad as she wanted the good Lord to strike her blind so she wouldn't have to look.

Piper shifted position then, moved out of her line of sight to reveal … *not soldiers.* A child. A little girl. And even from where she stood—even with her old blind eyes—Marian could see that the pore little thing'd been beat up something fierce.

~

Piper was too shocked, too relieved to think, couldn't seem to get her wits about her to say anything at all to the life-sized Raggedy Ann doll on the other side of the screen.

And that's what the little girl looked like, with hair the multi-colored hues of the flames that licked up off the logs in the fireplace on a winter's night—shades of bright red with streaks of yellow, copper and burnt orange. It lay in thick braids on her shoulders tied at the ends with pieces of twine.

Though her shiny hair was obviously clean, you could see dirt and little pieces of … something, little rocks, maybe, on her head and braids. Her shirtwaist dress was made of some threadbare fabric that might once have been pale blue. It was too filthy now to tell for sure, with a tear in the right sleeve and smeared with dirt. Her feet were bare and scratched up, as were her legs and arms.

Bright red freckles stuck out like sequins on her alabaster skin—but only a spray of them on her nose, nowhere else. The rest of her face was flawless—well, except for the ugly bruise that colored her right cheek greenish purple.

And the split lip.

And the black eye.

Piper sucked in a breath, the sense of déjà vu so strong it almost made her dizzy. She had looked like that—*exactly* like that when she was about this little girl's age, except her hair had been black instead of red. But the similarity wasn't about braids and freckles. It was about bruises, blood and fear. And whoever had blacked this little girl's *right* eye was likely left-handed. Piper's father had been left-handed, too.

"I'm thirsty," the little girl said simply, her voice emotionless. She stared straight ahead but didn't really seem to be looking at Piper at all. What she said next finally broke the spell and set Piper free. "If you've a mind, a glass of water and I'll be on my way."

"You'll do no such thing," Piper said, swinging the screen door open wide. "You'll come on in this house and sit down and I'll get you something to drink. And something to eat, too. I'll bet you're hungry, and I've got…"

Her voice trailed off. What did she have?

"Why, we've g-g-got fried bread, that's what." Marian's spoke from behind her. She was still standing in the kitchen doorway with Sadie wrapped like a coiled rope around her legs. "Least we will have soon's I f-f-fix it. With my tomato jelly."

The two women exchanged a look that said everything that needed to be said.

"Come on, now," Piper said, and gestured in the open door. "I got lemonade …"

The little girl advanced slowly. She didn't look so much frightened as disoriented and confused, looking around her like she'd just awakened from a dream and wasn't quite sure yet where she was. She stepped in off the rough board porch to the polished board floor only far enough so the screen would close behind her. Then she stood, looking around.

Piper felt a surge of emotions as tangled as last year's Christmas lights. She wanted to wrap her arms around the poor little girl and reassure her that everything would be alright now, that no one would hurt her anymore. She couldn't do that, of course, because clearly it would spook the child and because it wasn't necessarily true.

Get her some lemonade. Make her something to eat. Worry about the rest of it later.

"You sit down here on the couch and I'll—"

"A drink is all I'm needing. Just some water. Don't trouble yourself over me." She stood resolutely where she was.

"All right, you stay there and I'll get you some lemonade—or juice. Would you like some—?"

"Just water."

"Water it is then."

Piper turned and started for the kitchen. She saw Sadie peak out of the folds of her grandmother's dress at the older child standing in the doorway

If Sadie started to wail…

But that, of course, was exactly what she did.

She pulled her head out of the folds of fabric until one whole eye was clear and she got a good look at the little girl standing in the doorway.

Sadie let out a shriek, then, an inarticulate cry that almost seemed to have a word in it somewhere. She let go of her grandmother's legs, slipped out of the folds of fabric and raced across the room … *toward* the little girl. When she got there, she grabbed the child around the knees, looked up into her face and began chattering in the nonsense babble that always replaced speech when she was excited.

Piper's mouth literally dropped open. She felt it, and some part of her spinning mind registered how comical she must look, standing there with her mouth agape. Marian's hand flew to her throat and she stood motionless, too, staring in disbelief.

The little girl didn't freeze though. In fact, she thawed. All the tension seemed to drain out of her. She sank to her knees on the floor before Sadie.

"Well, hello, little pretty," she said. "What's your name?"

"Sabie!" She held up two fingers. "Sabie dis many."

Then Sadie launched herself at the little girl and threw her arms around the older child's neck with such wild abandon she almost knocked the little girl backward.

"Sabie house," she said, as language took over from babble. She let go of her strangle hold long enough to gesture at the room. "*My* house. I hab Rasmus, too. He my teddy bear." She held her chubby hands about two feet apart. "Dis big. He in my room, Sabie room. But Rasmus nose gone. Lost it." Then she threw her arms around the little girl's neck again, clinging in delight every bit as tightly as she had clung to Piper in terror only a few minutes earlier.

The little girl hugged Sadie just as fiercely. She closed her eyes and held the toddler tight to her chest.

"Such an angel you are," she said. "What a pretty, sweet, sweet angel."

Piper looked a question at Marian. The blank expression on the older woman's face likely mirrored her own.

Marian found her voice first.

"Go on then," she said to Piper. "Get a glass of water for …" she stopped. "Why, I'm forgettin' my m-mmanners. I'm Marian Addington and this here's my daughter-in-law, Piper." She smiled. "'Pears you done met Sadie. What's your name, Sweetheart?"

A distant look came into the child's eyes, as if she were struggling to remember her name. Or perhaps to think up a fake one.

"Margaret …" Clearly there was more but she stopped, offered nothing beyond that.

"Margaret's a right pretty name, but I b-b-bet you answer to somethin' shorter, doncha," Marian said.

The child nodded.

"Maggie?"

The little girl looked confused, then shrugged.

"Aye, Maggie's short for Margaret," she said.

Chapter Four

Grayson stared unblinking at Nguyen, then he resolutely closed his eyes, kept them shut, certain that when he opened them again, she would be gone. Now he couldn't see the world, but he could still smell it—sweat, smoke, dead pig. You couldn't deny a reality that stunk, though this one didn't smell nearly as bad as what he'd awakened to the day Haystack found him in Yan Ling.

The hand over his mouth is gone, but not the stink. Where had he been? And where is he now? He doesn't open his eyes, tries to assess his situation and position without moving.

He has bobbed up to the surface of awareness several times, but isn't sure if he has been unconscious or merely asleep. He is lying on his back on a straw mat, can feel it between him and the hard packed ground. He can smell the eye-watering stink of the Vietnamese dish made from rotted cabbage—mingled with the feces stink.

He is also aware of a headache that throbs in heartbeat bursts of torture. The pain forces a tiny groan out between his lips.

"You awake, GI?"

He opens his eyes, struggles to focus until he can make out the outline of a very small person, a child, a young girl, sitting on the ground beside him in a dimly lit hut.

"You thirsty?"

He is! So thirsty his tongue and the roof of his mouth come apart as reluctantly as two strips of Velcro. He nods and the little girl produces a tin cup. She lifts his head up so he won't choke when she puts it to his lips and he drinks greedily, long and deep. Now he can talk.

"Where am I?"

"I find you in dead bodies." After a battle, kids often swarmed over the bodies and stripped them bare. "But you still breathing. Cong coming so I roll you like log over into—" She uses a Vietnamese word he doesn't know, but her tone and the way she wrinkles her nose—and the stench that wafts up from his clothing translates it for him. "—to hide."

She points to the cross on his helmet beside the mat.

"You from Jesus. Don't kill."

Grayson thinks of the men who'd fallen as the commandeered M16 recoiled against his shoulder. He'd had the presence of mind even then to be surprised at how much it was like hunting back home. Deer, though, not squirrels. You stalked squirrels; you waited for deer to come to you. And when you caught one in your sights, you shot it and watched it fall.

Twenty-one. His kill number. Of course, some were only shadows. At the time, he thought shadows counted, but now he isn't so sure. In the crazy light, screams, dying all around, he had come to believe that the shadows were the fallen Viet Cong. That's why it counted. You shot them to kill them, and then you had to shoot their shadows when they rose up off the dead. So that counted, too, didn't it?

"I know missionaries from Jesus." The little girl grins a little then and he sees that she is missing key teeth in front. Six, maybe seven years old. Eyes much older, though. Like all the kids in this

country.

His first day on patrol—when he was a newbie like Dollar Bill —Grayson had handed out candy bars to children until he ran out, then mooched them off his buddies.

That night, Haystack had pulled an empty candy wrapper out of his pocket, remembered he'd given the contents to Gray to hand out to the hungry children and said, "You know, this country's full of little kids like those today."

"Yeah…I know. What's your point?"

"You can't love all of 'em."

"God does."

"And because He does, you have to."

"No, because He does, I get to."

Grayson looks into the dark eyes of the little girl sitting beside him in the dirt and tries to feel that same way again, longs to care. Nothing.

The sound of approaching footsteps outside and someone speaking Vietnamese stop his breathing. He sees a rifle-toting, backlit shadow appear in the doorway.

Please, Lord, not a POW. Kill me now!

Then he hears a braying-donkey laugh.

"They told me you stunk like a outhouse, but seein's believin'… no smelling *is believing," says a voice out of the shadow in the doorway and the donkey laugh brays again. It is followed immediately by a string of gasping expletives. "Where you been, Padre? You reek worse than a—"*

"I know what I smell like," Gray says, breathless, relief such a warm flood over him he fears for a moment he might wet himself. "When hiding places are in short supply, the least attractive is often the most effective."

Haystack is reluctant to step farther into the hut than just inside the door. Gray can't blame him.

"You wanna tell me where I am and how …?"

"You're in the village of Yan Ling—locals call it Ling—four or

five klicks from where they hit us. Gunships came right before dark and we made a run for 'em. Bartlett, the new guy, said he'd seen you go down, said you was dead." Haystack pauses. "He didn't make it. Took a round in the back as he was climbing up into the chopper. After the gunships sent the gooks on the run, corpsmen went back for bodies and said you wasn't there. That was yesterday morning."

Haystack has unconsciously backed up from the stink until he is outside the hut and Gray can actually make out his features. He looks awful. They all do. All those boys—farmers, mechanics and electricians. Bagpipes had been installing a television set in a motel room, turned it on to see if it worked and heard the announcement that the guard had been activated. They all looked the same now, indistinguishable in the same green/brown camo. All too thin, filthy, like they haven't slept well in weeks. Which they haven't. So different from the laughing young men who'd shown up once a month at the National Guard Armory in Spindle Rock, Kentucky, to "play soldier."

"I'll take you to a medic, but you might wanna …"

"Get cleaned up first? Ya think?"

"There's a stream that way," Haystack gestures toward the setting sun, "but if you're planning to use it, you better get after it. They're about to set out the Claymores and booby traps."

"I got soap," Nguyen says and disappears into the gloom of the hut to fetch it.

"And I'll see if I can find you something to put on that ain't quite so odor-iferous," Haystack beats a hasty retreat away from the hut.

Gray makes it to his knees without the world spinning crazily around him. His head still hammers in heartbeat bursts, but the pain is now localized high on his neck at the base of his skull.

"You wait, I help." The little girl appears at Gray's side and tugs ineffectually upward on his arm.

She is no assistance in lifting, but he uses her to steady himself and is surprised to discover that he can actually stand, swaying drunkenly, but upright.

The little girl doesn't seem to notice the stench at all, and in truth,

Gray has grown accustomed to it and it no longer makes his stomach heave and roll.

Goody, I smell like crap and I don't care. What's wrong with this picture?

He tentatively steps out into the late afternoon sun, quickly regaining his strength. Obviously, he has been unconscious for more than a few hours, has slept the clock around. Which means he's surely had more rest than any of the beehive of soldiers who cut a wide path around him as he approaches.

He puts the little girl in front of him a step or two, a hand on each of her shoulders, like the handles of a mule-drawn plow. Some of the soldiers are heating their K rations on the village cooking fires, and he imagines the aroma of coffee in the air, camouflaged for the time being by the latrine stink that causes wrinkled noses at 30 paces.

"What's your name, GI?" she asks.

"Gray," he said.

"Grape? You name grape? Like the pop?"

Apparently, the little girl has gotten her hands on Nehi somewhere.

"Yep, that'd be me, Grape."

"You Mr. Grape or just Grape?"

"Just Grape'll do. What's your name?"

"Nguyen," she says. Figures. Every third female in Vietnam was named Nguyen.

He is pleasantly surprised to find the stream is clear, about three feet deep with a sandy bottom. He takes off his boots and then tells the little girl, "You stand over there, Nguyen," indicating a spot on the rise leading down to the riverbank. "And turn your back."

"Why? You not want me see you—?"

"Because I said so! Toss me that bar of soap and face the village."

The child complies and Grayson pulls off his shirt and drops it on the sand, pulls his tee shirt over his head and---

GA. Letters printed on the inside of his tee shirt in black Magic Marker. Piper had put the marking there, said there was no way on earth he could keep track of which tee shirt was his when everybody else had one just like it and so she was going to mark his …. She'd only been babbling, saying whatever came into her head to keep from crying. She'd knelt over the neck of his tee shirt in forced concentration and traced the letters that must have looked like seaweed through the flood of unshed tears in her eyes.

He lets the tee shirt fall to the sand. His chest and belly are spotted with leeches. He has no spray with him—it is in his pack and his pack is … so he just pulls them off, one by one, feels his blood squish in his hands as he does. He knows the chances of infection go way up if you pull the slimy creatures off because pieces of them remain under the skin, but he has no choice. He lets his pants drop to his feet and pulls off his socks. Then he steps onto a large rock in the stream, but the rock is slick, he loses his footing and falls backward on his butt, gasping but invigorated by the cool water.

"You okay?" Neuyen calls out without turning around.

"Fine. All I need's a rubber duckie."

"What a bubber duckie?"

"Never mind."

Gray scrubs his skin until it is pink with soap, augmented by handfuls of sand from the stream bank. Two spots of jungle rot on his left hand and a swath of it from his elbow to his wrist on his right arm bleed bright red into the water but he keeps at it until he feels clean.

Haystack appears beside Neuyen on the rise above the bank.

"Gathered up some spares for you to wear 'til yours dry," he says and unceremoniously pitches a pile of odd mixed uniform parts down on the sand. "Ten minutes and you got to come in. CO wants to talk to you and Bones says you need antibiotic salve on your jungle rot, seein' as how you soaked them sores in—"

"I got it," Gray says, steps out of the water and picks up the "borrowed"—by no means "clean"—fatigues Haystack scrounged for him. Has to be some dead guy's gear. He pulls the shirt on—it is a size too small, tight in the shoulders—and glances at the nameplate.

"Campbell," he says, his voice hollow.

"Yeah, Campbell. Why? You know him? He bought the farm two days ago when—"

Grayson bursts out laughing. It makes his head scream in agony but he can't help it. Campbell. He is wearing the shirt of some guy named Campbell!

"Private joke or can anybody join in?"

"It's just…" The more he thinks about it the funnier it gets. "See, my mother was a McCullough. And for generations the McCulloughs and the Campbells …" He goes off on another laughing jag, clearly insipient hysteria, but he can't seem to get control of it.

"You mean like the Hatfields and the McCoys—that what you're saying?" Haystack asks.

"Hey, the Hatfields were from West Virginia, but the McCoys were your ancestors—they were Kentucky boys."

The absurd humor abruptly drains out of Grayson and he stops laughing in mid-bark, so abruptly that he feels light headed.

"Chop chop, Padre," Haystack says. "You're burning daylight." Then he turns and heads back over the hill. The Campbell shirt sends Grayson's mind over the miles to Piper. She was a Campbell.

Her face appears before him. Only it doesn't. What forms in his mind is a blur. Dark hair, but a face that …actually there is no face at all. He can't do it, can't conjure up her image and that should have scared him. But he is beyond caring about a thing like that. He'd wager that half the guys here, at least the ones who'd been here more than a couple of months, the ones who'd been on patrol, had met Charlie in the trees, had run for their lives through the tall grass with blades so sharp it was like running through razor blades, he'd bet those guys couldn't summon the images of their sweethearts to mind either. Because when you'd been here awhile, nothing but here felt real. The rest, the world and family, snow storms and Christmas and mist on the creek on a fall morning… none of that existed. Couldn't. Wasn't enough room in a man's head for the reality of here and the reality of *there. One or the other, not both. And if you clung to the reality of there, you wouldn't last a week here.*

Grayson picks up his reeking clothing, then steps back into the creek and begins to clean his pants, camo shirt and tee shirt the same way he'd cleaned his body—soap and sand. Slowly the reek of feces leaves his nostrils. He rings his clothing out and tosses it into a pile, then he stands for a moment, looking at the red sun as it slips below the treetops. He feels reasonably good. Well, if you don't count his cracked skull, bruised ribs, leech wounds, jungle rot ... oh, and trench foot. Yep, it'd been unmistakable as soon as he removed his left sock. When did his foot go numb? Who knew? When did it start to swell? Didn't know that either. But it is clearly swollen now, and an ugly shade of bright pink with several open sores. Have to get Bones to treat that when he got the antibiotic salve or he could develop gangrene.

He leans over, making his head throb, and grabs his pile of wet clothes. He'll hang them up somewhere to dry. Inexplicable as it was—absurd as it was—he is anxious to shed the shirt of the dead soldier named Campbell.

"You dress? We need get back Ling. They come mostly setsun."

"Sunset."

"Huh?"

"It's not set-sun, it's ... sunset. Uh-hay, et-say."

The quizzical look on the little girl's face strikes Grayson as funny, charmingly, innocently funny and he burps out a gentle, sincere laugh. "Un-hay et-say...sunset in a language called pig latin. It's a ... special language."

"Cong know pig latin?"

"I'm sure they don't."

"Then you teach Nguyen, okay, Grape?"

Her eyes sparkle.

A smile starts on his face but dies there and he is suddenly acutely aware of the jungle around him and the little girl—who are outside the perimeter. Unarmed. He scans the trees. There could be a sniper...

. . .

Like the sniper in the trees who'd tagged Haystack. Even with his eyes squeezed resolutely shut, Grayson was careful to keep his head down, out of the gook's sightline.

Not out of the sightline of the road, though. He was the only one of his squad who had an unobstructed view of it. And he knew what he would see there when he opened his eyes. Not an apparition, a ghost, a hallucination. A flesh-and-blood little girl with a smile on her face and tears on her cheeks.

All those thoughts flew through Grayson's mind in the space between one heartbeat and the next before he slowly lifted his eyelids.

Nguyen was still there.

~

Charleston, West Virginia
Thursday, August 14, 1969

Carter Addington lurched into semi-consciousness in sweat-soaked sheets. Some loud noise had awakened him from the dream. The same dream, of course. His father in the pulpit, his eyes blazing. Literally. Fire shot from two empty orbs beneath his bushy black eyebrows and blazed from his tongue as he spoke, the flames licking out of a mouth with too many teeth. Jagged teeth.

The phone jangled.

That's what had awakened him. Carter sat up and swung his legs off the bed to the floor, shook his head, trying to get his breathing under control so he could talk. Trying to get the face of his raging father out of his head!

But the image stubbornly refused to fade. The fire-breathing giant in the pulpit had focused those flaming eyes on him, seated alone in the front pew of that church in Stinkin' Creek Hollow where his father had pulled a snake out of a basket during a service for the first time. And where he did the same thing years later—for the last time. The church had burned to the ground, struck by lightning three days after his father's funeral. For a long time, Carter'd believed his father had sent the lightning bolt to reduce the church where he died to ashes. Sometimes, he still believed it.

The phone rang again and Carter snatched the receiver and barked, "What!"

"Sounds like I woke you up."

"Ya think!"

"It ain't that early! You city boys may get to sleep all day but I couldn't wait 'til noon to call or I wouldn't have the phone to myself." The only pay phone in Sadlerton was on the outside wall next to the front door of Bennett's Five and Dime. The man on the other end of the line lowered his voice. "We got trouble. Campbell trouble."

Carter ran his left hand through his close-cropped blonde hair in an unconscious gesture everyone who knew him would have recognized. It was Carter's frustration gesture. His annoyance gesture. His brow furrowed and twin pleats appeared at the bridge of his nose between his eyebrows, making his thin, angular face seem care-worn and severe.

Carter Addington had cold, sculptured, patrician good looks. His eyes were dark blue and seemed to change color with his mood. His face, long and lean, had a strong jaw and perfectly shaped nose. It *had* been perfectly shaped, that is, until it came into close personal contact with Riley Campbell's fist the day Riley's gang of thugs beat him almost to death for crossing clan lines—a McCullough daring to take up with a Campbell girl. Dating Piper had landed Carter in the hospital for three days. But it'd been worth it. Oh, my yes, it'd been worth it, alright! The broken nose had healed, leaving only a slight twist as a reminder. But the broken heart had never healed. The wound was as raw now as it'd been eleven years ago when she'd broken up with him.

"What kind of Campbell trouble?"

"I been hearing for a right smart while that the Campbells was gonna try their hand at the shine bidness."

"What?" Carter was incredulous.

"I seen Zeke ever day for a week up Blood Creek."

Jesse had Carter's attention now. Jesse was his cousin, not the sharpest knife in the drawer, but he was dependable and loyal. And he knew how to keep his mouth shut about his partnership with Carter in their joint moonshine operation.

"You think he knows?" Carter asked.

"That we got a still hid up there? Naw. What I think's he's decided to set up one of his own."

It made perfect sense. The springs in that hollow ran cold and pure—which is why Carter had put one of his own stills there three years ago.

"If'n he don't know we got business up there it ain't gonna be long 'fore he trips over it looking for his own spot. I figure he needs to be 'discouraged' from poking around."

"Give me a couple of days to think about it and I'll get back to you," Carter said.

"Don't take too long a'ponderin' 'bout it. That boy's meddlin' could bring a world of hurt down on our heads."

"I said I'll handle it!"

Carter hung up without bothering to say goodbye. What a way to start the day. He stood up and stretched. Tall and slender, Carter'd been called "graceful" by sports writers who could find no other word to describe the effortlessness with which the six-foot, six-inch point guard maneuvered a basketball down court, dodging defenders without breaking a sweat before he pulled up short and nailed a perfect jump shot. He'd been All-American at Duke his senior year—they'd called him the Demon Hillbilly and he'd pretended then like he'd been pretending his whole life that it didn't offend him to be referred to as a hillbilly.

Carter stepped to the window that displayed the city stretched out below his 10th floor apartment and considered his options. His shine business was small—by design. When Jesse'd approached him about forming a partnership, Carter saw the opportunity to make serious money with minimal risk, and the risk would remain minimal as long as his operation wasn't perceived as competition by the bootleggers in Franklin. Those boys played hard ball. Franklin County, Virginia, just over the state line, was the acknowledged moonshine capital of the world and produced more liquor than many legal distilleries. He'd read in the paper only last week that the feds had busted a feed store in the tiny town of Rocky Mount that was the single largest distributor of sugar on the East Coast! Carter had better sense than to take on big guns like that! But he couldn't afford competition right under his nose, couldn't allow his operation to be undercut by the Campbells! Zeke and Riley Campbell. Piper's brothers.

Her face formed on top of his own reflection in the window pane, with the high cheekbones she got from her Cherokee grandmother, no smile on the plump lips men went all stupid over and those chocolate brown eyes—welled with tears. That's how her face would look if there came a knock at her door one day and soldiers were standing on the porch looking solemn.

Oh, how Carter wished he could be there if that happened, to hold her and comfort her, to care for her as she grieved. And to be there for her when her broken heart was mended. Grayson had taken Piper from him. All Carter needed was a little luck—bad luck for Grayson—and he would be able to return the favor.

Carter was instantly ashamed. He didn't want his brother *dead*. Just out of the picture. And if things continued to move along according to Carter's plan, by the time Grayson got home from Vietnam in October, that's exactly what he would be.

Carter glanced at the clock beside the bed and groaned. He was going to be late for work.

Chapter Five

PIPER HAD GOTTEN the little girl called Maggie a glass of
water and had finally persuaded her to sit down on the
couch while she drank it. The child sat prim as a piano
student on a bench, knees together, back straight, on the
edge of the cushion, as if at the slightest provocation, she
would bolt toward the door and be out it and away in a
heartbeat.

"Sure I can't get you something else to d-d-drink, lass?"
Marian asked and Piper smiled at the faint echo of the
brogue the McCullough family'd brought to the new world
from Scotland generations ago. The mountains of West
Virginia had been settled by the Scots, the Irish and the
Welsh—with names like Gilfillin, Mawhinney, McCullough
and O'Riley—coming to mine coal as they'd done in the
old country, bringing with them a lilting speech that
became mountain dialect, traditional dances that morphed
into clogging, and the toe-tapping fiddle and banjo ballads
that were transformed into Bluegrass music. "I got lemonade. It's fresh made this morning. Not tart, g-g-got lots of
sugar."

"No thank you, ma'am. The water's fine."

Maggie reached down and ruffled Sadie's golden curls. Sadie was seated on the floor at her feet, scooted up to the couch so she was snuggled against the older child's legs. She had leaned her head over on Maggie and was holding one of her feet, the way you'd hold someone's hand so you wouldn't get separated in a crowd.

Piper shook her head. There was nowhere in her that could even begin to explain Sadie's response to the little girl with red braids.

Sadie's ears had perked up at the mention of lemonade.

"Sabie want lem-nade," she said. Sadie had recently taken to speaking of herself in third person. "Sabie thirssy."

"What do you say?" Piper intoned automatically.

"Sabie hab lem-nade, *pease?*"

Piper rose to get it.

"Well, if the little pretty one's having some … I guess I wouldn't mind a mite myself, if it's no trouble." Maggie said.

"I'll just be a minute," Piper said.

"I'll help," Marian said.

"Oh, I can manage, I don't need …" Her voice trailed off when Marian gave her a knowing look. "Well, maybe you could whip up some fried bread for tomato preserves."

The two women disappeared into the kitchen. Piper was the first to whisper as soon as they were safely out of earshot.

"I'll wager that child's from—"

"—Whoopie Country," Marian finished her sentence. "I s'pect her people's so far back in them hills the s-s-sun don't shine on 'em but one day a week."

In the deep, secluded hollows and inaccessible coves of

the mountains beyond them to the north was a land West Virginians called Whoopie Country (pronounced with no "w" sound). The people who lived there were a race apart. Isolated and fiercely clannish, they lived by their own rules, which sometimes didn't line up with the rest of the world's rules. *Usually* didn't.

"She looks like she's been on the r-r-run a right smart while," Marian said. "You see the dirt in her hair where she's been a-sleepin' on the g-g-ground."

"What are we going to do with her?" Piper asked.

"Well, the first thing is get some food in her belly and get her cleaned up."

"And after that?"

"We'll figure out 'after that' soon's 'after that' gets here. She could wear one of your n-n-nightgowns while I get that dress and—"

"You're not going to do anything but get yourself into bed for a rest before lunchtime," Piper said.

"Stop yer fussin', Missy," Marian said. "I'm—" She blanched, took a single step and sank down on the potato bin. If it hadn't been there, she'd surely have collapsed in a heap on the floor.

"Guess I d-do need to lie d-down for a bit," she said, her voice airless with pain.

Piper forgot about the two children in the parlor and concentrated on the pale, trembling woman in front of her. She crossed to Marian and reached out both hands.

"Try to stand. I'll hold your weight and you pull up." Marian wordlessly reached out trembling hands to Piper. "Only a little bitty step, hold on to me, we'll take it real slow."

Marian put one foot in front of the other, shifted her weight, winced and put out her other foot. One after the other, six-inch steps, Piper helped her out of the kitchen into the parlor where two girls who were expecting glasses of lemonade would just have to wait.

Sadie had climbed up onto the couch—or had been picked up and set there—and was on her knees beside Maggie. As she plucked pieces of twigs and leaves out of Maggie's braids, she babbled joyously, giggling, her words almost a song.

"…draw a picture of birdies fly hiiiigh in da sky, pretty colors, red and blue and lello…"

When Maggie saw Piper helping Marian, she jumped off the couch like it was on fire and rushed to Piper's side.

"You can rest your weight on my shoulders, Nan Marian," she said. At just a fuzz under six feet, Piper towered over Marian, who'd been five feet five as a young woman and probably wasn't five three now, bent over as she was with the beginnings of a dowagers hump. Maggie was shorter than Marian, more comfortable to lean on and Marian wrapped her arm around the little girl's shoulder without hesitation.

Sadie arrived one step behind Maggie.

"Sabie help Mabie," she said, looking up at Maggie.

Sabie and Mabie.

Piper scooped Sadie off the floor so she wouldn't inadvertently trip her grandmother. "Let's go fluff Nana's pillows," she said.

Maggie and Marian shuffled down the hallway into Marian's room, then Maggie turned the old woman so she faced away from the bed.

"I'll lean over and you hold on 'til your backside hits that nice soft mattress," Maggie said.

Marian eased herself down onto the bed and let out a sigh. Maggie knelt and slipped off the old woman's shoes. Then Piper gently eased Marian's shoulders down against the pile of pillows as Maggie guided her legs up onto the bed and covered them with the quilt.

Piper glanced at her watch, reached over to the table beside the bed for the brown prescription bottle and poured two small white capsules into her hand.

"Time for your medicine," she said. It wasn't time. It was at least 45 minutes before she was supposed to give Marian any more pain medication.

Maggie picked up the pitcher of water sitting beside the pill bottle and poured a glass for Marian, like she'd been taking care of the old woman all her life.

Marian said nothing. Probably couldn't. She took the pills from Piper and the water from Maggie, turned the glass up and washed the pills down.

"You rest now and I'll—" Piper began.

"I'll sit with her," Maggie said

"I sit wif Nana, too," Sadie said.

Maggie sank down into the chair beside the old woman's bed and Sadie plopped on the floor at her feet. "Like music do you?" Maggie asked. "I know a fair number of songs I used to sing before—" she stopped, looked confused.

"I've got a better plan," Piper said, taking charge. "You…" she pointed to Marian "…close your eyes and rest a bit. And you two…" she pointed to Maggie and Sadie "…come into the kitchen and have some lemonade and some bread and jam."

Maggie looked like she was about to protest. Marian did, too, in fact, but Piper set her "no arguing" look on her face and the protests died on both their lips.

"I'll sing for you later," Maggie said.

"You d-do that, Sweetheart," Marian said, her voice weak.

Piper felt for a moment like she'd wandered into somebody's dream. The little girl had shown up on the front porch surely it wasn't even ten minutes ago, and now she seemed as comfortably at home as if she lived here.

"Come along, little pretty." Maggie lifted Sadie up into her arms and balanced her on her hip like she'd been hoisting a toddler around her whole life. And maybe she had. Maybe she'd left a little sister or brother behind in the hills when she …

Don't go there now. Get her fed, get her cleaned up. Worry about "after that" when "after that" gets here.

~

SWEAT STREAMED out from under Gray's helmet into his eyes. The salt stung. Smoke from the burning village made him squint, too, but even squinting, he could see that the little girl in the sack dress edging slowly across the road toward him and the rest of the squad was terrified.

"Take me America with you," she pleaded, her voice hollow, like a robot. She had said that same thing—and meant it—so many times the words were haunting.

"TAKE ME AMERICA WITH YOU," Nguyen says, "and I not talk English, I talk pig latin."

She pulls the wrapper off the candy bar as if the foil itself is made of gold. She folds it carefully into a square, then into smaller and smaller squares until it's the size of a dime and she drops it into her pocket

"Most Americans can probably speak pig latin," Grayson says, "but nobody actually uses it to communicate—" He sees her brow wrinkle. "—to talk to each other."

"You teach me. I want learn. I want say what Cong can't say."

Grayson takes a deep breath.

"Okay ..." How do you explain about changing syllables to somebody who doesn't know what a syllable is? "Well, you take a word, like pig. You drop the "puh" sound on the front of the word and put it on the back of the word and then add ..." He sees the confused look on her face and his voice trails off.

"I don't think I can teach you, Nguyen."

"Yes, you can. You try; I learn. Show me."

And so he does. He no longer attempts to explain the process, just speaks the language and asks her to translate. By the end of the day, half the platoon is speaking pig latin to the other half.

"What's my name?" he says.

"You Grape."

"No, in pig latin."

"You ... grape-ray?"

"No, ape-gray. Keep trying, you'll get it."

"I learn pig-latin, you take me America, Grape, see Disneyland?"

"YOU TAKE ME AMERICA, Grape, see Disneyland," she said. Somewhere she'd come by a Mickey Mouse coloring book and she constantly begged him to tell stories about the characters. Today was different, though. Today, Nguyen was the one telling the story—with their special language.

"I want see Goofy and Minnie Mouse," she said. She took another step toward him. "You take me ... om-bay... with you."

Om-bay. *Bomb.*

Nguyen was wired!

And when the Cong detonated the bomb, the little girl would become red mist. Grayson had seen it happen once. Bill Hawkins had taken a direct hit from an 80 mm mortar and it vaporized him, spewed out a red fog of the minute particles of his humanity.

Nguyen continued to walk toward him and the rest of the squad, agonizingly slowly.

"You take urn-bay ing-lay see Mickey Mouse?"

Urn-Bay ing-lay. *Burn Ling!* The village. The Cong had strapped a bomb on Nguyen and if she warned the Americans, they'd burn her village—they way they always burned villages—with the villagers inside the huts.

Chapter Six

Carter Addington stepped out of the elevator on the top floor of the Northfield Coal Building, nodded at the cheery receptionist—"Good morning, Mr. Addington!"— and started down the hall toward his office.

When he passed by the desk of the secretary in the vestibule outside company president Nelson Warren's office, Stella was talking on the phone. But as soon as she saw him, she lifted one finger off the receiver in a "wait" gesture, then interrupted the person on the other end of the line.

"…Sir, excuse me, but he just came in." She paused. "Yes, sir."

She hung up.

"Mr. Warren has already called twice asking for you." She smiled. "But … I made excuses for you."

Stella had been flirting with him for months. She looked up at him now through a forest of heavily mascara-ed eyelashes under lids slathered with blue eye shadow. The pale pink lipstick and boyishly short hairstyle completed her Twiggy look. Or would have if she'd been thirty pounds lighter.

"Thanks, Stel. You're the best." Always a good idea to keep the help on your side. Information was power and nobody knew more about the goings-on in the office of the company president than Stella Coltrane.

He leaned close enough so Stella could get a good whiff of his English Leather cologne. He knew it was her favorite.

"What's up?" he asked softly.

She leaned toward him. White Shoulders perfume. *Not* his favorite.

"He was already in his office when I got to work this morning. He's been huddling with Benson from operations and Clayton from quality control ever since, talking about USBM inspections—because of what happened to that school."

USBM was the United States Bureau of Mines, the agency that exercised regulatory control over the mining industry. In theory, anyway. In practice, the USBM was more an extension of the industry than a watchdog. What was good for mining was good for the USBM.

"That coal slurry slide, you mean?"

"Yeah, the one in Whales." She pronounced it with an h, then glanced over her shoulder at the big oak door behind her. "You need to get in there."

The ornate door had a doorknob in the center, a big one, the size of a baseball, made of cut glass. A simple thing, really, but profound in Carter's mind. It had come to symbolize stature. One day, he would have an office with a glass knob in the center of the door.

Carter patted her hand and watched color flood her cheeks.

"Thanks," he said, then he strode toward the door. It

opened for him before he had a chance to reach for the knob, and a tall, balding man with a neatly trimmed mustache stepped aside and gestured him into the room.

The office itself wasn't as grand as the door leading into it implied. But its lack of grandeur spoke volumes. Hardwood floor polished to such a shine you could see your reflection. Dark wood paneling. Floor-to-ceiling bookshelves crammed with books—fancy leather-bound volumes worn from use, such an eclectic mix Carter couldn't get his mind around the kind of man who had read them all, as it was rumored the man occupying the office had. From the complete works of Shakespeare to How to Train a Coon Dog. One shelf had a stack of newspapers, from Charleston, sure, but the *New York Times,* too, the *Wall Street Journal* and the *Washington Post.* Today's issues. Already read and digested.

The most telling thing about the man who ruled Northfield Coal was the most incongruous. Hanging on the wall behind his desk was a huge portrait in an ornate gilded frame with a small shaded light protruding from the top that illuminated the picture below. The subject was Nelson Warren's son, Robert Nelson Warren, Jr. Bobby. He'd raised the boy alone after his wife died and doted on the child. About 5 years old in the portrait—probably 9 or 10 now—the boy bore the angelic smile and vacant expression common to retarded children.

The room was gauzy with smoke—cigar, pipe and cigarette. It hung in the air like morning haze on a creek.

A conference table, of some dark wood so black it might have been ebony, dominated the office. Twelve chairs gathered around the table. Warren sat at the end with his back to the entrance door. Two seats on the far side of the table were occupied by suit-and-tie clad men; one chair on the near side was pulled out. It was where

Haskell Benson had been seated before he got up to open the door for Carter. Benson gestured to the seat beside him and Carter crossed to it, picking up on the ongoing conversation that continued un-interrupted.

"…in this morning's paper."

That was the quality control man, Clayton. He sat next to Warren on the far side of the table, the concentrated frown on his face as permanent as a tattoo. He gestured with the lit cigarette in his left hand, lifted the newspaper in his right hand and began to read.

"Concerned that something similar to the disaster that may have killed as many as one hundred twenty-five school children in the village of Gaynor, Wales, on Monday might occur here, officials at the U.S. Bureau of Mines announced today that the bureau would prepare a list of similar waste banks in the Appalachian coal mining region and begin to inspect the ones whose failure could result in loss of life or extensive property damage."

Clayton tossed *The Charleston Gazette* down on the table in front of him as Carter slid into his seat beside Benson.

"You start talking about a hundred and twenty-five dead kids and folks get up in arms quick. All it takes is one person to go on some kind of crusade and—"

"A thing like this makes Mines inspectors nervous," Benson put in. "None of them wants to be the one everybody's pointing a finger at if … there's a problem."

"We have six large slurry piles," Clayton said. "There are three trailer houses below the one—"

"It's not the gob piles that are the problem," Benson interrupted, his voice firm. "What happened in Wales— that was a freak accident. From what I understand, they piled the slurry on top of a spring and then it rained a lot —somehow the stuff liquefied and slid downhill. None of our slurry piles is on top of a spring. Besides, I believe we've got much bigger fish to fry than those piles."

"And what fish would those be?" Clayton sounded miffed. He was a self-important little man and didn't like it when somebody stole his thunder.

"The impoundments," Benson said.

Carter sat up a straighter in his chair.

Strip mine canker sores first infected the West Virginia landscape before World War I and the blight spread like smallpox in the decades that followed as the coal companies determined it was more efficient and required far less manpower to rip the tops off mountains to get at the coal than to pay miners to dig it out. The environmental ramifications were enormous, of course, not the least of which were impoundment lakes. Strip mining created huge amounts of waste material, including the acidic sludge produced when the coal was washed. It was common practice for coal companies to bulldoze the coal waste, called slurry or "gob," across a hollow to form a dam and then impound the black sludge water behind it.

Since technically the structures were just gob piles, and the coal companies hadn't designed engineering plans for the construction of a "dam," federal regulations about the structure and safety of dams did not apply to them.

Apparently, Benson feared that might change.

"I think we have to consider the possibility—the *likelihood*—that the feds will go after the impoundments and not just the slurry piles," Benson said.

Nelson Warren sat deep in the leather cushioned comfort of his swivel desk chair. The droopy eyes below his shock of pure white hair belied his riveted attention. A trim man, tall and boney, he was as physically fit as any athlete. People said he actually ran up and down the road in front of his house—five miles every day—ten on Saturdays! He held an unlit cigar in his right hand, brought it to his mouth and bit down on it now and then as he listened but made no attempt to light it. Carter had never actually seen the man smoke, but he also had never seen him without an unlit cigar.

"I concede the point about the impoundments," Clayton began, "but how—?"

"I want to know about the locals." Warren cut Clayton off. His voice was deceptively soft, almost sounded kind if you didn't know better. "Any of them got a tit in the wringer about this business?"

Warren didn't turn his way, but Carter knew the question was directed at him. All such questions were directed at him, given that he was the only one of Warren's flunkies who knew jack about the people who actually worked in Northfield Coal's mines and lived in the mountains and hollows that surrounded them.

For generations, coal companies had built housing for their miners, called coal camps, along streams in steep-walled valleys, creating strings of small communities clustered up and down just about every creek in West Virginia. The Pocahontas Coal Field alone supported 120 camps, with 500-800 families in each one, up and down the hollows wherever the steep mountainsides gave way and the land around the creek spread out enough so you could build a house.

Even though most of the miners were now unemployed, untold thousands of people still lived in those coal camp houses—many of which now lay beneath a strip mine and *downstream* from an impounded lake. Among those people was Carter's family. The home where he grew up was perched on a mountainside in Sadler Hollow—less than a mile down the valley from Northfield Coal's Impoundment #1.

"Not that I'm aware of, sir," Carter said. He almost added that he'd bet his paycheck they didn't even know there'd been a disaster in Wales.

"What are they saying about it?"

Again, Carter caught himself before he said more than he could prove. Bluff Nelson Warren and you were asking for trouble. Craftier men than Carter had tried and lived to regret it.

"I haven't been home since it happened. I haven't talked to them, but Sadler Hollow'd certainly have something to say about it if anybody does."

"Then go home," Warren said. "Talk to the mountaineers up in the hollows." Unlike most of his executive staff, Warren was a native. Not of the mountains, of course, but of Charleston. Still, he knew West Virginians were *mountaineers,* not hillbillies. "I want to know what they're saying to each other." He turned back to Clayton. "And what they might say to a federal inspector if one happened to ask."

Warren must really be spooked!

Mountaineers wouldn't say crap to a mine inspector if he was covered in it. Warren knew that. They wouldn't spit on one if he was on fire. Wasn't a soul Carter knew in Sadler Hollow who'd give the time of day to any outsider, let alone a "fed-ral."

"I'll go home tomorrow afternoon and—"

"Today," Warren said. "Take a three-day weekend. I want a full report on my desk first thing Monday morning."

"Yes, sir," Carter said. He was careful to keep the joy out of his voice and the happiness off his face. "I'll leave right after lunch."

"You'll leave right now."

~

The president of Northfield Coal Company was still seated at the big conference table in his Charleston office hours later when Carter Addington pulled up in front of the house where he'd grown up in Sadler Hollow. In fact, it was at that very moment that Nelson Warren made up his mind to blow a great big hole in the dam on the mountainside above Carter's head.

It had come to Warren the way his best plans did—all of a piece, complete. He was not one to second guess himself, but even if he had been, this decision fit so perfectly into the complex puzzle of his plan to become one of the most powerful men in West Virginia that even a man given to vacillation would have seen the genius in it. It was daring. Even dangerous. But big rewards required big risks.

The idea had formed in his head as he studied the maps, geologic surveys and reports on the big black table in front of him. Everyone who had attended the morning's meeting in his office had left hours before, but Warren was again seated in his big leather chair, looking over his chief engineer's assessment report of all the dams. It was a document Warren had commissioned after the discussion at the meeting and he was relieved by what it revealed. The document reported that all the dams built by Northfield Coal were sound.

Well, all but *one.*

The short, bespectacled engineer stood behind the chair next to Warren, first on one foot then the other, his hands drumming unconsciously on the chair back.

Warren shot him an irritated glance. Peter Grigsby looked confused, then down at his hands and quickly shoved them into his pockets. Finally, Warren scooted the papers away from him, as a man might shove away his plate when he has finally stuffed himself.

"And all this means …?" he asked Grigsby. Warren knew full well what it meant, but he wanted Grigsby to say it, to explain it. That's what he paid the high-priced engineer for and he wanted his money's worth. He demanded his money's worth from all his employees—men who were "picks of the litter" in their fields. Well, except for Addington and Warren was stuck with him. The boy's uncle had called in a favor to land him the job and no one understood the reciprocity inherent in business associations better than Nelson Warren. He would see that Jim Addington repaid that favor with a generous contribution to his political war chest when he rolled out his plans next month.

In all honesty, the young man did bring more than Fritos and bean dip to the party. Addington understood the locals and God knows there wasn't anybody else in Warren's organization who could lay claim to that particular area of expertise. And you had to keep track of the locals, know what they were thinking as soon as they thought it. Before they thought it. Warren needed the halfwit mountaineers to mine his coal, of course, but they were like those birds that lived in the mouths of crocodiles, picking out the scraps, keeping them clean. A crocodile tolerated the bird's existence because it performed a useful function. Any time it got out of line, however, pecked a little too deep, the crocodile could chop down and swallow the bird in one bite.

"All your figures and numbers … give me the bottom line."

"Well, Mr. Warren, of all the company's impoundment dams, #2 above Sadler Hollow is the only one in critical condition. I've run all the equations, studied the—"

"Cut to the chase, Grigsby."

"It won't hold, sir. Impoundment Dam #2 is a disaster waiting to happen. There's too much water, too much pressure. The structure wasn't designed for it. When #2 starts to leak—and it *will* start to leak, no doubt about it—the water's got nowhere to go but downhill into Impoundment #1 at the top of Sadler Hollow. That dam's solid, but it's nowhere near tall enough. You pour a whole pot of coffee into one cup, it'll fill up and then overflow. Water leaking out of #2 is going to spill out over the top of the lower dam and flood the stream below … I believe it's called, *Naked* Turtle Creek."

Dam #1 had been built first. Coarse coal mining refuse, rocks, soil, anything and everything lopped off the top of Chicken Gizzard Mountain had been bulldozed into the valley where it narrowed at the top of the hollow above Sadlerton, creating a dam forty feet tall that stretched two hundred fifty feet between Chicken Gizzard Mountain on the north and Naked Turtle Mountain on the south. As the strip mine moved east, it expanded and the valley was wider in the spot selected for Impoundment #2. Stretching from ridge to ridge, the slurry pile dam built there was eighty-five feet tall, six hundred fifty feet across and was constructed of more than a million tons of coal waste. The dam held back one hundred forty-two million gallons of black waste water and sludge, five times the size of the lake behind #1.

"When you figure the pounds per square inch of all the water behind it, the failure of #2 is mathematically inevitable," Grigsby said.

"How long?"

"Sir?"

"How long before it goes?"

"If the drains I recommended for both dams had been completed ..." he began self righteously, caught the look on Warren's face and let it go. "How long is hard to say, sir. It depends on—"

"Estimate."

"I don't know. So many variables—"

"A guess, Grigsby. A ballpark guess."

"Well... it's been a wet month for August, sir. If the weather clears, it could hold six, maybe eight more months. But if the rain hangs on upstream, we're talking weeks. In a few weeks, it's going to pop a leak somewhere. Then another and another. And once a leak starts, there's so much water pressure you can't plug—"

"Is there any way to fix it?"

Grigsby looked relieved, less pained.

"Well, yes sir, there is. First, we'd have to drain most of the water out of the lake, which will take—"

"How much?"

"How much wha—?"

"How much will it cost to fix it?" Warren ground out the words between clinched teeth.

"Well, I ..." He caught Warren's deadly look.

"Hundreds of thousands ... half a million dollars. At least that. Maybe ... *probably* more. You'd have to—"

"And if we don't fix it, how much will that cost?"

Grigsby was genuinely confused.

"I don't think I understand the question, sir."

"If we choose not to fix it, the dam starts leaking and the water overflows the lower dam, how much will that cost?" He spit out the words carefully, like he was addressing a three-year-old. "The flooding downstream, destruction of property—buildings, bridges, roads… whatever."

Grigsby looked horrified.

"I'm afraid I don't have any idea, sir." He paused, then pushed forward timidly. "But … it's not only property. All those people who live below the dams, where will they—?"

"That's enough," Warren voice was back to its normal timber, like he was discussing the Giants chances in the world series or the square root of pi. "Leave these papers here with me."

"Yes, sir," Grigsby sighed the words out, anxious to get out of the room. Warren waved his hand in a dismissing gesture and the man practically bolted for the door. Without even turning around, Warren timed it perfectly. As Grigsby reached for the door knob, Warren called out.

"One other thing, Grigsby." He still didn't turn, merely pictured in his mind the man motionless at the door.

"Sir?"

"If you tell anybody—and I mean *anybody* about our conversation today…" He allowed the rest to hang there in the air between them. Let Grigsby come up with his own horrible end to the threat.

"Oh, no sir. Absolutely not, sir. Nobody. I won't breathe a word to anybody."

"See that you don't." Menace caustic enough to melt a hole in boot leather dripped from his voice.

Warren sat quiet for a time, eyes closed, after Grigsby pulled the door softly shut behind him. A casual observer might well have assumed he'd dozed off. But Nelson Warren's mind was whirring, spinning, calculating. Yes, it would work. Blow a hole in the big dam, #2, let the water behind it pour over the top of Dam #1. Perfect.

He opened his eyes, glanced at his watch and his face sprang to life. If he didn't hurry, he'd be late for Bobby's recital, and he'd suffered through months of practice as the boy prepared for it. Bless his heart, Bobby's stubby little fingers were not designed for piano keys. But he loved music, wanted to play, and that was all that mattered to Warren. And after tonight, surely he'd never have to listen to a hinky-tinky version of Twinkle Twinkle Little Star ever again.

Chapter Seven

CARTER HAD SPENT the day in Charleston running errands, then made good time from his apartment to Sadler Hollow late that afternoon. Going east, the city gave up quickly to forested mountains where he traveled along winding, rutted roads that snaked through narrow valleys with sides so steep they were almost vertical. *This* was West By-God Virginia.

Foreigners, defined as anybody you didn't recognize on sight and whose lineage you couldn't instantly trace back three generations, charged that West Virginia roads went "from nowhere through nowhere to nowhere" and there was some truth in that. But driving along the winding mountain roads was more than a journey through space. It was a journey through culture, from one civilization to another that was at once far simpler and immensely more complex than the other.

It was a journey through time, too, back thirty, maybe forty years. Carter always pictured West Virginia as the concentric circles inside a tree trunk or the orbits of the planets around the sun. The closer you got to the center of the mountains, the deepest, most remote areas of Whoopie Country, the further away from the twentieth century you'd traveled. He'd been there a time or two with his circuit-riding preacher father. In those remote hollows, people lived in houses perched on the mountainsides so precariously it looked like the weight of sunlight alone might topple them. They'd peered at him with more distrust, antagonism and suspicion than the folks in Sadler Hollow viewed strangers. But come to think of it, not a whole lot more. In truth, every West Virginia hollow was so isolated it was its own private universe, separated by light years from the hollow only a couple of miles away.

When he pulled up in front of his mother's house, the sun had gone down behind the mountain on the far side of the hollow and its shadow had stretched over the top of the little white frame house on the side of Naked Turtle Mountain—so named because there was a huge rock outcrop on the top that looked like a turtle's shell. The area below—shell-less—was therefore a naked (pronounced nekkid) turtle.

The folks in Sadlerton, which sat on the valley floor, only got four hours of direct sunlight a day—10 a.m. to 2 p.m. The home where he grew up got a little more because it was high up the mountainside and caught the last of the afternoon rays.

Though Sadler Hollow was in one of the outside rings, maybe Saturn or Jupiter, most houses had no electricity or indoor plumbing. Carter had spent a fortune to have a septic system installed for his mother three years ago and wasn't surprised to find the little Craddock boys on her porch the next day to try out her indoor privy. Electricity had cost more than plumbing. Gratefully, there was a line in the hollow on the other side of Naked Turtle Mountain —which as the crow flies was only a couple of miles away.

He'd never have been able to afford any of it, or wiring the house and the electric appliances, if it hadn't been for his shine business.

The elementary school he'd attended in Sadlerton had had electricity but no plumbing. It was a one-room structure where maybe a third of the students actually completed the eighth grade and went on to Cochran County High School in Chandler. Most of the girls dropped out and got married and the boys went to work in the mines. That he and Grayson had graduated from high school and then "got out" was nothing short of miraculous —with all the credit going to James Addington, their bachelor uncle. After he served in WWI, their father, Everett, moved into the West Virginia mountains to become a circuit-riding preacher. Everett's younger brother was less spiritual and more practical. He set about amassing a fortune and when the time came, Uncle Jim reached out and snatched his two nephews out of the 19th century into educations and a future.

Carter got out of his Camaro, then stood for a moment beside it, looking up the narrow hollow to the top where Northfield Coal's Impoundment Dam #1 rested in the crease between the ridges, shining black where the coal slurry caught a few rays of the sun before it fell below the mountain to the west.

He turned his gaze down the hollow toward the little community of Sadlerton. It was the largest of a half dozen coal camp communities—the only one with a post office and fire station—strung together like beads spaced out on a string, along Naked Turtle Creek, which had been a good-sized stream before the dams at the top of the hollow stopped the flow of its major tributary. When you counted the residents of Akin, Bent Twig, Alice Springs, Barberville, Copperhead and probably ten more communities that didn't have names, roughly five thousand people lived in Sadler Hollow. Add in Chandler at the far end of the hollow, the county seat of Cochran County, which had actually grown from a coal camp into a real town, and almost seven thousand people lived downstream from Impoundment Dam #1.

He looked up at the dam again and then back down the hollow as far as he could see.

"…inspect the ones whose failure could result in loss of life or extensive property damage…"

Well, that phrase certainly described Impoundment Dam # 1.

People in the hollow had been complaining about it ever since the coal company bulldozed the top of the mountain into the creek eight years ago. The dam was perfectly safe, of course, but these people didn't trust Northfield Coal and had good reason not to. Added to the disgruntled, laid-off miners, the folks who owned property had innocently sold the company their mineral rights for a paltry sum decades before, assuming there'd one day be a coal mine beneath their land. They never dreamed that the contract they'd signed granted the coal company the right to rip the top off the mountain, taking with it their homes and everything they owned. Put a bee in Sadler Hollow's bonnet about the dam failing and it would get ugly quick!

If the people who lived here actually knew what had happened three days ago in a little town on the other side of the planet, Warren would have good reason for concern. But Carter was sure they had no idea. Outsiders just didn't understand how isolated these people were. They didn't have electricity, let alone television sets piping Walter Croncite into their living rooms every night to tell them "That's the way it is …" More important, their universe was Sadler Hollow and whatever was going on in the rest of the world just flat out didn't matter. Carter would nose around anyway, of course. And find out absolutely nothing. He'd have a report crisp and neat on Warren's desk before the old man got into work on Monday morning.

Carter smiled. Meanwhile, he'd enjoy his three-day weekend with Piper. His mother, too, of course. And Sunshine. Precious Sadie was a little ray of sunshine, so that's what he called her.

GRAYSON LEANED against a tree beside the medical tent, outside the makeshift shelter he'd built right after first light out of a couple of rubberized ponchos and a piece of vine. He'd hated the smell of disinfectant, the copper stench of blood and the singed-hair stink of burned flesh in the tent, but the doc would only let him leave if he promised to stay near. Still watching his concussion, making sure ... what? That he didn't drop over dead from a brain bleed? Grayson figured half the GI's in-country were walking around with concussions. Cracked skulls were about as common here as jungle rot. But he'd done what the doc ordered just to get out of the tent.

And he did have to admit he'd definitely had his bell rung, and his brain was still so scrambled he didn't know exactly when it had happened. Or how. He could only recall opening his eyes in the medical tent, lying on a cot. Dollar Bill, KFC, Beanie and Bagpipes were talking to the doc at the other end of the tent but the doc shooed them away. That'd been night before last. He'd dozed off and on all day yesterday—remembered waking up screaming after a dream about ... no, it was gone. He'd slept through the night last night but still felt utterly, totally exhausted. Maybe it was the concussion.

It was early morning now. By noon when a whole fleet of Hueys, MEDIVAC choppers, came in full of wounded, the tent would be buzzing. Nobody would notice one missing chaplain. He'd wait until then to sneak off and look for his squad.

Until then, he was content to sit, figured if he sat still long enough and concentrated, maybe he could piece together what'd happened that had landed him in the field hospital.

He closed his eyes and tried, went back to the last thing he could remember clearly before waking up here. They'd come into that village by the river, on the back side, at night. The next morning, they were hit by gooks in the jungle beyond the village so he and Haystack had—

Haystack.

The image of him staring sightlessly upward, flies buzzing around the small round hole in his forehead filled Grayson's whole head. It was like he was looking at that huge movie screen where he and Piper had seen the *Ten Commandments*, but up so close to the screen that Haystack's face filled all his vision.

Haystack was dead. Sniper.

Grayson's memory took another step forward and a blurry form on the other side of the road resolved into clear focus. Nguyen! She was just standing there, looking at him. Then she began to advance slowly toward him and his squad. After that …

His mind recoiled so violently from the rest of the memory that his head bobbed slightly on his shoulders. Though he didn't know why, he did know that if he allowed himself to think about the little girl, he'd end up dinki dau. Crazy. Section Eight. No, the memory-movie ended with Haystack. Beyond that point was blackness.

He quickly opened his eyes, suddenly afraid the blackness existed outside his eyelids the same as it did inside. What he saw was boots. Just boots, that's all. It felt like way too much trouble to lift his head to see the rest of the soldier standing in front of him. Not now. Not with his ears humming, ringing. An explosion, there must have been an explosion so close it'd rung his chime good! He wondered idly if he'd ever hear normally again, if the hum in his ears that sounded like an old refrigerator kicking on in the middle of the night, would ever go away.

The soldier in front of him spoke, but Grayson couldn't hear what he said. He put his finger in his left ear and shook it. Sometimes that helped. Not this time, though. So he held his nose and blew hard. He felt a pop in his right ear and the muted sounds all around him became clear. He was instantly sorry he'd done it. Muted was better.

What had been mumble was now nearby conversations. He didn't have to hear the words to know what the conversations were about. Same talk, different day. How bad the food was. How bad the weather was. How bad their feet hurt. Expletives abounded, the f-word, inserted in every sentence and between the syllables of every other word. He could hear men groaning in the medical tent, the distant rumble of thunder, or gunfire.

"You Chaplain Addington?" the soldier standing in front of him asked. Gray heard him clearly that time so the ear-popping maneuver had worked better than he thought. He tried it again.

"Yeah, I'm Addington," Grayson said. He heard his own voice with relative clarity, so his other ear must be clear now, too. He looked up and saw that the soldier was a chopper jockey, a crewman on one of the early med-evacs that'd be taking the worst of the wounded in the tent back to Saigon.

The soldier looked at a clipboard, thumbed the top paper back and ran his finger down the paper beneath. "Addington, yeah, here it is. You've got orders to accompany the body of PFC Herbert Thomas Maddox back to Kentucky." Haystack. "Gather up your gear."

Grayson sat very still and felt the universe shift beneath him. He'd lost his short-timer's stick, hadn't seen it since … With no stick, and absolutely no idea what day it was, Grayson was unable to come up with an exact number. Less than thirty, he was sure. Twenty-two, maybe? Though he couldn't pin down his actual days-left-in-country, he did know one thing with absolute certainty: his time wasn't up.

"You got the wrong guy," he told the chopper jockey.

"You're Addington, right? Chaplain Grayson Allen Addington?" The soldier rattled off a serial number. It was the one printed on the silver dog tag that hung around Grayson's neck.

"Yeah. But I … why would…?"

"Whadda you care? You're getting out of here. Wish it was me. I still got 98 marks to cut in my stick."

Grayson's heart took up the rhythm of a snare drum in his chest.

"You're serious, aren't you," he said to the soldier in wonder.

The soldier nodded but still Grayson couldn't wrap his mind around the concept. Was it possible? Could he actually be … *going home?*

~

CARTER'S long strides carried him up the sidewalk to the front door of the house, which by the standards of Sadler Hollow was a large, well-kept structure. That meant it actually had a yard with a sparse stand of grass Piper mowed with the push-mower once a week. His mother loved roses and trellises on both sides of the wide porch steps sported climbing rose vines with blossoms that perfumed the warm evening air. There was a half whisky barrel by the front gate where blue, yellow and pink pansy faces looked up at the sky.

Ma had planted a vegetable garden along the south side of the house. Five grains to a hill of corn—"one for the woodchuck, one for the crow, one for the weather and two to grow." The garden had produced okra, too, squash and crisp black-eyed peas all summer, and pole beans climbed the fence on the back side of the house above ripe watermelons. The soil on the mountainside wasn't the best and there was precious little flat land around the house, but Marian Addington could make a garden grow anywhere.

The house needed painting but was in better shape than most. The fence had been in need of paint for so long the wood had worn almost bare and the sun had bleached it out a gray so shiny it was silver. But it was in good repair, stretched primly around the yard with the requisite squeaky gate in front with a mailbox on a post next to it. Piper's old white Rambler station wagon sat in the dirt driveway. Marian had no driver's license and had never owned a car.

The gate squealed its protest when he opened it and he took only a couple of steps, then stopped. Someone inside his mother's house was singing. The voice was as clear as a church bell on a cold winter morning and he thought instantly of the Vienna Boys' Choir he'd heard perform once on the Ed Sullivan Show.

He crossed the wood slat porch and opened the unlatched screen door, stuck his head in and called out, "Ding, dong. Avon calling."

The singing instantly stopped.

"Carter?" Piper called out. She emerged from the kitchen, wiping her hands on her apron. "What are you doing here?"

"Is that any way to greet the man who—at great risk to life and limb, I might add—won for your daughter the one and only Rasmus the Magnificent at the free-throw booth at the county fair?"

He blustered because the sight of Piper always took his breath away. She was wearing jeans and a stripped, sleeveless blouse that showed off her graceful, tanned arms. Her long black hair hung in loose curls around her shoulders and her eyes were so dark you could fall down into the depths of them and never come back up. She smiled, drawing her lips back in a heart shape that made his knees weak. She *was* glad to see him!

"It's Thursday and not even suppertime yet. Why are you here?"

"I've got a more pressing question. Who was that singing?"

As if in answer, a little girl emerged from the hallway leading to his mother's bedroom. She had Sunshine casually balanced on her hip. Though the toddler was small-boned and delicate, the little girl hauling her couldn't have been more than 9 or 10 herself.

"Unka Cardur," Sadie exclaimed when she saw him. She lifted her little hands shoulder high, palms up like a tulip, in a comical gesture of surprise. "You came baaaack." She did that every time she saw him—even if he'd only gone out to the road to check the mailbox.

The little girl holding Sadie had flaming red hair in

long braids and a spray of crimson freckles on her nose. Her eyes were the most amazing shade of green Carter'd ever seen. Well, one of them was. He couldn't see the other, the one almost closed with a huge, purple shiner. There was also an ugly bruise on her left cheek and her lip was split where somebody'd obviously popped her in the mouth.

"Shh," she said with her finger to her split lip. "Don't want to wake her now she's finally drifted off."

A peep would have disturbed the old woman whose pain never let her rest well and whose hearing was so acute she could be jarred from fitful sleep if a cricket tripped and fell in the front yard.

Sadie chimed in. Putting her chubby finger under her nose. "Be vewry, vewry quiet," she whispered, unaware how much she sounded like Elmer Fudd.

Carter was momentarily distracted by "kiiill da waaabbit … kiiill da waaabbit" ringing in his head.

"Marian's asleep?" Piper was incredulous.

"Just did nod away."

"But how…?" Piper looked a question at Carter.

"What?" He was totally bewildered.

"Marian hasn't gotten a wink of sleep without her pain medicine in weeks. I don't…" Piper's voice trailed off.

Carter turned and spoke to the little girl.

"Hi there. I'm Carter Addington, Marian's oldest son. What's your name?"

After a brief hesitation, she said, "Maggie."

"Maggie … what?" he prodded for a last name, but the little girl only looked at him. There was a moment of awkward silence. "Well, I'm glad to meet you, Maggie."

"Pleased to make your acquaintance, sir," she said. The lilt of the dialect in her speech was unmistakable. Clearly, she had come from deep within one of the inner rings of the circle. It seemed impolite to ask Piper what the little girl was doing here with the child standing right there with Sunshine … *Sadie!* It hit him that Sunshine looked as content in the little girl's arms as a puppy snuggled up to its mother. And unlike her nickname implied, Sunshine didn't warm up to *anybody*.

"Do you mind if I take the little one outside?" Maggie asked. "Wildflowers smell so good. We could pick some and put them in a vase in Nan Marian's room."

Nan Marian? Carter hadn't heard the term since he was a little boy and his mother told him stories about her own grandmother. The word for grandfather had been … what was the word? … tide! Nan and tide.

"It'll be dark soon." Maggie's tone changed to firm and intense. "I'll watch her careful! You needn't worry your head about that." She pronounced "about" so it sounded like "a boot."

"Fine then, run along." Piper's voice had a sort of hysterical cheeriness. "I'll fix supper and call you when it's ready. Do you like--?"

"I like everything," Maggie said. She set Sunshine on the floor and paused. "At least … I think I do."

"Sabie pick dis much flowers," Sadie spread her little hands as far apart as she could reach, then turned and raced for the back door. The child never walked if she could run.

When the screen door closed behind the two children, Piper let her breath out in a whoosh and sank down onto the arm of the overstuffed chair in the parlor.

"Uh … what just happened?" Carter asked.

"I have no idea. I've been living in the Twilight Zone ever since that little girl showed up on the porch yesterday morning."

"Who is she? Where'd she come from?"

"I don't know and I don't know."

"You look like a woman who could use a hug."

Carter walked over, pulled Piper to her feet and took her in his arms. It was a totally fraternal hug. Brother/sister. Carter prided himself on that—he'd been able to keep the platonic lid on his feelings. He would not make a move of any kind on Piper until Grayson was … out of the picture. He didn't want Piper to have to live the rest of her life with the reputation that she'd had a thing for the brother of her poor husband—and Grayson would automatically be granted poor-husband status because he'd been a soldier fighting a war.

She sighed in his arms, then stepped back and flashed him a distracted smile.

"It's been one of those—"

"Sit down." He pulled a chair out at the kitchen table and held it for her, then sat down in the one opposite it. His heart was racing. He couldn't do a thing about that. Merely being in her presence sent his hormones into overdrive, but he was very good at hiding it. He'd had years of practice.

For a moment, his mind threatened to mutiny, to rip the seals off the locked door of his memories and grant him a visceral re-enactment of the agony of learning that the woman he loved—the only woman he ever had or every would love—had eloped with his younger brother. But he shut the systems down and offered Piper a pleasant smile.

"Now, I want to hear the whole story. Blow by blow."

He listened attentively, asking a few questions here and there, as Piper recounted how the little girl had shown up out of nowhere on the front porch Wednesday morning. Described how Sadie had broken the ice. And after a couple of glasses of lemonade, three scrambled eggs and four pieces of fried toast—with Marian's special tomato jam—the child had allowed Piper to unbraid her hair, warm some water on the stove and fix her a bath.

"She closed herself up in the bathroom, very private. I gave her one of my nightgowns while I washed her dress and hung it out to dry. But when I was braiding her hair later, I saw huge bruises on her neck and down her back. Somebody beat her up—really badly. She's bruised all over."

"What did she say about it?" Carter asked.

"Nothing."

"What do you mean, nothing?"

"Come on, Carter, how many things can nothing mean? I asked and she didn't answer."

Piper mimicked her own concerned voice.

"So Maggie, Honey… what happened to you, your eye and your lip?"

"Nothing," she mimicked Maggie's reply.

"Something did. Something … or somebody… hurt you, blacked your eye and split your lip—who was it?"

"'I don't know' and 'I don't remember,' is all I could get out of her," Piper said. "And the thing is … I believe her, Carter. I don't think she does know."

"You think she has amnesia?"

"Maybe … or something like it. She didn't seem to be lying, covering up for somebody. It looked like she was trying to remember but couldn't."

"You don't suppose somebody hit her so hard she …"

"I asked her where she came from and she just pointed toward the mountains. As hungry and thirsty and dirty as she was, she must have been wandering around in these woods for days, could have come from…" Piper made a sweeping gesture. "…from anywhere."

"Not generic *anywhere*. With that lilt, definitely Whoopie Country."

"Which brings me to the what-do-I do-now part?"

"You can't just say, 'She followed me home, Mom, can I keep her?' She's not a stray."

"But I can't send her back to a place where somebody's going to beat her!"

"Piper," Carter said, his voice quiet, "that decision isn't yours to make."

She looked at him like she was about to go off again, but didn't.

"It's like she…like she's always been here. Okay, I know that's crazy, I'm only saying that's what it feels like." Her voice began to rise again. "How can I give her up to somebody who—?"

"Tomorrow you have to take her to the sheriff's office," he said, keeping his voice steady and calm. "I'll stay with Ma and Sunshine. With the weekend coming up, maybe Maggie could stay with us until—"

"Us? It's Thursday. You're here for the whole weekend?"

"I didn't just show up, I was sent."

Before he had a chance to say more, the back screen door opened and Maggie stepped inside, then held the door for Sadie. The toddler walked through it with the exaggerated slowness of a waiter balancing full wine glasses on a tray. Held out in front of her in both hands was a bouquet of wildflowers, complete with a generous sampling of thistle and weeds.

Maggie held a single perfect rose.

"For Nan Marian," she said. "Roses are her favorite, you know."

Chapter Eight

The Cochran County Sheriff's Department was in the courthouse at the center of the square in Chandler, eleven miles down Sadler Hollow from Sadlerton. An imposing, gray limestone structure, it boasted a shiny brass dome and war memorials out front that listed the names of the county's fallen. The one for World War I was the tallest. A bronze statue of a uniformed soldier, rifle at the ready, stood on a base of granite where the names were inscribed. The World War II memorial looked more like a giant headstone, wide, with no statue. The names inscribed there were on bronze plaques attached to the front and back sides.

Piper had grown to hate the memorials after Grayson went to Vietnam. She couldn't walk past without envisioning the one they'd build to honor the Vietnam dead. She had no doubt they'd erect a memorial. West Virginians were patriotic, proudly, loudly, fiercely patriotic. As a percentage of population, more mountaineers volunteered for military service than men from any other state. She could envision his name there, the first one, of course. Dead soldiers were always listed alphabetically.

U.S. Army Chaplain Grayson Allen Addington. Only his name, nothing left of him but letters etched into a piece of metal on a stone, snow capped in the wintertime and a landing/crapping spot for pigeons in the summer.

She gripped Maggie's hand tight and marched by the memorials without looking, climbed the wide concrete steps and pushed open the door.

Sheriff Clifford R. Bayless's office was on the ground floor. It was the office where property taxes were collected, so Piper had been there before, but that's not how she knew Sheriff Bayless. He'd been a deputy when she first met him. He was one of the officers who'd taken Riley away in handcuffs after he and his gang of thugs had beaten Carter half to death one night after a football game. He'd only been in jail a few days, of course. Though there'd been a dozen witnesses, Carter had refused to name Riley and his friends as his assailants. The McCulloughs and the Campbells didn't need the law interfering in their family business, thank you very much. They settled their own scores. But Piper always believed her mother and Marian had stepped in to keep the situation from escalating into more bloodshed. Darlene Campbell and Marian Addington had cut a deal that Carter wouldn't testify—or retaliate—if Darlene kept Riley under control. Nobody on the planet could have done it but those two women and what could have started an all-out war was swept under the rug and forgotten. Piper's mother's influence was so strong that the pact held even after she died a year later.

"Hidy, Piper," said Ramona Richards, the clerk who worked the front counter. "Where's that precious little girl of yours? I swear, that child's as perfect as a life-sized doll. I never seen the like."

Before Piper could answer, Ramona spotted Maggie. "And who's this pretty little thing?"

Piper had cleaned Maggie up the best she could, had mended the torn sleeve and holes in her dress, pressed it, even found two pieces of ribbon to tie the ends of Maggie's braids. There were no shoes in the house that would fit Maggie so she was barefoot, but so was every other kid in Sadler Hollow in the summertime.

"Is Sheriff Cliff around handy?' Piper asked, blowing by Ramona's questions about Maggie. "I sure do need to talk to him."

"Nope, sorry. He's up Wheeling for the day. Then he's going to visit his daughter in Pittsburgh. Won't be back 'til Monday."

It hadn't occurred to Piper that she might not be able to talk to the sheriff about Maggie.

"Can Phil help you? He's holding down the fort 'til the sheriff gets back." She gestured toward the open office door where a beefy man with a barrel chest and a head of salt-and-pepper hair combed straight back from his forehead was talking on the telephone. The nameplate on his desk read Deputy Sheriff Philip Higgins.

"Sure, I guess, Phillip's fine," Piper said. Deputy Higgins's daughter Allison and Piper had been friends in high school until Allison got pregnant when she was 15 and dropped out. He hadn't been a deputy sheriff then. He'd been a coal miner.

The deputy hung up the phone and Ramona went into his office to tell him Piper needed to see him.

"You sit out here for a little while, okay?" Piper told Maggie, then went into the deputy sheriff's office, closed the door behind her and sat down in the straight back chair next to the desk. After a few minutes of when-have-you-heard-from-Grayson and what's-Allison-doing-these-days, Piper told him why she'd come. She saw him study Maggie through the glass in his office door as she told her story.

"She don't know her name?"

"Or won't say, I don't know which."

"I can see she was beat up."

"She's got a whole lot more bruises you can't see."

"She showed up on your porch yesterday morning, so that means she's been missing from somewhere at least 24 hours."

"More like three days. Before she got to my house, she'd been out in the woods for at least a day and night and I think two's more likely. She was dirty, had twigs and sticks in her hair where she'd laid on the ground and she was about to starve to death."

"Why didn't you bring her in yesterday? You musta known somebody'd be looking for her."

"Because … oh, what can I say, Mr. Higgins… I mean Deputy Higgins. I … she'd been beat up and I couldn't stand the idea of turning her back over to whoever beat her." She lowered her head and whispered. "And I still can't."

"Well right now, far as I know, there ain't nobody to turn her back over to."

Piper raised her head.

"We ain't had a report of a missing kid anywhere in Cochran County and we'd have been notified if there was a kid missing in any of the counties around."

He looked back out at Maggie.

"Send her in here and let me have a little talk with her. Maybe I can get her to tell me her name."

Piper went out to where Maggie was sitting and sent her into the deputy's office. He closed the door behind her. She saw him come around his desk and sit down in a chair beside Maggie and she appreciated that. About ten minutes later, Maggie came out with a coin in her hand.

"Deputy Higgins said there's a machine in the basement with pop!" she said. Her eyes were bright. "And look what he gave me. Can I go—?"

"Sure you can."

Maggie unexpectedly threw her arms around Piper's waist in a tight hug, then turned and hurried out the door. Deputy Higgins had watched the scene from his office. He motioned for Piper to come in and sit back down.

"I'm thinking maybe she really don't know her name," he said. "But she's from Whoopie country alright, from somewhere so far back up one of them hollers Christmas gets there a day late. There's some Gregorys live near Chimney Rock … but I'm thinking the McIntyres, maybe. There's a passel of them and half of them's red-headed. I'll take the afternoon and do some nosing around."

Piper's heart ricocheted from her toes to her throat.

"What do you know about those people, the McIntyres?"

"They're dirt poor and ain't a one of 'em's dragging a full string of fish. That Maggie seems like a quick little thing, doesn't strike me as … I'll have to see what I can find out."

"And if you find … you'll take her back up there and leave her? After they beat—?"

"No, not if they beat her. The child welfare people from Charleston will get into it then, but you know as well as I do folks got a right to raise up their kids as suits 'em. Besides, she didn't say nothing to me about getting beat up, said she didn't know how she got them bruises." Piper opened her mouth to speak but he held up his hand. "I know, you can't hardly get kids to rat out their parents, no matter how bad they're treated."

Piper would have, if there'd been anybody interested enough to ask her. But she'd had no one to stand up for her, had been rescued by circumstance—and a bullet from William McCullough's gun. When her older brother told her their father was dead, her first thought had been: "I wonder if I'll be able to cry at the funeral."

"Let's take this one step at a time, Piper," the deputy said. I'm assuming you're willing for her to stay with you until—"

"Of course, she can stay with me!"

"I'll dig around and then I'll come by your place if I find anything. If you don't hear from me, come back into the office Monday morning and we'll figure where to go from there."

Piper left the office and started down the hallway to the stairs leading to the basement. Her hands were trembling, but the ball of terror in her stomach had eased some. Nobody had reported her missing! That was amazing. Three days and nobody'd even gone looking for her! But at least she hadn't been snatched away from Piper on the spot. That was something. Actually, that was quite a lot.

As Piper got to the end of the hallway, she heard a sound from below, echoing in the empty hollows of the marble floors and concrete walls. It was a child's musical laughter, carefree and joyful. What on earth had struck Maggie funny about a soft drink machine? Better question: How could a child like that not even be missed!

∼

THE HUEY TAKING Grayson to Saigon set down in a rice patty half way there to pick up a soldier who hadn't gotten out of the trees quick enough when the fly boys came over with napalm. He had no face, his features had melted like wax and he was screaming, wailing. They hooked him up and started pumping fluids laced with morphine into him through an IV. The corpsman squeezed the plastic bottle of liquid to push it faster into the guy's vein, but he kept shrieking, a sound that must have been shredding his vocal chords. On and on and on. Then he stopped, like turning off a tap. And the corpsman reached up and clipped off the IV. The only sound for the rest of the ride was the wind whooshing through the open doors.

Grayson was still wet from the shower, itching in the fresh fatigues, as the sergeant at Ton Son Nhut Air Base inspected his paperwork. The ink on it was as damp as the back of Grayson's neck. The sergeant nodded, then looked up at him.

"PFC Maddox's body shipped out yesterday. You'll connect in San Francisco and accompany him the rest of the way."

Then he pointed toward a transport. The doors were sliding shut. The ground crew had started to move the ladder away.

"You make it out to that plane and you'll be in Hawaii in thirteen hours—but you gotta factor in the seventeen-hour time difference and the international date line. Next flight's—" Grayson turned and started toward the aircraft. "Son, you're gonna need some American money and—"

Grayson didn't wait for the rest, merely snatched the voucher out of the sergeant's hand and bolted toward the ladder crew, waving his papers and hollering, "Wait, one more!"

There were no stewardesses serving lunch on Military Air Transport Service flights. MATS, affectionately referred to as Maybe Again, Tomorrow, Sometime. But cold K-Rations tasted fine, just fine! Because this wasn't an ordinary transport for Grayson—it was a Freedom Bird, the flight taking him home. He tried to sleep to make the time go faster. He did doze some, but it was hard to sleep through the whoops and groans of the soldiers engaged in a never-ending poker game. Or through the monologue of the black soldier with a gold tooth, which seemed unending, too. His wife was meeting him for a week of R & R in Hawaii and he talked too loud and described in way too much detail what he was going to do with her before he even took his boots off.

Chapter Nine

Carter and Piper sat together in the porch swing as evening draped a gauzy cape of twilight over the trees. There were no sunrises or sunsets here, of course. Night settled over the valley in ever-deepening shadows, a gentle exchange of dark for light as the pale blue sky cycled through navy to black to pitch and became a long, thin slice of coal sprinkled with starry sequins above their heads. The day had been hot and the cool evening breeze felt as refreshing as a spring rain.

The swing was old, sagged in the middle when two people sat in it, but held firm. The bare wood had been polished a smooth, mat gray by the backsides of the Addington/McCullough family. It was suspended from the porch ceiling with chains attached to S hooks and groaned a tempered eek-eek, eek-eek as it swung slowly back and forth.

Piper liked the sound. She remembered it from years ago. The first time Carter'd brought her home to meet the family, they had sat uncomfortably together in the swing. It was a couple of months before Carter's father had … died.

The old man had sat across from the couple, stiff in the cane-back chair and Piper had felt very small and vulnerable. She'd wanted to slip her hand into Carter's for support, but hadn't dared.

Piper stopped breathing. She'd almost done the same thing just now, had almost slipped her hand into Carter's! She rose abruptly, walked to the porch railing and looked out over the valley where shadows pooled and thickened in the growing dark.

"Maggie sure looks cute in those overalls," Carter said. Piper had remembered that the Craddocks had a little boy about Maggie's size. The family lived on Northfield Road —named, of course, for the coal company that built it— which ran the whole length of Sadler Hollow, through Sadlerton and the other coal camp towns to the county seat. She'd stopped at the Craddocks on her way back home and borrowed a pair of little Abe's overalls and a tee shirt. He was taller than Maggie, but Piper'd rolled up the pants legs and the overalls fit fine. "And I don't think I've ever seen Sunshine as … as…" Carter couldn't seem to find the words.

"As happy? Bubbly? Giddy, maybe?" She turned to face him.

"Yeah, as giddy as she was tonight playing house with Maggie. She and Maggie are like twins separated at birth."

They were silent.

"You're afraid Deputy Higgins is going to come get her tomorrow, aren't you?" Carter asked.

Piper turned back around. "Uh huh."

Carter didn't speak. The only sound was the chirp of the evening's first crickets under the porch and the comforting eeh, eeh, of the swing. Piper sighed and turned back to Carter.

"You saw her, the marks on her. You know how those people up in the mountains are."

She saw Carter fight a smile.

"Okay, so people in Charleston say the same thing about us. But Carter, I can't send her back to a home where they'll *hurt* her."

"What are you going to do, keep her here and hide her under the bed when anybody drops in. Be reasonable, Piper. Her parents are probably frantic. You have to—"

His gaze shifted to the road over her shoulder and his face darkened. She turned to see headlights on Turtle Road, a pickup truck trailing a plume of dust behind it like the tail on a kite. The truck rumbled muffler-free up the final hill and stopped in a cloud of dust in front of the house.

It was a beat-up truck. The black paint was peeling all the way down to rusted bare metal in spots, a spider web of cracks spread out across the windshield and the back bumper was affixed to the vehicle by an ingenious configuration of duct tape. A young man stepped easily down out of the driver's side of the truck. He was tall and slender, willowy, wearing a faded chambray shirt and battered jeans in need of patching at the knee. His West Virginia University cap was pushed back to reveal black curls peeking out from under the brim. The smile on his face was wide and stapled to his cheeks with deep-dish dimples just like Sadie's. He took a few steps toward the house, then stopped and the smile slid down off his face.

"Zeke!" Piper cried and hurried down the porch steps to greet the young man. He was considerably younger and taller than she was but one look at his face and it was clear he was kin.

She stopped in front of him, slipped her finger into his

shirt pocket and looked inside. Then she pulled the pocket on the right side of his jeans inside out.

"What are you—?"

"Just checking to see if you had a hug in there anywhere for your big sister."

He grinned in spite of himself and wrapped his arms around her. But he was looking at Carter.

"What's he doing here?" Zeke asked.

"Hello. This is his mother's house, Zeke."

"I mean why now, today? It's Friday. I thought he stayed down in Charleston 'cept on weekends."

"You don't have to talk about me like I'm not here, or deaf," Carter called out, and rose out of the swing. "I came home to see my Ma. You got a problem with that?"

The edge in his voice cut through the evening air like a saber. Piper felt Zeke stiffen. Anger rose in her throat and she pulled out of her brother's arms.

"Stop it! Both of you stop it." She looked up into Zeke's face. "Carter has every right to be here." She spun around and looked at Carter. "And my little brother has every right to come here to visit me. If either one of you has a problem with that, you can *both* leave."

The screen door opened and Maggie stepped out, almost as if she'd come specifically to interrupt the rising tension. And maybe she had. The swelling around her right eye was gone, though she still had a shiner. Sadie rested on her hip and she hiked the toddler up to keep her from sliding. She had pulled Sadie's hair back into two curly dog-ears that hung down her back.

As soon as Sadie spotted the young man, she squealed, "Unka Zeke!" Her face was instantly wreathed in a double-dimple smile and she wiggled down out of Maggie's arms. Then she raced across the porch, down the steps, held up her hands and cried. "Unka Zeke. Sabie go wheeee!"

Zeke took both her hands and spun her gently around in a circle, crying, "Wheeeee!" Her dog-ears flew out behind her like twin flags.

When he set her down, she held onto his hand and dragged him toward the porch.

"Come see my Mabie, Unka Zeke," she said. "Mabie loooves Sabie."

"Nan Marian's got fresh lemonade," Maggie said. She looked down at Sadie. "With extra sugar, just the way you like it." Beneath the flaming red hair her freckles practically glowed in the spill of light from the doorway.

Zeke unconsciously reached up and pulled his cap off his head the way he'd have done if Marian herself had stepped out on the porch.

Piper knew Zeke liked Marian, and that was saying something, her being a McCullough. Sure, it was hard to hold a grudge against an old woman whose grip on this life was so tenuous she might let go of it at any minute and rise up to the sky before your very eyes. But Zeke liked her because she'd welcomed him the day he'd shown up about a month after Piper moved in. Just there one day looking very young and vulnerable. Piper had wondered what she'd do if she saw him, *when* she saw him, because surely she would run into him eventually. Wondered what he'd do. After all, she was the one who'd left without a word when he was only 10 years old.

She needn't have wondered what either one of them would do or say. As soon as he got out of the truck in front of the house, the same battered truck Riley'd had when she left, Piper had run out the door, down the steps, and thrown herself into his arms, almost bowled the boy over. She'd hugged him fiercely and he'd hugged her back and then she'd started babbling and crying at the same time, explaining how she couldn't tell him she was running off with Grayson, couldn't tell anybody. If he'd let it slip to Riley… And then he'd stopped her and said he understood, and she realized she may have left behind the boy she'd raised as a son after their mother died, but she'd come home to a young man.

"You're *Mabie,* little pretty one?" Zeke asked Maggie, returning her smile.

"Maggie," she corrected.

Zeke turned to Piper. "Who—?" he began, but a slight shake of her head stopped him.

"Nan Marian said to ask if you brought Nellie," Maggie said. "Did you? And who's Nellie?"

"Sugar, I don't go nowhere 'thout my banjo," Zeke said.

"A banjo!" Maggie exclaimed. "Really? Will you play me a song on it? *Pleease!*"

Her little blond sidekick chimed in, "Peease, Unka Zeke."

Maggie turned to Carter. "You wouldn't mind a bit of music, would you now, Mr. Carter?"

Piper couldn't stifle a smile. Clearly, both men had been outnumbered, outmaneuvered and outgunned by two little girls.

"Well, no, I … " Carter began.

"Get Nellie," Piper said, "and let's all have some lemonade."

CARTER SAT beside his mother on the lumpy couch in the parlor with what he hoped was an appropriately benign look on his face as he watched Zeke show off his skill at Turkey in the Straw and Orange Blossom Special. If Jesse was right, the cocky teenager believed he'd be as adept at making moonshine as he was at playing the banjo.

Zeke was perched on the edge of the table with Piper seated nearby in a chair she'd pulled out from it. Sunshine was playing on the floor at his feet. Maggie was refilling their glasses of lemonade.

Carter knew his mother was in pain, could see it in the pinched set of her mouth and her squinted eyes. But there was a smile firmly planted on her face and she at least appeared to be enjoying the music.

Then Carter glanced at Piper and he softened. She couldn't seem to drag her eyes off the boy, caressed his face the way a proud Ma … Well, she was the mother he remembered best. Zeke'd been 4 years old when his father and Uncle William died in a hail of gunfire. Five when his mother'd had a heart attack—Piper said the *lack* of strain did it, that when the tension of living with a monster was released, something had just come loose inside her. Piper had stepped up and become a woman that very day—at 13. She'd told Carter about it when they'd started dating two years later, described how her little brother'd cried himself to sleep for weeks, woke up two or three times a night screaming from nightmares, how she'd finally moved his little cot into her room right up next to her bed and went to sleep every night for months holding her little brother's hand. She'd cared for Zeke all on her own, too, certainly had no help from that good-for-nothing older brother, mean as a sack of rattlers.

"Would you like this last wee bit of lemonade?" Maggie asked Carter, proper as a matre de in a fancy restaurant.

He held his hand out over the top of his glass. "I'm good, thanks."

"Are you, Mr. Carter?"

He turned and really looked at her then.

"What?"

"Are you good?" she said. "I want to be good, but I don't know how you learn a thing like that."

The child's eyes were such a luminous green that—her eyes! There were daisies in them. Flakes of yellow extended out from the black irises like the petals of a flower. Like a daisy.

"Do you?" she asked.

"Does he what?" Piper asked, then motioned for Maggie to follow her into the kitchen to fill the empty pitcher.

"Does he know how to play the banjo?" Carter replied. "And the answer's no, he does not. But he is a talented fellow for all that … and if you give him a minute, he'll think what it is he can do that will amaze and entertain."

"You talk real good," Zeke said, as he fit the pick beneath the strings on the neck of the banjo and pulled a package of cigarettes from his shirt pocket. "Sound like a city boy."

"I heard that," Piper called from the kitchen. "I worked hard to lose my accent, too. Do I sound like a city girl?"

"You don't sound funny like he does. Carter here … it's like he's some kinda college professor. Ain't exactly amazing, but it is entertaining to listen to."

On its face, there was nothing offensive about what the young man said, but the underlying sarcasm was thick enough to spread on toast. Carter grabbed hold of his anger, though, and pretended he didn't notice.

"I have a better idea. How about instead of talking, I ask questions and you talk. Actually, it's only one question. Have you heard about what happened Tuesday in Wales?"

Before he could answer there was a clatter in the

kitchen, the sound of breaking glass. Then he could hear Piper talking to Maggie.

"It's okay, Sweetheart, accidents happen. Go sit down and let me clean it up. I don't want you to cut yourself on the glass."

Maggie came back into the room, her eyes on the floor. "I dropped—"

"You didn't drop it," Piper called from the kitchen. "*I* did."

"One of your glasses slipped, Nan Marian, when I was handing it to Miss Piper, and it broke. I'm sorry."

"Now don't you worry 'bout a little thing like that." Marian patted the couch next to her. "Come sit here by me…" she turned back toward Carter, seated on the other side, "while Carter tells us about something that happened in Wales."

"No, I'm not going to tell you, I want you to tell me. What do you think about it?"

"I'll tell you what I think about it soon's you tell me what it is," Zeke said, lit the cigarette and sent a plume of smoke up toward the ceiling. "You ain't making no more sense than a drunk chicken."

Carter'd found out what he wanted to know.

"There was a disaster in the village of Gaynor, in a valley in Wales, Monday. A pile of coal slurry let go, lique-fied, and slag slid down the hillside into a village. A lot of people were …" He glanced at Maggie, who'd lifted her eyes when he began to describe the disaster, and edited the rest of what he was going to say. "…were hurt."

"And *you're* wondering if *we're* wondering whether #1's gonna bust loose?" Zeke said, and gestured toward the back of the house in the direction of the structure that was now nothing more than a deeper shadow on the dark mountainside. "Like maybe your boss is wondering if we're all upset about it. Might make us some signs like them commie war protestors and march around in circles?"

In spite of himself, Carter was impressed. Zeke had a good aw-shucks routine going but he was smarter than he looked. He might be a more formidable competitor in the shine business than Carter'd given him credit.

"Are you?"

"Why would I be upset about that dam? The whole thing let go, wouldn't get nobody's feet wet in Cricket Hollow." He looked from Piper to Sadie and then to Marian and Maggie on the couch. "But if I's *you*, I'd be upset. I'd be asking all kinda questions if *my* family lived in harm's way."

Carter felt his face flush.

"Are you saying—?"

"I'm sayin' if I's you, I never woulda went to work for Mr. Nelson Warren and the Northfield Coal Company in the first place, the way they done bled this whole county dry."

The boy'd said it in a normal, pass-the-salt tone of voice that Carter acknowledged was remarkably skillful passive aggression. You couldn't fault him. And if you lost your temper, he'd be the victim and you'd be the bad guy.

Two can play at this game, son.

"Well, that's the difference between you and me, I guess." He favored the teenager with a "Baby Bear" smile —not too hard, not too soft—just right. His voice was as even and level as the boy's had been. "I'd rather be the big dog than the bush he lifts his hind leg on."

PIPER WATCHED THEM SPAR, a jab here, a punch there. Back and forth. She'd dared to hope that maybe they'd both relax enough to realize they didn't have a thing against each other personally. If they'd been two strangers sitting together on a bus, they'd have enjoyed chatting.

Still, it wasn't as bad as it could be. As it used to be. Ten years ago, you couldn't have put a Campbell in the same room with a McCullough unless both of them had been dead for three days.

Carter and Zeke went at each other, but with *words*, not with fists and not with guns! That was something. Actually, it was quite a lot. But she was growing weary of the confrontation. The blasted testosterone! She stepped into the room and put her hand on her brother's shoulder.

"Thanks for the concert, Zeke, but you'd best be on your way. I got a little girl to put to bed, and you being in Riley's truck ..."

Zeke popped up off the edge of the table like a jack-in-the-box. If somebody chanced to tell Riley they'd seen his truck turn up Turtle Road ... He stubbed out his cigarette in the ashtray on the table and leaned down to snuggle Sadie.

"Bye bye," he said.

"Bye, bye, Unka Zeke," she said and gave him what Grayson had called her "gnat-snatcher" wave—opening and closing her little fingers as if she were trying to catch a bug in the air. She'd waved that way as a baby when she'd first learned "bye bye," and she never changed.

"Thank you for the lemonade, Mrs. Marian," he said as he gathered up Nellie.

"You come back real soon, Zeke."

He turned to go, then turned resolutely back.

"Carter," he said, and nodded his head almost imperceptibly.

"Zeke," Carter said.

"Can I walk out to your truck with you?" Maggie asked.

"Why, sure you can, Baby Girl."

Zeke shot a questioning look over the child's head at Piper. She answered with a shrug, then stood at the door and watched the tall, lanky teenager and the little red-haired girl walk out into the gloom. Maggie reached up and took Zeke's hand and was chattering away about something. What could the child possibly have to say to Zeke?

Chapter Ten

THE DRONE of the big transport's engines was pleasantly hypnotic. The black soldier's voice was still too loud, only now he was pontificating about how the International Dateline was finally giving them back the day it had taken from them when they'd flown to Vietnam. Grayson smiled sadly, remembering how Haystack had been genuinely upset at the thought of losing a day of his life. And his days had run out before he got a chance to get it back. Now the farm boy was on his final trip home to Kentucky, where Grayson would surrender his remains to the Monroe Funeral Home in Spindle Rock.

After that, then what? Surely, Grayson's orders would grant him a three-day pass. Getting in touch with Piper to tell her about it, however, was going to be a challenge.

The phone in the Sadlerton Post Office was something of a community phone. You could call there in an emergency and Mildred Magee, the post mistress, would see your message got delivered. In fact, Mildred and his mother'd been childhood friends, and the only other time he'd called home—to tell her and Piper he was safe after the deadly firefight that decimated his unit—Mildred hadn't just delivered a message. She'd hauled Piper down to the post office so he could call back and talk to her.

Only, he hadn't actually talked to her at all. He'd talked to some soldier on a switchboard somewhere and that guy had talked to Piper.

Grayson: Piper, I'm fine. I'm not hurt.

Intermediary: Piper, I'm fine. I'm not hurt.

Piper: I love you, Gray.

Intermediary: I love you, Gray.

After that experience, Piper had written to him and told him never to call again. And he hadn't.

It ran a little thrill up his spine to think of actually hearing Piper's voice, of the stunned surprise in it and how thrilled she'd be when he told her that he and all the members of C Company had gotten early-outs—their tours in-country had been cut thirty days. Nobody said why but the reason was obvious. When the only National Guard *infantry* unit in the whole country—the Kentucky 151st ARNG (Army Reserve National Guard)—had been activated, it had become the *only* National Guard ground maneuver unit in Vietnam, a unit of civilians that never should have … let it go. Piper wasn't expecting him until October. She'd cry when she heard his voice, he knew she would. And he'd have to make her promise she wouldn't drive like a wild woman from Sadler Hollow to Spindle Rock to pick him up.

But he couldn't call her from Honolulu. He'd get there at 7 p.m. Friday evening. If he'd calculated the time difference and date change correctly, that was 1 a.m. Saturday morning in West Virginia. Not only would the post office be closed then, it would be closed for the rest of the weekend. The only way he could get in touch with his family was to call Carter in Charleston. Failing that, he'd just have to call Uncle Jim.

When the military transport touched down in Hawaii, all the other soldiers aboard let out whoops and cheers. Grayson had an entirely different, totally irrational emotional response. It hit him out of nowhere. When he stepped into the Honolulu airport, he was instantly terrified, afraid all the scrubbed-up people inside the building would … smell his stink. His fatigues were clean, of course. *He* was clean—well, he had been 13 hours ago when he dived through the closing doors of the transport as it was about to taxi down the runway at the Ton Son Nhut Air Base.

But there was a stink in his nostrils so strong he couldn't smell the tropical flowers in the colorful leis a native girl placed around his neck. It was a stink of blood and urine and jungle rot pus. He knew it had to be his imagination. Still, he ducked into the first bathroom he saw and scrubbed his hands until the sores on them were bleeding. The stink remained, of course, because it wasn't on his skin but in his mind. He barely made the commercial flight that was his connection, stumbled down the aisle, collapsed in his window seat and sat there shaking, profoundly grateful no one was seated beside him. Then he turned and stared out into the endless blackness of ocean and night sky. When the airplane touched down at San Francisco International Airport, he could not recall a single thought that had crossed his mind during the whole five-hour flight.

~

PIPER LOOKED over the edge of her coffee cup and told Carter she felt like the rich aristocracy. He gave her a puzzled look and it struck her fresh that spending the night in his mother's house in the mountains was probably disconcerting for him. She'd never been to his apartment in Charleston, but he had talked about it—the fancy kitchen with appliances he had no clue how to use, the shower/bath combination and the balcony overlooking the Kanawha River. His mother's house clung to the slope of the steep mountainside like a bird's nest in a tree. The only flat land near it was a meadow about the size of a baseball field that belonged to the Tucker family who'd moved out of the shack at the far side of it years ago.

Marian's house had few amenities. It was clean, oh, my yes, the old woman had always kept the hardwood floors scrubbed and polished, the frayed curtains starched and ironed and handmade quilts covered the worn-through spaces on the parlor couch and chair. The kitchen was on the back of the house and opened onto a porch in the little back yard. Snuggled up to the house beside the porch was a woodpile and the storage shed where Piper kept the lawnmower. The table where they sat was at the far end of the parlor in front of the kitchen door, with windows on both sides, providing a view into the woods beside the house or down the valley out front.

The two bedrooms that had been the boys' rooms when they were growing up were much smaller now because the new bathroom with its big claw-foot tub had been hunked out of one side of them. Carter had added the bath when he piped running water to the house after his mother got sick. For years, he'd been begging her to let him fix up the house, but she'd allowed as how it'd been good enough for her and Everett and it was fine now—why there was a good well not ten feet from the back porch and a serviceable outhouse at the edge of the yard!

Marian occupied the small bedroom closest to the

bath; the other small bedroom was Sadie's, though she actually slept in a playpen alongside Piper's bed in the larger bedroom.

Maggie had insisted on making a pallet on the back porch and Piper suspected even that might have been more comfortable than the bed she probably shared with who knows how many siblings in some mountain shack. Carter slept out on the couch in the parlor—which was not nearly as comfortable as it looked, courtesy of two broken springs —one that poked up through the cushion on the right side and another that allowed the cushion to sink into a hole on the left. Carter'd always joked that the couch was like the mountains themselves—pretty from a distance but steep and craggy up close.

"Rich aristocracy? How you figure that?" he said. He hadn't shaved yet and she liked how the rough, stubble on his cheeks and in the indention of his chin gave him a rugged look. The blonde hair on his arms shone golden in the sunlight.

When she first moved with Sadie back to the mountains, Carter had dropped by once in awhile to check on them. But as his mother's condition worsened, he came more and more often. The proximity, the forced intimacy of cramped spaces, had been awkward at first. But not anymore. Now it seemed perfectly normal to look across the breakfast table at an unshaven Carter, his hair askew in an endearing sofa-induced tangle. He sometimes arrived in a suit and tie straight from work. This time, he had shown up in more standard fare—an old Duke tee shirt and jeans.

"Don't know anybody's not rich who has their own personal nanny," Piper said, and nodded to Maggie. "She gets to Sadie before Sadie even has a chance to figure out she wants something."

The two little girls were playing with Rasmus in the

small patch of yard beyond the front porch. Maggie had made a bed of red maple tree leaves for the stuffed bear and Sadie was chattering away to the nose-less creature.

"I heard her singing to Sunshine last night after Zeke left."

Piper could hear the dislike in his voice when Carter said her brother's name, but she let it go.

"I did, too, and the song … sounded like something Ma used to sing, but maybe I'm only imagining it."

"You ain't," Marian said from the hallway. Carter and Piper turned to face her and Piper thought she looked better this morning than she had in weeks. "My old granny called it *The Ash Grove*, but I've heared it called by other names, too. Come from the old country."

There was color in her cheeks and the lines around her mouth didn't seem quite so deep. It might have been wishful thinking, but it even seemed the old woman's voice was stronger and there was no palsy stutter.

"Maggie singing that last night—it put me to sleep same as it did Sadie, slept the night through," Marian said. "Granny McCullough used to sing it when I's little."

Marian's voice was scratchy, but the melody was true.

"The ash grove how graceful, how plainly 'tis speaking .
The harp through its playing has language for me.
Whenever the light through its branches is breaking,
a host of kind faces is gazing on me."

She moved slowly but without apparent pain from the hall to the table.

"Granny was a McFarland from The Isle of Skye, had a voice clear as spring water and a brogue thick as molasses. Me and William'd snuggle down warm in our corn-husk mattress and listen to her sing and the wind howl down through the holler."

Piper sat very still. She'd lived with Marian since

Grayson shipped out last October, had been married to her son for almost eight years, and in all that time she'd never once heard Marian mention her brother, William—the brother Piper's father had shot and killed. Piper's older brother, Riley, said William had ambushed their father and he'd only been defending himself. Piper figured the McCulloughs probably said the same thing about Rooster Campbell. Since both men had been dead when William's son, Jesse, found them, there would forever be speculation about who had started it. Not that it mattered now.

~

THE BIG TIRES squalled in protest when the plane touched down. Grayson blinked, then opened his eyes slowly, unbelieving. Bright airport lights twinkled in all the buildings like Christmas decorations. California! He breathed deep. The imaginary stink was gone. He was *home!*

The giddy joy Grayson felt made him wonder if his feet were actually touching the floor of the terminal as he walked toward the baggage claim area. He felt like he might just float up to the ceiling, light as a little kid's helium balloon.

He was surprised to see that even now, at four o'clock in the morning, the airport was far from deserted. A smattering of people dotted the wide concourse and clustered in groups at the gates.

He was approaching a group of young people, students maybe, hippies. The girls had long straight hair, parted in the middle and wore beads and peace crosses. The boys' hair was long and straight, too.

A toddler was holding the hand of one of the girls,

who didn't look a day older than 15 herself and as he approached, the little girl let go of her mother's hand and began to toddle—stagger forward. She was barely able to remain upright and when she went down with a plop right in front of him, Grayson bent to help her to her feet.

"Don't you *touch* her!" the hippie girl shrieked, leapt forward and yanked the child up into her arms.

Grayson was so surprised he just straightened and gaped at her. Then she took a step toward him and spit in his face!

"Baby killer!" she growled.

The girl behind her moved forward and tried to spit in his face, too, but it fell short and landed on his shirt.

Grayson couldn't move.

"Baby killer!" the second one yelled, then the five of them took it up as a chant. "Baby killer! Baby killer!"

Grayson turned away and started resolutely down the corridor—he wouldn't run!—and they followed along beside him for thirty yards or so, shouting and spitting. The people in the concourse and at the gates fell silent, watching, and he glanced at their faces as he passed. In some of them he saw sympathy. In most, just indifference, which somehow felt worse than being spit on.

He washed the spittle off his face in a bathroom, straightened his uniform, then marched with dignity out of the airport with his head held high, and caught a bus to Fairfield, where Haystack would be waiting for him at Travis Air Force Base.

But when he got there, Grayson discovered that Haystack had left without him.

~

MAGGIE HAD TAKEN Sadie back out into the yard to play while Piper washed the lunch dishes when the toddler pointed her chubby little finger at the meadow below the house.

"Wanna see Sabie's b'flies?" she asked. "C'mon. I show you."

She grabbed Maggie's hand and pulled her toward the gate in the fence like a dog straining on a leash. "Go see b'flies, Mabie!"

The two walked down the dusty road together, then Maggie hefted Sadie up onto her hip to carry her through the brambles that ran between the road and the meadow at the base of the hillside. A hedge of paw paw bushes marked the end of the brambles and Maggie set the wiggling child down on the ground beyond the hedge, then watched her plunge off through the waist-high weeds and wildflowers squealing, "B'fies! B'fies."

The meadow was alive with them, so many it looked like a patchwork quilt with moving patches. White ones, yellow and blue ones. Maggie had never seen so many butterflies in one meadow before.

Or had she?

The familiar lump formed in her belly, the ache without real pain that made her midsection throb with every heartbeat, every intake of breath.

Had she ever seen so many butterflies before?

She honestly did not know. Everything before she stood on the porch of Sadie's house on Wednesday was just … gone. Vanished in a gauzy mist she couldn't see through. She couldn't remember butterflies. Or sunsets, afternoon rain or parents, brothers and sisters. Rivers, creeks, meadows, mountains—nothing. Everything she'd seen in the days she'd spent in Sadler Hollow looked achingly familiar, like she'd just walked away from this house or just climbed down out of that tree only moments before. At the same time, it all felt distant and unfamiliar, like she had never seen a sky quite that shade of blue or a flower that smelled so sweet.

She was old enough to know that she ought to be terribly upset by it all. It should have terrified her to be somewhere but not know how she got there. How could she possibly connect so completely to people she barely knew but have no memories at all of the people before them in her life, and certainly there must have been people before? She hadn't brought herself into the world, after all, or raised herself for … how many years? She didn't know. But she did know that somewhere there was a mother and a father who belonged to her, though, who might right now be watching and waiting for her.

She reached up involuntarily and touched her healing split lip. Miss Piper and Nan Marian talked about the people who'd beat her, split her lip, blacked her eye and caused the painful bruises all over her body. She had no memory of them.

And right now, she didn't care.

That seemed more odd to her than any of it …that she didn't care. Maggie was perfectly content in the right now, the present. The past and the future were … mist.

What did matter to her right now was Sadie. An overwhelming love for the precious child had blossomed in Maggie's chest the instant she saw her, as if Maggie had gathered up all the love for the people in the "before" of her life and given every bit of it to the astonishingly beautiful little girl with wide purple eyes. Her love for the child seeped out into all the voids in her heart, filled all the empty spaces. The focus of her every thought, the intent of her every action was Sadie.

Sadie raced around the meadow gleefully chasing

butterflies, grabbing at them, giggling, her honey-gold curls, tumbled by the gentle breeze.

Maggie wanted to capture the moment, stitch it into the fabric of her soul, or seal it up tight in a Mason jar, imprison it there, a memory that would give off a golden glow even when the world turned dark and gray. She sat down in the shade of a small basswood tree and watched contentedly.

The afternoon wore on. Sadie tired of chasing butterflies and turned to picking handfuls of wildflowers that she deposited out of chubby, green-stained hands in Maggie's lap. Then she pulled the stems off the heart-shaped basswood leaves on the ground beneath the tree and they decorated the hearts with colorful flowers. Maggie showed Sadie an ant hill in the dirt and grasshoppers in the weeds. The toddler held her breath as she watched a ladybug creep across her finger and then take flight.

But she always returned to chasing butterflies.

Finally, Maggie followed Sadie into the center of the field and sat down Indian style facing the sun that now tracked down the western sky.

"Sadie," Maggie called to the toddler. "You'll catch nary a thing running after them like that."

Sadie returned to Maggie's side.

"B'fies go bye, bye," she said despondently.

Maggie took the toddler into her lap. "We must be still as little beasties hiding from a cat," she said. "Shhhh."

Maggie stroked Sadie's butter-colored hair and rocked gently back and forth. She began to sing a song, not a lullaby this time, though the haunting melody was soft and relaxing.

The sun moved toward the far ridge, backlighting a small armada of puffy clouds that had dropped anchor above the valley. Maggie's unbraided hair cascaded down her back and the sunlight set it ablaze, highlighted a half dozen different shades of red and auburn, gold and orange. When the breeze lifted and tumbled the curls, the effect was of flames dancing away from a burning log.

"Shhh," Maggie crooned, rocking back and forth. The sun was warm and squinty-eyed bright. There was a hum of bee-song in the air and the raucous cry and response of cicadas in the trees—the volume rhythmically rising and falling. Sadie grew very still and Maggie thought perhaps she'd drifted off to sleep. "See, pretty one. If you're still, you don't have to chase them. They come to you."

The air around them slowly filled with butterflies.

~

The protocol for escorting the body of a soldier killed in combat home from Vietnam was as detailed as the assembly instructions for a M102 Howitzer, with rules about what to wear, where to stand, how to stand, what to say, what not to say, how to act, when to breathe.

But there was no protocol for the snafu that happened with Haystack's body.

Grayson never got the whole story, though he pieced much of it together from the tirade he could hear through the door of the CO's office hours later. It involved a Tennessee soldier from the 195th Field Artillery who'd been seriously injured at The Birdcage—where he must have struck up a friendship with Haystack. That was no surprise, the big blonde kid was so likeable everyone who met him became his new best friend. Just released on a 30-

day leave from a San Francisco hospital, the Nashville soldier called Six Pack heard about Haystack's death from a friend who worked at the GR point at Travis Air Force Base. The Graves Registration point was a building where dead soldiers' bodies were processed before they were shipped out for burial. Six Pack had shown up at the GR point in his Class A uniform—dress greens. Why was unclear, though Six Pack's friend maintained it was just his way of paying his respects to Haystack. The story got even more sketchy after that. For reasons hotly disputed by the GR soldiers involved, they had mistakenly believed Six Pack was the body escort assigned to accompany Haystack to Spindle Rock and had turned over to him the paper-work—which included *two commercial airline tickets* to Louis-ville, Kentucky. Whereupon Six Pack had drawn himself up tall, executed a snappy salute and accepted both the tickets and the body. Within the hour, Haystack was on a flight home and Six Pack was on a flight that would cut the 2,000-mile journey to *his* home down to 150.

It took the CO quite awhile to unravel what had happened. When he did, he was apoplectic. Waiting outside his office, Grayson marveled at the most colorful, creative use of profanity he'd heard since boot camp. Gratefully, by the time Grayson finally stood in front of the Full Bird Colonel, the man's anger had been spent.

"You came all this way for nothing, Chaplain," the CO said, shaking his head. "And that was the Army's screw-up, not yours. We owe you an apology." He looked long at Grayson's haggard face. "In fact, we owe you more than an apology. I'm signing off on a 30-day pass."

Grayson's jaw dropped.

"I'll work out the paperwork so you can report to Ft. Knox, Kentucky at 0800 hours September 15." He smiled at the look of shock on Grayson's face. "In fact, if you haul butt, I can get you at least part of the way home. There's a daily round-trip supply flight from Chicago and you've got…" he looked at his watch "… 27 minutes to catch it."

Grayson focused on nothing but making that flight, wouldn't let his mind go off down any other rabbit trails until he was safely aboard and the wheels lifted off the tarmac.

Only then, did he let it hit him.

Thirty days. By the time the leave was up, his tour of duty in-country would be over. Grayson Addington would not be going back to Vietnam. He'd made it home alive.

Chapter Eleven

SATURDAY WAS CHORES DAY. Piper did the weekly change of linens, three loads of laundry—washed, hung on the line to dry, brought in and folded. She cleaned the bathroom and mopped the kitchen floor. Then she and Carter assembled the "big girl" bed in Sadie's room. It was time the toddler learned to sleep by herself. Piper didn't realize the whole afternoon had slipped away until she paused for a cup of coffee before she tackled the ironing.

Sinking down in a kitchen chair, she slipped behind her ear a strand of hair that had escaped from her ponytail and glanced out the window at the lengthening afternoon shadows and the children playing in the yard. The shadows where there; the children weren't. The yard was empty.

The coffee cup slipped out of her fingers and clattered to the floor. Piper was already out the screen door before all the coffee in it had formed a brown puddle beside the chair leg.

"Maggie…" she said, not calling her. She didn't have enough air to call out.

Her eyes darted from the yard to the fence to the dirt

driveway in the kind of herky-jerky motion that made it almost impossible to see anything clearly. A thousand horrible thoughts elbowed each other around in her head, all of them slathered with the black tar of guilt. What kind of mother hands over the care of her baby to a little girl she's only known for three days? Just because the child was sweet and likeable didn't mean—

She felt Carter's hand on her shoulder. He didn't speak, merely pointed. Down the mountain about a quarter of a mile away she could make out the form of the two children sitting in the middle of the only flat space of any size on the mountainside—the butterfly meadow, at least that's what Piper called it. She often took Sadie there to watch them.

Piper loved butterflies. They had come to symbolize for her all that was good and pure—and fragile in life. The Campbells lived at the top of Cricket Hollow on the other side of Chicken Gizzard Mountain from Sadler Hollow. Every morning, Piper woke to the spectacular beauty of mist on purple mountains marching row after row toward the horizon. And to the ugliness of poverty that bred hopelessness and anger like a fly breeds maggots. No shoes. No coat in the winter. Carrying water in buckets from the well, the stench of pigpens out back and flies buzzing in a nauseating hum inside the outhouse in the summer heat.

Her family had little. And that might not have been the source of such distress if the McCulloughs down in Sadler Hollow had not had more.

Jeremiah McCullough had been a bootlegger, made cash when there was no cash to be had anywhere. Her father had kept food on the table by raising pigs and digging coal, came home from the mine coughing up black spit, his fingers mashed, his clothes filthy. And he'd get drunk then, beat her mother and older brother. Her, too, when she didn't dodge out of his way fast enough. Quick and agile, she'd often escape the worst of her father's wrath to hide in the woods behind the house. Next to the woods was a small clearing alive with butterflies and it became her favorite place in all the world. She'd sit on a log, sometimes nursing a split lip or black eye, and watch the butterflies cavort effortlessly on the breeze. Free. Untroubled and beautiful. But if you caught one, even touched it, the fairy dust on its wings would come off on your fingers and it couldn't fly anymore. It would drop to the ground, flop around and then be still.

"They're fine," Carter said and Piper resisted the urge to relax back against his big frame as relief washed over her. "Are you alright?"

"Sure," she croaked. But she didn't feel alright. The dagger of terror that had impaled her heart when she couldn't see the children in the yard had left her weak and breathless. It wasn't the only thing, though. Carter's presence, the warmth of him near, the comfort of him towering over her, felt so ... normal... that she almost shuddered.

What was she thinking?

No, the question wasn't what was she thinking. The question was what *wasn't* she thinking. And she wasn't thinking about Grayson. Just his name in her head clanged around in some empty, hollow place. Carter was here. And Grayson was ...

"You're not alright. What's wrong? They're right there. Maggie should have asked, but..."

"It's not that. It's Grayson."

She felt Carter instantly stiffen. She hadn't meant to say that, hadn't meant to call up Grayson's presence between them. Only that was *all wrong*, too! She shouldn't feel guilty, as if she shouldn't even mention the name of

Carter's brother. Of her husband! Oh, it was all so mixed up and crazy, none of it made sense. All she knew for certain at this very moment was that she was glad Carter was here when she needed him. That might not be right, might in fact, be very wrong, indeed. But that's what she felt and there was nothing she could do about her feelings.

Except *not* share them.

"I thought … you know, how Grayson must miss … Sadie. How he'd want to be here to take care of her."

That came out awkwardly, but it was the best she could do.

"You think about him a lot—miss him a lot?"

"Of course, I do." She was determined to get past this, or get away from it. "Come on, let's go drag our runaway girls back home." Without looking at him, she strode with purpose out toward the dirt road.

As Piper and Carter set off down the road toward the meadow, Carter's telephone in Charleston was ringing. Grayson let it ring a dozen times, then hung up and waited for the pay phone in the Chicago Bus Terminal to give him his dime back.

He'd already tried Uncle Jim, whose maid had haughtily informed him that Mr. Addington would be out of town until the end of the month.

So it was Carter, then. Grayson would call back. He did a quick calculation—Chicago to Pittsburgh, 20 hours. It'd be right after lunchtime Sunday when Grayson got to

Pittsburgh. Carter'd be home. Where else would he be —church?

Grayson settled into his seat on the big Greyhound, flipped through the newspaper the previous occupant had left behind, then stared out the window and watched America fly by.

≈

CARTER AND PIPER could hear Maggie humming as they approached. She sat unmoving, perfectly still, with her head tilted slightly back, as if she were admiring the puffy white clouds tethered to the mountaintops like hot air balloons. She might have had her eyes closed; they couldn't see that from the back.

What they could see was butterflies, dozens of them, all around the children. A few had even landed on the girls.

A monarch and a yellow-and-black tiger swallowtail, the tips of its wings jutting out below its body like a bird's tail feathers were perched in Maggie's flaming hair. Pale gray gossamer-wings, gold-and-brown skippers and lemon yellow Sulphurs fluttered in the air above the nearby flowers and weeds which were liberally sprinkled with black-and-red American ladies and yellow-and-brown brushfoots. As they watched, a lone pearl crescent with purple-edged wings fluttered over to Maggie and lit on her shoulder, flapping its wings slowly in and out, in a motion Piper had thought as a child looked like the gills of a fish breathing underwater.

Piper took a couple of quiet steps to the side so she could see and it was as she'd suspected. Sadie was asleep in

Maggie's arms. No possible way would a single butterfly have come near that wiggle-worm, certainly not a whole flock of them.

Then Sadie opened her eyes. But when she saw the butterflies, she didn't snatch at them. In fact, she sat remarkably still.

"B'flies," she said. Her voice was soft, almost reverent. Her red lips parted in a wide smile that planted twin dimples in her chubby cheeks. Then she burped out a little giggle and a few of the butterflies took flight at the movement.

"They make me laugh, too." Maggie whispered. "It's like they've got so much happy inside they float up in the air from the warmth of it."

"Can b'flies laugh?" Sadie asked.

Maggie thought for a moment, then giggled, too. "Maybe they're always laughing but they're so little we can't hear them."

"Can they cry?"

"Well ... if they can laugh, I guess they can cry, too. But I can't think of anything sad enough to make butter-flies cry."

When she began to speak, the motion stirred the butterflies. By ones and twos they took flight and gradually disbursed. Sadie made to reach for them then but Maggie murmured "Uh uh," and the child stopped, her hand frozen in mid-grab.

"Bye, bye, b'flies," she said and offered a sad gnat-snatcher wave. "Mabie, why won't b'flies play wif Sabie?" Then she inexplicably started to cry.

Maggie turned the toddler around and hugged her. When she did, Sadie saw her mother.

"Mommy!" She held out her chubby arms. "Hold you."

Maggie turned around in surprise as Piper lifted the toddler. Sadie popped her thumb into her mouth and stopped crying.

"Maggie, you scared us half to death," Piper said. "You can't run off with Sadie and not tell anyone where you're going."

"I'm sorry!" She looked so stricken Piper wondered if she feared someone was going to hit her. "I didn't mean … I … but

I never let her out of my sight, watched her careful."

"I'm sure you did," Piper said. She smiled reassuringly and the child seemed to relax, though her face remained serious and earnest.

"If you turn your back even for a minute with a little one," she said, "something awful can happen."

Carter looked like a mule had kicked him in the stomach and Piper knew his mind had gone to Grayson and Becky.

"Did something bad happen to a little one in your life?" she asked Maggie.

Maggie stood and dusted the dirt off her coveralls. "Maybe," she said, and didn't seem to be evading so much as trying to puzzle it out.

A perfect opening, Piper leapt at it. Shifting Sadie to her other hip, Piper turned and started back toward the house. When Maggie fell in beside her, she said casually, "You're so good with children you must have little brothers and sisters. How old are they?"

"I don't know."

"You don't know how old they are?"

"I don't know if I have any." She peered up at Piper. "I should know that—and my whole name, where I live. But I just … don't."

She paused, stopped still in the road. "I do know I ran

away, though. I remember *that*. Running hard as I can and being so scared I want to vomit. But I don't know who blacked my eye and split my lip and I don't know *why* I don't. It's like ..." Her brow wrinkled in studied concentration. "It's like I'm a checkerboard. The red squares are what I know, but the black squares are holes, windows into ... nowhere."

"Have you looked in the windows?"

"Uh huh. But it's too dark to see anything. It's all ... gone, the before. There's only now."

Sadie looked back over Piper's shoulder into the meadow and said wistfully, "I see-ed b'flies." She turned to her mother. "Dis many b'flies, Mommy." She held up both hands, showed all her fingers, then pushed the strands of hair dancing in the wind away from her face, using her flat palms. "An a labby-bug. It hab little feet on my finger."

"Maggie, did you do something besides sitting still to ... is there a reason why all those butterflies landed around you?" Carter asked.

"I guess they wanted to," she said.

Chapter Twelve

A SCREECHING wail launched Grayson into awareness from a fitful sleep. Bright light blinded him and he tried to hunker down into the darkness, feeling around frantically for his rifle.

"Hey, man, cut it out. Quit pawing me!" The voice came out of the glare, muffled by the ringing in Grayson's ears. "What's your problem? You drop some bad acid?"

Gray tried to focus but sensory perceptions came at him so fast he couldn't process them. Cold metal. Bright lights.

A man, not a soldier, bearded, with scraggly long hair down past his shoulders was shoving him away.

The screeching wail cried out again and Grayson cringed back.

"Airbrakes, it's just airbrakes," the man said and got to his feet in the swaying bus. "Take both seats, pal, I'm moving."

The man reached up into the luggage rack and dragged down a duffle bag almost as scuffed and worn as Grayson's. Then he marched up the aisle, started to sit down beside a big black man reading a newspaper, but the man glared at him so he went forward one more seat and settled carefully next to an old woman on the other side of the aisle who was leaned against the window with her mouth open, sound asleep. The big black man who'd glared at Grayson's seatmate turned and looked back at Grayson. Grayson couldn't read the look, then the man faced forward again and went back to his newspaper.

Grayson forced himself to relax against the upholstered seat of the bus—something itched in that spot between his shoulder blades where it's impossible to scratch. He made himself watch the passing street lights outside the windows. The rhythmic, blinking white lights had a soothing effect, like the shiny watch of a hypnotist, back and forth, back and forth.

His mind was muddy, foggy. The past 50...60 hours was a blur of scenes, jumbled together in no particular order, like a handful of snapshots tossed on a table. The images, some of them, were clear, but the sequence, the connective tissue was gone.

As the bus passed beneath the last streetlight and out into the darkness beyond, Grayson thought about Becky. One good thing he could say about Vietnam, the only good thing he could say about it, was that when he was there he hadn't thought about his little sister.

Her small hand is warm in his and the bright July sunshine is hot on his back. He can smell the wildflowers and hear the raucous caw of blue jays and the cries of cicadas that sound like dull saws cutting through tin. As they get near the creek, he can hear the bees buzzing in the hollow of the shagbark hickory tree.

"You be careful of those bees," Ma'd said when he picked up the broom and headed out across the yard with Becky in tow. She always said that, like maybe he'd forget not to go near it!

Becky hears the bees and points a pudgy finger toward the tree.

"Dose bees!" she says, in the same scolding voice Ma'd used. Grayson laughs.

Once past the tree, Becky sees the creek, lets go of his hand and races toward it. He barely cuts her off and scoops her into his arms before she splashes in with all her clothes on.

"You can't go in the water with your clothes on, silly girl."

She squirms and wiggles and as soon as the last vestige of cloth is gone, the cubbby, naked toddler takes off for the creek bank. The water's only six or seven inches deep. Becky's favorite thing in all the world is to sit in the creek and splash. But the water's cold and she eases her way in, shivering all over in a comical way that makes Grayson laugh again.

He removes his boots, the special cowboy boots Uncle Jim had given him for Christmas. They're his prize possession and he sets them side by side on the creek bank, then rolls up the legs of his too-long pants—Carter hand-me-downs—and tiptoes into the chilly water.

"C'mon, Becky. It's not that cold," he says.

She moves a little deeper, into maybe two inches of water.

Grayson leans over and splashes water onto her bare belly. She squeals and runs back up on shore.

"I'm sorry, I won't do that again. I promise."

But Becky stays resolutely on the shore until Grayson wades out and turns away from the creek to the task at hand. Before he went in for lunch he'd arranged the rugs over the long, sturdy sycamore tree limb that sticks out like a clothesline about five feet off the ground. Four rag rugs, one from the parlor and one from each of the small bedrooms are draped over the limb.

Grayson picks up the broom he'd tossed aside when he made his dashing tackle for Becky and begins to pound on the first rug. Dust flies up in a haze around it and Grayson immediately begins to sneeze. He thinks, for probably the ten-thousandth time, that Pa ought to make Carter beat the rugs and let him milk the cow—dust didn't make Carter sneeze. But it was about rank. The grunt job went to the youngest; that was the way of things.

He hears a small splash and Becky squeals. He turns and sees that she is now sitting in the water, patting it with her hands.

Back to the pounding.

Whap.

Whap.

Whap.

The broom knocks dust into the air and Grayson breaks a sweat. That's when he starts to sing. "Hear that loo-nesome whippoorwill …"

He likes Hank Williams, listens to him on the big radio in Bennett's Five and Dime and at Uncle Jim's house. Uncle Jim has three radios and when Grayson and Carter visit—which isn't often because Pa says his brother isn't a good influence on the boys—he lets them listen to the Grand Ole Opry.

Becky giggles and splashes.

Grayson finishes the fourth rug and goes around to the other side of the rugs and starts again on the first one.

"He sounds too blue to cry …" Grayson takes up the song where he left off.

His voice isn't bad, he thinks. Maybe he could be a singer someday like Hank Williams. Pa wouldn't likely let him do that, though. Those singer folks didn't go to church or even say grace before meals, least that's what Carter says.

"The midnight train is whii-nin' low. I'm so loo-nesome I could cry."

He peeks around the corner of the rug at Becky. Sitting in the creek, she pats the water and giggles when it splashes in her face.

Then he … forgets about her.

At least, that's what his father says he did. Later, his father yells at him that he was so busy daydreaming, singing those awful, sinful songs and the like that he forgot about his baby sister in the creek.

Grayson honestly doesn't know. He doesn't know what happened.

He is beating the rugs, listening to Becky splash, beating the rugs, singing his song, beating the rugs and …

He stops to wipe his brow. And it's quiet.

Too quiet.

He steps out from behind the last rug, he'd worked his way all the way to the end, and looks at the creek.

Becky is lying on her back, her long blond hair flowing out around her head like a yellow fan. The water is just deep enough that it is flowing over her face. She is not moving.

"Becky!"

He screams. He runs to her, but he can't seem to move fast. It's like nothing will happen fast enough, like the twenty feet between him and the creek has stretched out into a mile.

He yanks the little girl up out of the water, screaming her name, but she is as limp as a broken doll. He shakes her, yells at her to wake up, to open her eyes, to look at him. He is crying now, sobbing her name, begging her, pleading with her to wake up and talk to him.

But she is silent. And cold. As cold as the water.

It is a long time before he turns with her cold, limp body and starts back with it toward the house. He walks right past the hickory tree. He hears the bees buzz as if from a great distance. Some of them sting him. He feels it, but it doesn't hurt. He just keeps walking.

It seemed to take forever to get from the rugs to the creek. It takes only seconds to get from the creek to the house. His mother must have seen him coming because she screams from inside the house and runs out the back door wailing, her arms out. She grabs Becky out of his grasp and sinks to the ground sobbing.

His father comes running from the side yard where he'd been chopping firewood. Carter appears from somewhere. His parents are yelling and crying and … and Grayson stands there with his arms at his sides, limp, with such a huge hole in his chest that he doesn't even feel connected to his bottom half, can almost feel the wind blowing through where he has been ripped open, cut apart.

Words don't make any sense to him, but later, he recalls some of them. Doesn't matter if he remembers because he doesn't have to. He will hear the same ones over and over again for the next seven years, while his father's face grows more gaunt, his eyes get wilder, his hair grayer, and the smell of liquor appears on his breath almost every night.

He will hear his father say—mostly on those evenings when the smell is strongest—that he'd trusted his baby girl to her older brother. He'd trusted Grayson to take care of her.

"How could you do it?" his father screams at him that July afternoon when the sun is hot and the blue jays are cawing in the trees. "How could you kill your own baby sister?"

The words echoed in Grayson's brain, clanging and banging like a wrecking ball slamming into the stone of his heart, knocking out hunks of it that flew through the air in slow motion.

The pain of remembering cored in like a dentist's drill. Grayson squeezed his eyes shut and shook his head, trying to shake the images loose. But they'd been welded to his consciousness and nothing short of his own death could dislodge them.

Gradually, he relaxed as the sway of the bus soothed him, drifted into a troubled sleep where shadowy figures leapt up from behind clumps of grass, fallen tree trunks and bushes—like targets in a penny arcade. The figures weren't gooks, though. They were Grayson's father.

"Hey!"

Grayson felt a large hand grip his shoulder and shake it.

"Hey, wake up!"

He was awake. But he wasn't. Not if awake meant fully in the here-and-now, responding to reality. By that definition, he was somewhere on the near side of sleep, a netherworld where then and now melded into a place that was neither, a landscape he knew well. He opened his eyes. Sunshine so fierce and bright it peeled back his corneas forced him to squeeze them instantly shut again. He squinted through a forest of lashes at the big black man who'd glared at Grayson's seatmate when he'd tried to sit beside him.

"You makin' all kinda noise, gruntin' and moaning," the man said. "You gotta shut up, quit disturbing the rest of the folks."

"Sorry," Grayson mumbled and opened his eyes to look full into the black man's face. He couldn't read the look the man'd given him before, but he could read this one.

The two men faced each other for a moment without speaking.

"How long you been back?" the black man asked.

"About …" Grayson looked at his wrist but there was no watch on it. "What's today?"

"You gonna be like this for awhile. Took me six months. And even now, sometimes …"

"When did—?"

"I don't talk about it," the black man cut him off. "And you'd best shut up about it yo-self. Found out the hard way that don't nobody want to hear the truth of it." He leaned a little closer. "You'd be doing yourself a huge favor if you was to decide right here and now that you ain't never gonna tell a soul what you seen over there."

The black man straightened and strode forward to his seat. Didn't look back, merely picked up his newspaper and started reading.

~

Even after all these years, it still felt odd to Carter not to go to church on Sunday morning. His childhood didn't contain a single memory of missing church. Not Sunday morning. Not Sunday night. Not Wednesday evening prayer meeting.

He and Grayson had sat with their mother on the front row. Their shoes polished, their shirts and pants starched and pressed. Ma had always smelled of Blue Waltz perfume. Pa had gotten her a bottle—it was heart-shaped—once on a trip to Charleston to visit his brother. It was the only perfume she owned so it was reserved for Sunday mornings. A big bottle of perfume could last years if you only dabbed on one drip a week.

He had once mouthed off to his mother that he'd sat through hundreds of sermons and couldn't recall the content of more than half a dozen of them—so what was the point in going every Sunday? His mother had responded that she'd fixed dinner for him and the rest of the family every evening for his entire life—how many of those meals could he remember?

"Your daddy feeds his flock every week. Some meals is more memorable than others, I'll grant. But every one of them meals was fixed for hungry people, folks who needed food, and whether they was particularly memorable or not, they fed folks and kept them going for another week and that's what matters."

Of course, later, when his father started to lose it, his sermons became more and more memorable—for the histrionics, for the theater, the terror, not for the content. In fact, the best Carter could remember, there had been little content of any kind in the last years, certainly not in the final months. People hollering and falling down, foaming at the mouth, shaking like they were having seizures. People shouting out in languages that Pa said were speaking in tongues but any fool could tell were only people babbling out in nonsense syllables while other equally addled people deigned to translate the babbled nonsense into English nonsense.

In the end, it was all craziness. Craziness and snakes, of course.

Carter knew his mother didn't share his relief on Sunday mornings. He knew that for her, every Sunday morning when she opened her eyes and was too sick to get out of bed and go to church, she felt anything but relief. But his mother's faith was real. Maybe his father's had been, too, early on, before Becky's death.

Carter sat up carefully in the early morning light. Then stood and stretched. He couldn't stifle a sigh. Later today, he'd have to go back to Charleston, and every time he came here, it was harder to leave.

"You look like a man who could use a cup of coffee."

Carter hadn't heard Piper come into the room from the kitchen and he jumped.

"I didn't mean to startle…" she spoke softly. "I actually believe we're the only ones up. Sadie never sleeps this late. And your mother hardly sleeps at all."

He crossed the room to her and when she turned back toward the kitchen he reached out and took her arm. He hadn't meant to do it, didn't plan the action in advance. His hand and arm had acted independently of his brain. He turned her slowly around to face him.

"Piper…" He found he had nothing to say. The moment drew out. His heart began to knock so hard his vision blurred and he could feel each beat in the big artery in his neck. She stood looking up at him with eyes the color of a Hershey Bar. He began to lean toward her and she toward him. Did she speak his name? He wasn't sure, with his pulse thundering in his ears.

"Good morning, Mr. Carter," Maggie said, and Carter felt his emotions slam into a brick wall at a dead run. "You're up early. Is it church you're planning on going to?"

The little girl stood in the doorway between the kitchen and the parlor. She had come in from the back porch so quiet she could have sneaked dawn past a rooster. The spring on the screen door that always squalled like a gut-shot yak hadn't made a sound. At least, he hadn't heard it through the pounding of his heart in his ears.

Carter forced himself not to step guiltily away from Piper. Merely looked at the child and said, "No, actually, I wasn't planning on going to church this morning. Were you? Does your family go to church on Sundays?"

"I hear Sadie," she said.

He and Piper both looked toward Sadie's bedroom door, where the child had slept in her big girl bed for the first time last night. Neither of them had heard—

Sadie cried then, a sleepy, whiney mewl. But Carter would have sworn she hadn't made a peep until—

"I'll get her," Maggie said, and scampered off toward the bedroom before Piper had a chance to move.

Piper took a step away from him then, moved easily out of his grasp.

"Like I said yesterday," she said. "My own personal nanny."

Chapter Thirteen

GRAYSON INTENDED to get off the bus in the Morgantown Greyhound station and call Carter, though he no longer had much hope of an answer. He'd tried without success after breakfast in the bus terminal in Pittsburgh more than three hours ago. Obviously, Carter was out of town, too. Swell.

But when Grayson stepped off the bus into West Virginia air, breathed it in, he found himself striding away from the station with his duffle over his shoulder, just walking, absorbing with all his senses the achingly beautiful mountains. He stopped at a corner and shaded his eyes from the sun that was balanced precariously on the mountaintop before it tumbled down the western side. The jungle had seemed a hideous, monochromatic wall of green, but the forested hillsides here were dappled, resplendent in varied green hues and shades, granting them texture and a depth that blended now with the dark velvet shadows of approaching evening. Grayson stood and stared, his eyes drinking in *his* world in such great heaving gulps he feared he might strangle.

Then he shifted his duffle bag on his back, felt the weight of it and exhaustion settled with a groan into his bones. The West-Virginia-air exhilaration grayed out and all he wanted was to sit down. He looked around, disoriented, hoping he hadn't walked too far from the station.

"You lost, soldier?"

He turned to see two men in a pickup truck. Two mountaineers. Ball caps pushed back on their heads, both had plugs of Skoal tucked under their lower lips. One had a full beard that had caught a considerable amount of snuff drool. The driver was clean-shaven, his face round, fat and jovial. He was the one who'd spoken.

"No, I ain't lost," Grayson said. *Ain't* lost? Where did *that* come from? His father'd never allowed West Virginia dialect from either of his sons. "I just got off a bus from Pittsburgh and I was … looking around. It sure feels good to be … home."

His voice had actually wavered a little. He hadn't realized how much he meant it until he heard the word come out his mouth. In fact, he hadn't even dared to admit he *was* home until now, this very minute. He wasn't waiting to go out on some patrol he might not come back from. He was on a street corner in Morgantown, West Virginia, and for him the war was over.

He knew his eyes were wet, hoped the men in the pickup truck couldn't see it. "I guess I am a little lost. Which way's the bus station?"

"You need a lift?" the bearded man asked.

"Sure," Grayson said. The sudden exhaustion had left his legs shaky. If it was more than a block or two back to the station, he'd have a hard time making it under his own steam. And since he couldn't reach Carter or anybody else until morning, a bench in the station would be his bed for the night.

"Lemme get that poke for you," said the bearded man. He hopped out of the truck, hurried around it and started to heft Grayson's duffle bag into the back of the pickup truck. "I'll ride back here with it, give you more room up front."

"You don't have to go to any trouble for me."

The man looked him square in the face.

"You been fighting for the United States of America and if'n I can give up my seat so you can set down comfortable, then I'm proud to do it."

Grayson's heart swelled in his chest so unexpectedly he didn't speak because he didn't trust his voice. That girl in the San Francisco airport with her hippie friends and her peace cross and love beads—she didn't speak for all of America.

He slid into the seat beside the cheery driver.

"Where you going, soldier?" he asked, as he ground the gears and shoved the lever into first.

"Back to the station to spend the night. I can't reach anybody to come get me until the post office in Sadlerton opens on—"

"Sadlerton!" He leaned his head out the window and called to his friend perched on Grayson's duffle in the back of the truck. "This feller's from Sadler Hollow!" He turned back to Grayson. "This here's yore lucky day, soldier. We're from Cedar Ridge, come down here yesterday to look at buying a boar but it was puny, had rheumy-looking eyes. We're on our way back home, be going in the direction of Sadlerton. We'll carry you right up to yore front door."

"I can't ask you to do that. It'd be miles out of your way. I'll just sleep in—"

"You'll do no such of a thing!" The big man pointed a beefy finger at Grayson's wedding ring. "I s'pect you ain't seen the missus in a right smart while. You can sleep in your *own* bed tonight if'n we take you."

Grayson certainly couldn't argue that logic. He smiled.

"I do thank you kindly, Mr. ..."

"I'm Lester Haggerty," the man said and favored Grayson with a nearly toothless grin. He gestured toward the back of the truck. "That there's Tuggs McIntosh."

"Grayson Addington," Grayson said. "But my friends call me Gray."

"Gray it is then," the man said as he performed an illegal U turn in the middle of the street. "You want a beer? They's a cooler of Iron City in the back. My Pa fought in the great war. Him and Uncle John kilt a passel of Japs in ..."

Grayson listened with the practiced ease of a man who'd tuned out untold hundreds of pointless conversations about high school and sex and baseball and sex and hot cars and sex ... He put his elbow out the window, felt the warm breeze in his face and wallowed a single word around in his mind, the way you suck on a peppermint to get out all the flavor, until it's such a little sliver it disappears altogether.

Home.

He must have dozed off. When he awoke, Lester had stopped talking and was happily humming *Stand By Your Man.* The fat man noticed that he was awake. "You's overseas, in 'Nam, wasn't you?"

Grayson thought about what the black ex-soldier on the bus had said to him. But he didn't need the admonition. His every memory was covered in razor blades. No way to get near any of them without being cut to the bone.

"Uh huh," Grayson said.

"You kill many gooks?"

Grayson considered getting out of the question by

playing the chaplain card. Cite the manual about non-combatants. But regulations didn't matter the night almost half the company was wiped out at Fire Base Eagle's Nest, which the Tennessee soldiers from the 195th Field Artillery who carved it out of the jungle had dubbed "The Birdhouse."

Gray hadn't picked up the rifle that night. Haystack had shoved one at him, grabbed it when that gunner from the 195th dropped it after a bullet stabbed through his neck. He'd just stood there, looking surprised and confused and then his fingers had opened up and the rifle fell to the ground. Fell in slow motion, the way Gray remembered it, as twin geysers of blood squirted out of his neck, one on the left where the bullet entered and one on the right where it exited. Squirt, squirt, squirt. The kid slowly sank to his knees and then pitched over in the dirt.

Gray had started to refuse the M16, to shake his head. But Haystack didn't have to say anything to convince him. Bullets zipping through the air and thunking into mud and sandbags and bodies, shrieks of agony and the smell of blood and urine and feces and death—they'd made the case Haystack didn't have to make. Gooks had gotten *inside* the perimeter of the compound!—40 or 50 of them, naked, cut up and bloody. They'd stripped to slither through the razor wire so their clothes wouldn't get caught on it and shake the pieces of Sergeant Hotchner's red underwear he'd hung on the concertina coils to announce their presence. They were firing RPG's (Rocket Propelled Grenades) and tossing satchel charges—small bags of TNT that weighed about a pound with five-second timers.

Haystack held out the rifle. Grayson took it. As easy as that. He was a crack shot from years of squirrel hunting. Shooting men was easier; the targets were bigger. He'd tried not to count but he couldn't help it. The gooks were like swarming bees; shoot one and three more appeared to take his place. They were everywhere at once. It would have been hard to shoot and *not* hit somebody.

One. The guy who stood up from behind the burning jeep. Took two shots before he stayed down. That was the trouble with the M16. It would drop a man but not necessarily kill him. The Army figured wounded soldiers drained the enemy's resources, took more time and energy than dead ones. So sometimes you had to shoot one of those zipper heads two, three times.

Two, the one on the end when the three came charging out between … Five. Nine. Eleven. Firing in the weird half light of flares, shooting shadows as often as real men. Grotesque, misshapen, elongated black shadow monsters in the squinty-bright, then rapidly-fading light. But he kept track of the shadows, too. They counted. You kill a shadow, it counted.

"I killed … some," Grayson said.

"It as bad over there as folks say?"

"Worse."

"But you went. You didn't run off like some commie coward to Canada. You done your duty." The man patted Grayson's shoulder. "You be proud of that, hear? You earned being proud."

Grayson didn't feel proud. He felt nauseas. The black man had been right, of course. You couldn't tell anybody what you'd seen. You couldn't tell people like the girl in the airport because she'd never understand how you could have killed anybody. And you couldn't tell people like this mountaineer because he'd never understand how you couldn't seem to save anybody either.

"Would you be offended if I said I didn't want to talk about it, that I can't talk about it, not yet?"

"You don't owe me no explanation." He paused.

"Whatever it was you done over there, you had to. You'd might want to remember that."

Grayson looked at the man, surprised. He was obviously sharper than he appeared.

"My daddy only talked about the great war when he was drunk. When he was sober, we all lied, said he'd never breathed a word about it. But he had. He said stuff … stuff it was no wonder he had to get drunk to say."

As the truck bumped along, every sight that greeted Grayson's eyes was more achingly familiar than the last. The mountains rose up protectively around him, hugging him snug and safe beneath a slice of bright blue sky that was sandwiched between green ridges like the white stuff in the middle of an Oreo cookie. In many places the valleys were so narrow there was only room enough for the pot-holed road, a creek, a railroad track and shabby, defeated coal camp towns where dilapidated houses clung to the mountainsides like the dried skins of spring cicadas.

Finally, the pickup truck rattled over a metal, one-lane bridge and made a sharp turn around a stand of cotton-wood and birch trees. Grayson's heart began to beat like the wings of a frantic, caged bird.

"This is it," he said. "That road right there—Turtle Road." Actually the road's proper name was Naked Turtle Road, just like Turtle Creek was actually Naked Turtle Creek. But Grayson's father had steadfastly refused to acknowledge that the road which terminated at his church and the creek a stone's throw from his back door might be in an "unsuitable state of undress."

"Stop here," Grayson said. "Pull off. I can walk from here."

Lester protested. "We don't mind to carry you all the way," he said.

"Thanks, but I want to walk from here," Grayson said.

"I *need* to walk from here. You know, get used to it … slowly."

Lester pulled to a stop at the dirt road that wound through the trees, then up the side of the mountain. Tugg handed him his duffle bag out of the back and climbed down to get into the front seat with Lester.

"Thank you for your service," Tugg said, a little awkwardly. Grayson suspected he'd been figuring out what to say for half the trip up into the mountains and screwing himself up to actually saying it for the other half.

"Thank you fellas for the ride." Grayson heard unexpected emotion in the words so he turned quickly and headed up the road. His army boots kicked up little puffs of dust as he walked back into his world and his life. It was about two and a half miles from the highway, Northfield Road, to his mother's house along a winding strip of dirt through the woods that switched north, then back south, again and again as it climbed the side of the mountain.

It was early evening, still, the in-between time before the owls and possums and raccoons ventured out but after the day creatures, the chickadees, the blue jays, woodpeckers, rabbits and squirrels had gone back to their burrows for the night. He could smell pine and spruce but the sound of the trees creaking like gates on rusty hinges was muffled by the explosion rumble in his ears, thundering in heartbeat bursts. The shadow of the western mountain reaching out its long, dark fingers across the valley felt like a warm balm on his scuffed and tortured soul and he peered into the purple shadows and mysterious green depths of the forest as he walked along.

Grayson pictured Piper's face. And he could see it here! No film covering everything, like it was wrapped in that sticky plastic stuff you put over the top of leftovers in the refrigerator. Here, he could conjure her face in front of him. And Sadie, like an moth captured in amber in his memory, forever eighteen months old. He'd seen pictures of the toddler, so stunningly beautiful she looked like a porcelain doll, but the pictures had been almost like looking at someone else's child. Now, the image he conjured up of the little girl seemed *real*.

He could see the house now, a car parked out front. Then the road curved around and it was gone from view. Gloom closed over the road but the house was ablaze with light. The house where his family was waiting for him.

As soon as the sun dipped down behind the mountain and the long arm of shadow stretched out to claim the house, Piper began to feel melancholy. Carter was leaving. She didn't like how much she had come to look forward to his presence or how his leaving seemed to take the light and life out of the house. She watched him slip his few belongings efficiently into the gym bag he always brought with him.

"I should have been a fireman," he said. "In under 30 seconds, I could gather up everything I owned and shinny down a pole."

"Is that what you wanted to be when you were a little boy—a fireman?"

"Of course not," he said. "I wanted to—"

"He wanted to be a preacher, like his daddy," Marian interrupted.

They both turned and looked at her.

"Thought you were taking a nap, Ma," Carter said.

"And you d-d-didn't want to wake me up so you tiptoed into the room and k-k-kissed me on the forehead."

Her palsy had been pronounced all day.

"You were playing opossum! Why didn't you—?"

"'Cause it was sweet. Now give yore mama a real hug and be on your way. I don't like you d-d-driving these roads at night."

Carter obediently crossed the room and gently hugged his mother. Piper saw her brow crease in pain, but she didn't wince and Carter didn't see.

Maggie had pleaded to be allowed to put Sadie to bed, and in the sudden silence, the sound of her voice singing a silly song about "puffy-tailed bunnies" floated into the room.

The song wrenched at Piper and she turned away so no one would see the tears that had sprung into her eyes.

"I'll walk you to your car, Carter," Piper said, then went out the front door and down the steps. He followed. The shadows were long; the sky darkening.

Carter opened the back driver's side door, tossed his gym bag onto the back seat and closed the door. Piper leaned on the front door, staring unseeing across the valley.

"You don't want to go to the sheriff tomorrow." It wasn't a question.

"You blame me? What if he says he knows who she is, that her family's been looking for her?"

She turned to face him. "What then?"

He put his hands on her shoulders. "Do you want me to stay and go with you in the morning?"

"No, of course not, I can—"

"I don't mind. I could—"

"Go back to Charleston, Carter, I'll be fine. It's just …" her voice broke.

She started to cry and he wrapped his arms around her and pulled her to his chest. He held her there, tight, patting her back. She could feel his warm breath in her hair and wanted to let go, let it all out. She didn't, though. She grabbed hold of her emotions and swallowed her tears, but remained in his arms, sniffling for a few more moments. Then she pulled back, with his arms still around her and looked up into his face. He reached down and tenderly cupped her cheek, using his thumb to wipe the tears from beneath her eye. The moment dragged out. She stood, staring up at him, and when his face slowly lowered, she closed her eyes and felt his warm lips on hers.

Chapter Fourteen

THAT's how Grayson found them.

He came around the last bend in the road and could see the house in the gloom. Light shone out through the front door, golden honey that flowed down the steps and out the walk. When he stepped around a stand of bushes, the golden light lit the side of the car parked in front of the gate. Lit the couple standing there, sparkled in Piper's dark hair as his brother looked down into her face. And then kissed her.

A gigantic hole opened under Grayson's feet and he felt himself teetering on the edge of it, the crumbling rim of an airless, black abyss in which there was no light and from which there was no return. Some part of him realized he'd felt that sensation before, when a little girl ... then it was gone.

The world slowed down. Seconds dragged out into an agonizingly long time during which images of his brother and his wife came to Grayson's mind unbidden, the two of them together ...

Then Piper pushed away from Carter, stepped back

shaking her head. Carter took a step toward her, said something, she shook her head again, turned away from him.

And saw Grayson standing there fifteen feet away.

Her face froze. Her body went just as rigid. Then her hands flew to her mouth, her face crumbled in an agonizing cramp of … of … he didn't know what. And she began to scream.

FOR A MOMENT, Piper had allowed herself to be swept away by a wave of loneliness and need—but only for a moment. She straightened then and stepped back out of Carter's arms. Carter moved to embrace her again.

"Piper, I'm not sorry. Please—"

She shook her head and turned away to go back into the house.

That's when she saw him. The soldier in the gloom. The ghost from her dream. Grayson stood in the fading light as she had seen him so many times before. He had come to her dead, his lifeless eyes staring, blind.

She screamed, a high-pitched, keening wail. Shaking her head no, pleading with the ghost with her eyes, she screamed again and began to stumble backwards.

"No!" she cried. "Oh, God, please no …"

The gloom grew muddy, black smoke rolled in all around, obscuring everything, covering the ghost, muting the sound of her screaming until she could hear nothing. Then merciful darkness took her.

Piper kept screaming, crying out "no!" then backed away from him in … *terror.* If there was anything Grayson could recognize with absolute clarity, it was fear.

She took two or three steps backward, wailing and crying, shaking her head and then her knees buckled under her and she fainted.

Grayson dropped his duffle bag and covered the space between them in seconds. Carter was closer, got there first, knelt beside her and reached out to—

Grayson grabbed his brother by the shoulder and shoved him aside. On one knee and off balance, Carter went sprawling on his back in the dirt. Grayson dropped to his knees beside Piper. He lifted her limp body off the ground and held her in his arms, rocking slowly back and forth crooning her name softly. Then he leaned sideways, sat in the dirt and cradled her in his lap.

"Piper. Piper, baby. It's okay. I'm home."

He heard activity around him. His mother's voice from the porch, crying out to Carter, "Carter, what's wrong— why's Piper screaming?"

But he ignored the voices, couldn't have paid them mind if he'd wanted to. The only thing that existed in the universe was the weight of the woman in his arms, her eyes closed, lips parted slightly as if she'd only drifted off to sleep. He could feel her warm breath on his face. It smelled of cinnamon and apples.

He eyes fluttered open, then closed again. Then they snapped open so wide the whites looked like egg-white around a yolk. She was confused, struggling, tried to push him away.

"Piper. Honey, it's me. Piper, I'm home."

When recognition finally registered on her face, her bottom lip began to tremble. She reached up tentatively and touched his cheek, then her eyes devoured his face.

"Gray ...? Grayson...is it really...?"

He couldn't speak. His eyes filled with tears and when he blinked, they slid down both cheeks. All he could do was nod his head. Then her arms went around his neck in a hug of such strength and force it was impossible to draw a breath. She pulled back out of the hug and began to kiss his face, crying his name, crying and laughing, tears on her cheeks and the most incredible smile, the most beautiful, loving smile he had ever seen. She kissed him then on the mouth, and he devoured hers, leaned into her, kissed her so hard and so long that when it was over they were both breathless and trembling.

"I thought ..." she whispered. "I thought you were a ghost. Dead and a ghost. I've dreamed it, the same dream over and over. You come to me before the men in dress uniforms in the black car. You're dead. You have blood all over—"

He put his finger to her lips.

"It was a dream. I'm real." He actually grinned. "I'll prove it." And he kissed her again, long and hard. He felt his heart kick into a gallop and all at once he felt more alive than he had felt in... Maybe more alive than he'd ever felt in his life. He had made it through hell! He had made it *home*.

When he finally pulled back, gasping, he heard his mother's voice from the porch.

"Grayson! Grayson Allen Addington, are you really out there like Carter says? Grayson, you come here to me right this minute! Do you hear me? Don't you make me come out there and snatch you bald-headed."

~

PIPER HELD onto Grayson's arm and he helped her to her feet. But she didn't let go of his arm then. Couldn't let go. She had to keep her hands on him, feel the warmth of him, touch him or she wouldn't be able to believe he was actually here, that this wasn't some dream she'd wake up from in the midnight dark, then reach over and feel the cold lonely side of the bed where he wasn't, where he hadn't been in so long.

She felt the muscles in his arm—thin! He was so thin! —felt them ripple and bulge when he reached for the gate. He smiled up at his mother on the porch and the pinched look, the tight set of his mouth relaxed. In the warm golden light spilling out the front door and down the porch steps, he was the Grayson who'd brought her flowers the night of his graduation from Southern Baptist Theological Seminary in Louisville, the Grayson who'd never left her side during the too-long labor that ended in a Caesarean section with Sadie, the young man in his dress uniform—a view of his face that was blurry because she'd stared at the picture through tears welling in her eyes so many times.

Piper remained attached to Grayson like an appendage as he hurried up the steps to his mother. Carter stood next to Marian, his face neither smiling nor frowning. Impassive. Piper only let go when Grayson reached out to fold his mother into his arms. He held her gently—how did he know to be so gentle?—but she'd almost bowled him backward with her own strength. Marian gripped his neck in a strangle hold, her eyes squeezed shut, tears seeping out the corners to slide down through the creases of wrinkles on her cheeks.

The old woman let go briefly, pulled back to see his face, then gripped him tight to her chest again.

"So you jest figgered—hey, I won't tell nobody I'm

comin' so I can scare my pore mama out of the few breaths she got left—that it?"

The palsy had vanished from her speech.

"No Ma," Grayson said. "I … it's a long story. But more important than how I got here is *I'm not going back!* Vietnam's over for me. I'll explain the whole thing later, and I did try to call…" He shot a glance at Carter and said no more.

"Well, don't hear that as a complaint, son. It'd a suited me fine if they'd a'done what your kindergarten teacher done—sent you home after three days with a note sayin' you didn't play well with others."

Marian pulled back out of his arms again but kept her hands on his chest, like she, too, didn't want to stop touching him. "That's probably why they sent you home 'fore your time was up. You always was socially awkward."

Piper's head was reeling. *Not going back!* Was it possible that Grayson was home for good? The idea threw a party in her head—complete with confetti, streamers and fire-works. She gobbled up the look on her mother-in-law's face. No pain showed there and she probably didn't actu-ally feel any at that moment, not with her youngest son in her arms, come home unhurt from the war. But more than that, the spirit of the old woman was back, the woman who'd once jammed a teenage Piper in the potato box when company showed up unannounced, then lifted the lid half an hour later and asked her why she hadn't peeled none for supper.

"Well, don't just stand there a'suckin' on a prune pit," Marian told Grayson as she dusted imaginary something off the front of his shirt and straightened his collar. "Come on in this house and let us fetch you some supper."

"Ma, I'm not hungry. I—"

"Don't be silly. Of course, you're hungry. Boys is

always hungry. We got left-over meatloaf…" She shot a look at Piper, who nodded "…and it might even still be warm. I can whip up some biscuits and—"

Marian hadn't made biscuits in months. It'd likely slipped her mind how painful it was. And Piper sensed Grayson had gotten a good enough look at the old woman now to know whipping up biscuits probably wasn't an option, that she was, indeed, having trouble standing.

"You'll do no such thing, Ma," he said firmly. "I'll make myself a meatloaf sandwich. But first, I want you to sit down."

He turned to face Carter, unaware that their greeting was a mirror image of Carter's and Zeke's parting on Friday.

"Carter," Grayson said, his face expressionless.

"Grayson," Carter said. There was a full beat of awkward silence before Carter turned to his mother, who was looking from one son to the other, confused.

"Grayson's right, Ma," Carter said, "you need to sit down." He took his mother's shoulders and gently turned her, pushed her toward the screen door and guided her inside.

Carter cast a glance at Piper, a look she couldn't read.

Carter!

Grayson's return had wiped every other thought and emotion out of Piper's mind in a great roaring flood of joy and relief. Now, the floodwaters receded enough for her to remember and she sucked in a gasp.

Carter had kissed her.

And Grayson had seen!

That's when Piper heard Sadie inside crying and Maggie's voice, soothing the child. Obviously, the commotion had trumped Maggie's efforts to sing her to sleep.

"I left my duffle in the road," Grayson said and headed back down the porch steps to retrieve it.

~

AN IMAGE FLASHED across the movie screen of Grayson's mind in excruciating detail, so clear he might have been looking at it through binoculars. No, through the lens of a microscope.

His brother. His wife.

A nameless emotion so fierce it sucked the breath out of his lungs seized him, the pain of it like the tiny cuts of shrapnel, a thousand different agonies all over the body, exploding in every nerve. Behind him, in the roar of his damaged hearing, he thought he could hear a child crying.

Grayson took only a few steps out into the road, then slowed, and the doors to a thousand fears flew open in his mind. The seeping shadows spilled into the road like ink spreading through the fibers of a blotter. The darkness seemed deeper because he'd been looking into the lighted house and for a moment, his heart kicked into a gallop.

Never look into a bright light!

Sergeant Hotchner had slapped him on the back of the head when he said it, then gestured out into the shadows of the jungles beyond the perimeter.

"In the three minutes before you can see again, Charlie's going to come strolling out of the jungle and slit your throat with a rusty Spam lid."

Grayson tried to shake it off, but he couldn't keep himself from scanning the shadowy undergrowth beyond the road, looking for the glint of metal from the light behind him, searching for a rounded puddle of darker shadow in the bushes.

Nothing.

Of course, there's nothing, you idiot. Knock-knock, Grayson. You're in West Virginia! You're home.

His head knew that, but still he snatched the duffle up off the ground and double-timed it back across the road to the gate.

Piper stood at the door waiting for him. She held a little girl in her arms, a child with honey-colored hair in a tangle of bed-head around her face and down her back—the most breathtakingly beautiful little girl he'd ever seen.

Grayson stepped into the house and set his duffle on the floor, not taking his eyes off the child in Piper's arms.

"Sadie," Piper said. "This is Daddy. Do you remember Daddy?"

The child noticed him for the first time then and froze. Grayson's heart melted into a puddle in his chest and he reached out to take her from her mother. But she recoiled from him, tilted her head back and shrieked, then buried her face in her mother's neck sobbing.

Piper looked chagrined and patted the child furiously on the back.

"I'm sorry. She … she's shy, terrified of strangers." She realized what she'd said and tried to backtrack. "I mean, if she's not used to you, she's afraid—men particularly, scare her."

Grayson heard something, a small voice, behind Piper.

"Want me to go get Rasmus? Or her blankie?"

It seemed familiar, a voice he'd heard before, though he couldn't place exactly when or where. But the sound of it made him uneasy, took his mind somewhere unpleasant, somewhere he didn't want to go.

Then Piper stepped aside and he could see who was standing behind her.

"Honey, this is Gray," Piper said to the child.

"Your name's Gray?" the little girl asked.

. . .

"YOU NAME GRAPE?" Nguyen asks, but she's not walking beside him through the little village of Yan Ling, ignoring the stench of his latrine- soaked clothing. She isn't wearing her habitual gap-toothed grin, either. Her face is a mask of terror and she is covered in blood. Not splattered with blood. Covered in it from the top of her head to the bottom of her bare feet. Her hair is dripping it. Her sack dress is soaked. A wash of blood flows down her legs into a growing pond around her feet. He drops to his knees in front of her, stunned.

Then he notices for the first time that there are … cracks in her face. In every part of her that he can see, in fact. She looks like a broken glass that has been pieced back together. But not all the pieces are there. Her left hand is missing. So are all the fingers on her right. He can smell the copper stench of her blood. He can smell the cordite of explosives, too.

A machine gun rattles off rounds behind him and he can hear the sound of shouting. More gunfire, screams.

"You can't be here. You're dead."

She turns to run away but he grabs her—by the right arm, the one that has a hand on the end of it with no fingers.

"Wait! Are you still—?"

He reaches out, tries to pull up her dress to look for the explosives strapped beneath it, but she wiggles, beats at his hands. Then someone in the smoke grabs her hand and pulls her out of his grasp.

"She's wired!" he yells and rolls away from her. " C-4 under her dress." Gunfire rattles in his ears again and he reaches for his rifle slung over his shoulder. But his rifle's gone! Where is his rifle?

The gunfire is closer! There's an explosion and he curls into a ball as the debris falls all around him. Someone grabs his shoulder, shakes him, calls his name.

"Grayson! Grayson, what's wrong with you?"

He opens his eyes.

. . .

CARTER STOOD OVER HIM, shaking him.

"Grayson, what's wrong with you?" Carter demanded.

The world slid back into place with a sickening sensation, like the pit of your stomach in those seconds after you leap out of the plane before your chute opens and yanks you upward.

He was lying curled in a ball on the hardwood floor, with his hands over his head, cringing. He sat up slowly, looking around wonderingly. The rag rug on the floor was bunched up where he'd slid it across the floor. Piper stared down at him, shocked and shaken. Sadie clung to her mother's neck. No longer screaming, Sadie's head was borrowed down out of sight and she made the hitching sounds of a child too frightened to cry. His mother sat on the couch. Her look of shocked confusion felt like a slap in the face.

Carter hulked over him. His brow was furrowed, pleated above his nose with twin lines. His lips were twisted down in a frown that might have been disgust. A flash of rage blossomed into a blaze in Grayson's chest and his hands curled into fists.

Then he saw a little girl who looked to be maybe ten years old clinging to Piper's leg and cringing away from him. Her hair was the color of napalm flames in the trees and a spray of red freckles on her nose stood out like sequins on her pale skin.

Grayson gestured toward the unknown child.

"Who..?" He meant to say more, tried to, but his voice locked up tight in his throat after the first word.

PIPER THOUGHT WILDLY that Grayson sounded like a hoot-owl on the limb of a sycamore tree. Almost blurted out, "Who-who!" in response, but she held onto the words, recognized them for what they were: incipient hysteria.

What just happened?

"Gray, what are you do—"?

"Who is she?" he asked, never taking his eyes off Maggie.

Maggie was equally transfixed. Only she was staring at Grayson in terror. And why wouldn't she be afraid? A big man yells at her for no reason, starts pawing her—it occurred to Piper this probably wasn't the first time and she felt sick.

"Why did you shout at her?" She couldn't keep the angry accusation out of her voice as she patted Maggie with her free hand. "Why did you—? She's only a little girl, a lost little girl."

"Lost?" He seemed to be having trouble forming words. He was panting. Sweat beaded on his forehead.

"She came here Wednesday. I opened the door and there …"

She turned to Maggie. "Honey, would you take Sadie into the bedroom, give her Rasmus and her blankie and—"

"She was about asleep when…" Maggie's voice was trembling and she watched Grayson out of the corner of her eye, prepared to bolt if he came at her again. "I'll rock her, but she's mighty upset."

Clearly, so was Maggie.

"Sing to her," Piper said and began to peel Sadie's arms away from her neck. The toddler clutched at her, started to cry, then noticed Carter standing beside Piper. She turned toward him and held out her arms.

"Hold you, Unka Cardur!" Her voice sounded

desperate and she lurched toward him, leaned so far out of Piper's arms that Piper was thrown off balance and Carter had to snatch the child out of the air before Piper dropped her. Sadie wrapped her arms around his neck and snuggled close to him for comfort. Then, from the safety of his arms, she cast a sideways glance at Grayson on the floor—only for a moment—before she turned away and planted her thumb in her mouth snug as a cork in a wine bottle.

Carter held out his free hand to Maggie.

"Tell you what—let's both put Sunshine to bed." He led the little girl into the bedroom without looking back.

Piper turned to Grayson. He was still sitting on the floor, leaning now against the pile of rug he'd scooted aside when he went rolling across the room.

"Her name's Maggie," she said. "She must be from way back up in—"

"Must be? Don't you know? How'd she get here?"

Was there accusation in his tone?

"I don't know."

Grayson stared at her with a look she couldn't read. He said nothing. She said nothing. The moment drew out, and Piper didn't know how to get from where they were now back to where they'd been only a few minutes before. She didn't think Gray did, either.

Chapter Fifteen

CARTER BROKE THE SPELL. He stepped out of Sadie's bedroom at the end of the hall, closed the door behind him and walked with purpose into the parlor. They could hear Maggie's muted singing behind the door.

"I have to get back to Charleston," he said.

"But Carter, aren't you going to—?" Marian began.

"It's late," he said, his voice curt and clipped. He looked at Piper and for a moment their gazes locked, then he turned to Grayson. "You two … obviously have lots of things to talk about."

Without another word, he strode to his mother, planted a peck on her cheek. She grabbed his hand and held on— but he pulled it free and was out the door and gone in seconds.

The room was quiet.

Grayson still sat at Piper's feet and the incongruity of having a sane, rational conversation with a man who'd rolled around on the floor like he was suffering some kind of … hallucination … struck her.

"What was this ..." she made an all-encompassing gesture, "all about? What happened to you?"

His voice was soft. "I don't know."

"I do!" said Marian from the couch and they both turned, startled. "I disremember what Everett called it, but he was still having them ... 'visions' when he and I got married, and he'd been back from Germany for nigh on six years then. Jumped sky high if'n the door slammed. And he had horrible bad dreams for years. After awhile, it got better, of course. But it took time."

She looked at her son tenderly.

"You seen some terrible things over there in Veet Nam, didn't you, son?"

Piper watched his face close, saw the shutters slam shut behind his eyes.

"I don't want to talk about it." He sounded cold, like a robot.

Then he got to his feet and leaned to straighten the rug. Piper took the other edge and helped him move it back into place in the center of the room.

"The little girl, Maggie, what's she doing here?" he asked.

Piper told him the story, searched his face for the sympathy she expected to see there but could find it nowhere in evidence on his features. He sat down beside his mother on the couch and the old woman took his hand in hers and sat patting it as Piper spoke.

"She'd been out in them woods at least a couple of days, I'd warrant, 'fore she come here," Marian put in. "Them bruises was two or three days old. And she was so hungry she liked to eat up everything we had in the house."

"But why is she still here?" Grayson asked. "If she got here Thursday, didn't you take her to the sheriff?"

"Of course, I did. But Deputy Higgins said he didn't have any reports of missing children."

"That still doesn't answer my question—why is she here and not in some—?"

"Because I said she could stay with me until they locate her parents." Why didn't he get it that she *wanted* Maggie here. It had made perfect sense to Carter. "Is that so hard to understand?"

"No, it isn't."

That maddening calm. No, not calm. Detachment. Disinterest.

"Tomorrow morning when I go into town for groceries, I'll stop by the sheriff's office and find out if they've made any progress finding the family that beat the crap out of her," Piper said. "Okay?" She turned toward the kitchen. "What would you like on your meatloaf sandwich?"

~

GRAYSON COULD HEAR HIS HEART, sledgehammer heavy, pounding and pounding, slamming blood to his brain to flush out unreason.

He knew he was missing something, but he couldn't make out what. He wasn't picking up on emotions, but he couldn't seem …

Bottom line: he was exhausted. It felt like he'd been traveling for weeks. On his body clock it was dawn—after a sleepless night. He took two bites of the meatloaf sandwich Piper fixed for him. It tasted like sawdust. The room began to swim in and out of focus.

A hand gently shook him. He was sitting on the sofa, his chin on his chest. The room was dark. His mother was gone. The house was quiet.

"Come to bed, honey," Piper said softly and took his hand to tug him gently to his feet. "You have to be very quiet. Sadie is a light sleeper."

He tried to tiptoe into the bedroom, but combat boots made that activity more or less ludicrous. He did manage not to stumble, though, sat down on the edge of the bed, got the boots unlaced and off his feet without sounding the baby alarm. He stood, dropped his pants to the floor and stepped out of them. Then turned to face Piper as he unbuttoned his shirt. She sat up in bed in a simple, white cotton nightgown that shone like a polished pearl in the moonlight streaming in the window. All the fatigue left him then. He pulled his shirt off and tossed it on the floor, knelt on the bed and took her into his arms. She felt so good, so soft and warm. She melted into him and—

Piper abruptly pulled back with a little cry and shoved him away.

"What…?" Grayson asked.

She reached over and flipped on the little bedside table lamp.

"Turn around so I can see your back."

He obeyed, faced the wall.

She touched his back lightly.

"What is *that?*"

There was revulsion in her voice.

"What is what?"

"That thing in the middle of your back."

He reached around and tried to feel it, but whatever she was talking about was squarely between his shoulder blades and he couldn't contort either arm sufficiently to reach the spot.

"Look in the mirror in the bathroom … and do… something. Get it off."

Grayson padded out into the hallway in his underwear

and down to the bathroom. The lone, dim bulb cast a bilious glow on the interior of the small room. He turned his back to the vanity mirror over the sink, then craned his head around and tried to see what—

It was a leech. That's what he'd felt, what'd been itching on the plane and the bus. But how in the world had it stayed stuck on him for so long? It only took a few hours, not even a whole day, for a leech to get full and drop off. This one was huge, a bulbous purple splotch beside his backbone. He looked around for something to use to get it off. Seeing no likely candidate, he went into the kitchen and pulled open a couple of drawers until he found what he was looking for. Carrying the butcher knife back to the bathroom, he again turned his back to the sink and mirror and stabbed the creature with the knife. When black blood squirted out of it onto the mirror, the sink and the floor, he jumped back, tripped over Sadie's potty chair sitting beside the toilet and landed with a clatter and thump in a heap on the floor.

Sadie began to wail.

Grayson sighed, got to his feet and turned his back to the mirror again. The creature didn't wiggle and squirm. It hung limp, dead, which perhaps explained why it hadn't fallen off. Something had killed it and it ... Grayson let the thought go and carefully began to scrape the knife across his back to peel the dead leech away. He knew he was asking for an infection, but he'd deal with that in the morning when he could see. Right now, he only wanted it gone!

He flicked the dead leech into the toilet and flushed it, tried to dab his bleeding back with toilet paper but couldn't reach the wound and felt blood trickling down into his underwear. Because of the blood thinner leeches injected into a bite, it was sometimes difficult to stop the bleeding.

He used more toilet paper to clean up the mess in the bathroom as the wound continued to send a sticky stream of warm ooze down his spine. Exhaustion was making him dizzy and he didn't do a very good clean-up job before he stepped out into the hallway. Piper had taken Sadie into their bedroom and was pacing back and forth with the child in her arms, patting her back and whispering soothing sounds.

He pointed to the parlor and mouthed: "I'll crash on the couch."

Grayson hoped she'd tell him not to, that she wanted him in bed with her where he belonged. But she didn't, only blew him a kiss and went back to comforting Sadie.

He closed the door quietly behind him—not that the closing door would awaken anybody the wailing child hadn't already roused—went to the kitchen and tossed the knife in the sink, then stood for a moment, looking out the window. The moon was bright. Though not yet quite full, it silvered the trees in an other worldly sparkle. He held his breath, listened, wanted to hear the melody of night time, the rub-bub, rub-bub of tree frogs and the creaking of crickets. Nothing. Either the frogs and crickets were on strike or the thunder in his ears had won the battle of the bands.

He went back into the parlor, then thought about his bleeding back and fetched a towel from the bathroom to lie on. He stretched out on the couch—lumpy, with a sagging place on one end and a big protruding bump on the other. He made a note to be grateful for small favors. The roaring of his damaged hearing helped mute the sound of Sadie's wailing. Grayson had time to think about the black soldier on the MSTS flight who'd described in detail what he planned to do with his woman, and considered that sleeping on the couch wasn't how he'd planned his first night home after spending a year on the other side of the planet. Then he closed his eyes and was instantly asleep.

~

Carter had to pull over before he reached the highway because his hands were shaking so violently he couldn't keep the car on the road.

He killed the engine and lights and sat in the darkness, silence roaring in his ears. Then he let out a yell, a cry of anger and pain and frustration, a sound almost more feral than human and pounded his fists on the steering wheel so hard some rational part of his brain wondered how he'd drive the car if he broke it.

He stopped pounding and sat quietly. The breeze off the creek carried the night smells of mud, wet leaves and dead crawdads. He could hear frogs and crickets and could barely catch the rushing water sound. Since the construction of the dam, Turtle Creek only carried the water from small mountain streams and Butler Creek, which ran south along the bottom side of Chicken Gizzard Mountain and emptied into the dry creek bed a quarter of a mile below his mother's house. Even after a heavy rain, Turtle Creek was seldom more than five or six inches deep now.

But you could drown in less than six inches of water.

There's the sound of the creek and Becky splashing in it along with the whump, whump, whump Grayson makes as he slaps the broom against the rugs hung over the tree limb.

Becky sees Carter and starts to speak.

Shhh, he whispers, shakes his head and puts his finger to his lips.

She puts her pudgy finger to her own lips and stands with the water running over her bare feet watching him.

Grayson's cowboy boots are sitting on the creek bank where he set them after he waded into the water with Becky. Carter edges down into the creek and starts toward them.

Carter shook his head so violently he had the sensation of flinging the memory out of his mind. Not now! Not *tonight!*

But the other thoughts that flooded into his mind to take the place of The Worst Memory Of His Life, as he'd come to call it over the years, were very little better.

Grayson! How could he…? He wasn't due home for two more months!

But he was here now. And he wasn't going back!

When they'd heard about the massacre at Fire Base Eagle's Nest, Carter had actually hoped his brother had been one of the casualties. He hated himself for wanting it, but that would handed him his every desire in life on a silver platter.

And now…

Carter needed more time. It was *working.* He was winning her. He was slow, patient, kind—everything he wanted to be to her for the rest of his life. And tonight she'd kissed him! Okay, he'd kissed her. But she'd let him, she leaned into it.

And then…

He slammed both fists down on the steering wheel again and heard a sound that might have been something cracking. He leaned back in the seat, ran both hands through his short hair and groaned. Images flooded into his mind unbidden of Piper welcoming her husband home from the war—into her heart. And her bed!

No! He would *not* give up. He'd already lost her once. It

had ripped his heart right out of his chest when Piper broke up with him. At the time, he was certain it was temporary, that he'd win her back. Then, after her brother Riley's thug friends put him in the hospital, he understood she'd been avoiding him to protect him. He went off to Duke certain that as soon as she was out of high school she would ... But the day after she graduated, she eloped with Grayson!

At least, he seldom saw her after that. The couple moved to Louisville for Grayson to go to seminary and Ma rode a bus to visit them on holidays. Carter didn't accompany her.

He'd had lots of other women then. Managed to wall all thoughts of his lost love out of his heart and mind.

But everything changed when they called up Grayson's National Guard unit and Piper moved back to the hollow to care for Ma. Carter put on a full court press then, was with her every chance he got—under the guise of visiting his mother, of course. And he should have had *60 more days.* Carter was absolutely certain that by the end of October Piper would ...

He let out a sigh that actually trembled slightly on the end and for the first time in five years wished he had a cigarette. He seldom thought of smoking after he quit, but when Piper's precious little brother lit one the other night, Carter had felt the familiar yearning.

Zeke. He made a humph sound in his through. Somebody ought to—

And then it came to him. A plan. Not in pieces, vague, with bits to figure out and work out. It came to him whole, like it'd been designed by somebody else and mailed to him. Or like he'd been working on it himself for months. A plan that would solve both of his problems with one decisive act.

He started the car, gave it the gas and fishtailed in the dirt of the road. When he turned left on the highway leading into Sadlerton instead of right toward Charleston, he peeled out and left rubber on the asphalt.

Jesse McCullough lived down in the valley by the creek and the railroad track, not up on the side of the mountain like the Addingtons. That was because Rev. Everett Addington had built his family a house on his own little piece of land and most of the houses in Sadlerton were what was left of the company town, the coal camp that had belonged to Northfield Coal Company.

Carter remembered when he was in the third grade, Northfield had painted all the company houses in Sadler Hollow a sickly yellow color nobody liked. A week later, in American history class, they'd been studying how settlers had come to America to find land of their own and freedom to choose how they lived. His best friend, who lived in one of those yellow houses, had raised his hand and asked, "Why ain't West Virginia in that America?"

Now, of course, most of the houses were sagging wrecks that showed no sign of any color whatsoever, only the ash gray of unpainted boards. Over time, layoffs, mine closings, mechanization and strip mining had decimated the workforce who lived here. All up and down Sadler Hollow were former coal camp houses with yards where barefoot kids in tattered clothes played in the dirt and where men with hollow faces and hopeless eyes sat on porches looking out at nothing, men who hadn't had steady employment since the mines started closing in 1956.

On the way to Jesse McCullough's house, Carter passed the homes of three other cousins—well, one was a second cousin. The whole hollow was full of McCulloughs.

He also passed Bennett's Five and Dime where he'd stood on the slat porch in 1960 as a junior at Duke and shook hands with John F. Kennedy. Kennedy had spent six weeks in West Virginia that year campaigning for the primary. As a wealthy Yankee Catholic, he'd had to demonstrate he could carry a blue-collar, protestant state. Six weeks in West Virginia was the equivalent of spending a year in a state as big as California, and Kennedy had gone everywhere, to schools, farms, coal camps, even went down into a coal mine and talked to miners. He'd won the primary handily, but more importantly he'd won the heart of West Virginians forever. When he came back as President in 1963 to celebrate the state's centennial, he'd stood in the pouring rain in Charleston and said, "The sun doesn't always shine in West Virginia, but the people always do." No state was more heart broken at his passing than West Virginia.

The almost-full moon shone a silver light that erased some of the ugliness of the house until Carter's headlights illuminated the dark porch where Jesse and his two oldest boys sat on the steps. Jesse had a beer in his hand and Carter was certain he'd already had more that a couple of others.

"Come on up and set a spell," Jesse called out as Carter got out of the car. "What brings you down here to mingle with the pore folks?"

Carter was used to the jab. He'd heard it his whole life. He was a McCullough, all right, but he was also the son of the Rev. Everett Carter Addington, the circuit-riding preacher who'd come here from Richmond, married the beautiful Marian McCullough and then earned his place in the community by a lifetime of selfless devotion. Though Carter and Grayson lived the same lives of poverty and deprivation as everyone else in the hollow, being Addingtons meant they got out.

Carter now lived with a foot in two totally disparate

worlds. Charleston boasted one of the highest per capita incomes in the East—in large part due to the wealthy coal operators, who'd raped the land in the mountains and lived like kings in the untouched beauty of the city on the Kanawha River. Unfortunately, mere proximity to that wealth was not sufficient to produce it and Carter was making his fortune using the skills of the forbearers on his mother's side of the family, who for generations had manufactured the best moonshine for a hundred miles in any direction.

Jesse turned to Buster, the older of the two boys and said, "Go get your cousin Carter a beer."

Carter held up his hand. "Thanks, but I can't. Got to drive back to Charleston tonight."

"And you can't drink one beer and still keep the car 'tween the fence posts. You gone soft, Carter. City livin's made you a pansy."

The two boys laughed at that.

Carter stepped up on the bottom step of the porch.

"We need to talk," he said.

"G'on in the house, you two," Jesse said to the boys. "'Fore you do, bring me 'nuther Iron City."

The screen door banged shut behind them.

"You come all the way to the holler just to talk?" Jesse asked. "Couldn't wait 'til I called?"

"I was already here, seeing to Ma."

"Seein' to Piper, don't you mean?"

The boy came out on the porch and handed his father a beer, then went back inside. Jesse tilted his head back and chugged the final few gulps of his last, crumpled the can and tossed it at a barrel on the weedy yard by the porch. He missed and it clunked into the side of the barrel and clinked to the ground atop the pile of other misses. Jesse picked up a can opener, poked two quick holes in the top of the fresh can and held it out to Carter, who shook his head.

"Grayson's home."

That was a conversation stopper.

"No lie? When'd he get here?"

"Tonight."

"Oh … and you's up there with Piper. Didn't catch you doin' nuthin'—"

"You want to watch that mouth, Jesse," Carter growled, "or you're going to find it on the other side of your face."

"I's only cuttin' up with you, Carter. Jeeze."

"You're not drunk are you?"

"No, I'm—"

Carter snatched the beer from Jesse's hand, turned it up and began pouring it on the ground.

"What the—?" Jesse reached out to grab it, but Carter glared at him and he slumped back on the porch in a pout.

"You ready to listen to me now?"

"I's ready 'fore you poured out my beer. Beers cost money you know."

Carter pulled his billfold from his pocket, yanked out a couple of bills and tossed them at Jesse.

"Here, buy yourself a case after you hear me out. But this is important and I want you sober, and *listening.*"

"You shore got yore panties in a wad tonight, Carter. Yeah, I'm listenin'."

It didn't even take five minutes for Carter to outline his plan. It was simple and brilliant. With any luck, it'd solve both their problems with a minimum of effort—effort Jesse was more than happy to expend—and neither of them would suffer the consequences of their actions. It was perfect. Even Jesse thought so, and there were sharper knives in the drawer than old' Jess.

"When you want me to do it?" Jesse asked. If he'd been a coon dog, his tail would have been wagging eagerly.

"Obviously, the sooner the better, but I've got to work out my end of it. When I know, I'll call and leave a message for you at Duffy's, only the number of the date. You remember to bring me some red mud."

"I'll put some in a mason jar and screw on the lid, keep it nice and soft and spreadable." Jesse's lips stretched in a grin that revealed missing teeth. "Yore little brother might a'been lucky 'nuff to make it home when most of them Kentucky boys ended up face-down in a rice patty, but his luck's 'bout to run out."

Chapter Sixteen

Piper didn't like the way Grayson treated Maggie. Didn't, in fact, even like the way he looked at her. There was a wariness in … no it was more than wariness. It was hostility. He was belligerent to the child and he had absolutely no reason to be.

It's not supposed to be like this.

Not after all the waiting and worrying. Every night for months, she'd fantasized about Gray coming home, but then she'd stopped. Partially because it hurt too bad to reach over and find his side of the bed cold, the pillow puffed where no head had dented it. And after she'd returned from Hawaii, she didn't imagine his return because she didn't know what to picture anymore.

She hadn't been prepared, hadn't been ready and suddenly here he was. And it wasn't—

"I tried, but I messed it up." Maggie had come up silently beside her. "My fingers won't … do that."

Piper stood at the front porch railing, dressed in cut-off jeans and a pale yellow shirt as a cool morning breeze gently blew ebony curls back from her face. She was gazing out over the valley where the sun was just burning the mist off the small streams that slipped down the mountainsides and eventually emptied into Turtle Creek as it sliced through the middle of the hollow.

Maggie held up the braid she'd been working on and it did, indeed, need help. Piper quickly pulled out the awkward twists and winds of the three strands of hair and began to braid it. The child's hair was more than simply red. It was a riot of different shades and tones with strands of copper, gold and orange—individual notes that blended in a symphony of color.

"Mr. Grayson went down to the creek." Maggie said. "He took a towel and a bar of soap, said he was going to scrub himself raw and couldn't do a proper job of it in that wee tub." She paused. "Least that's what he told Nan Marian. He didn't talk to me."

The women in the house had been tiptoeing around like cat burglars all morning so as not to disturb Grayson where he slept on the couch. It was almost ten o'clock before he finally woke. When he did, he was instantly awake, didn't merely open his eyes but sat bolt upright, looked around frantically, then slowly relaxed.

Marian was seated at the table, making a stab at snapping beans from the garden into a pot in her lap. But she had little strength and the movement was painful. Piper knew that all she really wanted was a to sit somewhere near him so she could stare at Grayson sleeping on the couch.

Piper couldn't blame her. It was all she could do to keep herself from hovering over him, touching him. She didn't want to leave the room because the joy of seeing him there filled her heart to overflowing.

Maggie had kept Sadie quiet by reading to her in her room from the big book of "Grimm's Fairy Tales." And by taking her out to the back porch to teach her a new skill.

"Lookit me, Mommy," Sadie'd cried. Her smile stapled deep dimples into her cheeks. She squeezed both her eyes tight shut and popped them instantly back open again. "I winkin'."

Then Maggie and Sadie took a watering can out to "gib the begables a drink—they thirssy."

When Piper settled the toddler in for her morning nap she hoped Sadie would sleep long. The child had been up and down all night and she would miss her afternoon nap when Piper went into town for groceries. Piper'd planned supper in her head as she walked the floor with the fretful child, wanted to fix Grayson's favorite meal—fried chicken, mashed potatoes and milk gravy. A big salad with not-thirssy-anymore vegetables from the garden—tomatoes, carrots, red and green peppers and sweet onions. She had broccoli, too—he liked it steamed, crisp, not squishy—corn on the cob and okra fried in corn meal. Pie, of course—chocolate, his favorite.

She'd stood in the kitchen doorway and stared at Grayson, sleeping deeply on the lumpy couch. When he sat up, wide awake, she'd meant to offer to make him what-ever he wanted for breakfast. Then Maggie came in the house with Sadie and the watering can and everything went south.

Sadie took one look at her father and ran screaming out of the room. Maggie took off after her, and Grayson bluntly asked Piper if she was going to take the little girl back in to the sheriff's office today.

It had been stiff and awkward after that. She sensed that Grayson didn't really understand what she was upset about any better than she understood why he was behaving as he did.

"Hold still one more minute ..." She was discovering Maggie could be as much a wiggle worm as Sadie was.

"There," Piper said as she finished the bow. Maggie scooted off the porch and into the house trailing a "thank you, Miss Piper" behind her as she went.

Piper turned and saw Grayson coming toward the house. That explained Maggie's quick exit. His damp hair fell in the beloved widow's peak over his forehead. He was wearing a tee shirt and jeans. Both were too big for him. He'd lost so much weight! And His skin was red where he'd scrubbed it. In fact, his right hand was bleeding.

"What did you—?" she began, reached out and tried to take his hand, but he pulled it away.

"Washed a little too hard. I've got, it's a fungus we called ... jungle rot. Everybody gets it. I didn't expect to bring it ... I figured I'd be back stateside long enough for it to heal before I came home."

He looked into her eyes.,

"I'm sorry about last night. It was ... a leech. Jungle's full of them. They're flat as paper, can get in the tops of your boots, up your sleeves even when you keep the cuffs on your shirt tight. You can't feel them bite you—they inject some kind of natural anesthetic. That one was right where I couldn't see it or feel it."

He seemed to be studying her face, looking for…what? Revulsion, maybe. Well, it *was* disgusting. Some kind of fungal rot and a leech—yecht! But she had no intention of letting Grayson know how she felt.

She reached out and took his hand, which he reluctantly allowed her to touch. She turned it over, examined the bloody sores on the bottom edge of his palm stretching from his little finger to his wrist, then saw there were bloody places on both elbows, too.

"Did you try hydrogen peroxide?"

"No, there's this white powder called Dapsone to treat

it, but I didn't stop to grab any when I was running to catch that plane."

While Piper made his meatloaf sandwich last night, Grayson had explained what'd happened to bring him home and described his marathon journey.

"I bet hydrogen peroxide will do the trick, but if it doesn't, we'll find something that does." She squeezed his hand and he looked from it to her face.

"It's okay, Honey," she said tenderly. "You could have come home wounded, missing an arm or a leg or … do you honestly think I'm upset over a little fungus!"

He smiled and the relief she saw on his face broke her heart.

"But I am upset over one thing you *didn't* bring home."

He looked confused.

"All those pounds you left on the other side of the planet. But since you left those behind, I shall have to find some brand new ones to put on you."

He grabbed her and hugged her fiercely. Was he trembling? His voice was husky.

"I'm sorry about the rest of it, too. I had a flashback. After a firefight, sometimes, a guy'd suddenly get this blank look on his face and start hollering and you knew he was reliving it. More vivid than remembering—*re-living*. You can't control it, don't know when—"

"It'll pass, Honey. It'll take time. And that's one thing we have an abundance of now." She pulled back out of his arms and looked up into his face. "We've got the rest of our lives, Sweetheart. You're home, safe—for good! Nothing else matters. Whatever is wrong, we'll work it out together."

His eyes were moist, he leaned down and kissed her. Tenderly at first then with growing passion. She leaned into him, melted into him, got lost in the feel of his arms around her, his lips on hers.

She didn't hear the door open behind them, wasn't aware of Maggie's presence until Grayson finally released her breathless. Then the child spoke.

"Did you have a good wash in the stream?" she asked politely.

Grayson went rigid, then turned in something like slow motion to gawk at her. Piper wondered what exactly it was that he saw when he looked at the child. It was clear he *didn't* see Maggie because his reaction made no sense.

"What do you want with me?" he asked, his voice hard and cold. "Why are you here?"

Nguyen stares up at him with wide, wondering eyes.

"You wash good in stream, Grape?" she asks. And for a moment he catches a whiff of the putrid stink of human feces that still clings to his skin though he'd scrubbed at it as hard as he could with soap and sand.

"What do you want with me? Why are you here?"

But of course, he knows. She wants him to help her, to protect her. After all, she'd helped him. She'd risked her life to hide him, had cared for him. Now she wants him to hide her from the enemy. But he can't do that. There's a reason he can't help her, but right now he can't remember what it is. He reaches up and rubs his throbbing temples.

"You think I can just load you up in my backpack and haul you out of here. Is that what you think?"

She says nothing, merely looks at him. But she isn't …substantial, it's like you can reach right through her. Wraithlike. Nguyen is like a film, like an overlaid image, a double-exposed photograph. There is Nguyen, her eyes dark, her black hair hanging in her eyes. And there is the little red-haired girl—Maggie—with braids and freckles. The child before him is both and neither, a ghostly image in a real world.

GRAYSON GRITTED his teeth and closed his eyes. Gradually, he began to hear the cicadas in the trees, feel the sun on his arm—hot but not jungle sticky. The breeze was surprisingly cool. There was no stench, he couldn't hear gunfire or the incessant noisy creatures of the jungle. Haystack had always been curious about them, wanted to know what animal or bug made the eech-eech-eech sound and what made the argh-wah, argh-wah sound and what … But Gray'd had no desire to get up close and personal with the teeming hordes of strange flora and fauna beyond the campfire light.

He took a deep breath, let it out and slowly opened his eyes. Before him stood a little red-haired girl staring up at him with wide green eyes, an odd shade of green with yellow flakes. He'd barked at her and she was cowering back from him, like he might hit her, and he felt instantly guilty. When she spoke, her voice was soft and tentative. Compassionate.

"Yer bum's out the window, Mr. Carter, sir," she said.

"Huh?"

"She said your butt's out the window," his mother translated from the doorway. She leaned against the frame, her face pale. "Means you're not making no sense. And you ain't."

"It's … all happening too fast. I'm sorry."

"You know what you need," Piper said. "You need to take off into the woods, get away by yourself for awhile. Why don't you go squirrel hunting? I know the season doesn't open for another couple of weeks, but who'll care?"

Hunting? How could he possibly—

But he *could*. Strange as it seemed, the thought of holding the old .22 that hung over the mantle sounded comforting. He'd actually feel … normal with a rifle in his hands. Oh, he understood that response might not be rational, but emotionally … yeah, he'd like to go hunting. Not today, though. He was too tired.

Piper must have seen him slump.

"Today's probably not the best time, but …" she paused. "Marian has a doctor's appointment in Charleston on Thursday. All the women could go into town, leave you here in peace and you could spend the whole day in the woods."

"Yes," he said. And as he heard the word escape his lips he felt the growing conviction of it in his heart. He'd rest up, putter around the house for the next couple of days. Get re-acclimated. He'd seen the dead tire swing leaned up against the trunk of the oak tree, a piece of broken rope dangling from the limb above. Sadie wasn't too young for a tire swing, was she?

Sadie. He'd dreamed for months of gathering the child up in his arms and nuzzling her soft hair, inhaling her glorious baby smell, but she wouldn't let him near her.

She held out her arms to Carter, though…

Carter. He and Piper had to talk about what he'd seen when he walked up the road in the twilight last night. As he'd examined the memory, he'd realized that in point of fact, Carter had kissed Piper, not the other way around. True, she hadn't instantly reacted, but she *had* shoved him away, clearly upset. It was plain he'd taken advantage of her at a weak moment.

He felt his hands begin to ball into fists at his side but he forced himself to relax. Not now.

Sadie. Piper. And Carter. Yeah, he had a couple of

bridges to mend, alright, and another that might need to be blown completely out of the water!

He resolutely planted a smile on his lips.

"Honey, I wouldn't have thought of going squirrel hunting, but I think I'd like that very much."

He leaned over and planted a kiss on her nose, then glanced at Maggie.

"You're taking Maggie with you when you go to the sheriff's office today, right?"

"Of course," Piper snapped and stepped away from him. "Wouldn't want to trouble him to come get her." Then she shooed Maggie into the house and followed her.

He'd stepped in it again. Surely, Piper didn't think she could just keep the little girl!

"Piper sees herself in Maggie, son," his mother said, her voice quiet and pain-filled. "And wasn't nobody there to rescue her from Rooster Campbell."

She turned slowly and started toward the couch and he hurried inside to take her arm and ease her down onto the cushion where the spring wasn't broken.

Maggie came down the hallway with Sadie, who'd just awakened from her nap. As soon as his daughter caught sight of him, she started to wail.

~

Nelson Warren moved the unlit cigar from one side of his mouth to the other and read again the last line of the report from Carter Addington about the reaction in Sadler Hollow to the landslide in Wales that had buried an elementary school.

"Based on the interviews I conducted, no one in Sadler Hollow has in mind to seek out a federal inspector and complain that Northfield Coal's slurry dams are unsafe. But they don't like the dams, never have, and they don't trust them. If one of the dams developed a substantial leak, say, and the rising creek flooded their homes, they'd yell foul. The houses in Sadlerton are clustered close around the creek, and while the people there would remain tightlipped to a federal inspector, they're a little more accustomed to strangers than mountaineers deeper in the mountains. If they were approached right, they might cheerfully give an earful of complaints to a newspaper reporter."

He put the sheet of paper back down on the pile of them in the neat manila folder and sat back in his chair.

Bottom line: if—*when*—Dam #2 started leaking and water began to pour over the dam at the top of the hollow, there'd be flooding in Sadlerton, maybe in every other coal camp downstream, too. Northfield would be on the hook for millions in damages. Every lazy mountaineer who "threw his back out" trying to wrestle the five junk cars and the door-less refrigerator out of the front yard and up to higher ground would file a lawsuit. The company would be tied up in court for years. But Addington had put his finger square on the issue of primary importance to Warren. When the leaking dam flooded the homes of a bunch of dirt poor coal miners, Northfield Coal would be eaten alive by the state press and probably some of the national media, too.

And he couldn't have *that!* Not right now.

Nelson Warren had never cared what the press had to say about Northfield Coal—good or bad. He still didn't, but it mattered now that he had aspirations beyond the presidency of the second largest coal company in the state, ambitions that would transport him out of Charleston, West Virginia and deposit him in Washington, D.C

Those plans likely hinged on how he was perceived by the press—and that, of course, meant how his coal company was perceived.

He was a Charleston native, the son of the man who built Northfield Coal with the sweat of his own brow in the coal mines. Nelson had never sweat in a coal mine, though he had worked in one briefly as part of his grooming to take over the company, which had prospered under his leadership. Now 51, Warren was ready to cash in his business success for a heaping helping of power.

West Virginia Senior Senator Laythrope P. Cavanaugh, who had strung an amazing five consecutive terms in office together, had recently announced to his inner circle that he would not seek re-election, and the man that group endorsed would be elected to replace him. By hook or crook, as the saying goes, their political machine would make it happen. Nelson Warren was in that inner circle. Trouble was, he wouldn't be their first choice as a candidate. There was a feisty young lawyer who was making quite a name for himself in Wheeling. He'd stepped into the limelight when he agreed to represent—pro bono—twenty-five victims of an apartment building collapse in a class action suit against the huge real estate conglomerate whose shoddy workmanship had been at fault.

He'd won that case handily, garnered millions in damages for his clients, and had come out the other side with a gleaming Champion of the Masses image. Warren had to trump that image. And as he stared down at Carter Addington's report, he was certain his strategy would do just that. If he executed everything perfectly, he'd be able to swoop down and rescue way more of the great unwashed than that snot-nosed Wheeling lawyer.

When some *vandal*—teenagers who wanted to see what a couple of sticks of stolen dynamite would do, maybe, or some out-of-work miner with an ax to grind—blew a hole in Impoundment Dam #2, the lives of thousands of people would be affected. He'd call in every chip he had with the newspapers—even the Charleston television station—to give maximum coverage to the efforts of *blameless* Northfield Coal to rescue suffering families with two feet of water in their living rooms! Not *forced* by law, but only as a compassionate neighbor, a good corporate citizen.

Under his hands-on leadership, of course, the company would immediately launch a valiant though futile effort to patch the leak in #2 before water from it filled up Impoundment #1. (But he would insist that they evacuate the endangered citizens below the dam "just in case.") And when the worst-case scenario did, indeed, come to pass, Northfield Coal would respond to the rising flood waters by providing temporary housing, warm blankets, hot coffee and untold numbers of photo ops featuring company president Nelson Warren passing out bowls of chicken soup to bedraggled grownups and cookies to their damp kiddies.

The amount of money to fund such an operation would be negligible. The company wouldn't be on the hook for any real, concrete damages—nothing of substance, merely bright-colored, photogenic Band Aids.

And the payoff for this magnanimity would be a seat for Nelson Warren in the United States Senate!

He'd already set in motion the first part of his plan, scheduled an inspection tour Tuesday of Logan County mines where there would be substantial stores of dynamite on hand. He smiled, reached across the wide expanse of his desk and punched the button on the intercom.

"Sheila, call the school and tell Miss Watson that I'll be coming by to have lunch today with Bobby."

He leaned back in the chair and wallowed the plan around in his mind. Sure, some people were going to get their feet wet, no doubt about it. More than a few of the residents of Sadler Hollow would likely be wading in their parlors real soon—not in ordinary flood water either. The sticky, almost viscous black sludge behind the dam would be a nightmare to clean up. And he was sorry about that, he really was. But that was the price of doing business.

Chapter Seventeen

PIPER WAS PREOCCUPIED AS SHE, Maggie and Sadie bounced down the steep, potholed road from Marian's house toward Northfield Road, which wound through the valley first on one side, then the other of the railroad. The highway and the railroad hugged Turtle Creek; in some narrow spots there was room for nothing else. But in the places where the valley widened, coal camp houses were jammed together like stands of mushrooms.

When they pulled into a parking space down from the courthouse, Piper looked at the two memorials and such sweet relief flooded over her that she wanted to laugh out loud. When they got around to erecting a Vietnam memorial, Addington would *not* be the first name listed. And after his 30-day pass, he'd be doing nothing more dangerous than ministering to the soldiers at Fort Knox or Fort Campbell in Kentucky, maybe even Fort Hood in Texas—didn't matter. He'd be safe!

"Hey, Piper, I hear Grayson's home," Ramona Richards said as soon as she saw Piper. "That a fact?"

Word traveled fast in Sadler Hollow.

"He sure is!" Piper beamed. "Came walking up to the house last night and liked to scared the be-jeebers out of all of us. We didn't know he was coming."

Ramona looked at Sadie, who quickly buried her head in her mother's shoulder. Maggie had fixed Sadie's hair that morning in a ponytail and it hung down her back in golden curls.

"I swear, that child gets purdier ever time I see her. Them big ole eyes and them curls. When she gets older, Grayson's gonna have to beat the boys away with a stick."

"Sheriff Cliff in?"

"No, he ain't. Sorry. That daughter he went to visit in Pittsburgh—she's pregnant you know, and she went into early labor. Had a premie. Little boy didn't weight but four pounds and they're all scared he ain't gonna make it. I don't know when the sheriff'll be back."

"Come on in, Piper."

She turned and saw Deputy Higgins standing in the doorway of his office.

She handed Sadie to Maggie. "You sit out here with Sadie, okay? She'll be good." The into-everything toddler would make no effort to get down and run around in a room with so many people she didn't know.

As soon as Piper closed the door behind her, Deputy Higgins sat down in one of the two chairs in front of his desk like he'd done when he spoke to Maggie on Friday. Piper's heart sank. He had bad news! They'd found her family and he wanted to break it to Piper gently.

Her heart tried to jackhammer a hole through the side wall of her chest.

"...so...?"

"Nothing," Higgins said and held out both hands, palms up. "Couldn't find a soul who knew a thing about her."

The relief that instantly surged through Piper was so profound for a moment she was afraid she'd sighed out loud.

"Spent all afternoon Friday and most of Saturday going up and down Fearsome Creek Hollow, knocking on doors and asking questions. I wasn't 'xactly a welcome sight, as you can well imagine."

Piper could. Nobody in a uniform would be a welcome sight in Fearsome Creek. The only people welcome there were the ones who'd lived there for at least four generations.

"But I don't think they was hiding nothin'. Once they found out I was there on account of a lost child, some of 'em—a *few* of 'em—even tried to be helpful. But nobody'd ever heard of a child named Maggie. They all trotted out their red-headed younguns for my inspection. The McIntire's have got four—two boys, two girls. And they got that orangey, carroty red hair. Can't imagine they'd have a sister with hair's pretty as hers." He gestured toward Maggie and they both looked at the child, who was keeping Sadie occupied with a rousing game of peek-a-boo.

"Well, if she's not from there, where …?"

"I checked with the elementary schools in Fayette, Nicholas, Greenbrier—even Pocahontas counties. Classes don't start for another couple of weeks, but no red-headed kids her age named Maggie or Margaret were enrolled in any of them county schools last year. I called the sheriffs departments, too, and the state police. There's been only one missing child case in the past three months in the whole state. A little boy in Charleston, and turns out his daddy run off with the kid 'cause Mama had custody. They found him twenty-four hours later and threw his papa in the iron house. I even went to the FBI."

"The FBI?"

"It ain't like there's some national list of all the missing kids in the country—and if you ask me, there dad-gum sure oughta be!—but the FBI gets called in if there's a ransom demand or the kid's transported across state lines. They don't have nothing that matches that little girl sittin' out there."

"Then … what …?"

Piper hadn't really let her mind play with the possibilities. She'd assumed the little girl was from Fearsome Creek Hollow or somewhere equally remote, and that people mean enough to beat up a child were such sorry human beings they wouldn't bother to report her missing. Piper hoped the state would take that into account along with the beating and not return her to her family. She never considered any alternative scenario.

"I have a theory," the deputy said, "I think she mighta got dumped on the highway, on Route 50, maybe 119 or even 19. Some family traveling through, could be from anywhere. They stop by the side of the road to answer a call of nature, and she seen that as a chance to run off."

"But why wouldn't they …?"

"Maybe they figured when folks see how beat up she is, they're gonna have to answer for it so they just kept going."

"Route 50? That's … what? Forty, fifty miles from here?"

"Not as the crow flies."

"*Over* the mountain? You think she …?"

"Or maybe she hitched a ride with somebody, or hid in the back of a truck. And there's another possibility, too. Maybe she wasn't beat up at all. That's the first thing you think when you see a black eye and a split lip, but there's lots of ways a kid could have got injuries like that. An accident, maybe, and—"

"She was in a car wreck? And soon's the dust settled,

her folks drove away in their dented-up car and left her by the side of the road?"

"I don't know what to think. Alls I know for sure is ain't nobody laying claim to that little girl."

"I do. I'll claim her, keep her, I mean."

"It ain't that simple, Piper, and you know it. I gotta call the Child Welfare people in Charleston."

"No! Please don't do that. Not yet. What's the hurry if nobody's looking for her?"

"What's Grayson think about coming home and finding he's done become a daddy again?"

"He only got home last night. He's still got jungle rot on his hands and a leech on his back. He doesn't know what to think about anything yet."

She hadn't meant to say all that, to raise her voice.

"I'm sorry Mr...Deputy Higgins. It's been a real emotional rollercoaster at our house. We didn't even know Grayson had got leave until he showed up. And I've been so worried that the people who beat Maggie ..." She paused, took a deep breath. "Seriously, why on earth would this child be better off in some orphanage or foster home in Charleston than right here in the mountains where she belongs? At least until you can find out ... what happened to her."

"I done thought about that Piper. And I tend to agree with you. Now, if Sheriff Cliff was here ... he goes by the book. But me...shoot, I'm just a coal miner who don't have to go down no more. And I'm inclined to let well enough alone for the time bein'. If it ain't broke, don't fix it. But all that could change when the sheriff's back. Likely will change when he gets back."

Piper stood, anxious to get out of the deputy's office before he changed his mine.

"You know where to find me—and Maggie—when you

want us. But right now, I got to get to the grocery store. I got me a man at home who hasn't had real fried chicken in so long he's forgotten what it tastes like."

"How is Grayson? He doing all right?"

No, he most definitely wasn't doing all right. But she didn't intend to share that fact with every man, woman and child for thirty miles in every direction. Though they would hear about it eventually, she supposed. They heard about everything else.

"He's still shook up a good bit. And he's way too skinny. But other than that …"

The deputy put out a hand and laid it on Piper's shoulder. His face was solemn and sincere. "You tell him we're real proud of him, hear!"

Piper left Sadie and Maggie in the car with the groceries while she called Carter from the pay phone outside Bennett's Five and Dime. What with Grayson showing up out of the blue last night, she'd totally forgotten to confirm that Carter was still on to go with her to Marian's doctor's appointment Thursday. He always went to the appointments, then took them all out to lunch afterward.

But it was more than that and she knew it. She *wanted* to call him. She wanted to tell him what the deputy had said about Maggie because she knew he'd be thrilled.

His distant, professional, "Hello, this is Carter Addington, how can I help you today?" changed to warm and concerned as soon as he heard her voice. She felt a little thrill in her belly at that, which sent her mind reeling so it was hard to stay on topic, tell him what the deputy had said.

She watched the girls playing in the car while she talked. Maggie pushed in the lock button on the car door, then Sadie pulled with all her strength to unlock it, loved the clunking sounds it made, did it over and over again. Maggie never tired of the game. Piper had never seen a child as patient with younger children as Maggie was.

"Higgins thinks Maggie climbed over the mountain?" Carter was incredulous. "You're kidding!"

"You got a better idea?"

"No, I assumed … Well, she's here now and she's with you where she belongs. That's what we need to focus on right now. Let the future take care of itself."

Oh, how she loved that about Carter. He was positive and encouraging. And practical. No sense in worrying until they had to.

She confirmed Marian's appointment time and then told him Grayson wouldn't be coming.

"Oh?" His voice was a shade chillier..

"He needs some time alone. You know, to readjust, so he's going to take the day and go squirrel hunting."

Carter had no response.

"Carter, are you there?"

"Yes, I'm here. Squirrel hunting, huh. Sounds like just the kind of relaxation he needs. Well, I'll see you girls on Thursday."

Piper left the grocery store and drove to the Dollar General Store. She bought a couple of pairs of size ten shorts, two tee shirts and two pairs of underwear for Maggie. The child had to have something to wear besides the dress she'd come in and a borrowed pair of overalls.

But the whole time she was in the store she was anxious, as she had been in the sheriff's office and the grocery—anxious to get back home to Grayson! She planned to fling herself into his arms the moment she saw him.`

When they turned on Turtle Road, she caught Maggie

looking intently up at the top of the hollow at the dam. Her face was troubled.

"Something the matter?" Piper asked.

"It's dark up there," Maggie said, her voice so soft Piper could barely hear her. "Dark and scary."

~

Carter hung up the telephone from his conversation with Piper wearing a grin so wide it split his face like an ax stroke, almost cleaved the top of his head off altogether. He picked up the receiver and placed another call. When the proprietor of Duffy's Tavern, answered, Carter said he wanted to leave a message for Jesse McCullough.

"I sound like Jesse's secretary to you?" Amos Burdette said.

Amos always made protesting noises when Carter called, which he did at least once a week. Carter didn't know if it was for the benefit of some audience in the bar who might have overheard or if he was just making sure Carter understood that the communication service he was rendering was worth the weekly $5 Carter paid him.

"Who took a leak in your Cheerios this morning, Amos?"

"I got better things to do than yap on the phone, that's all."

"Well, this message is short. Tell cousin Jess that Carter said the number is 'twenty-one.'"

"Come again?"

"A number. Twenty-one. Legal drinking age. The number between twenty and twenty-two. Twenty-one's the message."

"Okay, if he comes in, I'll tell him." He hung up.

Jesse would come in alright, to find out the date of the ambush, when he was to hide out somewhere along Blood Creek and shoot Zeke Campbell. That was the plan that had formed in Carter's mind last night. Oh, Jesse wouldn't hurt the kid, only wing him, but it would indeed send a message. To Zeke and his older brother, Riley, that it might not be a plan to try to horn in on McCulloch shine. It'd send a message to Piper, too, once she found out that her shell-shocked husband had plugged a hole in her precious little brother!

Carter had been at his desk at 6 a.m., to ensure the "report" about Sadler Hollow was on Nelson Warren's desk when he got to work. It had been thorough, detailed and totally bogus, full of made-up information and fabricated interviews—a pile of the warm, sticky substance you find on the south side of a horse going north. But writing it into the wee hours of the morning had kept his mind off Grayson and Piper. It also kept him from worrying about the one big hole in his scheme--how on earth was he going to make sure Grayson didn't have an alibi for the time when Zeke got shot? Then Piper handed him the whole thing on a silver platter. With cranberry sauce on the side.

Not only would Grayson have no alibi for Thursday—when everyone else in the house would be gone all day. But he was going squirrel hunting. Could you beat that!

Carter leaned back, flipped a cigarette out of the pack he'd bought on his way to work this morning, lit up and inhaled deeply. Grayson would be using their father's .22 rifle that hung in the rack over the mantle. Jesse'd be using a .22 to shoot Zeke, too. Perfect!

Chapter Eighteen

PIPER DIDN'T FLING herself into Grayson's arms the moment she saw him. When she got home, she found Grayson sound asleep, lying on his side, almost curled in a fetal position on the bed. She didn't wake him. About six o'clock, she reluctantly put the chicken away in the refrigerator rather than frying it. He awoke about sundown and she forced some vegetable soup down his throat before he was out again. He stirred around midnight, came partially awake, obviously in the grip of some monster nightmare. He flailed at the covers and called out so loud he woke Sadie. Maggie was instantly there to soothe her this time, though. Maggie had moved her pallet off the back porch to the floor of Sadie's bedroom, offering an odd "I need walls around me" by way of explanation.

Grayson slept through until ten o'clock the next morning, woke groggy and disoriented. He ate breakfast, apologized for conking out the way he'd done, made a manful effort to be cheerful and energetic, but was asleep on the couch by the time Sadie went down for her afternoon nap.

He was still asleep when Sadie awoke and that was

arguably the best thing that could have happened to their relationship. He lay unmoving on the couch and for half an hour Sadie refused to go anywhere near him. But eventually she relaxed and began to play on the floor at his feet. Piper watched her carefully check him out, timidly get a little closer and a little closer. By the time he began to stir late in the afternoon, Sadie was accustomed enough to his presence that she didn't shriek and run away when he sat up and dug his knuckles into his eyes like a sleepy child.

Again he apologized. During supper, per her whispered instructions, Grayson pretended Sadie wasn't even there. The technique paid off. When he unexpectedly burst out laughing, the child was startled by the loud noise, but then went back to her mac-and-cheese.

Grayson took a long, hot bath while Piper got Sadie ready for bed. She could see how he ached to take the child in his arms, but he didn't even try to kiss her goodnight.

"See you in the morning, Sweetheart," he said. And to everyone's surprised delight, Sadie responded, "Night, night, Daddy," and gave him a gnat-snatcher wave.

Piper luxuriated in a hot bath, too. Her heart took up a stacatto rhythm as she dried herself on the lone bath towel and slipped into her white cotton nightgown.

How she had ached for him, longed for him all those long months he was gone. Now they would be together, make beautiful love and fall asleep in each other's arms. She stepped into the bedroom where Grayson had left a single lamp burning on the bedside table. He lay in his boxer shorts, propped up on pillows. Sound asleep.

Piper swallowed the bitter taste of disappointment, went to the bed and sat down quietly beside him. She reached out and touched his chest where his ribs were clearly visible, then leaned closer and examined him. His chest, arms and legs were a patchwork of healing scratches and bruises in various shades of purple, green and yellow. The jungle rot sores were beginning to heal on his hands, but something was wrong with his left foot, too. There were larger healing sores on it and a clear ooze had formed on them—probably because the bath had washed away crusted scabs.

What had he been through? What horrors had he seen?

She understood that once he'd really relaxed, residual fatigue had hammered him like a bad case of the flu. He needed rest to heal. She watched him sleep for a time, then got up and went into the parlor and made herself as comfortable as she could on the couch so she wouldn't disturb him.

Piper awoke Wednesday in the early morning light to the feel of warm lips on hers. She opened her eyes and Grayson was kneeling beside the couch, a night's growth of dark whiskers on his face, his hair in bed-head disarray. But his eyes! Grayson, *her* Grayson, had finally come home.

"Shhhh," he said. He took her hand and pulled her to her feet, then led her across the hardwood floor to the bedroom and closed the door quietly behind them.

Piper saw the fire in his eyes, thought irrationally, "Wait, I have to brush my teeth." This wasn't how she'd imagined it—low light, her skin fresh from a warm bath, his face smooth and clean shaven.

He took her into his arms and kissed her, tenderly at first, then with more urgency. Her breath caught in her throat as she felt sudden heat wash over her. He moved her backward toward the bed without taking his mouth from hers, then eased her down on it. She had time to whisper three words breathlessly before the world exploded in months of built-up passion.

"Welcome home, Grayson."

MARIAN SAT UP IN BED, looking out the window at the back yard, what there was of it. Grayson was fooling with the old tire swing that had hung from the limb of the oak tree since he was a boy, fixing it up for Sadie. She shook her head. That boy's eyes were so full of hurt and fear, death and anger it was all she could do to look into them. He was cut up inside with razor blades, so many wounds he was near drowning in the blood. She closed her eyes.

I do thank you most humbly, Lord, for answering my prayers, for bringing my boy back home safe! And for letting me see him once more before I pass over. My time's near. 'Course I'm not tellin' you nothing you don't know. You got my days all counted out in that book of yours. You know the exact instant I'm gonna let out a breath and then not draw another one back in.

All's I know is it's gonna be soon.

My, won't it be fine to look you in the eye!

Meantime, I'm gonna soak up every second I got with them I love. In this here place I love.

She opened her eyes, lifted them from her son and traced the mountainside rearing up behind him to a bare cliff face topped by Turtle Shell Rock. Chicken Gizzard Mountain, on the other side of the gob dam, had once been even taller. Before they strip-mined it and bulldozed the waste off in the creek. Now the ridge on that side was flat, not a whole lot taller than the dam.

She sighed and mentally erased the ugly coal slurry dam between the sides of the valley. She put back the top of Chicken Gizzard Mountain the coal company had lopped off and the trees, even inserted a hawk in the picture in her mind, circling high above the valley floor. She set Naked Turtle Creek back in the almost dry creek bed, sliding down the ridge that was so steep it looked like a waterfall. As soon as she placed the creek inside its banks, no more than a bubbling brook a few inches deep in the wide spots, her mind went immediately to that day the way a yo-yo rises up the string to your hand.

Grayson standing in the back yard by the porch holding the limp body of his baby sister in his arms. Someone screaming, a shrill, shrieking wail. It seemed far away but when her throat began to close up, she'd realized the scream was hers.

Running in slow motion, dropping to her knees, the look of such pain in Grayson's eyes. She wanted to reach out and comfort him. But comfort comes from the heart and hers had been sucked out of her chest down into a black hole where the shining eyes of ferrets and weasels glowed yellow in the darkness.

It wasn't until long after that day that she wondered about the boots. Carter had been standing in the edge of the woods holding Grayson's cowboy boots. She'd seen him and had only a moment to wonder what he was doing with them before she saw Grayson staggering toward the house.

Pain ate up the memory for months. But it surfaced eventually. Carter was forever playing practical jokes on his little brother. He'd unscrew the top of the salt shaker before he handed it to Grayson, put a dead mouse under his pillow or steal his only two pairs of pants out of his dresser drawer and put them up a tree.

So it was pretty clear what he was doing that morning with Grayson's boots. But how did he get them away from Grayson? And *when?*

The how wasn't obvious but the when was. Grayson had been wearing his boots when he left for the creek that morning with Becky. So if Carter snatched them, it would have to have been ... Her heart went into her throat when she allowed her mind to follow that assumption to its logical conclusion: Carter had been there at the creek when Grayson was beating the rugs and Becky was playing in the water.

Why had he never told anybody about it? What did he see, or do, that he was unwilling to share with the rest of the family?

Carter had changed after that. Of course, the whole family had, and none of them for the better. Everett slid slowly away into some place where she couldn't reach him, some ugly place where everything he believed about God and the Scriptures became twisted into a monstrous perversion that ended up killing him. Grayson became the object of his father's wrath and growing instability and it was like the little boy crawled into a hole and pulled the dirt in after him.

And Carter? He never played another practical joke on anybody. All the laughing, prankish joy was gone from him. Something else took its place. Something that looked, felt, sounded and smelled like guilt.

Now that she was coming to the end of her days, she found she desperately wanted to understand that one simple mystery: why was Carter holding his brother's boots? But she knew she would go to her grave not knowing. Oh, she could ask Carter. He might even tell her. But satisfying an old woman's curiosity wasn't worth that kind of pain. Rip open those old wounds and the whole family would hemorrhage.

Marian was tired. The kind of tired that wasn't heavy, didn't weight her down like the exhaustion of caring for a family. This tired made her feel light, airy. As if she was barely attached to the world at all.

She closed her eyes and slept.

PIPER WATCHED Grayson through the screen of the back door as she dipped the pieces of chicken she'd just skinned into milk and then into flour to fry. Sadie was on her hands and knees at her feet, her long hair cascading off her shoulders to the floor.

"Sabie a doggie, Mommy," Sadie said and made a barking sound.

"Good doggie." Piper leaned over and petted the doggie on the head. Sadie tried comically to wag her little butt.

Grayson had the old rope untied from the tire and turned now to climb up to where the broken piece of rope dangled from the tree limb.

A slow smile spread across her face and she actually blushed at the memories that flooded her mind, but the color in her cheeks wasn't embarrassment. It was remembered passion. And delicious anticipation.

Today—finally!—she had gotten her husband back! They'd made beautiful love early in the morning, dawdled over a big breakfast—which he gobbled down as if he hadn't eaten a bite in a week. Sadie had watched him warily from her high chair, but his ignoring her was definitely working. Now, she was curious about him instead of afraid. It wouldn't be long before she'd be running into his arms, crying, "Hold you, Daddy!"

They'd intended to take a walk before lunch, but Grayson's energy failed and he took a long nap instead. Eager to do something when he woke up, he took the .22 rifle down from the rack over the fireplace and cleaned it for his squirrel hunting excursion tomorrow.

Whenever she came near, he reached out to touch her, as eager for the feel of her as she was for him. He whispered in her ear promises of what tonight would bring, then kissed her ear to seal the pact.

In all this glorious day, there was only one dark cloud. Maggie. Grayson was not unkind to her. He was polite, but he regarded her warily when she came into the room, seemed to be uncomfortable when she was around, as if her presence sucked some of the joy and peace out of his homecoming.

"Arf! Arf-arf!" said the doggie crawling around at her feet.

She reached down and patted Sadie on the head. "My what a fine doggie you are."

A few minutes later Maggie came into the kitchen to display her handiwork. Marian had shown the child how to crochet and the little girl had become a regular doily-making machine.

"I messed up this part," she said, pointing to a lumpy spot, "but Nan Marian says I'll soon be ready to make an afghan." The child's face fell. "But there won't be time for her to teach me."

Was Maggie talking about how long she had left here or how long Marian did?

The doggy barked and Maggie leaned over and patted her head affectionately, then nodded toward the back yard and asked, "Is Mr. Grayson going to fix up that old swing?"

"Uh huh. But it looks like a two-person job to me. Why don't you go see if he needs help."

Maggie looked dubious. "I don't think he wants *my* help," she said.

"Give him time, okay? Now shoo." Piper urged a reluctant Maggie to the screen door and practically shoved her out.

~

Grayson had climbed the gnarled old oak tree and shinnied out onto the big overhanging limb, holding his army knife in his teeth. One end of the rope that he'd untied from the old tire was knotted around his waist. His intent was to slice away the remains of the broken rope, tie one end of the rope around his waist to the limb and let the other end dangle. Then he'd shinny back down, attach the dangling rope to the tire leaning against the tree and voila', the tire swing would be fixed.

He used his legs to grip the tree limb, took the knife out of his mouth and set to work sawing back and forth across the old rope. It didn't cut readily. Obviously, he needed to sharpen his knife.

"Can you fix it?" called a voice from below him. He looked down and there stood Nguyen.

The cool air of a West Virginia early evening was replaced by the sticky, stinking heat of a jungle night. He could hear the cries of the unknown animals in the dark jungle as well as the laughing voices of the other members of the company playing poker.

"Can you fix it?" Nguyen asks.

She is seated in the dirt at his feet, looking up at the stars sprinkled like salt on the velvet sky. Sergeant Hotchner has just told him they've been ordered to move out, leave Yan Ling to the enemy. Abandon the village. And Nguyen.

Now Grayson must think of a way to explain to the little girl that they will be leaving in two days.

She points up at the stars. "Is that the …" she pauses, then continues, concentrating, "…the ig-bay ipper-day?"

"Yeah, the Big Dipper." He tries to keep his voice light and cheery. "And over there is the constellation—"

"You leaving, Grape?" she asks quietly.

He looks down at her, stunned. How had she found out the unit was pulling out? Even the sergeant didn't know until a couple of hours ago.

"Yes, we're leaving." His voice is tight.

"And I not go with you—right?"

Now he fears his voice will crack. Emotion wells up in his chest.

"That's right, Nguyen. You can't go with me."

"Can you fix it?"

Grayson sits down on the dirt beside her and lifts her into his lap.

"Nguyen, I'd take you if I could. Do you know that?" He rocks her tenderly back and forth, then stops and holds her at arms' length. "You do know that, don't you?"

"Take me where, Mr. Grayson? I don't have any idea what you're talking about."

THE WORLD BEGAN TO SPIN. He could hear the jungle creatures. And West Virginia cicadas, each with its own voice—deep or shrill—blending in a constant chorus. He looked around. It was twilight and the shadows shifted and moved. When he looked back at the little girl in his lap, she no longer had shiny black hair and brown eyes. Her hair was red, her eyes an odd shade of green and a spray of red freckles decorated her nose.

But she looked at him with the same almost-adult compassion on her face he'd seen so many times on Nguyen's.

He shook his head and blinked.

"Do you know where you are, now, Mr. Grayson?" the little girl asked timidly. "You're home, here at your Ma's house."

Piper stood in the back door, staring through the screen into the back yard. She had watched Grayson climb down out of the tree and take Maggie tenderly into his lap. He'd held her close in the kind of familiar way a father holds a beloved child. But now he was looking at her quizzically, as if he'd only just now noticed she was sitting there.

He shook his head, then stood up so abruptly Maggie spilled out of his disappearing lap in a heap on the ground. He turned away from her and strode purposefully toward the house.

"Grayson…what—?" Piper began.

He didn't respond, merely brushed past her into the kitchen. Sadie looked up when he came into the room. And Piper was sure she saw the beginnings of a smile on the child's lips. Then she must have seen the stern, severe look on her father's face because her face crinkled up like a piece of crumbled notebook paper and she began to cry. Grayson ignored her, walked past her as if she weren't even there, went through the parlor into their bedroom and shut the door behind him.

It all happened so fast, Piper felt like a tornado had sailed through the house from the back yard and almost wondered why there weren't papers and debris still hanging in the air in its wake.

She left Sadie on the floor crying and went to the bedroom door, reached for the knob and then thought better of it. She called through the door instead, "Supper'll be ready in a few minutes, Gray, honey. I'm making—."

"I don't want anything," he called back through the door. His voice sounded muffled, like he had his face buried in a pillow—or had been crying. "I'm not hungry."

"But you said you wanted—"

"I said I don't want any supper," he snapped. "Please, just leave me alone."

Piper walked slowly back into the kitchen and turned off each of the burners on the stove. Then she picked up the crying toddler and bit her lip to keep from joining Sadie in tears.

Grayson stayed in the bedroom—sleeping, Piper assumed—until after Piper had bathed Sadie and put her to bed. When he emerged, he was "gone" again. Piper had given that label to the distant look in his eyes, the "not-there-ness" in which he could engage in conversation, be kind, polite and totally in another world where she couldn't join him. A world full of monsters.

He had let her in. For a brief time yesterday, it'd been like it had always been between them, so close emotionally you couldn't slide a piece of tissue paper between them, and so close physically it was like they really were one person, like the Bible said—the two shall become one flesh.

But that had vanished in his conversation with Maggie.

Marian went to bed early. It would be a long, hard day for her—the trip to Charleston and being poked and prodded by the doctor. Maggie tiptoed into Sadie's room and curled up on her pallet on the floor a short time later. Piper and Grayson went to bed soon afterward. They made love passionately—but it was physical passion with no emotional connection. The act left Piper feeling emptier and lonelier than she'd felt when the bed beside her was cold and Grayson'd been in a foxhole somewhere. Did they dig foxholes anymore? She didn't even know. She knew nothing about what had happened to him. And she *wanted* to know.

Tomorrow would be different, she vowed. Tomorrow after she returned from Charleston, she would begin the process of prying open the locked doors in her husband's heart, of letting light shine into the darkness there.

She fell asleep with that vow on her lips and awoke with Grayson's lips on hers.

She opened her eyes. The sky outside the window was that odd shade of blue-black that told her the sun had risen out on the flatlands. It had cleared the horizon and it was dawn there, but the sun wouldn't shine down into the hollow for hours.

"I'm going now," Grayson said. "I'll see you when you get back from Charleston." He paused. "And we'll talk. There are things … we need to talk about."

"Why so early? Don't you want some break—?"

"I've been awake for hours. I need to get out of the house, get some air." He paused again. "Piper…I'm sorry for … how I've been. I love you."

He hugged her fiercely and then was gone.

She sat up in bed and looked out the window, watched him get his gear—Army fatigue pants and shirt and black lace-up boots—out of the storage shed beside the back porch. Then her eyes followed him as he crossed the yard and started up the hill, his Steeler's cap cocked back, the rifle in the crook of one arm, a knapsack with the lunch she'd made him and his canteen in the other, a silent shadow that quickly melted into the darker shadows of the forest.

She felt uneasy when he was gone, her mind spinning webs of anxiety like spiders. It was a long time before she was able to go back to sleep.

Chapter Nineteen

Jesse McCullough went puttering down Carlisle Road, looking like he didn't have nowhere in particular to go to and wasn't in no hurry a'tall to get there. Just like he done ever time he went out to check the five stills he and Carter had hidden high up in the hollows.

He had lots of kin in this neck of the woods so he had reasons he could give if he had to come up with an explanation of what he was doing out here.

'Course he wasn't never going to have to explain nothing to nobody. Even if he'd put a great big ole sign on his pickup truck saying, "I'm goin' out to bottle up some hooch" wouldn't nobody call the law. Mountaineers didn't care if you made moonshine. They was the ones who bought it off'n ya! Besides, nobody called the law about nothing. If you had a problem, you solved it yourself, didn't expect some outsider with a badge to fix it for you.

He wasn't going out to work the stills, anyway, just watchin' over 'em. Carter'd shut them down for the summer and sent the boys off to make a different kind of hootch. Kentucky was broke out with bourbon distilleries and ever one of them aged their whiskey for seven years in white-oak barrels. Had to be new barrels with every batch so the old ones was sold off to wineries in California or for folks to cut in half and plant flowers in. But if'n you's to "borrow" them barrels for a week, say, 'fore they was shipped out, put some water in 'em and leave 'em out in the hot sun … you could leach out some mighty fine liquor. Mighty fine!

Jesse was a big man with a shock of sandy blonde hair that hung down over his ears and the collar of his shirt. He had been strong and tough when he was younger, but the strength was gone now, muscles had slid down into a beer gut and he'd got three front teeth knocked out in a bar fight. Even Jesse had to admit he wasn't much to look at anymore. But Angie Faye had got so fat she didn't have no right to complain about nobody's looks. Jesse hadn't had regular employment since … maybe it was four years ago when he was a scoop operator in Northfield #2. He knew miners'd been out of work longer than he had. Some of 'em was hurting turkeys, too, 'cause they didn't have the moonshine business he and Carter had to keep them afloat.

Truth be known, Jesse, didn't cotton much to Carter Addington. Never had. But kin was kin, and when he needed somebody to help him get the moonshine business he'd taken over from his daddy on its feet, Carter was the obvious choice among all the cousins scattered around the holler. That'd been seven years ago and now it was Carter who ran the operation. And Jesse wasn't sure exactly how that'd happened. Oh, Carter was college educated and knew how to run a business, but Jesse still had his nose out of joint about it. Jesse was the one done all the hard work, overseeing the making of the shine. Only thing Carter done was the part that didn't get your hands dirty, the money end of it, sales and distribution.

Maybe that's why Jesse'd brought Buster along today —'cause he didn't like Carter calling *all* the shots. Naw, that wasn't why. He'd brought the kid because he needed him, but he couldn't very well tell Carter that!

He shot a glance at his oldest son next to him on the dirty, torn truck seat. The boy was leaned up against the door with his skinny arms crossed over his chest, his head thrown back, sound asleep. His mouth was hanging open and he was drooling a little—made him look like a half-wit.

"Hey." Jesse reached out and poked the boy in the ribs. You could see his boney chest through a hole in his tee shirt. "Wake up. You're droolin' like a retard."

The boy opened eyes a shade of blue Angie Fay called "robin's egg blue." He had no eyelashes you could see— they was pale blonde like his hair. And if he'd had one more pimple, he'd a'had to hold it in his hand. Wasn't no unmarked skin from his hairline to his chin.

"I wasn't asleep," Buster mumbled, wiped his chin and scooted up to a sitting position.

"Was you drunk last night?"

The boy was only 16, but he'd got wall-eyed on hooch the first time when he was 12 and Jesse was all the time catching him sneaking a beer.

"I was just restin' my eyes." Sounded like a pouty 2-year-old.

"'Cause you gotta be alert, clear-headed. You ain't gonna get no do-over on this here."

The boy said nothing, pulled his WVU cap down over his eyes and leaned back against the door. He'd be asleep again in thirty seconds.

Maybe Jesse shouldn't have brought him. But he had no choice. The job had to be done and he couldn't very well admit to Carter that *he* couldn't do it, that his hands wasn't steady enough no more, shook so bad sometimes he spilled coffee or beer in his lap.

Didn't want Carter the businessman to start wonderin' what it was exactly he needed Jesse for.

Jesse passed the Lassiter place—wasn't nobody home—and turned his old Ford pickup up Goose Creek Road. Soon as the truck started bouncing along the rutted dirt road, Buster sat up sullenly and looked out the window. Jesse drove several miles up the dirt track that traversed the steep ridge until he got to a stand of cedar trees where he pulled off the road and drove the truck far enough back into the woods that you couldn't see it.

"We walk from here," he said.

Buster reached back and took Jesse's .22 rifle off the gun rack above the seat. Jesse picked up the small Mason Jar on the passenger side floorboard among the empty beer bottles, and shoved it down in the front pocket of his over-alls, cursing himself for not having the good sense to fill the thing up with mud when he'd come here yesterday to scout out the ambush site.

It was a hike up the mountain and down the other side where Blood Creek wound down from the spring. Jesse figured somewhere near that spring was where the Camp-bells intended to set up shop—if they hadn't already! Spring water was the best for moonshine, of course, and they couldn't very well use the creek water farther down. Folks said there was a lot of iron in the dirt on this side of the ridge, made the sticky clay soil red, which, of course, was why the stream running down through it was called Blood Creek.

The McCullough's first still, the smallest, was in the other direction, over the next ridge in Tree Frog Hollow. It used the water from a spring that bubbled up clear as rainwater. Three other stills were scattered close around it on Stag Ridge. The fifth, the biggest, was hidden in these woods. Daddy'd always said their likker was better'n other folks' hooch because the water was better and Jesse was certain Daddy'd been right.

There was no trail, so Jesse and Buster had to make their way through the woods to the top of the mountain. Carter'd said the ambush had to be along Blood Creek so's Jesse could bring back mud Carter could use to make it look like that's where Grayson'd been. But there was a lot to consider in picking the exact spot.

When Carter told him Grayson was actually going squirrel hunting today, Jesse could only marvel at the good fortune that seemed to grace everything Carter Addington touched. 'Course, everybody knew the best squirrel hunting in Cochran County was north of Aunt Marian's house, not south toward Blood Creek, but if Grayson really was as goofy as Carter said … well, nutcases was likely to do most anything.

Jesse had studied on it and determined the best spot for Buster to shoot Zeke was in the lower leg, below the knee. That was the safest, so if his aim was off a hair, he wouldn't accidentally hit something vital. Nobody wanted to kill the kid! But even a .22 shot to the leg was going to do some damage, no way around that. It was gonna bleed. So what if the kid lay there and bled to death? Had Carter thought about that? No, he had not! But Jesse had. Ever morning for the past couple of weeks Riley'd drove Zeke out to the bottom of Roberts Hill and let him out, then came back to get him about two o'clock. So if Jesse waited until Zeke was going back down the mountain to meet his brother, then Riley'd get concerned about Zeke when he didn't show up. Riley might even hear the gunshot! Either way, Riley'd go looking for the boy and find him before he could bleed out.

Jesse had made it to a small clearing on the top of the ridge, huffing and puffing. Sweat soaked his shirt and the headband of his Pirates cap. Buster hadn't even broke a sweat and was breathing normal, but Jesse had to pause to catch his breath or he'd pass out.

Buster looked nervous.

"You all right?" Jesse asked.

"I'm fine."

But he wasn't.

Jesse said nothing, merely wiped the sweat out of his eyes and started down the other side of the ridge. But now he was the one getting nervous. When he'd first told Buster about the plan, the kid'd jumped at the chance. He was gonna *shoot a Campbell*, kin of the man who'd ambushed his granddaddy. Made him feel like a man. But now that it was actually starting to sink in that he really was going to shoot somebody, the kid was getting hinky.

THE RIFLE FELT good in Grayson's hands and that surprised him. He would have sworn that once he got home he'd never touch a firearm again. Instead, the gun felt more than just normal. It felt safe. He had felt almost naked without it. Surely, this would pass. Surely, so many things would pass.

He'd jumped at the chance to go hunting for reasons Piper didn't understand. He needed to engage in some activity he used to enjoy, to crawl back into that skin again and grow accustomed to the feel of it. And he needed to get away by himself to try to sort out his tangled emotions and memories.

He stopped, took a deep breath of air scented with pine, spruce and cedar.

Sometimes, it seemed to Grayson that the contents of his entire mind had been divvied up and stored away in boxes, and he couldn't allow himself to see what was in the black ones. Oh, he'd had a black box before he ever went to Vietnam. Becky's black box. But now his mind was littered with them—small square land mines—and he had to edge carefully from one part of life to another to keep from stepping on any of them.

Grayson continued on a diagonal up the mountainside. The best squirrel hunting in Cochran County was here, though he didn't intend to shoot anything. He didn't know much about the new Grayson Addington, the man who had come home so changed from the war. But one thing he did know for certain. He would never again kill another living creature.

He hadn't come this way for the squirrels. He'd come this way because it was a shortcut to his father's church.

The air gradually filled with birdsong. The coo of morning doves, the "chick-a-dee" of chickadees, the chirps and tweets of bluebirds, killdeer and larks mingled with the ever-present hum in his ears. He topped a rise and the simple white building came into view up ahead. There was a steeple on the high-pitched roof and wide porch steps. Turtle Road dead-ended at those steps.

As Grayson drew closer, he could see the abuse of disuse the building had suffered. Paint had peeled down to bare wood, the front door hung on one hinge, the roof sagged and all the windows were broken out. But the beautiful stained-glass window Uncle Jim had paid for above the porch roof was miraculously untouched. Grayson could only imagine what the inside must look like, but he didn't intend to find out. He'd last been in the building the week his father's wild-eyed, raving lunacy had reached such a fever pitch that Grayson's mother had taken the boys' hands and walked with dignity out of the church and said she'd never go back. The next week, his father had died from a snakebite during services in the Stinkin' Creek Pentecostal (pronounced penny-costal) Church, way back in a remote hollow.

Grayson sat down on the splintered porch steps and looked back down into the valley where silver mist rose off all the creeks and a sudden love of the mountains welled up in his throat so powerfully he feared he might burst into tears. He had never felt at home anywhere else. Oh, he had lived in Louisville, Kentucky during seminary when he and Piper first married. He'd liked it there. It wasn't awful. Neither was Spindle Rock, where he'd taken his first church, gotten involved with the young men in the community and signed up for the Kentucky National Guard infantry company there so he could minister to them. Never in his wildest dreams did it occur to him—or to anybody else—that the unit would actually go to war.

He was at a wedding rehearsal for Bobby Clarkson and Emily Filiatreau when Emily's grandmother rushed into the sanctuary in hysterics and herded the whole wedding party down to the church basement where there was a television set.

They stood in mute surprise as U.S. Secretary of Defense Clark Clifford announced the call-up of nine National Guard units, two of them in Kentucky—the 138th Artillery, Battery C in Bardstown and the 151st Infantry, Charlie Company in Spindle Rock.

Emily started to cry, wailing that the unit call-up would interfere with the honeymoon they'd already paid for in Acapulco. Then Bobby's groomsmen—fellow Guard members—began to process the ramifications in their own lives. Porter was a dairy farmer. If he had to leave … just *leave*, who was going to milk his cows twice a day? Who would care for Mattingly's ailing wife who was expecting twins? Who'd help Haggarty's elderly father cut tobacco?

Grayson went home and told Piper and they had dropped to their knees in prayer.

When was the last time Grayson had prayed? Maybe it was the Sunday service the night before Clarkson, Porter, Haggarty, Mattingly, Hawkins and … the other Kentucky soldiers died when The Birdhouse was overrun.

But even then, he'd only been mouthing words. Saying what he was supposed to say. He'd stopped believing … when? When had he realized he'd spent the better part of his life perpetuating a grand hoax?

He leaned the rifle against the porch steps, set the knapsack in the dirt and tried to puzzle it out. Because it mattered. A man ought to know where that crossroads was. When his life had been steaming down a channel in one direction at full throttle and then without warning stopped, turned and went down another river altogether.

Had he stopped believing even before he left for 'Nam? Wasn't he merely going through the motions even then?

No, he'd believed, but it had been passive belief. Belief set in neutral. Just coasting. And you couldn't take that kind of belief into battle with you. That kind of belief wouldn't sustain you when Mattingly got his arm blown off and the squirting blood splashed in your face, and you hunkered down in the hole with him, trying to stop the bleeding. And then it did stop.

That kind of belief was nothing but the dregs left when real belief had leaked out a hole in the bucket. When Grayson really needed it, reached into the bucket for it, to scoop some up in a cup and feed it to men desperate for it —to drink some of it himself—the cup scraped on bare metal. Made a sound Grayson could hear now, deep in his soul.

So what could he say to Piper? He was a minister. That's what he'd trained to be, what she expected him to return to now. How did he tell her it meant nothing anymore? That the black bags they zipped the boys in to ship them home were no more silent than the God of the universe when you cried out to him to protect—

Sadie! Almighty God, Please protect her!

The day the trucks transported his unit away from Yan Ling, leaving Nguyen behind, he'd dropped to his knees in a walking black-out.

He hadn't thought about it since. What he'd seen in the blackout was utter darkness. Then the darkness moved, writhed, rumbled, twisted and roared. A malevolent darkness from the pit of hell roared down the mountainside, its gaping maw open, hungry, eager to gobble up Sadie as she played happily in the yard beside the house.

A sudden silence fell, like a giant bell jar had been lowered around Grayson. The birds stopped singing. The aged creak of trees in the breeze grew quiet. And Grayson found himself turning slowly to face the giant coal slag dam that formed an ugly smile between the ridges. As he stared at it, he felt a kind of fear he'd never felt in 'Nam. Oh, he'd been terrified knowing Charlie was hidden somewhere in the jungle waiting to kill him. But that fear was perfectly rational and what he felt now was totally irrational. What he feared now was mindless evil, death with a black grin, smiling malevolently out over the little valley it intended to devour.

Chapter Twenty

THERE WAS a rock outcrop that hung out over Blood Creek about half a mile from the road where Riley Campbell would be waiting for Zeke. The creek bank narrowed there. Zeke would have to walk beneath that overhang, it was the only clear path back down the mountain. Buster and Jesse would snuggle down among the rocks on top of the overhang, rub dirt on the barrel of the rifle so it wouldn't shine in the sun, and after the boy had passed beneath them, Buster could take a steady aim and put a bullet in his calf.

The overhang was the only place they could remain hidden and still get close, and they had to get close because a .22 wasn't dead-on accurate beyond about 30 yards. The shells it fired made little holes, and traveling so fast, the bullets usually went all the way through. It'd be nice if there wasn't no bullet to be pulled out of Zeke's leg 'cause there was ways the law could identify what gun had shot a particular bullet. 'Course, a thing like that wasn't never gonna matter 'cause the Campbells would take Zeke to the doctor and get him patched up, and if the sheriff asked, they'd say he'd got shot accidental. They wouldn't go broadcasting around that somebody'd got the drop on him in the woods!

From the top of the overhang, Jesse and Buster could high tail it back up over the mountain and down to the truck on the other side. Even if Zeke turned immediately and looked up—which he wouldn't because he'd be more concerned about the bullet hole in his leg!—there wasn't no way he could see who was up on top of them rocks.

Yes, siree, Jesse'd planned it all out perfectly.

Problem was, nothing that day went as Jesse McCullough had planned it.

Marian sat on the examining table in Dr. Rutherford's office. What little butt she had was numb from sitting there for so long. That was the least of her aches and pains, of course, aches and pains that wouldn't be around much longer because neither would she.

She tuned back into what the doctor was saying. He was talking to Piper as if Marian wasn't even there. What was it about doctors—when they had something bad to say, they wouldn't look you in the eye and say it, straight out? They had to wrap it up in technical mumbo jumbo and tell it to somebody else so you's just eavesdropping.

"Dr. Rutherford." She interrupted his spiel and he looked piqued. But she didn't care. This was getting old and apparently she didn't have time for all this lollygagging.

"You're saying I'm gonna be dead 'fore the end of the month—that it?"

"As I was telling your daughter-in-law, Mrs. Addington,

it depends on several variables and on how you tolerate the new—"

"But I'm dying and it ain't gonna take long. If that's what you mean, son, quit beating around the bush and spit it out."

Dr. Rutherford said nothing for a moment, seemed to consider, then merely nodded his head.

"In essence … yes, that's what I mean. Given your—"

"How long?"

"Well, it depends on—

"How long?"

"A week … would be a fair estimation, I'd say." Marian saw the color drain so completely out of Piper's face even her red lips turned blue. "We need to get you admitted to—"

"The hospital?" Marian was incredulous. "Young fella, did yore mama have any kids that lived? You know I ain't going into no hospital. Onliest place I'm going is home to my mountains, so you need to help me down off this here table. I got to get about the business of living what's left of my life so I can commence to dying."

The nurse helped her to the floor and fussed around getting her sweater situated back on her shoulders. The doctor was talking in low tones to Piper—who had tears streaming down her cheeks, pore thing!—and Marian caught phrases like "pain medication" and "keep her comfortable" and things like that.

"You need to blow your nose and wipe your face 'fore we go out in the waiting room and them little girls think something awful's happened," she told Piper tenderly. Wouldn't do no good though. You could read that girl's soul in them big brown eyes. And when her temper flared —and Piper *did* have a temper—she could pull them black eyebrows together to give you a look as would cause internal bleeding.

Marian resolutely struggled to fix on her own face what she hoped looked like a smile on the outside—'cause it sure enough didn't feel like one on the inside. Hard to pull off something simple as smiling when you had to remember which muscles to pull up and which ones not.

She concentrated. There. That was probably a fair-to-middlin' smile, seemed to fit where it was supposed to in all the right places on her face.

Piper obediently wiped her cheeks, squared her jaw and draped a smile between her ears that hung limp as a broke clothesline.

EVERYTHING STARTED to go south on Jesse when he got to the site of the ambush and discovered he couldn't climb up to the top of the overhang. It'd looked simple enough when he'd scouted out the location. Buster clambered up it easy as a spider. But Jesse couldn't heft his considerable bulk up there to save his soul. He huffed and puffed, struggled to climb to the perch for the better part of an hour.

Buster sat on top of the rocks and watched.

"You ain't gonna make it, Pa," he finally said. "You better go find someplace else to hide."

Buster was right but Jesse didn't like leaving the boy all by his lonesome. What if he locked up and couldn't shoot? Or missed?

"You sure you can—?"

"I'm sure."

Buster didn't sound sure. He sounded scared.

The boy hunkered down behind the rocks and Jesse pulled the Mason jar out of his pocket and shoved several handfuls of red mud down into it, secured the lid, wiped his hands on his pants and headed back up the side of the mountain above the overhang. He finally settled himself in a thicket of crepe myrtle bushes. From there, he could see Zeke approach down the trail, but had no line of sight for the actual ambush.

Time passed slow as mold growing. Jesse must have checked his watch a dozen times over the course of the next hour. He figured Buster must be getting powerful nervous. He didn't have a watch to judge the passing of time and it musta seemed like a hundred years to him.

Jesse actually heard Zeke coming before he saw him. The kid was whistling. Jesse sat perfectly still in the bushes and watched Zeke approach down the trail. About 25 yards before Zeke passed beneath the overhang, he vanished from Jesse's sight.

Then there was silence.

The louder-then-softer cries of cicadas assaulted Jesse's ears. What was taking so long? Zeke should be in position by now. Had Buster let him get away before—

Crack!

The shot sounded like a cannon in the still of the woods.

A few seconds later, he heard the rush of running footsteps and Buster flew past him without stopping in a headlong dash to the top of the ridge. Jesse took off after him, but didn't catch him until the boy paused at the top of the ridge to wait for him.

When Jesse came out of the trees, Buster was standing in the small clearing puking up his breakfast, making sounds like somebody grinding the gears in a bad transmission. His face was so white the zits stuck out on it like polka dots and Jesse's .22 lay in the dirt beside him.

It was at least a minute before Jesse could catch his breath enough to speak.

"Did you—?"

"I shot him," Buster said. There was something like wonder in his voice. "I got him ..." He left the rest hanging.

"...but?"

"But nothing. Let's get out of here."

Buster grabbed the rifle, turned before Jesse could stop him and headed back down the mountainside to where their truck was parked in the trees. Jesse could do nothing but stumble along behind.

The truck was so well hidden Jesse almost ran into it. Buster was sitting in the passenger side of the truck, his face expressionless. The .22 was hanging in the gun rack.

Jesse got in on the driver's side still gasping, pulled the mason jar full of mud out of his pocket and laid it over in the floorboard.

"...what ... happened?" he gasped.

"I told you. I shot him. Can we go now?" Buster's voice was trembling a little.

"We ain't going nowhere 'til you spit it out—what's wrong?"

Buster turned to him and his blue eyes welled with tears. That scared Jesse plum to death.

"I shot him ... I just don't know *where!*" Buster's voice was thick, like his throat was tight from holding back crying. "He tripped, Pa! Just as I was pullin' the trigger, he stumbled a little, almost went down on one knee. I shot and he fell forward, so I know he was hit. But I don't know ..."

Then he did start to cry, sobbed out the rest, "I'm feared it might nota been in the leg!"

Jesse's heart was slugging away in his chest, hammering

harder than it had after he'd run all the way up the side of the mountain. He was nauseas, afraid he might have to lean out the door and puke up his breakfast, too.

Had Buster ... had his son *killed* Zeke Campbell?

CARTER PUT his arms tenderly around Piper and let her cry. His own head was spinning. Of course, he knew his mother was terminally ill, but terminally ill and "a week to live" weren't the same thing at all!

Marian and the girls were seated at a table in the Howard Johnson's Restaurant that overlooked the Kanawha River near the doctor's office. He could see them through the window. Marian had an untouched omelet in front of her but she was smiling, feeding small pieces of blueberry pancakes to Sunshine, who smashed most of the sticky pieces into the high chair tray rather than eating them. Maggie sat beside Marian, looking up at her. The expression on the child's face was unreadable. Piper said she hadn't told Maggie what the doctor said, but he had the sense the little girl had figured it out.

"How did Ma take it when he told her?" he asked Piper and she pulled out of his arms and looked up into his face. She never wore makeup, so there was no mascara smeared down her cheeks—like he'd seen on every woman he'd ever broken up with and there had been more than a fair number of those. She glanced in the window at the trio seated at the table inside, careful to keep her back turned so if they chanced to look up they wouldn't see her face.

"He didn't tell her; she told him," Piper said. "She just nailed him, asked him how long." She stifled a sob. "And he said ... a week."

She buried her face in his chest again, and he couldn't help the thrill that ran through him at the feeling of her in his arms. But this was all … messed up, not like he'd planned. At this very moment, Jesse was probably somewhere in the woods taking a bead on Zeke. The playing out of that whole scenario—blaming Grayson, convincing Piper—he'd never intended that to happen as his mother was dying! If he could get in touch with Jesse…but, of course, he couldn't. It would happen today, whether it was convenient or not.

"I'm coming home," he said into Piper's hair.

She drew back and looked up at him in surprise.

"If Ma's only got … I'm coming home after work tomorrow, staying with her until …"

"What about …?"

"Grayson? Don't worry about that. He and I … we'll be fine."

But they wouldn't. As soon as Piper heard about Zeke, and Carter blamed it on Grayson, oh, no, they most certainly wouldn't be fine at all.

For the first time since Carter conceived the plan he hoped would drive a wedge between Grayson and Piper so deep it would split their marriage apart—he questioned whether he actually should go through with it. Whether he could go through with it. His mother, *their* mother was dying.

THE TWO-HOUR DRIVE from Charleston back to Sadler Hollow was quiet and that was good because Maggie needed to think. Sadie had fallen asleep next to her on the back seat with her thumb in her mouth and her head in

Maggie's lap, and Maggie idly brushed the little girl's hair back from her forehead as she watched the mountains outside the car windows grow steeper and steeper.

Nan Marian and Miss Piper had said little since they came out of the doctor's office, but Maggie had seen the looks the grownups exchanged, heard the whispers. She knew. Nan Marian's time was drawing to a close, and like water circling the drain in the sink, the time would spin faster and faster until it was gone.

Though the light in Nan Marian's eyes was fading, that's not what was stealing the light and color from Maggie's world. It was something else. Something terrible that filled her with such foreboding she sometimes couldn't quite draw a breath.

It had come to her in a nightmare as she slept on her pallet on the back porch the night Mr. Grayson came home. The thing in the dream rumbled and roared … and then was silent. She had awakened panting, sweating and afraid. And cold. The kind of cold that wrapping up in a warm blanket or sitting in a tub of hot water wouldn't fix. It wasn't a cold that came from the outside in, feeling snow slide down your collar when you lay on the ground in it and flapped your arms to make snow angels. It was cold from the inside out. That cold didn't leave when she woke up. She'd moved her pallet into the house then, not wanting to sleep outside by herself in the dark anymore. That didn't help, though. Every night since, she'd had the same dream. Every night, the cold sent out icicles into her blood that didn't thaw.

Since she couldn't remember her past and didn't know what her future might hold, she pictured in her mind that she lived in the space between tall, thick oak doors with brass doorknobs and no keyholes. She didn't know what lay on the other side of either one. She had come through one once, running away from the people Miss Piper'd said had beaten her. She would go out through the other into the future eventually, though she was terrified of living in a place where grownups hit children. And *Sadie!* How could she bear to leave Sadie? That's why every moment between the two doors was such a precious gift and she treasured every breath, every touch of Sadie's hand—every bird call, note of fiddle music, titter of laughter and smell of honeysuckle.

But the darkness, the rumbling dark Thing was now stealing the joy from her small world "in between." She wanted to ask somebody about what it might be, but knew no one would understand.

When they rounded a curve into the far end of Sadler Hollow, she saw a bright red light on the road ahead. It was a flashing light that grew brighter and brighter as it approached until an ambulance passed in a roar of siren and was gone. Maggie turned to look out the back window and watched until it was out of sight.

Chapter Twenty-One

PIPER GOT Marian settled in bed, made her as comfortable as she could. The old woman refused to take additional pain medication, though the trip to Charleston had obviously raised her pain level to something near unbearable.

"That nasty medicine makes my tongue thick and my eyelids droop. I ain't gonna sleep through the last days I got on this earth."

"Mommy, come see," Sadie cried and Piper stepped out of Marian's room to find the child standing on the back of the sofa. "Sabie fly like a birdie." Before Piper could say a word, the little girl hopped down from the back of the sofa to the cushion with the protruding spring, flapping her arms frantically. Then she bounced up and down on it.

Well, that explained how the spring got broken.

"Sadie, no," she said and started toward her. "You can't—"

Out the front window behind the sofa, Piper saw a car pull up in the dirt driveway. Her recurring nightmare slammed back into her chest with such force she actually grunted out loud. Two officers in dress uniforms, solemnly getting out of the vehicle, then walking with respectful gravity up the walk to—

But it wasn't a black military car. It was dark blue and had a big bubblegum machine light set in the center of the top. The man who got out of it was Cochran County Sheriff Clifford Bayless. He was a broad shouldered, barrel-chested man with eyebrows that looked like tangles of black barbed wire over his deep-set gray eyes, and a mole the size of a piece of popcorn—and about as lumpy —on his left cheek.

He was unsmiling, had the same grim look on his face the soldiers would have had if Gray—

Gray was here, home, safe!

Then it hit her that the sheriff was about to break her heart nonetheless. He wasn't here to deliver bad news about her husband on the other side of the world; he was here to deliver bad news about the little red-haired girl who had taken Sadie the birdie into her bedroom to play dolls.

They'd found Maggie's family. Sheriff Bayless had come to take the little girl away and Piper didn't think she could stand that.

Piper crossed the parlor and stepped out onto the porch, closing the door firmly behind her. She met the sheriff halfway up the walk.

"Piper," he began, "I have some bad news for you."

"No!" Piper said.

He looked confused.

"I know why you're here and ..." She squared her shoulders. "You can't have her."

"Have wh—?"

"You didn't see the bruises, the black eye and split lip. They beat her, Sheriff Cliff. Somebody smashed their fist into her face." Piper felt herself edging into hysteria but she couldn't stop. "You go in there and take a look at that little girl your own self." She stepped aside and make a sweeping gesture toward the house. "Go on. She's mostly healed up now—but you look at her face and tell me you can hand that child over to somebody who'd—"

"Piper, hold on. I—"

"You hold on, Sheriff. If you think I'm going to let you—"

"I'm not here about the little girl."

"What?"

"Phillip told me you'd found a lost—"

"She's not lost. She ran away!"

"—a run-away child, but I don't know any more about her than he did."

"Then why…?"

"It's your brother, Piper. Zeke. I'm sorry to have to tell you this, but he's been shot."

The air turned as thick as creek mud and Piper couldn't seem to get any of it into her lungs.

"Is he—?"

"It happened this afternoon in the woods. Riley found him and brought him in and they sent him on to Bishop Memorial in Charlestown."

Piper gasped.

"I saw! The ambulance, I saw it. It flew past us …" Her mind was reeling. "How bad is he hurt?"

"I'm not sure, but you gotta know they wouldn't have turfed him out to Bishop if it was only a flesh wound."

Piper's gut tied in a knot so suddenly she felt like she'd been kicked in the stomach with a steel-toed boot.

"Well, I … I have to go … to Charlestown. *Back* to Charlestown to the hospital."

But what about Marian? She couldn't leave her here alone. And Sadie and Maggie?

"Grayson went hunting and until he gets home—"

"Looks like he just did."

The sheriff was looking past her toward the hillside above and behind the house where Grayson had come out of the woods with his rifle in the crook of his arm.

Piper let out a gasp of relief. Grayson was home and—

Grayson had almost made it to the back fence when he stopped abruptly, merely stood there staring at them. Then he slowly lifted the rifle and pointed it at them. There was a heartbeat pause before he lowered his face to the sight.

For a big man, Sheriff Bayless was lightening quick. He reached out a burley arm and shoved Piper so forcefully toward the house that she lost her balance and fell backward on the ground. Then he yanked his handgun out of his holster, crouched behind the whisky barrel of pansies, held the weapon out in front of him with both hands and pointed it at Grayson.

Piper tried to scream, "No!" But the breath had been knocked out of her. She stared at Grayson. Every detail of his image was seared into her brain. His hunting hat cocked back on his head, his army fatigues—she'd washed and pressed them and cleaned his boots last night. The .22 held with such ease and confidence in his hands. She saw him squint down the barrel.

"Grayson, drop that rifle! Drop it!" the sheriff called.

Dear God, no! Had Grayson survived a war just to be gunned down in his own backyard.

Piper heard a sickening click sound as the sheriff thumbed the hammer back on his pistol.

"*Now!* I won't tell you again."

THE MORNING HAD GRADUALLY WARMED as the sun marched up into the sky, finally cleared the mountain and shown down into Sadler Hollow. Then it turned hot. August-in-West-Virginia hot. Grayson was a long way from the church by then, and when the sun hit him, he stripped down to his tee shirt and tied his long-sleeved camo shirt around his waist. He'd been cold ever since he got back. Thermostat was off and sometimes the long sleeves of his fatigues felt good, even in the stifling summer heat of August.

Besides, they hid the jungle rot that ran from his wrist to his elbow on his right arm. Piper'd been right— hydrogen peroxide was drying it out even without a daily dose of Dapsone, but the pus had gone crusty and it was still disgusting and he didn't want anybody to see it. So far, Piper hadn't noticed the open sores on his left sole from immersion foot. He'd caught it early, got out of the boots and into dry socks in time so it didn't go gangrene on him. Still, it was repulsive. He didn't want to see it and he sure didn't want his wife to.

Piper's face formed in his mind in splendid detail. The feather of dark eyebrows above her brown eyes and her full lips. She was real. And somehow he had to shovel out all the slime, the goo as disgusting as the rot on his hands and foot that lay between them so he could be with her again, really be there.

But he didn't know how.

He looked around for a place to sit in the shade and enjoy the view spread out below him as he ate his lunch. Piper had packed him an apple, a chocolate-chip cookie and a peanut butter and jelly sandwich in the knapsack. He'd always loved peanut butter, even the kind that came in a small tin in K-Rations. The other soldiers hated it, though, and would toss the tins into the fire pits where the cans would heat up and then explode. The GIs called them peanut butter ambushes.

He spotted a sugar maple tree that lifted a leafy umbrella over a bed of moss and lichen around its lumpy roots dug into the rocky soil. He leaned his rifle against the trunk, then settled himself among the lumps into what was a surprisingly comfortable seat.

He ate the sandwich, washed it down with swigs from his canteen, and chomped the apple as a chicken hawk flew high overhead, up above the black scar of dam. He didn't allow his eye to follow the bird that far. He'd done enough staring at that ugliness this morning. Though it was totally irrational, he'd made a decision as he sat on the porch of the abandoned church building. He was getting his family out of that house as soon as he could. Once he knew where he'd be stationed after his leave was up, he'd move the three of them—Piper, Sadie and his mother—into off-base housing. No … maybe it would be the four of them.

There was Maggie, after all.

He pulled the cookie out of the knapsack. What about Maggie? He and Piper couldn't cart her off somewhere even if the sheriff couldn't find her family—which was crazy! Who doesn't report a missing 10-year-old child?

He grabbed his emotions before they could follow the rabbit down that hole. Gray didn't want to get angry at Maggie's parents because that meant he cared for her. And he couldn't care for her!

He started to take a bite of the cookie.

Ookie-kay.

That was the first pig latin Nguyen ever learned.

The two of them sit together beside a small fire they'll have to put out before dusk. Haystack, the red-haired kid named McKenzie they called Bagpipes, a skinny soldier called Beanpole or Beanie and KFC, the chicken farmer they'd dubbed Kentucky Fried Chicken are preparing to cook their K-Rations—small cans the size of tuna fish cans, full of chopped ham and eggs, ham slices, beef, or turkey loaf.

Haystack reads off the label: "Says this here was made during World War II. I hate eating food's older than I am."

Beanie smiles. His father is a dentist and he looks like the poster boy for Crest Toothpaste.

"Don't nobody tell no jokes when Beanie's in a hooch with me," Haystack says. "You can read the label on the K-Rations from the glow off his teeth."

Grayson turns to Nguyen as he digs into the accessory pack that came with his K-Rations.

"Pig latin. Ig-pay atin-Lay. You try it." He removes a white plastic spoon, some instant coffee, sugar and nondairy creamer, two Chiclets, a small roll of toilet paper, moisture-resistant paper matches, and salt and pepper before he finds the cigarettes he's looking for.

"Ig-Lay Atin-Lay," Nguyen says.

"No, the first sound of the word. Ig-pay."

He looks at the four-smoke mini pack of Pall Malls. The Winstons, Marlboro's and Lucky Strikes are better, easier to trade. He holds up the Pall Malls.

"What do I hear for this fine assortment of death, four Pall Mall cancer sticks for your coughing pleasure?"

"I'll take 'em," say Haystack and Beanie at the same time. Then Haystack holds up a round, chocolate cookie tin and tosses it toward Grayson, who catches it and throws back the cigarette pack. Beanie groans and Haystack fishes out one of the smokes and hands it to him.

The company has been encamped here outside Yan Ling, Nguyen's village, for more than a week. They could be here another week, a month, or they could be ordered to pack up and haul butt in 20 minutes. Those decisions are made by folks higher up the food chain than a simple foot soldier like Grayson.

And that's what he is. A foot soldier. That's how he sees himself now. He is a chaplain who packs every instrument of death the other soldiers carry—an M16, ammo, grenades and a viciously-sharp Bowie knife.

Nguyen has hardly left his side since he came to in the hut and he's found out a mountain of information from her constant chatter. She is an orphan. "Father step on mine. Not find all of him." Her mother died of some kind of jungle fever, so she is being raised by the village. Everybody's child. And, consequently, nobody's child. She does as she pleases, ranges far from home. That's how she had come to be the first to the bodies of Grayson's unit, discovered that the one with a cross on his helmet wasn't dead, and then rolled him over and over like a log into the latrine when she heard the Cong in the jungle nearby.

He pops open the round tin with the cookie inside.

"Want a cookie?" he asks and hands it to her. Then holds up the beef loaf and turkey loaf tins, trying to decide which is the least distasteful.

"Ookie-kay," Nguyen says.

He turns and stares at her. "What did you say?"

"Ookie-kay."

"That's it!" He gathers her in his arms in a big bear hug, then turns to the others.

"Did you guys hear that?" Back to Nguyen, "Tell 'em what a cookie is."

"Ookie-kay," she says and giggles. All the soldiers within earshot burst into spontaneous applause.

GRAYSON LOOKED at the cookie in his hand and whispered "ookie-kay" because his throat was too tight to say the word out loud.

Then snapshots of the little girl who said the word play

across a screen in his head like he's turning the pages of a picture album. Nguyen, giggling when Bagpipes pretends to pull a quarter out from behind her ear. The solemn way she looked at him sometimes, like she knew what he was thinking. "You miss her, don't you, Grape? Your girl, Sadie?" And he did, but he couldn't see Sadie then. Or Piper. All he could see was what was is front of him, the dark-eyed little girl who was so full of life. She had brought him back from the hole he fell into after The Birdhouse. As long as he could see the light in her eyes, he could get up one more day, pull on his boots one more time, carve one more notch in his short-timer's stick.

The pig latin phrase beat softly in the back of his head, like the sound of surf crashing rhythmically on rocks. There was more. Something else. But it was in a black box and he had no intention of stepping on one of the black-box mines and having his guts splattered all over Cochran County.

No, thank you.

He stood, picked up his knapsack and his rifle and headed into the trees, the woods a balm to his wounded soul as soothing as a clean white bandage on a burn. He felt the world become more and more real as the hours passed and the sun slid across the open space above the valley and down behind the mountain to the west. As the world he had left behind faded, a scab started to form over the lacerations in his soul. The wounds of war take a long time to heal, but it had to start somewhere and for U.S. Army Chaplain Grayson Addington it had begun today under the tender ministrations of the West Virginia mountains.

Perhaps for the first time since he stood in the rain at The Birdhouse and looked out over a smoking ruin of humanity, at the bodies of young men who had cows back home to milk and girlfriends to marry, he dared to hope that there really was a world beyond that. And that he could return to that world and live a life there.

Tonight he and Piper would talk. About Maggie, and moving, and what happens next in the life of a minister who no longer believes in God.

He saw the sheriff's cruiser angling up the road to the house as he descended the mountainside. They must have found Maggie's family. And he was surprised to discover how that saddened him. High above, a chicken hawk bleated out a cry that sounded as mournful as he felt.

When he came out of the woods and crossed the small clearing behind the house, he could see Piper standing on the front walk talking to the sheriff and he circled around the back yard fence and headed in their direction.

He was tired. The gun felt heavy. And he was hot. He reached up and pulled at his T-shirt collar. All at once it was sticking to his neck. It was so hot.

The mountains dissolved into jungle between one heartbeat and another. He had stepped on a black box and the mine there might very well blow him apart.

He smells smoke and dead pig and his own fear sweat. And the copper, metallic stench of the blood that has puddled behind the hole in the back of Haystack's head.

Nguyen stands on the other side of the road near the trees.

She's smiling but the smile's not real, not genuine. It never reaches her dark, terror-filled eyes as she continues to walk slowly toward him, agonizingly slowly.

KFC and Dollar Bill are behind him, crouched by a cart next to the bloated carcass of the pig. The others are strung out farther back.

"She's wired," Dollar calls out to him in a hoarse whisper. "The

…" He growls a mouthful of expletives. "Cong've got her packed in C4."

"Gray, you can't let her get any closer," KFC pleads. "She'll blow us all into the middle of next week."

Gray, not Padre. Padre is a chaplain; Gray is a soldier.

There is, of course, only one way to stop her from getting close enough for the blast to reach them.

"I want see Mickey Mouse, okay?" Her voice is tear-clotted now. "See Goofy. See …" she pauses, "… Oot-shay ee-may."

Oot-shay ee-may. Shoot me.

"Gray, you gotta do it, you gotta stop her," Bagpipes rasps in a fierce whisper. "Now!"

Grayson is, of course, the only one who has a clear line of fire. As in a dream, he lifts his rifle. Then he becomes a piece of solid granite that only looks like a man. This is beyond the pale of doin' the necessary. No, he can't send a bullet to rip open that little girl's chest, the child who has been the only light in his darkness.

"Padre—she's gonna blow!" Dollar cries.

"She'll kill us all," Beanie yells and Grayson can hear raw terror in his voice.

There is more sadness than fear in Nguyen's.

"Oot-shay e-may," she says. Her phony smile is so wide it is a slash across the bottom of her face, like it's been cut there with a bayonet. Tears stream down both cheeks. "You do that for me, Grape." She pauses. "Ease-play."

Grayson fits the rifle to his shoulder and bends his head to fix the sight on the little girl's chest. He curls his finger around the trigger and unconsciously sighs out a relaxing breath as he'd learned to do hunting squirrels.

"GRAYSON, drop that rifle! Drop it now!" somebody shouted.

The bright sun faded, as if someone had opened up a beach umbrella like the one he and Piper'd had in the sand in Hawaii. A cool breeze ruffled his hair, stuck his sweat-soaked shirt to his skin. And he heard … a chicken hawk?

"Now!" the voice called out. "I won't tell you again."

And then the haze fell away like scales from his eyes and he saw Piper, sprawled on her back in the front yard and the sheriff crouched behind the half whisky barrel full of pansies, pistol in both hands, pointed at his chest.

Grayson slowly lowered the rifle and set it carefully on the ground.

PIPER LEAPT to her feet and raced to the clearing where Gray stood with his hands hanging limply at his sides. She threw herself into his arms with such force she knocked him backward a step and the two of them very nearly went tumbling into the dirt.

"Gray! What were you doing? Why'd you … you looked like you were about to…"

"I'm sorry," he said, his voice hollow and unnatural.

With astonishing speed, her fear and confusion morphed into anger.

"You're sorry! You point a rifle at me and—"

"What do you want from me, Piper? Do you think I meant to—?"

"And the sheriff almost shoots you—" *Shoots* you! "Zeke's been shot."

Gray looked at her like she'd slapped him.

By now, Sheriff Cliff had reached them, huffing a little. He picked up Gray's rifle off the ground but didn't give it back to him, merely stood there holding it.

"You wanna tell me what that was all about?" he asked.

Piper had no time for this.

"Zeke's in the hospital in Charleston. I don't know how bad it … I have to …"

To what?

"Go!" Gray said. "I'll see to things here, Ma and the girls."

The girls. He said *girls!*

Without another word, Piper turned and ran back to the house to get her purse and car keys.

Chapter Twenty-Two

THE SHERIFF DIDN'T MAKE a move to give his rifle back to him so Gray reached for it. For a moment they both held onto it, Gray trying to take it, the sheriff reluctant to give it up. Then the sheriff let go and Gray placed the rifle in the crook of his arm, barrel pointed at the ground.

"What was you doin', son?" the sheriff asked.

Well, I was actually pointing my rifle at an eight-year-old child I loved dearly.

He did! He loved Nguyen. And he had—what? Shot her? He didn't know. That part was gone, still in the black box. Obviously, the bomb the Cong had strapped on her had gone off because he'd awakened with a concussion and explosion-roar rumbling in his head. So Nguyen was dead. Then he had been yanked out of Vietnam like Beanie's father pulling a tooth. Painfully. With blood still dripping.

"Gray, can you hear me?"

He realized he'd stood there ignoring the sheriff's question.

"I'm sorry, Sheriff Cliff. I'm still … not over what happened."

"'Course you ain't, son." He gave Gray a knowing look. "And you ain't gonna be for awhile. Maybe not for a long while."

Grayson remembered then that Sheriff Bayless had served in Korea.

"That's why it ain't a good idea for you to be carrying a gun around. Not 'til you're … more yourself."

"Guess not. But it felt, you know … right—"

"You mean *normal*? Safe, maybe? I know how that feels. It'll pass." Then he stopped. "But you was a chaplain. You didn't have no gun, didja?"

Gray took a deep breath. Might as well start coming clean. "Not when I got there. Not at first. But later, yeah, I had a gun." He paused for a beat. "And I used it."

There was compassion in the big man's eyes. Then something else began to form there, too, that Gray couldn't identify. Wariness? Suspicion?

Zeke!

"What happened to Piper's little brother?"

"He was out in the woods this afternoon and somebody shot him's all I know. Clinic called me 'bout the gunshot wound and by the time I got there, they was loading him into an ambulance for Charleston."

"How bad …?"

"Bad, I think. He wasn't talking, least not to me. And Riley was … a madman."

Gray nodded. He had no trouble imagining the little weasel foaming at the mouth.

"You see anybody strange in the woods?" the sheriff asked. "Or hear anything out of the ordinary?"

"I didn't see anybody period, strange or otherwise."

Piper rushed out of the house and ran to the car,

calling to Grayson over her shoulder, "I don't know when I'll be home." She jumped into the driver's seat and slammed the door.

"Don't you go tearing outa here and run over somebody," the sheriff hollered to her. "Be careful, drive safe. If you got any message for Gray, you call me and I'll see he gets it."

Gray wasn't even certain Piper heard the sheriff. She said nothing, just started the engine and sprayed dirt out behind the old white Rambler as she took off down the road.

~

PIPER'S only memory of the two-hour drive to Charleston was that it felt like one of those dreams where you're running down a long, dark hallway toward a door, but no matter how fast you run, the door stays in front of you, just out of reach.

When she burst into the waiting room outside the hospital's surgery suites, there were maybe a dozen people there. Some of them she knew—mostly relatives—others were folks she recognized but couldn't place. But the first person she made eye contact with was Riley. It was the first time she'd seen or even spoken to him since she eloped with Grayson. One look told her nothing had changed in those eight years. By the time she was 10 years old, she was a full six inches taller than he was. She still was and he was still mad about it.

The chip on her older brother's shoulder had started to form when he was 7 and she was only 4. Granny Lucille Campbell had come to visit and when she spied the two children playing together in the yard, she'd bawled: "Why, lookit that. Riley's such a puny little runt even his baby sister's almost big as he is."

That single remark changed Piper's relationship with her brother and his relationship with the world for the rest of his life.

Piper's mother had been a Donahue—a family of pale-blonde, small-boned people. Her mother'd never seen the top side of five feet tall. Her grandfather had been only five-four and when her mother was a teenager, she could wear the old man's boots—size seven.

The Campbells, on the other hand, were big and raw-boned, tall and rangy, with the black hair and eyes of the Cherokee blood in their ancestry.

Rooster Campbell was 6'4" and probably weighed near 300 pounds on the day William McCollough put a bullet in his belly. Zeke was 6'5", Piper was a fuzz over six feet herself.

But Rooster Cambell's oldest son, Riley, had taken after the Donahue side of the family. If he stood up straight and tall, which he always did, he could have nudged the bottom side of five feet six. His size, or lack of it, had molded his character as profoundly as the hands of a potter on warm clay. "Small but scrappy" as a little boy became "meanest dog in the junkyard" as a teenager and "devious, back-stabbing little weasel with a hair-trigger temper and a mean streak the size of Pittsburgh" as an adult.

The perfect size for a coal miner coupled with his absolute fearlessness should have numbered Riley Campbell among the elite, the handful of miners the company always kept on when everybody else was laid off. He never earned that distinction, however, because he didn't play well with others. Fellow miners actually walked off the job rather than work with him.

When Riley saw Piper, his blond eyebrows knit

together in the deep creases above his nose and his lips curled in a snarl.

"What're you doing here?" he growled.

She ignored the remark.

"How's Zeke? The sheriff said—"

"That some McCullough shot him in the back? 'Zat what he said? 'Cause that's what happened. One of them—"

"The back? How ... where is he?"

"In surgery, been in there four hours already. What do you care?"

Piper lost it. She was bigger than he was and he didn't scare her one bit, wouldn't have if he'd been twice her size.

"Zeke is my little brother, the *only*..." she glanced around the room pointedly, "member of my entire family who has said hi, bye or kiss my foot to me since I moved back home." She spoke the next words slowly, distinctly, accusingly: "... while my *husband* was fighting a war on the other side of the world!"

Though the Addingtons were McCulloughs, most Campbells gave Grayson a pass when he became a minister like they had his father. And he was a soldier, too. Had been in combat! Everybody knew about the massacre of his unit and the room fell uncomfortably quiet. Even Riley had no comeback. In fact, it appeared that most of the fizz had gone out of him. Like a shaken soft drink, he'd spewed all over Piper, but now was flat and mostly calm.

Piper knew he wouldn't be for long. The moment Carter walked into that room, Riley'd go off again like a bottle rocket.

The woman working the information desk on the ground floor had been maddeningly slow locating where Zeke had been taken. There'd been a phone on the desk and Piper had asked to use it.

To call Carter, of course. That he was the one person she wanted to see right now, that she'd instantly turned to him in a time of crisis, that she needed his comfort … all those things said something, but she refused to consider what it might be.

She now realized it had been a terrible mistake to call him, and if there were any way she could un-do the blunder she would. But there wasn't.

"What did the doctor say about Zeke's condition? About what damage—?"

"Said he wouldn't know nothing 'til he got in there where he could look," Riley said, now sounding tired and depressed. And more than a little scared. "He was up Blood Creek … coon hunting …. and I's waitin' for him and when he didn't show up, I went looking. He was laying face-down on the ground, wasn't even much blood and for a minute I thought …" His voice trailed off. "He never did wake up, never said nothin' about what happened."

Piper thought to wonder how Riley'd gotten the limp body of his huge little brother out of the woods, but had no chance to ask. The doors leading from the operating room opened and a doctor in scrubs entered.

"I'm looking for the family of Ezekiel Ray Campbell," he said.

"That's us," Riley said and hurried with Piper across the room. "He's our little brother. How is he?"

"I believe he will live." the doctor said, and the breath Piper'd been holding exploded out of her lungs in an inelegant whoosh that almost made her cough. "His injury is not life-threatening. "

The beginnings of a celebratory rumble among the people gathered in the waiting room were cut short by the "but" that followed.

"But the bullet did do substantial damage."

"What kind of damage?" Piper's voice was airless.

"To his spinal cord. The bullet entered his back between the fourth and fifth lumbar—"

"Talk English, doc," Riley barked.

"His spinal cord was severed," the doctor said. "There really is nothing we can do about it. Your brother is paralyzed from the waist down."

The communal gasp was so perfectly synchronized it sounded rehearsed.

"He will need a wheelchair to—"

"Wheelchair?" Riley didn't bark. He sounded confused, uncomprehending.

"I'm sorry Mr. Campbell." Then he turned to Piper. "Miss Campbell, your brother will never walk again."

Piper literally staggered backward like she'd been struck. When she did, she saw the doorway leading to the hallway out of the corner of her eye. Carter was standing there, a look of shock, surprise and horror on his face.

Piper gasped for air like all the oxygen had been sucked out of the room, groaned and shook her head in disbelief.

Riley lunged at the doctor, actually grabbed the man by the lapels, and yelled into his face, "Well, you fix it! You hear me, doc. You fix Zeke, you make his legs work—"

Several men in the waiting room grabbed Riley and pulled him off the doctor. When they did, he spotted Carter. With an inarticulate cry of rage, Riley ran toward him, actually growling. Carter didn't flinch. Riley leapt at him and the force of his running start knocked Carter backward against the wall and the two of them fell in a heap in the floor.

The crowd surged that way. A couple of her bigger cousins—Rosco and Ed, Aunt Lucille's's boys, grabbed Riley. Each took an arm and literally lifted him up off Carter. But he was struggling and fighting like a wild man, screaming. "You shot him, I know you done it. You murdering McCulloughs, sneak up and shoot a man in the back."

Carter staggered to his feet and loosened the tie at his neck, ready for a fight if there was going to be one. But not spoiling for one, and when he saw that the others would control Riley, he relaxed the hands that had balled into fists.

"I didn't shoot anybody," he said. To Riley, but more to the cooler heads that had prevailed. "I live here in Charleston. I've been at work all day. You can check."

Though there was no love lost between Piper's cousins and any member of the McCullough clan, everybody knew Carter was a big shot here in Charleston in Northfield Coal. While they might not like that, they were reasonable enough to understand that he was probably the least likely candidate to be the shooter who'd pulled the trigger on a rifle in the mountains earlier in the afternoon.

Piper sealed the deal.

"Marian had a doctor's appointment here this morning." Marian, who was dying. "Carter had lunch with us after. I hadn't been back in the holler half an hour before the sheriff came to tell me about Zeke. There's no possible way Carter could have had anything to do with it."

Riley's eyes still spit fire, but he relaxed, shook off the hands that held him.

"Then I guess that lets you off the hook, don't it?" he said. He stepped forward and poked Carter in the chest with his finger as he spoke. Carter didn't flinch.

"But it was a McCullough done it. You know it and I know it. And soon's I find out which one of you it was, I'm gonna kill him."

He turned and stormed out of the room. The others wandered off, talking softly among themselves and Piper noticed that the doctor was still standing by the doors where he'd entered, staring in shock at the scene he'd witnessed.

She hurried to him.

"Doctor …?"

"Bledsoe," he said, his voice a bit shaky. "Dr. Arthur Bledsoe."

"I'm sorry about Riley, Dr. Bledsoe. He's … please, tell me about Zeke. Is he awake? Can I see him?"

"No, he's been deeply sedated and won't come around until sometime in the morning. He won't be fully coherent for about 12 hours, actually." He looked at her sympathetically, perhaps because of Zeke or perhaps because she was obviously the only sane person in a family of lunatics. "You need to go home and get some rest. Come back tomorrow after lunch. He'll be awake then and … you'll want to be here with him when I explain his condition."

Carter walked her to her car in the hospital lot. Neither said anything until he opened the door for her.

"Piper, I'm so sorry."

"It's not your fault."

He said nothing for a moment, then seemed to recover his voice.

"I'll be there tomorrow to help in any way I can," he said. "To stay, until …"

Marian! And Zeke. Piper sagged under the weight of both agonies and Carter reached out and drew her to him, hugged her tight.

"Take one thing at a time. It's all you can do. It's all any of us can do."

Piper slid in behind the wheel and drove slowly away. She saw Carter standing alone in the parking lot, saw a burst of light as he lit a cigarette—he'd started smoking again after five years! She wondered why.

By the time Piper got home, it was after eleven o'clock and she'd spent almost five hours on the road. Her head hurt, her back hurt, but mostly, her heart hurt.

Grayson got up from the porch swing where he'd obviously been waiting for her, probably for hours. He said nothing, just gathered her into his arms and held her, patting her back.

Unexpectedly, she started to cry. She could not have identified the specific source of her tears, but found that once she started, she couldn't stop. She cried for Zeke—18 years old and the rest of his life in a wheelchair! And for Marian, saintly Marian who had only days to live. She cried for Maggie who would most certainly be returned to her own family soon. For Grayson, poor, lost Grayson. For herself. And for Carter.

Her tears ratcheted up to sobs that racked her whole body. Grayson stood quietly and patted her back. At first, it seemed a comforting, gentle thing to do. But as she continued to cry, his response never changed. And after awhile, it felt as repetitious and without feeling as mindlessly patting a dog's head. It was that, in fact, that sobered her, like cold water splashed in her face. She stopped almost in mid-sob, stepped back out of his arms and looked up into his face.

It was kind. Caring. But he didn't appear to be the least bit upset. And she wanted *upset!* She *needed* upset.

"Zeke's paralyzed," she spit at him, angry for no reason. "He'll be in a wheelchair for the rest of his life. Eighteen years old and he'll never walk again!"

"I'm sorry, Piper."

Sorry? That's it?

"Did you hear what I said? My little brother's been crippled for life."

"I heard you. That's terrible."

But she didn't think he thought it was terrible at all. She thought she could have told him that Zeke had been eaten alive by a polar bear and all that was left of him was his big toe, and Grayson would have said, "that's terrible," in that same maddeningly calm tone of voice.

"What's wrong with you, Grayson?" She stabbed at his chest the way Riley had stabbed at Carter's. "You used to have a heart in there. You used to *feel* things. It used to matter to you that people hurt, that they were—" she thought of Marian, and involuntarily looked toward her closed bedroom door.

"Dying?" he finished for her.

Her voice caught in her throat and she couldn't speak, just nodded her head as tears welled in her eyes and slid down her cheeks.

"She told me," he said, in that same dead, flat tone. "Said the doctor gave her a week … maybe less." His voice cracked when he said it and tears welled in his own eyes. But his face remained impassive.

She was suddenly pounding her fists on his chest, over the edge into hysteria.

"Say something, Grayson! Anything. Cry, yell, scream, fall down in the floor sobbing. *Something.* Your mother's going to be dead by this time next week. Don't you care?"

He grabbed her wrists and held them so tight the grip felt like crushing metal shackles.

"Don't you think I wish I could just let go," he hissed with such intensity it felt like he was screaming the words. "Let it all out. I don't know how anymore. I've … seen too much." He paused, seemed to consider something, then plunged ruthlessly, almost savagely ahead. "Freck, that's what we called Joey Mattingly, the freckle-faced kid with the pregnant wife."

She remembered Joey. His wife—his widow—was

struggling to raise twin boys alone. Joey'd been killed in the massacre at Fire Station Eagle's Nest.

"He was in the hole with me, grenades and mortars going off all around us, and he reached over and slapped me hard, right in the face." He stopped and she felt it coming. "I turned and the hand and arm that slapped me wasn't attached to his body."

She tried to pull away, shook her head, didn't want to hear any more but she couldn't find her voice to tell him to stop.

"And Hawk …Bill Hawkins, he became nothing but red mist when …" Grayson came back from somewhere then, regained control. He stopped squeezing her wrists, but didn't let her go. "Piper, I've seen death and I've inflicted it. I've seen men shot dead and I've shot men dead. And when that happens, you have to … you can't…"

He let her go then, turned his back on her and grabbed the porch railing, maybe for support. She knew now was not the time, knew she should keep her mouth shut and go to bed, knew—

"You *killed* people? Is that what you just said? Shot … ? You were a *chaplain*."

He turned slowly back to face her and he'd crawled back into that suit of armor, that impenetrable chain mail that held the man she loved hostage. If, indeed, he was still alive at all.

"I was a *soldier*," he said.

And that was it. All she could stand. Too much, in fact. She said nothing, merely stepped back away from him, turned and walked like a zombie into the house, down to the bathroom at the end of the hall, closed and locked the door behind her.

~

Grayson watched Piper walk away from him and wanted to run after her, to gather her in his arms, to be loving and tender and …

But he stood rigid and watched her go.

When a flare lit up the night sky, it was so bright you couldn't look directly at it and even when it fizzled and blinked out you could still see it. Your eye had recorded the image and you could see the light even though it wasn't there.

Their love, their life, their marriage was like that. It had burned so bright its image was seared on his heart. And he could still see it. But it wasn't really there anymore.

He and Piper weren't really there anymore.

And he had absolutely no idea how to get back what was gone. If that was even possible. He'd thought so this afternoon in the woods. Things had been so clear there, real, touchable. Now, only shadows again.

He'd intended to have a long talk with Piper, get some things out in the open, start really communicating again. All that had blown up in his face the minute he walked out of the woods and the black box exploded.

Then his mother told him she was dying.

"Doctor said a week, maybe more, maybe less. I'm thinking less," she said matter-of-factly.

When she saw the stricken look on his face, she'd reached out a bony hand and patted his. "Death lies sleepin' in us all, a'waitin' for the rooster to crow. Well, that ole bird's tunin' up right now. Remember what your daddy used to say, 'We all got the same odds—a 100 percent chance of dying.'"

And then, more tender.

"You know I'm ready. Me and Jesus is gonna sit down side by side in rockers on a porch somewhere and talk for hours … days. He's gonna explain all I don't understand. And I'm gonna look at his face and maybe laugh or sing and dance, or cry. Somethin' grand, I know that."

What could he say then? That he didn't believe there was anything after your last breath but blackness and emptiness.

So he'd offered her the scraps of a smile, patted her hand and swallowed the lump in his throat.

"You got terrible things in yore eyes, son."

"Yeah, I know.

"You wanna tell me about 'em?"

"No."

"Then tell God about 'em. Not that he don't already know. It's not like you pray to give God information he ain't got. I heard you preach on that onct. Remember?"

"I don't remember any of my sermons, Ma. Not a single one."

She'd leaned over and squeezed his hand, looked deep into his eyes.

"They'll come back to you. I promise they will. You wait and see."

But she wouldn't be around to find out if they did or not. She'd be dead in a few days.

The pain of that realization hit him fresh as he stood where Piper'd left him on the porch, felt like a bayonet in his side. He sank down into the porch swing, put his face in his hands and tried to cry. He couldn't. He tried to pray. He couldn't do that, either.

Chapter Twenty-Three

CARTER KNEW he looked awful but he didn't care. He wasn't trying to impress Stella with his charm or Nelson Warren with his business acumen. They were both going to make the acquaintance of the unvarnished Carter Addington on this sunny Friday morning.

Oh, he'd shaved, put on a clean shirt. But it was what his father'd have called putting lipstick on a pig. He had not slept more than half an hour and the matched set of dark suitcases under his eyes were prepared to testify to that effect to anybody who looked at him.

Any illusion he might have had about not looking as bad as he felt was quickly dispelled when Stella lifted her head to greet him, but didn't speak, merely stared at him.

"I need to see Mr. Warren," he said.

"Do you have an appointment?"

"No, but I'll only take five minutes. It's important."

When Carter stood in front of Warren's desk, he was too tired to make nice.

"I'll get all my loose ends tied up by the end of the day because I need to take some time off next week," he said.

"Probably all of it. My mother…the doctor told her yesterday she only has a few days to live."

"I'm sorry to hear that, Carter," Warren said, and he actually sounded like he meant it. Folks in the office said he had a tender side, a human side. They'd seen it when he was with his little boy. But Carter had never seen anything but the steel-plated businessman, shrewd and clever, a man you'd be well advised not to cross. Or trust.

"Thank you, sir." He turned to leave but Warren wasn't finished with him yet.

"She lives up there in Sadler Hollow, right?"

Warren knew perfectly well where Carter's mother lived.

"Yes, sir."

"Just down from Impoundment Dam #1."

"Yes, sir—what's your point?"

"Oh, no point. I'm still curious about the reactions of locals—"

"The locals have more pressing things to think about right now than the dependability of that dam." Warren didn't ask what that might be, merely sat expectantly, waiting for Carter to tell him. "There's a feud …" His voice trailed off. Where do you start, how do you explain something as tangled up as that?

"A feud…?" Warren prompted. He shifted his unlit cigar from one side of his mouth to the other, clearly interested in what Carter had to say.

This was not a topic Carter ever wanted to talk about, certainly not now, with Zeke lying in a hospital unable to move! But he described as succinctly as he could the generations of hostilities between the McCullough family, who'd settled Sadler Hollow, and the Campbell family, who had lived on the slopes of Chicken Gizzard Mountain and down Cricket Hollow on the other side. He explained that it had long since ceased to matter what had struck the original spark. After awhile, the embers of hatred were never more than a gust of wind away from bursting into flames and consuming whoever happened to be handy.

"I was 15 the last time there was bloodshed," Carter said. "My mother's younger brother, William, and Rooster Campbell ... got into a fight."

"About?"

"Walnuts."

"Walnuts?"

Carter gritted his teeth.

"The Campbells had a black walnut tree that grew by a creek and the water washed the nuts downstream." Carter kept his voice emotionless, like he was reading the ingredients label on a bottle of aspirin. "Whenever my cousin Jesse and his friends were in the woods, they'd fish the nuts out and eat them. One day, Rooster appeared out of nowhere, accused the boys of stealing and took back the two walnuts they hadn't cracked yet—at gunpoint! Jesse ran home and told his father, who grabbed his gun and went after Rooster. By the end of the day, both men were dead."

Warren raised his eyebrows at that.

If he says it's 'just like the Hatfields and the McCoys,' I swear I'll hit him.

He didn't. But he did seem particularly interested in the latest turn of events in the story.

"And this Riley Campbell who jumped you in the hospital, he's a ... loose cannon?"

"He's too short to be a cannon," Carter replied and made no attempt to keep the contempt out of his voice. "More the size of a pop gun. But he's a mean, nasty, vindictive little weasel. He yelled at me that when he figured out which one of the McCulloughs did the shooting, he'd find the man and kill him."

"Would he go through with a threat like that?"

"Absolutely."

~

After Carter Addington left, Warren told Stella to reschedule his 9:30 appointment and hold his calls. He swiveled his chair around to the big window behind his desk and stared sightlessly at the Kanawha River and the mountains rising up behind it as he carefully examined the fabric of his grand design to make sure there were no holes in it, no frayed edges or loose threads.

The plan was solid. It had been a good one before Carter Addington walked into Warren's office this morning. Now, it was a great one. Now, Warren had a scapegoat. Somebody to blame. A focus for all the anger the disaster he planned to inflict on Sadler Hollow would generate. The Campbell clan.

Somebody took a potshot at poor Jake or Zach or Zeke —whatever his name was—Campbell in the woods and now the Campbells were out for blood. When a dam blows up that will flood out a whole hollow full of McCulloughs, which way will accusing fingers point?

He actually chuckled out loud at his good fortune. He couldn't have designed a better set of circumstances than a clan feud to take the fall for his handiwork. And it would be *his* handiwork. He intended to blow a hole in Impoundment Dam #2 all by himself. Warren had spent enough time in the mines to know his way around a stick of dynamite. Get someone else to do the dirty work and the decision would come back to bite you in the backside somewhere down the line. No, he'd do what had to be done with his own hands. Sometime soon, while the feud was still hot and emotions were running high. Sometime when no one would be around. A weekend.

This weekend.

A huge smile pulled back the corners of Warren thick lips, revealing the chewed-up end of the unlit cigar clenched between his teeth.

~

Jesse McCullough sat in the rocking chair on his front porch, his ball cap pulled down over his eyes, his feet resting on the porch railing, sound asleep.

All of a sudden, the chair tilted sideways and he slid out of it in a heap on the floor. He came up sputtering and cussing … until he saw who'd shoved the chair over.

"What. Happened?" Carter ground the words out one at a time through clenched teeth. Jesse was so surprised and rattled he forgot all the responses he'd cooked up in his head and spit out the truth.

"Swear to God, Carter, we didn't mean to hurt—"

"We?" Carter roared. "Who's we?"

Jesse got to his knees, then stood. He wanted to rip his own tongue out by the roots. He'd never meant to tell Carter about Buster. What was the point of using the boy so Carter wouldn't know Jesse'd got the shakes if he couldn't keep his own mouth shut about it?

"I won't ask again, Jesse," Carter spoke the words softly, but there was more venom in them than in a bushel basket full of rattlers.

"Me and Buster."

"You took a 16-year-old kid out to watch you shoot Zeke Campbell!"

"Not exactly."

"Then what *exactly?*"

"He didn't watch." Jesse saw Carter's hands ball into fists. "I mean, he didn't go to watch me, he went to … I didn't shoot Zeke, Carter. Buster did."

The look of shock on Carter's face would have been comical if there'd been anything about this whole situation that was funny. His eyes got huge and then it was like all the air whizzed out of him, a balloon with the end untied. He sagged back against the railing, maybe to keep from falling if his knees buckled.

"You're telling me …?"

"I couldn't. I didn't want to say. I'm… it's embarrassing, but I got me the shakes.?"

"What are you talking about?"

"This!" Jesse said and thrust his hands out in front of Carter's face. For a moment they were still, then his right hand began to tremble. A couple of seconds later, the left followed.

"What's wrong with you?"

"I ain't got no idea." Jesse righted the rocker and sat down in it. "Started about a year ago and's been getting worse ever since. If I'm doing something, moving my hands, I'm fine. But if I have to hold 'em still …"

"I've never seen your hands shake. If I had, I sure wouldn't have—"

"I keep my hands in my pockets a lot. Ain't nobody noticed, 'em shake. Well, 'cept Angie Faye and she's all over me to go have it seen about. But it don't hurt nothing and—"

"Why'd you tell me you'd shoot Zeke when you knew you couldn't? What possessed you to take a 16-year-old boy …?" It was like there was so much for Carter to get his mind around he didn't know where to start. Which was good. Maybe this wasn't gonna go as bad for Jesse as he'd been scared it would. "What happened out there, Jesse? You were just supposed to wound him!"

"It's true then, what I heard? That he's paralyzed?" Carter only looked at him. "Cuz, I'm jest glad he ain't dead! He tripped! Buster had took a bead on his leg. I figured that was the safest place to shoot him, less likely to miss and hit something ... but then Zeke stumbled, kinda went down on one knee just as Buster pulled the trigger."

"Did he see you?"

Jesse wasn't about to admit that he wasn't 100 percent sure what Zeke did or didn't see because he was fifty yards away when Buster pulled the trigger!

"He couldn't have. Back was to Buster. To us. And when Buster fired, Zeke fell forward. Never turned around." That's what Buster'd told him when he finally got the kid calmed down enough to think clear. "Sides, we ambushed him from that overhang about half of a mile from the road. Waited 'til he was going back out so's Riley'd get worried when he didn't show up and go looking for him. Didn't want him to lay there for a couple of hours and bleed to death."

Jesse waited for Carter to acknowledge that it was smart of him to think of that, but that was probably too much to ask, the frame of mind his cousin was in.

"Anybody see you going in there, or——?"

"Didn't nobody see us doin' nothing! I was careful. But even if somebody hada seen, you think they'd tell?"

"An 18-year-old boy's never going to walk again for the rest of his life," Carter growled. "Yeah, for that, I think even a McCullough might tell."

"Ain't nothing for anybody to tell."

"What about Buster? Is he going to go out and brag to his friends how he——?"

"He's so scared he spent all last night and most of today in the outhouse! First he was pukin', then he was … told Angie Faye he ate somethin' gamey."

Carter was quiet. Thinking. Jesse could tell he was so upset there was a whole lot he wasn't sayin', but that was fine with Jesse. He didn't enjoy getting yelled at. Finally, Carter let out a breath.

"Okay," he finally said. "Where's the mud from Blood Creek?"

Jesse hopped up out of his rocker and down the stairs to his truck, pulled out the Mason jar and handed it to Carter. He took it without sayin' nothing, turned and started back to his car. Then he stopped and turned back around.

"You do understand how bad this is, don't you, Jesse?"

"I'm sorry it turned out this way, Carter. We wuz only tryin' to do what you told us to do."

"Yeah," he said, turned back around and headed toward his car. Jesse heard him muttering under his breath, "…what *I* told you to do…"

"BUSTER?" Carter said aloud in an awed whisper as he drove down Northfield Road.

The idiot kid would tell. Only a matter of time. Not right now, but in a week or a month or a year. Jesse was loyal, stupid but dependable, safe. But Buster? Buster'd get drunk and brag to his friends. Or strut it out in front of his girlfriend to show what a big man he was. The boy was even dumber than his father. He was incapable of carrying a secret like that to his grave.

Eventually, whoever Buster told would tell somebody

else and the genie would be out of the bottle. And when it hit the fan, Buster—and maybe even Jesse, too, to save his kid's hide—would fall all over himself to point the finger at Carter.

Yep, it was only a matter of time.

Carter swerved to the side of the road, opened his car door and lost his lunch. When the reflexive heaving finally subsided, he closed the door and leaned his forehead on his hands on the steering wheel, panting. He'd wanted to give Piper's cocky little brother a flesh wound that'd heal in a few weeks and barely leave a scar. It'd all seemed so simple.

Now what?

He looked down and saw that his hands were shaking worse than Jesse's.

He took a deep breath, let it out slow and settled back in the seat.

The Mason jar of red mud was in the floorboard, the mud he'd planned to use to convince Piper that Grayson had lost it and ...

He stopped breathing. That was it, of course, his way out.

Carter'd never given a moment's thought to the criminal consequences of shooting Zeke. He knew the Campbells wouldn't go crying to the sheriff over a flesh wound. But it was different now. The law was involved. The sheriff had been called to the health department clinic in Chandler as soon as the nurse on duty saw it was a bullet wound. The Philippi Detachment of the West Virginia State Police was investigating, too. If Carter managed to lay the blame on Grayson—and everybody bought the story—it wouldn't matter what some stupid teenager bragged to his drunk friends someday. Nobody'd believe Buster, because the "real" shooter would be ...

Where?

In prison.

Grayson would go to prison. And Piper would be Carter's.

Carter sat very still as realization settled over him. He'd never intended to do anything but take his brother's wife—not because he had anything against Grayson but because he loved Piper. He couldn't help it; she was the only woman he'd ever loved, no matter how hard he'd tried to forget her. She cared about him, too. She did. Only a little while longer, another month or two. If Grayson hadn't shown up early, Carter could have won her heart. None of this would have been necessary if Grayson …

Could he send his own brother to prison?

He sat there by the side of the road for a long time. The shadows thickened. Finally, he stirred, started the car and drove slowly down the road. It wasn't like he made some kind of decision. It was simply that he accepted the nature of reality. Forces had been set in motion he couldn't control anymore. People had been hurt; more people were going to be hurt. He hadn't planned it that way, but sometimes things didn't work out like you planned. And the truth was his conscience was encrusted with worse transgressions than this.

He pulled up in front of his mother's house and killed the engine, wondering idly if Piper'd told Grayson he was coming. And staying. It wouldn't be hard to do what he had to do. Grayson's hunting gear, boots, pants and hat would be in the shed. That's where Ma had always demanded such things be kept to keep her house full of men from tracking up her clean floors. As soon as everyone was asleep, Carter would slip out to his car, get the jar of mud and rub it deep into the tread of the soles on Grayson's boots, maybe smear some on one knee of his pants, like he'd knelt down in the mud when he was taking aim. The only possible explanation for red mud on Grayson's boots was that he had tracked it home from Blood Creek the day before.

Once Piper saw it, the fireworks would begin.

~

Zeke's big hand felt so cold. Piper held it between both her hands, tried to warm his whole body by sheer force of will. She couldn't. She couldn't make him walk again by sheer force of will, either.

Dr. Bledsoe had warned that when Zeke learned his paralysis was permanent, he would go through all the stages of grief—denial, bargaining, anger and finally, acceptance. He said there was no way to tell how long it would take the boy to complete the journey.

Right now, he didn't seem to be in any of those stages. Well, maybe denial, but it was more like stunned disbelief.

"I's whistling the tune to the *Andy Griffith Show*," he said. His voice was so weak it made her heart ache. "Seen it on a television in the window of Sears once in Charleston and the show starts with some fella whistling. That's what I was doin', walking along whistling, kinda stumbled—and it wasn't even a second later, not even a *second*—I opened my eyes and I was here. And I wasn't whistling no more."

Piper didn't know what to say so she said nothing, just patted his hand.

"It's funny what that little girl said, not even a week ago."

"What little girl?"

"The one looks like a Raggedy Ann doll. Maggie. I been thinking about it ever since I woke up."

"What are you talking about?"

"The night I come over and Carter was there, you remember she walked me out to my car."

Piper nodded. She remembered that she'd thought at the time it was an odd thing for Maggie to do.

"She was chattering away about Nellie, about how good I played. She asked if I loved my banjo and I said I sure did. Then she said, 'Would Nellie be enough? If all you could do was play Nellie, could you be happy?'"

"What did you tell her?"

"I said if I's on a boat in the middle of the ocean and all I had was Nellie, I'd be happy alright—'cause I'd use her for a paddle!"

"You do still have Nellie," Piper said softly.

"Yeah, I got me a banjo. Gonna be hard to play her, though, if'n I can't tap my foot to the rhythm."

He turned his face toward the wall and said nothing more.

Chapter Twenty-Four

GRAYSON CAME in from checking the oil in the Rambler—it was about a quart low—and paused in the doorway. Carter was on the floor playing with Sadie. He pulled her tattered pink blankie over his head, then yanked it off and cried "peek-a-boo."

Sadie squealed with laughter, then snatched the blanket and draped it more or less over her head.

"Where's Sunshine?" Carter asked. "Where did she go? I can't find her any—"

Sadie could stand it no longer and pulled away the blanket.

"Sabie right here. Peek-a-boo." Then she begged him, "Again-again, Unka Cardur!" and the sequence started all over.

His daughter had finally warmed up to Grayson night before last for the first time since he got home. After Piper raced out of the house for her second trip into Charleston, he'd helped his mother to bed early. The old woman was fading so fast she looked like a flower in that fast-frame Walt Disney's Wonderful World of Color show he and

Piper had watched on the 13-inch black-and-white television they had in Spindle Rock. The picture on the TV relentlessly rolled and was only visible through the snow when you correctly positioned the aluminum foil dangling between the rabbit ears of the antenna. But they had sat spellbound before it as the whole life of a flower played out in 30 seconds. A bud, full bloom and then it withered and turned brown. Ma was withering. He had the sense that her very breaths could now be counted in a finite number.

With Ma in bed, he'd set about winning Sadie's affections using the method that had been working successfully so far. He ignored her. He plopped down on the floor in front of the couch and began to read an old newspaper he'd found lining the bottom of the potato bin in the kitchen, where his mother had once stashed Piper to hide her presence from uninvited McCullough guests. The date on the newspaper was July 7.

When he'd explained his plan to Maggie, she had flashed a radiant smile that crinkled up the freckles on her nose. And it felt somehow like he was seeing the child for the first time, surprised that he hadn't noticed how adorable she was. The little girl really did look like a Raggedy Ann doll, with long red braids tied in blue yarn and coveralls rolled up above her bare feet.

"Sadie's curious as a little yellow kitten," Maggie said. "You be an itch and she'll have to scratch it."

Then Maggie busied herself in the kitchen noisily re-washing the already-washed dishes.

Sadie was accustomed to playing happily near him. The longer he sat, the closer she nudged toward him, Finally, she brushed her long hair out her eyes with that endearing gesture, using the palms of both hands.

"Sabie can wink," she said. "Mabie taught me." She

squeezed both eyes tight shut, crinkling her whole face, then instantly popped them back open again. "See!"

Grayson choked back a laugh.

"I don't believe I've ever seen a finer wink."

Sadie's dimpled smile melted him, but as badly as he wanted to reach out to the precious little munchkin in front of him, he picked up the newspaper and continued reading. Sadie went back to her kitchen set and he thought he'd lost her. But she came right back and held out a toy plate.

"Wanna doughnut? I maked it on the stove."

The plate was empty, so he picked up the pretend doughnut and pretend munched on it, then patted his belly.

"Mmmm. That was good."

"Wanna nuther bite? It be's yummy in your tummy. "

"Sure." He took another bite. And so it went.

Half an hour later, she was sitting happily in his lap as he read to her from one of her favorite story books—about a baby bird who fell out of the nest and went looking for his mother. Every time he'd wail pitifully, "Are you my mother?" Sadie would burst into a peal of dimpled giggles.

He gave Sadie a bath. She splashed water all over the bathroom and somehow Grayson managed not to think about another little girl who loved to splash water, too. Then he carefully brushed the silky, honey-colored curls that reached past her waist and rocked her to sleep.

Maggie stayed quietly in the background, but was waiting outside Sadie's bedroom when he tiptoed out and closed the door softly.

"She'll be a daddy's girl in no time," she said with a huge smile and he was surprised at how much it meant to him that she was on his side.

The next morning, despite tension in the house thick enough to spread on toast—Sadie had dragged him proudly into the bathroom to show off her proficiency in the "big girl potty," and when Piper left for the hospital in Charleston, he and the "girls" had spent a remarkably pleasant day together. Maggie had remained inside most of the day, reading the Bible and singing silly songs to his mother—and sometimes *with* his mother. The day had been a scorcher, the hottest since he got home, and Maggie had fanned Marian for hours to keep her cool with the Japanese fan Piper had brought home from Hawaii. Grayson had played outside with Sadie, pushed her in the tire swing and helped her pick a bouquet of wildflowers for her grandmother.

Piper had come home a wreck, wouldn't talk about Zeke and how he'd taken the news about his paralysis. Then Carter had shown up about nine o'clock with a suitcase and announced he'd be staying until … Grayson hadn't liked the look of—maybe not joy but … relief?—he saw on Piper's face when his brother walked into the house. As if now she had someone she could depend on through the difficult days ahead.

Grayson was biding his time before he confronted his brother about what he'd seen the day he arrived, the kiss Carter had forced on a not-altogether-reluctant Piper. Maybe they all three needed to talk about it, get it out in the open. But there'd be time for that later after … Right now, they all needed to focus on his mother and make the most of her precious remaining time.

Ma had awakened this morning so weak she didn't leave her bed. And so very pale.

When Sadie woke up to find Unka Cardur in the house —"You came back!"—she had abandoned her newfound attachment to Grayson like yesterday's newspaper and followed Carter around like a puppy. But later in the day, she'd brought Grayson *Are You My Mother?* And begged him to read it to her "again-again."

Maggie had awakened that morning with the look of a baby bird coming out of the shell. She didn't have much to say, appeared to be distracted and preoccupied, as if she were considering the world around her afresh, with new perspective. He caught her several times standing in the back yard, staring at the mountain behind the house looking deeply frightened. Perhaps she'd finally remembered the family that had beaten her. Grayson refused to consider what it would mean—to her and to everyone else in the family—if she had.

Piper had barely slept at all. Grayson knew; he hadn't either. Now, she seemed to be in shock, going through the motions of caring for her family but with her mind somewhere else entirely. As she was finishing up supper, he'd gone out to check the oil in the old Rambler because she'd said she wanted to return to Charleston Sunday to see Zeke.

"I hab Rasmus, Unka Cardur," Sadie told his brother, raced to her room and returned with the well-worn bear. "Play peek-a-boo wif Rasmus!"

Carter obliged and Piper looked on smiling. Grayson didn't think he'd ever felt quite so ... unnecessary. So disenfranchised.

When supper was done, Maggie scooped up Sadie and got her ready for bed as he and Piper did the dishes and Carter sat with his mother.

"Tell me about Zeke," he began. "How did he take—?"

"No! I can't. If I talk about it ... I don't want to break down in front of ..." He squeezed her soapy hand and she laid her head briefly on his shoulder in response.

Before Maggie put Sadie to bed, she carried the

toddler around the room for the ritual "give night-night kisses." When she got to Grayson, the toddler threw her arms around his neck and planted a wet kiss on his cheek. As Piper got Marian settled, Grayson got out the whet-stone and began to sharpen his knife. When Piper came out of the old woman's bedroom, she looked like she was about to cry and Grayson tried to think of some safe subject to distract her.

"The car's a quart low on oil," he said. "You need to stop somewhere on your way—"

"You don't need to stop," Carter interrupted, almost eagerly. "I'm pretty sure there are a couple of cans of Valvoline in the storage building." But then he made no move to go get it, so Piper turned and headed out the back door.

Finished with his knife, Grayson poured himself a cup of coffee and was sipping it at the kitchen table when Piper walked slowly back into the house. She wasn't holding a quart of oil, though. She was holding Grayson's hunting boots and pants.

His eyes went from the boots to her face and he saw instantly that something was terribly wrong.

"Piper, what—"

"Where were you Thursday?" she demanded, her voice cold and hard. "Where did you go hunting?"

Grayson was confused, by the question and the tone of her voice.

"Well, I went up to the church first, and then … actu-ally, I don't really know where I went. I wasn't looking for squirrels, just wandered around—"

"Until you got to Blood Creek. And you sure enough weren't hunting for squirrels there!"

"Blood Creek? No, I couldn't possibly have gone that far because—"

"Oh, yes, you did." She thrust his boots at him, bottom side up. "The proof's right here!"

He looked at the soles of the boots. Dried red mud was caked in the treads. He was stunned. He must have gone to Blood Creek. It was the only place in the county with red mud. But how on earth …?

"Well, I guess … looks like I must have gone to Blood Creek. I don't remember … but what difference—?"

"And here!" She pointed to mud on the right knee of his pants. "Here's where you kneeled down to take aim!"

Piper's face was bright red; her eyes spit fire.

"No, I must have tripped, fallen down or something because I didn't shoot a single squirrel all day."

"Oh, you weren't aiming at squirrels. You were aiming at my little brother. And you shot him in the back!"

Grayson was so dumfounded he stared at her gape-jawed. Carter had gotten up from the couch during the exchange and now stood next to Piper, the same look of accusation on his face.

"What? I didn't shoot Zeke! Why would you think I did?"

"I don't *think*. I know." Piper launched the boots and pants at him and burst into hysterical sobs. Carter gathered her into his arms and snarled at Grayson over the top of her head.

"Zeke was at Blood Creek when he was shot—when he was *ambushed*."

Grayson leapt to his feet.

"What possible reason would I have to shoot Zeke? That's ridiculous."

"For the same reason you went off on Maggie the first time you laid eyes on the child," Carter hissed the words at him in a growling whisper, keeping his voice down so Marian and the girls wouldn't hear. "You groped her, pawed her, told her she couldn't be here, that she was dead."

Piper pulled back out of Carter's arms, and spit words at Grayson. "You pointed your rifle at the sheriff and me!" Her eyes instantly opened wide in realization. "You'd have shot us that day, wouldn't you! But Sheriff Cliff pulled a gun on you."

"Zeke didn't have a gun, though," Carter took up where Piper left off. "He couldn't have defended himself even if he'd had one because you sneaked up on him and put a bullet in his back."

Grayson felt like one of those shiny silver balls in the machine when the pinball flappers bat it clanging from one post to another.

"You're both crazy!" he stammered.

"No, Grayson, *you're* crazy!" Carter stepped away from Piper and poked his finger in the air inches from Grayson's chest. "Something happened to you over there in that jungle. All your buddies getting dead and you walking away without a scratch—"

Grayson lunged at Carter, grabbed fistfuls of his shirt in both hands and shoved him backward until he slammed into the refrigerator, knocking the casserole dish on top of it to the floor where it shattered in an explosion of broken glass that flew like shrapnel across the kitchen and out into the parlor.

"Don't you *dare* talk about a war you didn't fight or about soldiers you're not fit to—"

Carter swung, a ranging roundhouse that would have decked any man it connected with, but Grayson easily dodged the blow, spun around and grabbed Carter's arm, bent it backward at the elbow until Carter grunted in pain and went down on one knee, gasping.

"Piper," Marian called from the bedroom. "Did you

drop somethin' and b-b-break it? You be careful, don't you cut yourself c-c-cleaning up that glass."

They all three went rigid, stopped breathing.

And into the bizarre wax museum walked Maggie, a pale, ghostly apparition in Piper's short white nighty, so long on her it dragged in the floor like a train behind her. She took the measured steps of a sleepwalker, her skin so chalky the spray of red freckles on her nose looked like drops of blood. Her eyes were unfocused, her face set. She didn't appear to notice that Carter was on one knee with Grayson twisting his arm, or that Piper's face was a mask of conflicting emotions.

"We have to go," she said, her voice hollow and flat. Like a recording. "Now. We have to go *now*. The black monster is coming after us."

Piper went to the child and put her hands on Maggie's shoulders. Grayson released his hold on Carter and Carter sat back on his heels and rubbed his arm with his other hand.

"Honey, what are you saying?" Piper asked. "Maggie—"

At the sound of her name, Maggie's head snapped back like somebody'd slapped her. Life and color and animation returned to her face.

"Oh, Miss Piper, we have to get away! Right now. We have to get up high."

She didn't wait for Piper to respond, but turned and ran the few steps to where Carter was still kneeling, got right in his face.

"Mr. Carter, you go get Nan Marian, be easy with her because she's in fearsome pain." She turned to Grayson, who stood now beside the refrigerator. "I'll get Sadie up and dressed while you start the car." Back to Piper she ran, like a little magpie. "Hurry, we have to *hurry*." That's when

Grayson saw it. He took two quick steps and lifted the little girl up into his arms.

Piper reached out to stop him as Carter jumped up, both obviously intent on "protecting" Maggie from the madman, but Grayson halted them with a single word.

"Look!" he said and nodded toward the floor. Bloody footprints made a trail on the shiny hardwood where Maggie had cut her feet on the broken glass of the casserole dish *and never even noticed!* Then everyone started talking at once.

"Piper, you get something to—" Carter said.

"Grayson, put her down on the table and I'll—" Piper said even as Grayson did exactly that.

"Have you got tweezers?" Grayson asked. "We need—"

In the midst of the babble, Maggie continued to plead with them to leave, that a huge black monster was coming to get them. In the next few minutes, the grownups grabbed hold of their emotions and held them rigidly in check while Maggie became more and more hysterical. They quickly discovered that there were only two small cuts on her left heel and a hole in her right big toe—lots of blood but little damage. The child didn't wear shoes, had none and the bottoms of her feet were as tough as leather. While Grayson picked out the glass and applied Band Aids, Carter swept up the broken glass and reassured Marian, who had heard the ruckus from her bedroom. Piper went to soothe Sadie, whose wailing gratefully appeared more whiny-sleepy than upset.

Grayson could hear Carter telling his mother that Maggie "had a bad dream, that's all. Must have been a doozy of a nightmare."

Indeed, it must have been because instead of calming down as reality blew away the cobwebs and vapors of imagination, the child was getting more agitated by the minute. She continued to babble even after Piper returned and tried to reassure her. Finally, Grayson took her by the shoulders as she sat with bandaged feet dangling off the edge of the kitchen table, got right in her face and said forcefully, "Maggie, stop it!"

Piper stepped forward to protest, but Carter caught her arm. Tears streamed down the child's face, but she appeared to be "back" from wherever it was she'd gone. Now, she just sounded like a frightened little girl.

"Please Miss Piper, you have to … Mr. Carter, please! Believe me. The black mon—"

"Nothing's going to get us!" Piper said.

Grayson could see that Piper was on the edge. He reached down and gathered the little girl in his arms.

"Come on, honey. You're going back to bed—right now," he said.

She made one more attempt to plead with him as he carried her down the hallway, but he silenced her with a finger to his lips as he tiptoed into Sadie's room and settled Maggie on her pallet on the floor. Her eyes begged him … but he planted a kiss on her forehead—surprised at the swell of tender affection he felt for her—and slipped back out of the room.

When he stepped into the parlor it was clear Piper and Carter had been talking. Equally clear, that he was odd man out.

Carter started to speak, but Piper touched his arm—Grayson hated the intimacy of the gesture—and said to him, "Could you please give us a minute."

Carter shot an angry look Grayson's way, then turned and went out the front door and down the walk to his car. Grayson could see the flame of his lighter as he lit a cigarette and leaned against the hood.

"Piper, please, listen to—"

"Don't!" Her rage gave the word an edge of pure hatred. "*You* listen to *me*. I'm going to make a pallet and sleep on the floor in your mother's room. What happened here tonight, what was said—none of us will speak another word about it as long as your mother …" Her voice broke. He could tell the sudden emotion surprised her, and instinctively reached out to her. She slapped his hand away like it was a spider that had crawled up on her arm.

She leaned toward him, her voice a ragged, guttural growl that didn't sound like anyone he'd ever met, certainly not the wife he'd fought desperately to stay alive to come home to.

"But after … I'm done! That's it, we're through!"

"Piper, I didn't do anything!"

"Save your lies for Sheriff Cliff. I want you out of my life—and

Sadie's. It's over between us, Grayson."

And just starting between you and Carter.

He didn't say that out loud, of course. Before he could say anything at all, Piper went into his mother's bedroom and closed the door softly behind her.

A scream tore open the silence, made a sound like fabric ripping. Grayson sat up, disoriented. Then he heard Piper's voice, wailing his name. He leapt out of the bed and raced down the hall where he found Piper standing in the middle of the Sadie's room, turning slowly around in a circle.

When she saw him, she fell into his arms.

"Grayson, they're gone! Sadie and Maggie are gone!"

His mind registered the horror and desperation in her

voice at the same time it registered the feel of her against his chest and the fact that she'd instinctively called out to him and not Carter.

Carter spoke from the doorway.

"Did you check—?"

"Everywhere! At first, I thought Maggie had …" It appeared Piper realized where she was because she stepped back out of Grayson's embrace. She didn't let go of his arm, though, dug her fingers into it. "But their things are gone." She gestured vaguely. Grayson didn't know what specifically she was referring to, but he got the point. "Maggie's run away and she's taken Sadie with her."

"Piper!" Marian cried out from her room. Her voice had an airy, hitching sound that suggested she'd been calling before but nobody heard her. They all three hurried to her room, where they found her sitting on the side of her bed, trying to rise. "What was you screamin' about, child? What's wrong?"

"It's nothing for you to worry about, now—" Piper began.

"Stop treatin' me like I'm lame, halt and addled!" Marian snapped and shocked them all into silence. She saw their surprise. "I ain't got time for nice. I been busy dying, ain't paid attention maybe like I ought. But I know there's all kinda stuff going on in my very own home and I want to know what it is right now!"

Grayson steered the conversation to the safest, most immediate concern.

"Maggie's run off … with Sadie."

Though clearly upset by the news, Marian didn't look particularly surprised.

"All day yesterday that child wasn't right," she said.

"The sun hasn't cleared the mountain yet," Carter said. "How far could they have got?"

Marian reached over and tugged open the drawer on the bedside table. Other than a pair of spectacles and some tissues, it was empty.

"Flashlight Piper got me 'cause the lamp don't give 'nough light to read my Bible—it's gone," she said.

"With a flashlight for the shadows under the trees—no telling how long they've been gone," Carter said.

Piper uttered a little peep of a cry and Grayson saw Carter start to reach out to her and then draw back.

"What are we standing around talking for?" Piper said. "We have to find them!" She turned to run out of the room, but Grayson put his hand on her arm.

"If they've gone more than half a mile, Maggie's likely carrying Sadie by now," he said. "They won't get another fifty yards in the time it takes us to think this through."

"Gray's right," Carter said. "They could be anywhere. We need to try to narrow down the search area if we can."

"But…" Piper looked from one to the other pleadingly, then settled back, pursed her lips in concentration. "Okay, Sadie's coveralls and a pink shirt are gone—and her shoes. Maggie's barefoot!" She looked at the jumble of Maggie's pallet. "… she's wearing her blue shorts, a tee shirt … and Maggie took Sadie's blankie, maybe wrapped the other stuff in it, made a sack."

"What other stuff?" Carter asked.

"The cabinet's open in the kitchen and I think a Mason jar's missing."

"For water," Grayson said.

"Cheese, all that was left of the bread, a couple of slices, some apples—maybe there was an orange," Piper said. "Why would she do a thing like this?"

"Because we wouldn't listen last night," Carter said.

"About that nightmare she had?" Marian asked.

"That's right!" Piper said. "She wanted us all to run away—and when *we* wouldn't, *she* did!

"Why—?" Marian began.

"She said some monster was after us, just kid stuff. Imagination," Grayson said. "She said we had to 'get up high.'"

"The top of the mountain, maybe?" Marian said.

"Maybe," Grayson said. He put his hands on his mother's shoulders. "You need to lie back, now, Ma. We'll find them." He eased her down on the pile of pillows that held her frail body in something like a sitting position in the bed. He could see in her eyes she wanted to protest, but she didn't have the strength.

"We need to get dressed," he said to Piper and Carter, "and go outside and look around the yard, see if we can find any indication which way they went."

"It's up," Marian said, her voice barely above a whisper. "I b'lieve that. Up the side of the mountain."

Dressed only in the underwear and tee shirt he slept in, Grayson picked up the boots with red clay on the bottom and his pants that had been left on the kitchen table, carried them out to the storage shed beside the back porch and got out his fatigue shirt . As he was lacing up his boots, Piper and Carter came out the back door and he gestured with his chin to the open gate in the back fence.

"I was playing out here with Sadie yesterday," he said, "and I'm sure I closed it."

"She wouldn't have gone out the back gate if she was going down the road to town," Carter said.

"But which way?" Piper was near tears. She hurried ahead of them to the fence and frantically scanned the mountainside. "Shouldn't we tell somebody, go get Sheriff Cliff?" There was only a heartbeat of awkward silence at the mention of the sheriff. Finding the missing children was what mattered now; there'd be time for the other later. "We can't search all these woods. We need help!" She glanced up at the sky. Clouds were moving in. "What if it starts to rain?

"*We* are not going to search anywhere," Grayson said gently. "You're going to go sit with Ma while Carter and I go find the girls."

She started to protest, but for once the brothers displayed a solidly united front.

"How about this," Carter said. "Gray and I'll spread out, search until …" he looked at his watch "…meet at Hickman's Thumb at noon. If we haven't found them by then, we'll come back and go for help." He looked to Grayson for approval; Grayson nodded.

Grayson took Piper by the shoulders. "We'll find them, okay. It'll be all right." She looked at him, her eyes so full of unshed tears he knew a single blink would send them streaming down her face.

"Okay, 'til noon," she said.

"Ma's worried sick," Carter said. "She—"

"I know. I'll … Just find them!"

She turned and hurried back into the house.

Grayson faced Carter. The glug, glug sound their "united front" made as it drained out of their relationship was almost audible.

"My money's on south," Grayson said emotionlessly. "North toward the church is steep and beyond it's the ridge and Turtle Shell Rock. You can see from here that's un-climbable. And straight up the mountain from here is steep, too. I don't think two little girls could get up that incline on this side of the dam. If the kid's bent on 'up', she'll go south and try to angle up to the top."

"Sounds reasonable," Carter said. "You got a plan?" There was just the hint of sarcasm in the remark that might have been directed at Grayson's combat fatigues, canteen and belt, but he let it go.

"How about I go up to the creek bed below the dam, cross it, then angle south along the base of Chicken Gizzard Mountain toward Hickman's. You go due south. I think we'll run across them way before we get to the rock."

"Suits me." Carter turned to go.

"Carter, one other thing." His brother turned back guardedly. "Why don't you call out to Sadie, not Maggie. Maggie will likely try to hide, but if Sadie hears your voice, Maggie won't be able to shut her up."

What he didn't say was that he intended to remain silent. Sadie might be talked into hiding from him.

"Good idea." Carter turned without another word and started off toward the woods. As he got into the trees, Grayson heard him begin to shout. "Sunshine! Where are you, Sugar? Suuunny!"

Grayson stood for a moment, considering. He almost went back into the house for the rifle—his heightened survival instinct told him it wouldn't be a good idea to go into the woods unarmed. But if he took the rifle now, when there was no compelling need for it, he'd lose a round in his battle against irrationality. Besides, he didn't want to face his wife holding the weapon in his hand she thought he'd used to cripple her little brother.

He turned and headed uphill into the trees.

Chapter Twenty-Five

Piper watched out the kitchen screen door as the brothers talked briefly, then set out in different directions. She thought she heard Carter calling to Sadie, then both men disappeared from sight.

She stared for a moment at the thick woods that blanketed the mountainside and felt a wave of despair. How could they possibly find two little girls in hundreds of thousands of acres of …?

"Piper, honey…" Marian's voice was so weak!

Piper paused outside Marian's doorway and forced a smile to her lips.

Marian was looking out her window and turned as Piper entered.

"Sugar, that fake smile m-m-makes you look like a shark—all teeth with eyes cold as frozen d-d-doorknobs."

Piper collapsed into the chair beside the bed, put her head in her hands and waited for the tears to overwhelm her. But they didn't come. She sat with her gut tied into so many different knots she was certain of only one thing.

Untying them would cause even more pain than she felt now.

Marian reached out her trembling hand and placed it tenderly on Piper's shoulder. It was like being touched by a cloud.

"We need to talk, you and m-m-me," Marian said.

Piper lifted her head.

"What's all this n-n-nonsense about Grayson shooting Zeke?"

Piper merely looked at her mother-in-law, but could find no words anywhere inside to speak.

"Surely, you can't p-p-possibly b'lieve—"

Marian's face abruptly crinkled in a grimace of pain. She grunted and her hand slid off Piper's shoulder. Then she clasped both hands over her belly and moaned softly.

"It's past time for your medicine," Piper said, reached for the biggest of the three brown prescription bottles on the table, opened it and dropped two small white tablets into her palm.

The old woman shook her head.

"No," she gasped. "Too dopey. It'll … pass."

Piper ignored her protest. She filled a small glass with water from the pitcher beside the pill bottles, then held it and the tablets out wordlessly to Marian. After a moment, the old woman reached out a trembling hand for the pills and Piper helped her wash them down with a gulp of water.

In less than a minute, Marian began to relax, the tension eased out of her shoulders and she settled back on the pillows.

"I'll be right here," Piper said. "You sleep now, and when you wake up, we'll talk."

Marian was already asleep.

Piper got up, walked out of the room and found herself in Sadie's room. She picked up Rasmus off Sadie's pillow—"nose gone, lost it." Holding the teddy bear tenderly, she lifted the toddler's nightgown Maggie had dropped in the floor when she dressed Sadie, held it up to her nose and inhaled deeply. The little-girl smell of it brought tears to Piper's eyes at last and she began to cry. Not sob. Her hurts were too deep for anything as simple and cleansing as a good cry. Everywhere her mind touched, sliced her open to the bone. Sadie. Maggie. Marian. Zeke. Grayson. Even Carter.

The weight of it all pressed her down and she found herself on her knees beside Sadie's big-girl bed. She leaned her head over on her hands and began to pray.

Lord, please … what?

What do I say? What do I ask for? That you make Marian well? That you make Zeke walk again? I know you can, but do you anymore? And Grayson! What do I pray for him. He killed people. Something inside him died over there, too. Can you resurrect that? He shot Zeke!

Or did he?

Could Grayson possibly have—of course, he did! He went hunting and he was at Blood Creek. How many men packing .22s just happened to be at Blood Creek on Thursday afternoon? It wasn't like there'd been a squirrel-hunters convention in the woods. She sank back off her knees and sat on the floor in Sadie's room, clutching her baby daughter's teddy bear and nightgown. Some time later she was roused by a sound—it was a vehicle pulling up out front.

She leapt to her feet and ran for the front door. She could send whoever'd come to visit to find the sheriff, tell him two little girls were—! She saw the truck.

Zeke?   For a moment her mind stumbled. Zeke was here? She could imagine him getting down out of the truck, strolling up to the door with a cigarette in the corner of his mouth and Nellie hung around his shoulder. Grinning. Always grin—

Though the illusion vanished, the truck was real. It was parked in the dirt in front of the house but the man coming through the gate wasn't Zeke. It was Riley.

Piper's heart leapt into her throat. Her knees felt so weak she feared they'd drop her in a heap on the floor.

No. Oh, please Lord—No!

She stood at the screen door, but couldn't open it. Couldn't speak, either, like she'd imagined all those times she'd have stood there unable to speak as the two officers in dress uniforms advanced up the sidewalk, their faces solemn.

Riley's face wasn't solemn. There was, in fact, a light in his eyes she'd never seen before. He didn't look like a man who'd come to tell her their brother had …

"Riley," she managed as he got to the porch and stopped, stood staring up at her with an odd look—was it … satisfaction? "Has something happened to Zeke?"

"Yeah, somethin' happened to Zeke. He got shot and he can't walk, that's what happened to Zeke."

"I mean, he didn't … there wasn't some problem, complication? He's not …?"

"Dead? No. He ain't 'xactly lovin' life though, if you know what I mean."

"Then why are you …?"

Riley could help them look! Three instead of two! She shoved open the screen door and raced out onto the porch.

"Oh, Riley, I'm so glad you're here. Sadie's gone! A little girl, Maggie, who's been staying with us, took Sadie and ran away this morning. They're out there…" She gestured up toward the mountain. "… somewhere. Grayson and Carter are looking for them. They're meeting at Hickman's Thumb so you could catch them there and …"

Riley should go for help!

"No, no you have go get the sheriff so they can organize a search party and—"

"Ain't gonna be getting the law," he said. She noticed for the first time that he had a rifle in his hands. A deer rifle.

"Riley, what are you doing here?"

"Come to see your husband." He spit out the word like it tasted bad in his mouth. "Me and him's gonna have ourselves a little 'family meetin'.' I ain't gonna do no talkin', though." He held up the rifle. "This here's gonna say everything I got to say."

"Riley …?"

He squinted up at her. His cold, blue eyes looked dark, the dull gray of a stormy sea or of clouds bearing heavy snow. "Heard all about what happened 'tween you and him and Sheriff Cliff on Thursday. How he come out of the woods and drew down on the two of you, woulda shot you, too, if the sheriff hadn't pulled a gun on him 'fore he had a chance. Too bad ole Cliff wasn't there to face him down 'fore he put a bullet in my brother's back."

"Surely, you don't believe Grayson would—"

"You know, there was a time I woulda thought not, him being a preacher n' all."

There was almost an air of joviality to the conversation. A smile thin as a filleting knife played across Riley's lips. It dawned on her slowly, laboriously, like lifting something heavy, that Riley was enjoying torturing her. Payback for untold imagined slights over the years. Payback for the sack full of resentments that was his most prized possession. For marring a McCullough. For being a foot taller than he was!

"But the way I hear it, the preacher man ain't the one come home. The one come home from Veet Nam is a crazy man. That crazy man's the one done it."

He paused and the genial façade vanished, leaving behind a coiled spring so taut she could almost feel the vibrating tension.

"But when I put a bullet in him, the man who's heart's gonna stop beatin' will still be Grayson Addington."

"Riley, no!" her hands flew to her mouth. She saw that he enjoyed the look or terror on her face.

"I ain't decided 'xactly what I'm gonna do yet. I don't know if I'm gonna shoot him in the back—right where he shot Zeke. 'Course, this being a 30.06, it'll tear a hole right through him 'stead of paralyzing him." He lifted the rifle then, pointed it at her face. She fought the urge to flinch and won, just stood looking down at him. "But I'll probably put a bullet right there, center of his forehead, right 'tween his eyes."

"You won't get away with it," she said. Ice had formed in her veins and her voice didn't shake. "You murder the Reverend Grayson Addington—a war hero—and they'll strap you into Old Sparky in Moundsville, turn on the juice and fry you."

"You think I care?" He screamed at her now, the restrained rage set free. "I ain't got no intention of 'getting away with it.' I'm gonna shoot Grayson Addington dead, drag his body out of the woods like a gut-shot buck and brag about it. Let 'em come and git me, take me away. Don't matter to me. Long's I get revenge—long overdue revenge—I'll die a happy man!"

And he would, too. Riley didn't care. All that mattered to him, all that had ever really mattered to him, was making the world and everybody in it pay for the raw deal he'd gotten in life. He was probably secretly glad Zeke had gotten shot. It'd given him the excuse he needed, the cause he could champion. Zeke had given Riley Campbell the opportunity to be the star of his own movie, and Riley would cheerfully play the part all the way to the electric chair.

He strode back to his truck, reached in the open driver's side window, took the keys from the ignition and dropped them into his pocket. Then as casually as you'd kick a can out of the way, he pointed the rifle at the front tire of Piper's Rambler and fired. She jumped at the roar. Had Carter and Grayson heard it in the woods? What if they had? They were unarmed!

He chambered another round and fired again, blowing out the front tire on Carter's Camero.

"Case you was thinking 'bout going for the law. Filling the woods up with county mounties or State Po-lice."

"… but Sadie's *lost!*"

"If nobody finds her, there'll be one less McCullouch in the world and it'll be a better place for it!"

He moved the rifle to the crook of his arm and started toward the back yard and the woods.

"Riley … please! Grayson didn't—"

He turned on her, fast as a rattler, raised the gun and pointed it at her chest.

"Shut up! Rolling around in the sack with the man who put a hole in your kin. I oughta … One. More. Word. … and you get dead today, too."

She said nothing else. Just watched helplessly as he walked away from the house. He stopped right before got to the woods and re-loaded the rifle, then he disappeared into the trees.

~

GRAYSON HEARD a gunshot and stopped moving, breathing. The far-away sound came from behind him, down the mountain. He thought. Perhaps not. The roar that still rumbled in his ears like constant surf distorted sound to the point that the shot could have come from just about anywhere. He took another step and another shot rang out. He spun around—instinct!—and scanned the trees, listening as the sound echoed off the mountainside.

He saw nothing. Heard nothing else. But he didn't think his hearing was lying to him about the gun that had fired the shots. It wasn't a .22 or a shotgun. It was a deer rifle. Probably a 30.06.

Though nobody paid any attention to squirrel season, deer season was strictly enforced. And deer season didn't open until the end of November.

His whole body ached for the weight of a rifle, the comfort of a weapon in his hand. Why had he talked himself out of going back for the .22, not that a .22 would be any match for a 30.06 in a firefight.

Listen to yourself Grayson! A firefight? Get a grip. You're in the woods on a West Virginia mountainside, not—

He didn't let his mind go any further, didn't want to call up images of that other place for fear he'd be transported there against his will, like he'd already been shanghaied again and again since he got home. How long would it be like this, with reality blinking on and off like a Joe's Beer Joint sign?

He shook it off and began to angle south in the general direction of Hickman's Thumb—a more or less thumb-shaped granite outcrop thirty feet across and twenty feet tall that jutted out of a sheer ridge into a meadow. He scanned the undergrowth and the shadows—which were getting deeper now with the cloud cover overhead. By force of habit, he moved silently through the trees, looking for even a tiny splash of out-of-place color. Piper said Maggie had taken Sadie's blankie—which was pink.

He didn't call out to the children, but moved quietly through the trees. He had already come far enough to be seriously spooked! Of course, maybe Carter'd run into them a mile from home! Grayson hoped so, because if his brother hadn't seen them either when the two met up … Grayson didn't want to go there.

So many places in his mind he didn't want to go! Every day, new black-box land mines. His own wife actually believed he shot her little brother! How crazy was that. No crazier than the red mud on his boots when he'd have sworn on all he held sacred he hadn't been anywhere near Blood Creek.

And "his own wife" might not be that for very long.

"I'm done! That's it, we're through! I want you out of my life and Sadie's life. It's over between us, Grayson."

Only it wasn't. Piper's understandable hysterics aside, she was his still, for the time being. That was clear this morning as soon as she began to scream. And she would remain his wife as soon as he could convince her—

A sound. He stopped, listened. Far away, he couldn't tell from where …

"Suuuny! Where are you, Honey?"

His heart sank. Carter hadn't found them either! Where could two little girls possibly have gone all by themselves?

"Suuuny, come to Unka Car—"

The cry cut off abruptly in mid-word. Something had interrupted him. Maybe Carter found them! And maybe that wasn't what it was at all. Grayson began moving again silently through the trees in the direction he thought the cry had come—Hickman's Thumb.

~

CARTER HADN'T BEEN GONE from the house for an hour before his throat was raw and his voice gravely from calling Sunshine's name. But he knew his brother'd been right— even if Maggie tried to hide from the searchers, she'd never be able to shut Sadie up once the toddler heard Unka Cardur calling her.

The image of her face, giggling and crying out, "Again-again!" brought an entirely different kind of ache to his throat. If anything happened to that precious little girl…

Like maybe losing her father, you mean? Like watching her father get hauled off to prison … for a crime he didn't commit?

Carter shook his head wearily. He had been listening to that voice and all the other voices inside him try to shout each other down all night, as he lay on the lumpy couch trying not to hear Piper sobbing into her pillow on the floor in his dying mother's bedroom.

What had he done? And how could he possibly un-do it?

He didn't know much, but the answer to question number two was pretty clear. He couldn't!

"Suuunny!" he called, picking his way across the slanted hillside. He could see Hickman's Thumb in a flat space up ahead. How had Maggie carried a toddler through these woods? And her feet were cut! Okay, not seriously. But she was a little kid—weren't little kids supposed to be wimps? "Where are you, Suuunny?"

Nope, much as Carter'd like a do-over, the eggs were

scrambled. Carter, Jesse and Buster went to prison. Or Grayson did. For something that wasn't his fault.

...wasn't his fault...

A sudden realization lit up his mind like a lighthouse beam on a reef. Maybe Grayson wouldn't go to prison after all! He'd been in some kind of blackout or flashback or whatever they called it, hadn't he? He wasn't responsible. It wasn't his fault!

Yes!

Grayson's chilled soul warmed to the idea like hot breath on frostbitten fingers.

A good lawyer could make hay out of all of it. Grey'd been a chaplain, for crying out loud! And his unit got massacred. National Guard from one small community gets called up, shipped into war without enough training and eighteen of them come home in body bags. And there's Grayson, right in the middle of it. Their chaplain, the man charged with getting brokenhearted soldiers through all that pain and suffering ...

The engine driving Carter's thoughts screeched to a stop and all the thoughts behind slammed into it—bam, bam, bam. Grayson *had* been through hell. And now he was about to get blamed for something he didn't do. Something Carter did.

And it wouldn't be the first time, either.

SPLASHING WATER.

Giggles.

The whump, whump, whump of a broom hitting a rug.

Shhh, Becky. Shhh.

Grayson's boots on the creek bank.

Carter snatches them, turns and runs back across the creek.

Becky reaches out to him.

He shoves her aside and keeps running.
Knocks her down *and keeps running.*

CARTER HAD MADE it to Hickman's Thumb and he leaned against one of the smaller boulders, panting. Not because he was out of breath but because the images had taken his breath away, clamped an iron band around his chest and squeezed.

Could he really do the same thing again?

There was movement off to his right. He turned, calling out, "Suuunny! Where are you?"

The only response was a quiet so profound it roared in his ears. The silence all around him was more than just a condition. It had substance and the air was heavy with it. An eerie chill raised gooseflesh on his arms.

"Suuunny, come to Car—"

Something moved in a nearby thicket. The leaves of the bushes rattled.

Carter instinctively straightened and began to back away slowly. More leaves rattled. He sucked in a ragged breath.

A deer leapt out of the brush and bounded off through the woods. Startled, Carter jumped, maybe even grunted in surprise as the white-tail doe vanished in the trees. Feeling foolish, he chuckled at his own edginess and turned back toward the big outcrop in the center of the pile of boulders.

Riley Campbell stood ten feet away grinning, holding a 30.06 pointed at Carter's chest. His hammering heart leapt into an even faster rhythm then, so fast he couldn't detect the individual beats, just a steady hum beneath his ribs.

MAGGIE TENDERLY BRUSHED a tendril of honey blond hair back from Sadie's forehead and continued to murmur. It wasn't a song, really, or even a tune. It was only a sound, like the buzzing of bees around a hive. She lay beside Sadie who was stretched out on her pink blanket in the shade of a huge azalea bush on the far side of a flower-covered meadow from a huge rock jutting out of the ridge. Maggie lay close to the sleeping toddler, her lips brushing Sadie's left ear, humming her tuneless noise so the sound of Mr. Carter calling Sadie's name wouldn't awaken her.

The spot she'd chosen for Sadie's nap was secluded, with brambles on three sides forming a natural fence. The low-hanging branches of the bush, which would be covered with huge pink or purple blossoms in the spring, granted the whole area a cool gloom. The poor little thing was worn out from walking, even riding on Maggie's hip had exhausted her. And since she'd awakened the little girl as soon as it was light enough out to see and skipped her morning nap altogether, it wasn't surprising that the child was falling asleep on her feet. As soon as Maggie spread out the blanket on the ground, Sadie'd popped her thumb in her mouth and was out in seconds—well before Maggie began to hear Mr. Carter calling in the distance. His voice got closer and closer, so she gently bunched the blankie up against Sadie's right ear and hummed for all she was worth in her left.

Maggie couldn't let him find them. Not now! She'd tried to warn them but they wouldn't listen and the darkness in Maggie's head kept getting bigger and bigger. It had grown so huge during the night she couldn't even close her eyes for the fear of it, had finally done the only thing she could think to do.

She had to save Sadie from the gobbling monster. The others were grownups, she'd rationalized, they'd be able to escape.

Carter's voice got louder and louder. It hadn't roused the sleeping child yet, but he was getting closer. Should she gather Sadie up and try to make a run for it before she heard him. Because if that little girl heard her Unka Cardur calling …

She turned the humming up a notch and tried to keep the sound constant, without a hitch between breaths. She grew as still as possible. Her heart thumped in her chest so loud she was afraid that sound would waken the sleeping child. She wanted to cry, but couldn't. She was so frightened, so alone. It was all she could do not to whimper. And so *tired!* The big blackness in her mind, rumbling and boiling that threatened to eat her alive had kept her wide awake all night.

Her eyes began to close. She fought it but her voice faltered and her vision blurred. Struggling to keep her eyes open, she saw through a forest of eyelashes something … yellow. There were weights on her eyelids and they closed, but with great effort she blinked them back open. A yellow butterfly? Did a yellow butterfly flutter out of the meadow and land on the ground beside her? She closed her eyes, blinked them open again more slowly. A white one came next. Two more yellows, a monarch and a blue landed on the limb of the azalea bush above her head. Before long, butterflies were everywhere, covering all the low branches of the bushes that stretched out to hide them.

Then the slow opening and closing of their wings synchronized. All the wings opened at the same time and closed at the same time, like breathing in and out. But instead of generating a tiny movement of air with each beat, the wings generated silence. Open and closed.

Quieter and quieter. Within seconds, Maggie could no longer hear the cicadas buzzing in the bushes on the high side of the meadow. She couldn't hear the trees' gentle creak or the birds chirp. And Mr. Carter's voice—if, indeed, he was calling out at all anymore, was completely gone. The two little girls were wrapped in butterfly silence so profound Maggie could not even hear the sound of her own humming. Was she humming? Was she even awake? Or was she dreaming? She didn't know. The world dissolved in a pale yellow light.

Chapter Twenty-Six

Even with his damaged hearing, Grayson could make out the voices coming from Hickman's Thumb long before he was close enough to be seen. The taut wire of his survival instinct, vibrated, hummed and he slipped into combat mode.

He crept from tree to tree, getting closer and closer, angling down to the rock formation from higher up the mountain. At first, he couldn't hear what was being said, but he picked up on the hostile tone and recognized Carter's voice. When he was finally close enough to understand, he knew who else was talking.

"…can't be serious! You don't really believe my brother would … ?"

"Don't believe it. Know it! And he's gonna pay for what he done. The both of you are."

"I thought we'd already been over that part, how I am the one McCullough in all of West Virginia who couldn't possibly have … "

"Oh, I checked you out, don't think I didn't. I asked around and you was where you said you was. I ain't gonna shoot you 'cause you shot Zeke. I'm gonna put the both of you in the ground because one Campbell's worth two McCulloughs—three, four, more'n a dozen! The two of you dead won't even skim the surface of the debt. But it's the best I can do right now and I am proud I get to honor the blood of my daddy and my brother by spilling as much McCullough blood as I am able."

Riley ordered Carter to go over to the base of one of the large boulders scattered around the north side of the Thumb and sit down on a rock next to it, told him they'd wait "real quiet like" until they heard Grayson calling for his little girl.

"You make one sound. You grunt, you hiccough, you even fart to warn him and—"

"Why shouldn't I?" Carter challenged. "You're going to kill me anyway. What's to keep me from yelling my head off as soon as I hear him—"

"…holler for them little girls that's lost out here in the woods, the one that's got McCullough blood in her, too? If I can't have the two of you, I'll find that youngun and put the bullet in her that was meant for her daddy!"

Grayson flattened himself against a tree and tried to think. He had to figure out what to do, and it had to be the right decision. Panic would get them all killed. He took a deep breath and recognized the calm that settled over him.

Doin' the necessary.

The nearest weapon was at the house. It'd taken more than three hours to get here. Even going straight back home instead of angling up the mountain and back down, he couldn't hope to make a round trip in much under four hours and he didn't think Riley's patience would hold out that long.

If you're outgunned, you have to outsmart. That's what Sergeant Hotchner always said.

Grayson was unarmed except for the Bowie knife on the belt of his fatigues, which was no match for a rifle at any distance greater than three feet!

Well, there is was then. He had to figure out a way to get within three feet of Riley. If Grayson could climb the Thumb, he could get above Riley. Even from that position, he wouldn't be able to jump down on Riley unless the little man moved right up next to the granite slab and stood directly below him, down on the far end where the rock was less than fifteen feet tall. But Riley couldn't get to Grayson either, couldn't climb with a rifle in his hands. And the rock was so wide, he couldn't back up far enough to get a shot at Grayson on top of it.

Grayson studied the terrain. With sides as smooth as an ice sculpture, the granite Thumb jutted out from the ridge into a clearing. But on the north side there was a tumble of boulders and smaller rocks beside it and Grayson could climb those to the top. Except that Riley and Carter were leaned against one of the boulders on that side and there was nothing but meadow—grass and ground cover maybe two feet tall—between the Thumb and the forest.

How could he possibly get from the trees to the rocks without being seen?

Rangers.

Grayson had sat around many a fire listening to stories by and about the rangers, men who slithered like ghosts through the jungle into enemy encampments. Faces blackened, special camouflage, those guys only ate Vietnamese food so they'd even smell like the gooks!

He remembered what one of them had said one night.

"It's not about heavy cover. If you've got any cover at all, you can hide. The trick is *don't move.* The eye's drawn to movement. You go slow enough, take an hour to go a foot, nobody will see you."

There was one spot where a bush extended out toward the rocks from the trees. There was ten or twelve feet of grass, two feet tall maybe, between the bush and the nearest rock. The sky was a sheet of slate gray. Over the course of the next few hours, the sun would begin to sink behind the mountain and its shadow would extend out over this end of the meadow, not making it dark, but making it dark*er* than it was now. Shadowy. He was dressed in camo, could rub dirt and lichen on his face and in his hair and use grass and weeds to break up the contour of his head and body.

Twelve feet in … say two hours. That'd be rocket-fast for a ranger.

Was he nuts*?* Riley was facing the other way, but one wrong move, or maybe Riley just decides to walk this direction to take a leak—Grayson would be a sitting duck.

So Plan B was?

There was no Plan B. Either he bailed out, left his brother to die, or he gave this a shot. Grayson's heart began to bang, a stone pestle pounding a stone mortar, hammering his courage into dust. He turned and crept off into the woods to find dirt and lichen before he could change his mind.

CARTER MADE a couple of vain efforts to talk some sense into Riley but the trigger-happy little man jabbed the rifle in his direction and told him to shut his face and keep it shut. No noise.

And so they waited.

Carter was soon amazed by how patient Piper's squirrelly older brother could be. He sat quiet. Didn't fidget, didn't pace or skulk around, peeking from behind the rocks at the woods. He was a man in a deer blind, waiting for the unsuspecting buck to walk into his sights so he could drop it with a shot through the heart. Riley figured to hear Grayson calling Sadie as he got near. It would be easy to get the drop on him.

Carter sat coiled, waiting for an opening. Any moment of inattention, he intended to jump Riley. It'd probably get him killed, but it was better than dying and taking Grayson with him.

Piper needed one of them to come out of this alive!

"Care if I—?"

Riley yanked the rifle up and glared at him.

"...smoke?" he finished in a whisper.

"Suit yourself," Riley whispered back.

So Carter smoked. One cigarette after another. The minutes crawled by. He sneaked a look at his watch— didn't want to call attention to the fact that they'd been waiting a long time. He knew what Riley apparently didn't. Piper must not have mentioned that he and Grayson were supposed to meet here at noon and it was already past two o'clock. Where was he?

Carter took the last drag off his next-to-the last cigarette and flicked it away with his finger, watched it sail with a breeze past the grassy area about thirty feet behind Riley.

Something there caught his eye. Could that possibly be … ?

He looked instantly away, fussed around putting his lighter back into his pocket, then fiddled with the package that contained the lone remaining cigarette.

Making himself wait until he had counted slowly to 500, he reached up and scratched his forehead, momentarily hiding his eyes so Riley couldn't see where he was looking.

Was it…? No. Maybe …

If there was even a chance, he needed to make sure Riley didn't happen to glance that way.

"Since it's not likely I'm going to see another sunrise," he whispered, so quietly Riley instinctively leaned a little toward him to hear, "would you indulge my curiosity. I'm just wandering … the Campbell clan totally out of the shine business?"

Riley grunted a laugh under his breath.

"Maybe." He eyed Carter. "How 'bout you indulge my curiosity," he whispered softly. "I've heard rumors you might be involved in the trade—personally. Didn't b'lieve none of 'em, of course."

"Well, you shoulda," Carter whispered back. "I got five stills. I put the first one in Tree Frog Hollow. The spring there's as clear as rainwater. Uncle William always said McCullough shine was the best hooch around because the water was better than anybody else's. And he was right."

Carter had Riley Campbell's undivided attention now.

CARTER SAW HIM! Or saw something. Grayson was almost sure because all at once his brother engaged Riley in an animated whispered conversation that Grayson's muffled hearing reduced to a few intelligible words.

He ignored it, concentrating on the infinitely slow ballet of movement that had transported his body a little over seven feet in the past ninety minutes. He controlled his breathing; chest barely moving. Face sliding across the ground, eyes open a slit, measured blinks that took at least thirty seconds each.

He had emptied his mind of all thought, calmed his heartbeat, placed his whole being in a kind of suspended animation that was absolutely here, feeling every grain of dirt, twig and leaf he touched, with no thought beyond the next pebble his cheek encountered as it coursed slowly down his face.

He had come to the most psychologically challenging part of the journey. His whole upper body was now completely out of sight behind a rock. All that remained in the short stand of grass was his legs from the knee down and sock feet. He must not change his movement now, though, must continue to crawl with the same agonizing slowness, face in the dirt, eyes squinting.

His heart took up a heavier beat and he allowed himself the luxury of allowing his chest to expand with his breaths. Not inching along. *Millimetering* along.

∾

Maybe it hadn't been such a good idea to get Riley talking about shine. It had definitely captured his entire attention, but he was getting more and more agitated by Carter's revelations.

"You lyin'!" Riley spat at him, his voice low and tense. He had grown too upset to whisper. "You tellin' me you got stills in three places up on Stag Ridge? No possible way. Ain't no water up there."

"Wrong, wrong and wrong," Carter said, matching Riley's volume, providing cover for any small sound that might ... if Grayson was really out there. But how could he be? Carter hadn't dared look a second time and all he'd seen was a lump, kind of a dark shape, a shadow. No, couldn't have been Grayson. And why would it be?

Grayson should have been here hours ago—and Carter was convinced his brother had, indeed, gotten to the rocks then. Grayson wouldn't have been calling out to Sadie. He'd have come up quietly, seen what was going down, and done the only sensible thing—run. A man's intent on shooting you and you're unarmed—you run, no shame in that! Why would Grayson risk his life for … still, Carter thought he'd seen something, so he kept up the charade with Riley. What else was there to do?

"No, I'm not lying. Yes, I got stills on Stag Ridge. And yes, there's water there. A spring, but we had to dig down for it. Spotted some water dripping out a crack in a rock. Took almost six months to dig it out, but now it produces all the water we need, cold and clear."

"An you 'xpect me to b'lieve that? That you McCulloughs can call water out of a stone? Can you fly, too?"

"Well, yeah, as a matter of fact we can," Grayson called out from the granite outcrop above their heads and Carter was afraid Riley was going to shoot him in surprise. The little man leapt to his feet, his eyes huge and swung the rifle in the direction of the voice.

"How'd you get up there?" he gasped, swinging the rifle back and forth, trying to cover the whole top of the rock at once.

Grayson didn't answer.

"You hear me? I said how'd you get up there?"

Still no answer.

"Answer me…" he turned and pointed the rifle at Carter. "…or I'm gonna plug a hole in your brother's belly so he bleeds out slow and painful."

"I told you," Grayson said. "I flew."

But the voice didn't come from where it had before. It was impossible to see the flat top of the huge slab of granite from below, of course, and Grayson was now at the far end of it.

Riley swung the rifle in that direction.

"You stay right where you are, you hear me?"

There was a clatter of rocks halfway back toward them from where Grayson's voice had just come.

"I said stay put." He turned the rifle on Carter and cocked it. "Your brother's got less than a minute's worth of breathing unless—"

"You're not going to kill Carter," Grayson said. He'd moved again, but not all the way to the far end of the rock. Riley swung the rifle in the direction of the voice, tried to adjust.

"I ain't? Really? Well listen to this gunshot and then tell me I—"

"Because my brother is your ticket out of the electric chair."

Grayson was in a different spot. Not far this time from where he'd just been, but enough so Riley wasn't exactly sure where he was. And Riley wasn't demanding he be still anymore.

Carter watched the drama with increasing admiration, almost as a spectator. Grayson had done such an astonishing thing, to show up out of nowhere like he did, that Riley was clearly rattled. And in little and big ways, Grayson was keeping him off balance.

"How you figure that? Like I told that sister of mine who's gonna be a widow before the sun sets, I ain't trying to get away with nothing. I'm gonna kill the both of you and then go to Suzie's Place,

buy beers all around and tell the world where to come and find your worthless bodies. Shoot, if I's an injun, I'd scalp you and show 'em the hair."

"No you're not," Grayson said calmly. "Because you don't want to scream out your last breath in agony when they turn on the juice and fry you in Moundsville. Ever seen a man fry, Riley? They bite their tongues off and their eyeballs squirt out of the sockets and dangle on their cheeks."

Carter watched Riley's face grow pale. He'd turned to cover Grayson's new position without a word of protest. Grayson had moved to the far end of the rock again but didn't raise his voice, and Riley unconsciously took a couple of steps in that direction to hear him. "Only that's not going to happen to you, Riley, because you're going to walk away from this a free man, going to grow old bragging to your grandchildren how you made the McCulloughs pay for shooting your little brother."

Riley said nothing.

When Grayson spoke again, he'd moved really quickly halfway back down the rock so he was right above Riley, and he spoke in a menacing whisper.

"And you're not going to scalp anybody, Riley. You don't have a knife. *I'm* the one with a knife."

WHEN MAGGIE OPENED HER EYES, the sun had moved down behind the mountain, taking the light in the cloudy sky with it. The two children no longer lay in the shade of the azalea bush but in a deep shadow beneath it.

There were no butterflies and Maggie wasn't sure if there ever had been or if she had just dreamed it.

She sat up and looked tenderly down at Sadie still asleep beside her. Though she had no memory of *before*, Maggie was absolutely certain she had never in her life loved anyone as much as she loved this child. Sometimes the ache of it welled up in her chest and she could hardly catch her breath.

Brushing her lips softly across Sadie's cheek, she whispered, "Wake up, little pretty."

Sadie opened her eyes—purple eyes!—and looked up at her.

"Mabie loves Sabie," Maggie said softly.

Sadie reached up, put her arms around Maggie's neck and hugged her sleepily, a small smile denting shallow dimples in her cheeks.

"I need go potty," she said.

She stood and Maggie helped her down with her panties, holding her so it didn't splash on her legs. Then Maggie gathered the pink blankie into a sack, putting in the last small piece of cheese, half an apple and the flashlight with the empty Mason jar. They'd filled the jar with water out of a small creek they'd crossed long before they got to the big pile of rocks she could see across the meadow. But the jar had no lid and she'd spilled the rest of the water hours ago.

When Sadie saw the jar, she whined, "I'm thirssy."

"We'll get you a drink soon as we can," Maggie said brightly. "We need to walk a little first." She reached into the blanket sack and retrieved the half apple. "This'll wet your lips." She'd given all the food to Sadie, had eaten nothing herself. "You wanna walk or you ride?"

"Hold you."

Maggie hefted Sadie up onto her hip and headed into the woods away from the meadow. As soon as she awoke, black had bloomed menacingly inside Maggie's head. In fact, it felt like the black was seeping out into the world around her. Maybe the woods really were dark, but she didn't think so. She thought the dark was coming from her. She had to get Sadie away. Away and up.

She put Sadie down on the ground.

"Come on, Sugar. Can you run with me?"

It was flat here, for a little while, before the land began to climb again. And they had to move fast. The black was coming.

"Run with me, Sadie! Come on!"

The black smile in the distance grinned down on them as the two little girls, one with flaming red braids and the other with blond curls, ran through the trees toward the rising mountainside.

~

RILEY CAMPBELL WAS SPOOKED. Grayson could hear it in his voice. But he was interested, too. It hadn't entered his pea brain that there was any way he could make it out of a double murder alive.

"How you figure I kill you and Carter and they let me walk?"

"You're not going to kill both of us. You're just going to kill me. If you can, that is. You're going to let Carter live—hey, you said yourself he's the one McCullough you know *didn't* shoot Zeke—because Carter's going to save your miserable little life."

As soon as he finished speaking he hurried halfway down the rock.

"You don't think I can kill you? How you figure that? I'm the man with a gun, and if you'd been packing you'd a shot me a long time ago. You got a knife, you say? Well, bring it on. We'll see how you fare—"

"And that's how Carter's going to save your life."

"Talk sense or I'm gonna—" he began, as he moved to stand below where Grayson was speaking.

Yes! Riley was totally unaware that Grayson now controlled where the little man stood.

"Carter's going to make you a free man because he's going to tell the sheriff that Riley Campbell didn't ambush a U.S Army Chaplain who came home from the war with a pocket full of medals. He shot a madman with a knife who was trying to kill him. He shot Grayson Addington in self defense."

Riley said nothing at all. Good! He was thinking. And while he thought, Grayson moved. All the way to the low end of the rock where the space between it and the nearest boulder was the narrowest. When Riley stood there, he was at the closest possible point to the outcrop.

"You're saying … you're gonna come at me with a knife so I can shoot you?"

"No, that's not what I'm saying." Grayson said from his new position and held his breath. Sure enough, Riley walked down to the end of the rock below him to hear the rest of what he had to say. "I said I'm going to jump you and if you shoot me first, it's self defense. But if I get you …"

He let his words trail off. Let the silence drag out before he picked up the big rock he'd set aside for this purpose and threw it as far as he could down the length of the flat top of the granite outcrop. It hit, made a crunching sound and rolled toward the edge.

Then Grayson took his life into his hands. Betting that Riley had started to move toward the sound and had turned his back, Grayson stepped out in plain sight and leapt off the rock.

Riley was directly beneath him. He was, indeed, facing the other end of the rock, but he heard Grayson's movement and was turning back as Grayson leapt. He tried to fire but couldn't get a shot off before Grayson was on him.

There was no fight. Grayson had eight inches, and even as thin as he was, 50 pounds on Riley. He drove Riley into the ground and the freshly sharpened blade of his knife was at the little man's throat before Riley could suck in the breath that'd been knocked out of him.

"If I get you," Grayson growled. "I slit your worthless throat. In self defense, of course."

He dug the blade into Riley's neck and watched the blood begin to flow.

Chapter Twenty-Seven

As GRAYSON ADDINGTON drew the razor edge of his knife across Riley Campbell's neck, Nelson Warren sat at a workbench in his garage a hundred miles away and put the finishing touches on a bomb.

He mopped the concentration sweat from his brow with a monogrammed white handkerchief and sat back to survey his handiwork.

Not bad!

He had put considerable time and energy into figuring out what it would take to cause the proper amount of damage—which would not, of course, be catastrophic. He only wanted to blow a hole in Impoundment Dam #2— not a large hole, really, just one too big to repair, though his crews would make heroic efforts to do so. One so big that if —no, Grigsby had said *when*—the dam started springing leaks of its own, nobody'd even notice. Or if they did, they wouldn't blame Northfield Coal. Oh, no, no, no. They'd blame somebody whose last name was Campbell!

Shoot, the hole in the dam might release enough pressure to prevent more leakage, so when the sludge water was all drained out it wouldn't cost an arm and a leg to repair the thing. But all that was a long way out. It would take several weeks, maybe a month, for the lake to drain. One hundred forty million gallons was a lot of waste water. And the sticky, oily mess the black water would leave behind … it'd take way longer than a month for the unfortunates downstream to clean that up.

Warren had already established that he intended to take Bobby fishing on Sunday morning, so it would be no surprise when he couldn't be located immediately to be notified about the explosion. But as soon as he returned home to the bad news, he would rush to Sadler Hollow to inspect the damage and then offer every resource at his disposal to facilitate the evacuation of residents below Dam #1—as a precautionary measure only, of course. He'd express his sincere hope that workers would be able to repair what *someone* had done to the dam. But if the damage was too extensive … well, that was out of his hands.

Warren wallowed the unlit cigar from the left side of his mouth to the right, and gingerly inspected the sticks of dynamite he'd rigged together to blow from a single fuse. A long fuse. He intended to be well up on the hillside above the dam before the actual explosion. The hillside afforded a view of both lakes and both dams.

Warren had the perfect place to set the charge in #2—the drain pipe Grigsby was forever mewling about. Two years ago, rains had been fierce and the little chief engineer had persuaded Warren to construct an emergency spillway in the dam to relieve the pressure. Like the hole in the top of a sink, if the water ever came dangerously close to the top of the dam, it would hit the pipe first and drain out. They dug into the eighty-five-foot-tall structure on the downhill side about twenty feet from the top to set a pipe three feet in diameter all the way through it. They'd made it four hundred feet into the five-hundred-foot width of the dam, laying pipe as they went, before budget cuts put the project on hold. In a tight economy, there were better uses of men and resources than digging a hole in a dam.

Nelson intended to set his charge inside Grigsby's drain pipe, place the dynamite at the far end and feed the fuse out behind him as he crawled backward to the entrance. A fuse that long would give him plenty of time to get to safety before the charge blew.

He studied the bomb. Had he used enough dynamite?

He wasn't sure. He'd watched miners set blasts when he was in training, but he'd never actually done it himself. And he couldn't very well ask somebody to show him how. The sticks he'd snatched during his inspection of a strip mine in Logan County were far bigger than the ones they'd used long ago in the mine where he'd worked, more powerful, too, he was sure. But how much more powerful —that he didn't know.

What if his bomb only damaged the dam but didn't knock a hole all the way through it? That would be worse than doing nothing at all. Federal inspectors would be crawling all over the dam then, thicker than flies on road kill.

He picked up three more sticks of dynamite, paused, picked up two more and bent back to work.

~

"Grayson, wait! You can't just slit his throat."

Carter had leapt forward and snatched Riley's rifle up off the ground when he'd dropped it. He now stood with it pointed at Riley, who lay on his back with Grayson on top of him, sinking his knife into the skin of Riley's neck.

Grayson turned and looked up into Carter's face, and with the tiniest movement, a lifted eyebrow, widening eyes, an almost imperceptible nod, gave him the "brother look," and Carter read it like a blind man with his fingers on raised dots.

"He'll die too quick," Carter continued. "That's not how he planned to take you out."

"You're right," Grayson said, and reduced the pressure on the blade that had made a thin, red smile under Riley's chin. "You're definitely going to be taking a dirt nap today, as we used to say in 'Nam, but I'm not going to plant you quick. I want to enjoy this."

He got up off Riley, then reached down, yanked the little man to his feet and flung him like a rag doll up against the rock. Riley's eyes were dark pools of threat and hatred, the color of a murky well in which a possum or rat had drowned. But he stared at Grayson now in surprise, horror and wonder. Grayson knew he must look a sight! Dirt and mud covered his clothes and every exposed body part, grass, leaves and moss were mashed into his hair, stems of grass stuck out of his shirt collar, cuffs, the waistband of his pants and the tops of his filthy brown socks like straw on the Scarecrow in the Wizard of Oz. His appearance alone had Riley totally spooked. And that was good. Real good.

"Remember that time I told you about when we were questioning gooks?" Grayson said to Carter.

"Which time? The time you cut the guy's ears off and stuffed them down his throat?"

"No, the other time." Grayson ambled over to where Riley cowered against the rock face. "The time we castrated the guy and—hey, look at that, Carter." He pointed to a widening dark stain on the front of Riley's pants. "Mr. Campbell isn't a big boy—he didn't go wee wee in the potty."

Grayson laughed, the sound as metallic as coins dropping into the slot of a pay phone.

"In 'Nam, if we found a guy like you in our unit, we killed him ourselves. It's called 'friendly fire.' But there's nothing friendly about cutting bullies down to size. They're all the same, nothing but gutless little cowards."

He was standing right beside Riley now.

"And speaking of cutting…" He held up the knife with Riley's blood dripping down the dirty blade.

Riley looked pleadingly at Carter.

"He's crazy, Carter. You can see that. Nuts. You got the gun. Shoot me!"

Grayson leaned close, smelled the twin stinks of urine and fear sweat and fought off a wave of memories.

"No, Riley, I'm not crazy. And you're waaaay more than just a coward. You're stupid! You're an idiot and a fool! You very nearly gave whoever really *did* shoot Zeke a free ride past go and $200."

Grayson leaned even closer, inches from Riley's face and dropped each word like an individual stone into a pond. "Because. It. Wasn't. Me!"

There was genuine shock and surprise on Riley's face. Not disbelief, though. Very good!

"But … you was coming out of the woods … you almost shot the sheriff with the .22 you was carrying. Ramona told Crystal." The sheriff's big-mouth secretary. Figured. "And she told—"

"I went squirrel hunting, you moron!" Grayson roared. He said the next words slowly "Where the squirrels are." Everybody knew the best squirrel hunting was on the west side of Naked Turtle Mountain—not around Blood Creek.

"But I didn't shoot any. I never fired the rifle. Which the sheriff will find out when he gets around to looking into such things. And when he matches the bullet they pulled out of Zeke's back, he'll see it *didn't* come from my gun."

"That's a stupid Campbell for you," Carter scoffed from behind Grayson. "Ends up in the electric chair for killing the two people who *didn't* shoot his little brother. Real sweet revenge, Riley. Give that man a cupie doll."

Grayson could see the gears turning in Riley's head.

"Then who did shoot Zeke?" he bawled.

"I've been back in Sadler Hollow for six days," Grayson said quietly, then rumbled, "How would I know?" Riley flinched back from him. "*I* know it wasn't me and *you* know it wasn't Carter. Who does that leave?"

"It was a McCullough!" Riley bleated in fearful defiance.

Grayson sighed. "Maybe it was. Or maybe it was some guy Zeke cheated at poker, or the boyfriend of some girl he flirted with. Or space aliens! What I do know is I came this close to dying today for something I didn't do." He held the knife up in front of Riley's nose. "And that piece of Spam, my friend, is on your sandwich!"

"Look, Grayson, I didn't know … I thought …" Riley was groveling, sniveling. "I mean, you was in the woods, you tried to shoot the sheriff. What was I supposed to … anybody woulda thought…" But he was sincere. If there was one thing Grayson was good at—or used to be anyway—it was reading people, and Riley meant what he was saying.

Inwardly, Grayson relaxed. Whew! He had accomplished what he'd set out to do—convince the little weasel that he was innocent. Because if Grayson couldn't do that, the only way he and his family would ever be safe from Riley was to kill him. And Grayson did *not* want to kill his wife's older brother—not when she already thought he'd paralyzed the younger one.

Riley slumped against the rock when Grayson stepped back and turned to Carter.

"What do you say Carter? He was going to kill you and he knew you didn't do it. What should we do with him?"

"We make him pay!" Carter growled. Riley looked stricken. *"Unless … he helps us find Sadie."*

"I will! I will. I'll comb these woods, look under every rock, up every—"

"No, you won't. You'll hightail it out of these woods and go get help," Grayson said.

"We've only got a couple more hours of daylight," Carter said, then turned with the gun toward Riley. "Because we wasted the whole afternoon on you!"

"If we can't find them before dark … I want an army of searchers out here at first light," Grayson said. "And if you don't arrange that, I will come looking for you when this is all over." He cleared the distance between him and Riley in two long strides, gathered the little man's tee shirt up in his fist and slammed him back against the rock. "I learned things in 'Nam, Riley, ways to kill a man slow. I will find you and I will make you wish that the worst thing that happened to you before you died was your eyeballs popping out on your cheeks."

"I'll bring the Sheriff, the state police, I swear," Riley gushed. "Why, shoot, I could get a dozen of the boys from Suzie's Place to help me find my sweet little niece got lost in the woods."

Grayson rolled his eyes, but he let go of Riley's shirt and the little man danced away out of his reach.

"Go on, now—get!" Carter said. "If you don't hurry, it'll be dark before you get to the house."

"And you tell your sister—my wife!—when you get

there that we're okay, and that we're not leaving these woods until we find Maggie and Sadie."

Riley cast a longing glance at his rifle in Carter's hand, but knew better than to ask for it back. Merely turned and took out running through the woods.

Grayson and Carter stood and watched until he was out of sight.

"Think he believed you?" Carter asked.

Grayson turned to him. "Do you?"

"Yeah, I do. I think he—"

"Not what I'm asking. I'm asking, do *you* believe me? Do you think I shot Zeke?"

The question caught Carter totally off guard. He looked shocked and—understandably, Grayson supposed —upset by it. Then he dropped Grayson's gaze, looked at the ground and said, "No, Gray, I don't think you shot Zeke."

Grayson started to ask if he'd help convince Piper of that, but the subject of Piper was not a can of worms that needed to be opened right now. So he asked instead. "Think we can trust Riley?"

"What choice do we have?"

As it turned out, Riley Campbell did not betray their trust. He wanted nothing on earth as much as he wanted to get down that mountain and gather up a herd of cops and volunteers to look for those two little lost girls. But then, Riley'd wanted to kill Carter and Grayson, too, and that hadn't worked out like he'd planned, either.

Chapter Twenty-Eight

MAGGIE WAS SCARED, but Sadie was too little to know there
was anything to be scared of so if Maggie acted like everything was fine, Sadie'd never know. But everything wasn't
fine. It was almost dark and with the cloudy sky, there was
no full moon, no starlight. When the sun disappeared
below the horizon out there beyond the mountains, it
would be as pitch black in the woods as the inside of a
lump of coal.

It already was that dark inside her head.

She had Marian's flashlight. It had been sufficient to
make their way without tripping through the minimal
undergrowth in the forest early this morning. But in the
profound dark after sundown, the pitiful little puddle of
light it made when it peeled back the darkness would
barely keep them from falling off a cliff.

Where were they going to sleep? What were they going
to eat?

Maggie did not know how much longer she could keep
staggering forward, carrying the two-year-old first on her
hip, then her back and when it was flat enough, perched on

her shoulders. Though her bare feet were tough, they were scratched and bruised from hours of walking on the uneven, rocky hillsides. Sadie now stubbornly refused to take a step on her own, merely whimpered and cried.

She'd pop her thumb out of her mouth long enough to whine, "Sabie not wanna walk. Sabie wanna go home." Then huge tears would form in her purple eyes and slide down her rosy cheeks. "I want Mommy and Nana."

This wasn't what Maggie had expected, not how she'd planned it at all.

She'd had no idea how hard it would be to get to the top of the mountain! It hadn't looked all that far from the house, and when she left she hadn't been able to think beyond getting there—just up!

Maggie had known she couldn't climb straight up the mountainside. It was too steep, even if she hadn't been carrying Sadie. She knew she'd have to cut across the mountain, angling ever higher and higher up the side until she reached the top. But once she got deep into the woods, "up" wasn't always possible. The uphill way was often blocked by bushes and brush, rockslides or fallen trees. Or just un-climbable. When she finally struggled to the top of a crest, she'd see a taller one ahead. And another. They'd used up precious daylight sleeping and for the last hour or so they had been forced by the terrain ever downward, not up. What would she do when the battery on the flashlight gave out? Sit huddled with Sadie under a bush all night—in the dark?

She stopped and hiked Sadie up on her hip. Rested her weight for a moment on the stump of a tree.

Sadie moaned in a pitiful, tired wail, "Sabie hungry."

Maggie had not eaten a bite of the food she'd brought from the house. She'd given it all to Sadie. Now, there was nothing left.

Then Sadie burst into real tears, sobbing as if her little heart would break. "I want my m-m-mommy!"

Maggie's voice cried out in anguish, too, silently, in the dark, hollow cavern of her mind where all the light had been gobbled up by the thing that was coming ... coming... *Please! I can't find my way.* She closed her eyes and begged simply, *Help!*

When she opened her eyes again, she saw it.

True, she'd been looking down at the circle of flashlight beam on the ground, picking her way around the tree roots and rocks. She hadn't been looking ahead. Still, she could have sworn it hadn't been there a minute ago. Up ahead, through the trees, was a light!

Carter was the one who finally said out loud what they both were thinking but didn't want to admit.

"Gray, we gotta make camp while there's still light."

Long shadows melted into the dust and it was fast approaching that moment of change from light to dark when both and neither are all around.

"They're still out there somewhere." Grayson's voice was anguished. "We have to keep looking."

"If we couldn't find them in broad daylight, you think we're going to stumble across them in the dark?"

Grayson said nothing.

"I think we need to go back up to that little meadow we passed through a few minutes ago. There's a creek and maybe we can bag something to eat with this." Carter held out the deer rifle.

Grayson looked awful. He was still covered in the camouflage dirt he'd smeared on himself hours ago. More than that, he looked spent. He was the one, Carter reminded himself, who'd performed a miracle rescue, and the energy that must have taken was energy the thin man standing in the failing light didn't have to spare.

"We have to keep looking," Grayson said. But he didn't believe it and Carter didn't even bother to argue with him.

"You sit down before you fall down," Carter said. "There's deer around here, saw one this afternoon at Hickman's, and I might get lucky at dusk in that meadow."

White-tailed deer stayed hidden in the shadows during the daytime but came out at dawn and dusk to feed in open areas. Since deer season didn't open until November, the woods were well-stocked, the animals not yet skittish.

"I'll do it," Grayson said, his voice flat and expressionless from exhaustion. "I'm a better shot."

Again, Carter didn't argue, merely handed Grayson the rifle and the two started back through the woods to the meadow.

THERE WAS ONLY one light on in the little cabin Maggie and Sadie approached through the woods. The rest of the house was black. Maggie had no idea what she'd say to the people who lived here, how she'd explain why she and Sadie were wandering around in the woods at night.

As it turned out, she didn't have to explain anything. She knocked repeatedly on the back door, but no one answered. It was, of course, unlocked, so she opened it carefully and called out "Is anyone home?"

No response.

Though she felt like Goldilocks in the fairytale book she read to Sadie, she walked into the kitchen uninvited and began to look around. She flashed the beam of light on the walls first, searching for switches. There were none. The house had no electricity. Then she shone the light along the rustic wood countertop and swept it across the kitchen table. That's where she spotted the apple pie.

Sadie made for it, climbed up into a chair, stretched out across the table and buried her hands in the lattice crust before Maggie could stop her.

"Sadie, wait!"

But Sadie shoved the sticky hunks of dripping apples into her mouth with total abandon and after only a moment of hesitation Maggie laid the flashlight on the table and joined her, not realizing until that moment how famished she was. They'd eaten half the pie in the space of about two minutes before she noticed the note on the table beside it. She licked the sticky off her fingers and held the flashlight to read it.

"Thelma go on and take the pie I done made it and we cain't go to the potluck after church cause my sister Mamie come git us. Ma's took po0rly again Me and Harolds gone to see to her."

Joy spread over Maggie's face. The house would be empty all night! No one would be here until before church tomorrow morning. She and Sadie had a place to stay.

They continued to shove gooey hunks of pie into their mouths for awhile, neither speaking, only making contented slurping, smacking sounds. Then Maggie licked her fingers clean a second time and picked up the flashlight.

"Let's go find that light we saw from outside," she said.

It wasn't difficult to locate. The light shone out from a kerosene lamp that sat on a table in front of the window in a back bedroom. Maggie stared at it in wonder. Nobody just walked out of a house and left behind a lit kerosene lamp! Why hadn't the lady who'd written the note leaned over the lamp and gone whoooosh before she got into the car with sister Mamie and drove away?

Better question—why was the lamp burning in the first place? It'd been daylight when the lady and her husband left.

She and Sadie would still be out there in the dark, cold woods if this light hadn't shown them the way. To shelter, safety, warmth, food. Maggie sank down into a rocker beside the bed and struggled not to burst into tears of relief. Sadie climbed wordlessly into her lap and stoppered her sticky lips with her thumb.

GRAYSON LOOKED BETTER. He'd cleaned the shocks of grass out of his shirt collar, pants and socks, washed his face and hands in the cold creek water, then dunked his head to get the dirt, twigs and moss out of his hair. He came up sputtering and gasping but obviously refreshed.

Carter watched him in the flickering campfire light, glad he no longer looked so alien. Throughout the late afternoon, he'd had to struggle not to stare at his brother. Grayson's wild appearance was a product of what he'd just done and Carter wasn't even entirely sure what that had been, much less how he'd managed to pull it off. But he understood perfectly the result. Grayson had saved Carter's life.

If their roles had been reversed, would Carter have done the same?

Had he, in fact, ever in his life been the kind of brother to Grayson that Gray had been to him? When Becky died, everything had come apart, the world had split open like a giant ax had cleaved it in two. Gray was on one side of the fissure in their family and Carter was on the other. Over the years, the crack continued to split wider and wider until their father finally toppled over the edge into the dark abyss and the two brothers were so distant from each other they could never again connect. What had happened that day so long ago had … what *had* happened? If he only knew for certain, he … would what? What was there to be done, then or now?

He reached over and turned the makeshift spit where the hunk of venison hissed and sputtered in the flames. The chunk of meat they'd ripped out of the flank of the little doe Grayson had felled with one shot wouldn't be cooked very evenly—probably burned on one side and half raw on the other, but the two men were so famished their mouths were watering at the smell.

Carter had snagged a couple of handfuls of dried-up, late summer blackberries from a bush on the edge of the meadow and now he made small piles of them, using the huge, heart-shaped leaves of a Catawba tree as plates.

Grayson crossed back to the fire and sat down beside his brother on a log that formed a perfect bench.

"It's so dark out there. And it'll get cold. We've got a fire and something to eat and they've got …" His voice seemed to catch in his throat. When he continued, it was in a ragged whisper. "They must be so *scared.*"

"We'll find them tomorrow," Carter said, trying to sound more confident than he felt. "But if you don't eat something you won't be in any shape to look."

He watched Grayson struggle to collect himself. After a moment or two, Grayson asked, "Is it done?"

"Maybe. How would I know? You were the one who helped Ma in the kitchen."

The mention of their mother punched both men in the gut. She could be dying with neither of her sons there to tell her goodbye. Or already dead.

The moment dragged out, then Carter seized the conversation and yanked it forcefully into the right-here, right-now.

"I never tried to cook a chunk of deer meat over an open fire like a hot dog."

"Even raw, it'll taste better than K-rations. Well, some of them weren't bad, but the ones with ham and eggs would have gagged a maggot. Didn't cook them over a fire, though. We used C-4 explosives."

"To cook dinner?"

"Yeah, we'd stretch it out into thin strands, then light the strands with a cigarette lighter. Burned hot and clean and didn't make smoke for the gooks to sight in on."

Carter felt utterly overwhelmed, totally unable to countenance what had happened to the younger brother he had once teased and played jokes on.

It got quiet. Carter stared into the flickering flames of the campfire, watched them twist and cavort, Spanish dancers dressed in bright red and orange dresses. Grayson looked out over the fire into the darkness of the forest beyond.

"This part's charred at least." Carter's voice sounded too cheery even in his own ears. "I don't know if that means its done inside but we can give it a shot." He reached to pick the spit stick up off the rocks they'd pilled on both sides of the fire. "I need your knife."

Grayson said nothing. Didn't more.

"Gray?"

Carter turned and looked full into his brother's face. Grayson's eyes were open, but they were moving, like your eyes move when you're asleep and dreaming. Tears pooled there, then he blinked and they spilled down his cheeks.

"Grayson," he said softly. You weren't supposed to wake up a sleep walker, were you? Was this the same thing?

"Ooshemy," Grayson mumbled, his eyes darting, watching a movie Carter couldn't see.

Then he said it again, clearer: "Oot-shay e-may." Pig latin. Shoot me.

PIPER HAD PACED FOR HOURS. Had walked miles without ever leaving the house. She had worn a path from the back window in the kitchen to the side window that looked out over the side yard to the front door, across to the front window that looked out over the valley, down the hallway to Sadie's room and back down the hall to the kitchen. Around and around the mulberry bush the monkey chased the weasel …

As she walked, her mind raced, wondering what she should do. After awhile, after the sun went noon, then slid down the western sky, she wondered what she should have done.

With a car, she could have roared down to the Craddocks, where she'd borrowed the coveralls for Maggie. The nearest neighbors, they lived in the first house on Northfield Road before town. She could have screamed at them to go get the sheriff—they didn't have a phone either —then roared back up to the house. She would have been gone twenty minutes down and twenty minutes back up. A little over half an hour. She could leave Marian that long. After she took her medicine, she sometimes slept for hours.

And sometimes she woke up five minutes later in agony, and Piper sat by the bed and talked to her, read to her, stayed with her. What if she woke up and Piper wasn't there. What if Marian lay in the bed and died alone?

Of course, when Riley blew out her tires, that had

made all her decisions for her. There really was nothing Piper could do.

Except wait.

And worry.

And pray.

Only no words formed, no prayers came. All she could manage was to sob out their names, one at a time, with all the pain and fear and love attached to them and agonizing over what could be happening to them at that very moment.

Sadie.

Grayson.

Carter.

Maggie.

She'd been so frantic with fear and worry about Zeke, but that receded now. Whatever lay ahead for the boy, at least he was safe, alive. That hadn't seemed like much a few hours ago; now it was all in the world that mattered. And Marian was alive, too, at least for a little while longer.

But the others …

So around and around the house she went. Around and around in her head the horror images chased each other, monsters with vicious teeth and yawning mouths and the smell of moldering corpses on their breath.

Marian slept after the pills Piper gave her when Grayson and Carter left. When she awoke, her eyes were cloudy and she didn't seem to know where she was. She called Piper Evelyn, her sister's name, asked about Grayson and Carter as if they were boys off playing in the back yard. Talked about "plating" Becky's hair before church on Sunday.

The old woman's incoherence terrified Piper. No matter how bad her pain or how sick she got, Marian had remained Marian. She had been *there*, alive. Now, she moved in and out of semi-consciousness and semi-awareness.

By mid-afternoon, Marian's breathing had become labored. She moaned in pain. Then cried out. It was too soon to give her more medication. Should Piper give it anyway? There was no one to ask. No one to help her.

Finally, she gave in, gave Marian more medicine, but not a full dose. The old woman's moaning eased and she slipped into an uneasy sleep.

Piper went back to pacing.

As darkness descended on Sadler Hollow, it descended into Piper's heart as well. Her baby was out there in the woods in the dark. Her husband might be lying dead there, too. Alongside Carter.

Or was Riley still looking for them. After all, his truck was still parked outside; he'd never come back for it.

~

Riley hadn't come back for his truck because he couldn't walk. After awhile, he couldn't even crawl. Eventually, he stopped moving altogether.

He had left the Addington brothers at a dead run, anxious to put as much distance as he could between himself and the two men lest they change their minds and decide to use on him the gun he'd intended to use on them. Or worse. For the first fifteen minutes, he'd raced mindlessly through the woods, the skin on the back of his neck crawling as he flinched away from the bullet he feared any minute would ripe into his back.

But it didn't, so he slowed down. For almost an hour, he'd been merely jogging. That's when it happened. A root caught his foot and he tripped and pitched forward head first down a steep slope. He saw the drop-off coming, clawed at the dead leaves and the dirt, dug in his hands and toes, trying to stop his downward slide before ...

He fell almost twenty feet into a rocky creek bed. Broke his right arm and his left leg in two places. Riley shrieked in agony, screamed for help until he had completely shredded his vocal chords and couldn't make a sound. But he'd run so hard, so fast, he'd put a lot of distance between him and the Addingtons. So much that they couldn't hear him.

He actually dragged himself about fifty yards, clawing his way along the creek bank. Then his strength gave out. He knew his only hope was the search that would be mounted in the morning for the two missing children. His truck was still at Piper's. Eventually, somebody'd figure out that Riley was still in the woods, too, and come looking for him.

He had to hold out until then, that was all. He was near a creek so he had water. He was tough, he'd make it.

But just like Riley Campbell's other plans, that one didn't work out either.

Grayson was getting more and more agitated, babbling pig latin. Carter was afraid to touch him, hoped the mental convulsion would run it's course, but finally could no longer stand the pain on Gray's face and the anguish in his eyes.

Facing his brother on the log bench, he shook Gray's shoulder gently.

"Grayson. Bro. You okay? Grey, talk to me."

Grayson froze, then looked confused. He turned his gaze from the dark forest and stared hollow-eyed into his brother's face.

"Grayson ... what—?"

Gray's eyes didn't focus for a few moments, then he actually saw Carter instead of whatever freak show was playing at the drive-in movie of his mind.

"There was a little girl, a pretty little girl. Her name was Nguyen," Grayson said, his eyes locked on Carter's. "I just remembered that I shot her."

He started to cry then, dropped his chin and put his face in his hands. Carter moved instinctively, reached out and took his little brother in his arms. Grayson began to sob, great heaving, wrenching sobs that went on and on. Carter held him tight, didn't pat his back or anything, just held on. And he found he was powerless to stop the images of another little girl from forming in his head, and tears ran down his own cheeks and dripped into his brother's hair.

Chapter Twenty-Nine

As it did every morning, dawn on the flatlands changed the slice of velvet black sky above Sadler Hollow to navy blue. The rising sun cycled the navy through countless other shades of blue, each more pale than the last. But this morning, Piper couldn't see the transformation. She couldn't see anything at all through mist that didn't merely obscure the landscape but totally erased it.

The cool creeks that rushed down the mountainsides breathed mist into the humid summer air every evening, swirling white gauze with ragged, tattered edges. The creek mist sometimes lingered until the sun cleared Naked Turtle Mountain to burn it off. But true fog was fairly rare, and fog as thick as pudding and this far up the mountainside was something Piper'd never seen in her whole life.

She stepped out onto the front porch and couldn't even make out the gate in the fence. If she hadn't been beyond sobbing she would have burst into tears. How could you find lost children in the woods when you couldn't see them, when searchers and children alike were slogging through white quicksand?

~

Maggie stood on the front stoop of the little cabin in the woods and stared in disbelief at two things. No, stared through the first thing at the second thing. Mist, thick as the white bubbles of dish soap in the sink, had scrubbed away the features of the nearest trees, making them vague and indistinct. Beyond them was nothing.

What she could see through the mist that was closer than the trees was vague and ghostlike, too. But it was there. It was real. A *road*. Not a dirt track that meandered up the mountainside for miles and ended at this house. Before her lay a road that continued past the house and *up* the mountain. No more clambering through tangled undergrowth and stumbling over rocks. The road would take them effortlessly *up*.

And they had to hurry! As soon as she opened her eyes this morning, the darkness began to grow in her head.

Maggie fed Sadie fresh bread she found in the cabinet, smeared it with butter and jam from the icebox, and then took her out to the privy. She'd cleaned her up the best she could with well water last night before bed, brushed the leaves and twigs out of her hair with a comb she found on the dresser.

"Where's Mommy," the little girl wanted to know. She was tired and cross. "Sabie wants Nana and Unka Cardur … and Daddy."

"We'll see them real soon," Maggie assured her. But would they? *In the fog,* could anyone escape the monster that was coming, even grownups?

Maggie wanted to write a note to explain what had happened to the pie and the other supplies and to thank the folks who lived here for their unintentional hospitality. But there was no time. They had to go *now*. Leaving the

Mason jar and the flashlight inside on the table, she shoved Sadie in front of her out the door and hurried toward the road across the patch of dirt that passed for a front yard.

It was *coming*.

~

GRAY MUST HAVE SLEPT. He would have sworn he hadn't closed his eyes for more than a moment, but he must have because when he opened them, the world was gone. Though there was a creek nearby, this was wasn't mere creek mist. This was *fog*. He could barely see Carter, curled up on the ground beside the dead campfire.

As the night hours had dragged by on terror-leaden feet, filed with nightmare images both real and imagined, he had clung to one hope like a drowning man to a hunk of driftwood. In the morning, the woods would fill with searchers. It wouldn't just be he and Carter trying to find little needles in a hundred-thousand-acre haystack. They'd have help.

Nothing lit a fire under mountaineers like word of lost children! Every human being above the age of twelve who wasn't blind or lame would drop whatever they were doing and join in the rescue effort. There'd be hundreds of people, state police helicopters, tracking dogs. Two little girls on foot couldn't possibly have gotten so far they couldn't be located before they had to spend another night in the woods!

He envisioned folding little Sadie in his arms, smothering her with kisses—whether she wiggled and struggled to get away or not. But now ... how could you find anybody in this soup! It'd be gone by noon, maybe long before that, hard to tell, but the search needed to start at first light. This would cost them *hours.*

"What in the world …?" Carter had awakened. Maybe Grayson had said something out loud that roused him. Anymore, Gray had trouble sorting out what was reality and what was memory, let alone what he'd said aloud and what he'd merely thought.

Carter sat up and looked around like a still-wet baby duck in half an eggshell. "Maybe this is only creek mist," he said. He didn't believe that any more than Grayson did.

Grayson got to his feet, stiff and sore, feeling like a man of 50 rather than 26. He was paying now for the hours of constant tension in every muscle in his body yesterday as he crawled slowly through the grass.

"I'm not going to wait around for it to burn off," Grayson said. He slipped his arms into the long-sleeved fatigue shirt he'd used as a pillow, grateful for the warmth in the chilled, damp air. Then he sat on the log and began to pull on his boots. "We can follow this creek upstream. And up seems to be the direction of choice for our little fugitives."

He lifted his eyes and saw that Carter was staring at the boots. Grayson looked closer now, too, examined the bottoms. All the red mud had worn away. But how had it gotten there in the first place?

When Carter saw that Grayson had caught him staring, he stood quickly, turned and began to dust off his pants.

"We'll get above this soon—we're pretty high now," Carter said. Then he turned back to Grayson, his face set in grim lines. "I wonder … I've been thinking about Ma. If she …"

"Yeah. I thought about her all night, too." Her pained face was among half a dozen rip-your-guts-out images.

"When we hook up with the other searchers, maybe you …"

"I'll go home," Carter said. "You won't need me, I'll go sit with Ma."

Without another word, the two men turned and began trudging along beside the little stream. Up. Ever up.

~

Nelson Warren had intended to be headed back to Charleston by now, planned to do what he'd come to do at dawn, but he was only now arriving at the Impoundment #2 dam!

As soon as he drove into the mountains, he'd found the hollows and low spots awash in puddles of fog so thick he could only inch along. It had delayed him for hours. But now that he was up here above it all in the crisp morning sunshine, he thought to be grateful for the fog. The odds of being discovered, of somebody braving that soup to show up at an isolated dam site before church on a Sunday morning were long enough even for a non-betting man like Nelson Warren.

He had approached the strip mine site from the east side, through Cricket Hollow, and now stood on a hillside that granted him a view of both impoundment lakes and both dams. Beyond the dam on Impoundment #1, Sadler Hollow was filled almost to the brim with what looked like a puddle of Elmer's Glue.

Warren pulled his new Grand Prix Pontiac off the dirt track bulldozed for the coal trucks that had hauled away millions of tons of black sunshine from this site. He parked near the dam but behind a hill, didn't want some random piece of flying debris to ding the shiny black-over-silver paint job.

He opened the trunk and got out everything he'd loaded up in his garage the night before. Coveralls and boots, a miner's helmet and headlamp and a backpack containing the dynamite and fuses, which he very carefully shouldered and then set out across the dam to the spot where the end of the pipe protruded about four feet from the back side. He stopped, looked back at the hillside and let his eye measure the distance from the pipe to a point well above where debris from a small explosion might land. He'd have to be quick to get away from the dam and up to that point before the charge went off. Good thing he was a runner!

He looked down at the pipe sticking out the back side of the dam. What happened here today would be the beginning of a tidal wave of events that he'd ride like one of those California surfers all the way from backwater West Virginia to Washington, D.C.. He started to whistle.

Grayson and Carter began to come out of the fog in less than half an hour. Up ahead, the white gradually brightened. Like headlights seen through night mist, shafts of suffused light filtered down from the treetops to the ground. They left the creek bank then and climbed up out of the mist to the top of a rise and looked back down over the valley where a giant cotton ball had replaced all the features of the hollow.

"Well, attention Kmart shoppers," Carter exclaimed, and pointed through the trees to the left. "Is that …?"

"Strawman Road? Has to be! Can't believe we came this far."

Strawman Road had been so named because of the big scarecrow Jethro Donovan had set up in his little patch of corn next to where the dirt road curved away from North-field Road and snaked up to the top of Chicken Gizzard Mountain, where a mining road that lead to the strip mine and the impoundments split off it to the left like a casual part in a man's hair.

When the two men came out of the trees that hugged tight to the dirt road, both of them stopped at the same time, for the same reason. Before them in the powdery dust of Strawman Road were footprints! Two sets of small feet—one very small wearing shoes, the larger one barefoot—had passed this way. Beside the smaller set, the dust was smeared, like perhaps a blanket had been dragging in the dirt.

The trail lead up, of course.

Carter opened his mouth to call out, but Grayson stopped him.

"They'll stay on this road, no reason for them to go back into the woods—except to hide. We need to try to sneak up on them."

Carter didn't look like he agreed, but he didn't argue, merely nodded, turned and began a slow lope up the road. Grayson fell in beside him.

Maggie never heard them coming. Everything was muffled, muted by the darkness in her head that had grown, ballooned. Now, it was black around her vision, like she was looking through a tunnel and Sadie's voice sounded like she was down in a well.

Sadie had already grown too tired to walk and Maggie had just picked her up to carry her when the little girl suddenly wiggled out of her arms, dropped her filthy pink blankie in the dirt, and went running back down the road the way they'd come, Maggie had no idea what Sadie could have seen that—

Then she turned and there they were. Mr. Carter and Mr. Grayson were coming around the last bend in the road. Mr. Carter knelt down on one knee and held out his arms and Sadie crashed joyfully into him. But Mr. Grayson reached down and snatched her out of Mr. Carter's arms and covered her with kisses, tickling her and laughing, and then she started to laugh, too, and squealed, "Daddy!" Mr. Carter stayed where he was, kneeled in the dirt, and watched them.

For a few minutes nobody paid any attention to Maggie. She stood where she was, her heart hammering so hard in her chest it made her tee shirt move in the front with every beat.

They hadn't understood before and they wouldn't now. They'd stop her, or try to, and she couldn't let them do that.

CARTER STOOD up slowly and looked at Maggie. He'd never seen a kid so forlorn. No, more than that. Frightened, too. Seriously scared. He took a couple of steps toward her and she backed up a step, like she might actually turn and bolt into the woods. Then she fixed her eyes on Sadie and instead of running, she began walking slowly toward them.

Grayson noticed her when she was about twenty feet away. Carter saw his face harden and knew he had every right to be furious with the little girl. She had, after all, taken his daughter and run off into the woods with her. He steeled himself for Grayson to unload on the kid, but his brother didn't do that. Instead, he looked at her for a long moment then wordlessly handed Sadie to Carter and got down on one knee in the dirt, so when Maggie got there, they'd be eyeball-to-eyeball.

WHEN GRAYSON SAW Maggie walking slowly toward them, he felt anger well up in his throat. This waif from who knows where had shown up at his house, charmed his wife, his mother and his brother, then kidnapped his daughter! There was something wrong with the kid, seriously wrong with her and he didn't intend to let her anywhere near his family again. If the sheriff couldn't find out where she belonged, they'd have to find a foster family for her. He was through.

Then he looked into her eyes. The terror there was a beating, living, palpable thing. He'd only once before in his life seen a little girl so afraid. And 5 seconds later, he had shot her.

All the anger and recrimination turned to vapor and floated away. Maybe her fear was irrational—boogie-man, bad-dream stuff—but it was absolutely real to her and it had been so powerful it had driven her out alone into the woods. He hadn't been able to comfort a terrified Nguyen, but he could be tender to this frightened little girl.

"Maggie, Honey, I won't hurt you," he said. "Nobody's

mad at you. We've been so worried about you and Sadie. Come here and let's talk about it."

Maggie approached and as soon as she opened her mouth it was clear she was not afraid of him and Carter. Well, maybe she was, but she was more afraid of whatever internal monster stalked her.

"We can't stop now," she cried, her voice shaking. "It's coming! We have to get Sadie away or it will swallow her whole. We have to go, go——"

"Up," Grayson finished for her. "I know, that's what you said. But Honey, you had a bad dream, that's all, a horrible nightmare. It's daylight now. Everything's fine. It wasn't real."

"Yes, it was real—it *is* real!"

"What's real?" Carter asked. "What are you so afraid of?"

She took a deep breath, clamped her teeth together like she was trying to calm herself.

"There's no time for talking now. The black monster is coming. He's going to roar down and gobble Sadie up, swallow her whole, and everybody else in the hollow, too."

The color faded out of Grayson's world and for a moment he felt himself falling away, felt the cool morning air begin to turn jungle hot. But he fought it, shook his head, and the flashback faded into a vivid memory instead. The walking blackout he'd suffered leaving Nguyen's village. In it, there was darkness, but the darkness moved, was a living thing with evil intent, a *black monster* rushing toward Sadie as she played in the dirt outside his mother's house.

Maggie's voice came as if from a great distance.

"The monster's grinning now, smiling black on the mountain. But any minute it's going to …." She took another breath and then she was pleading. "Please not precious Sadie! You can't let it get her. We have to take her and run!"

She reached out and grabbed Carter's hand and actually tried to drag him up the road with her.

"Honey, you're not making any sense," Carter said, standing his ground. "There is no monster!"

"Yes, there is," Grayson said.

Maggie dropped Carter's hand and stared at Grayson, astonished.

Grayson had to concentrate to keep his voice from shaking.

"Did you hear what she said? The black smile on the mountain. She's talking about the dam. The black water behind it—that's the monster." He turned from Carter to Maggie. "Isn't it Maggie—that's what you're afraid of."

"The monster's behind the smile," she said, getting more agitated by the minute. "It's coming. We have to *go!*"

Grayson got to his feet, struggling to make sense out of something that made no sense at all. What he'd seen that day outside Yan Ling … Maggie had seen the same thing night before last in a nightmare. What had it been? A shared … premonition.

He felt chill bumps pebble his arms.

"She's afraid the dam's going to burst," he told Carter. "She's afraid any second we're all going to drown."

As Grayson turned and squatted down again in front of Maggie, he heard a noise behind them. He looked over his shoulder and saw an old red pickup coming slowly up the hill.

"Maggie," Grayson began. "I understand you're afraid of the dam. I don't blame you. I am, too, sometimes. But it's not going anywhere. It's been there a long time, and it's strong, tough."

Was he trying to convince Maggie or himself?

He reached out and took her hand. "We'll be fine. I promise."

The pickup pulled up beside them and stopped, belching a cloud of dust from the road and gray smoke from the exhaust. At the wheel was a woman somewhere between 65 and 500 years old. Her face was cratered with deep wrinkles, her eyes sunk into hollows spider-webbed with sagging flesh. The cheery smile she flashed them was missing teeth and the ones left were little more than stumps, blackened, like the remnants of a forest after a fire.

"Hidy. I'm Edna Turpin," she said. "You folks out for a Sunday morning walk, trying to get up high so's you can see the fog? It's a doozy, ain't it?"

She didn't seem a bit put off by the men's appearances —dirty and unshaven, their hair tousled. But they probably looked like most of the men she saw every day.

Then she got a good look at Sadie in Carter's arms and she actually gasped. "Oh, my goodness, I ain't never in all my days seen a little girl any purdier than that 'un. Them eyes and that sweet angel face, and blond hair like her daddy's." Sadie instantly cringed away from Edna deep into Carter's arms and stuck her thumb soundly in her mouth.

Edna turned to Grayson, who'd taken Maggie's hand. "And that there littl'un is—"

Maggie yanked her hand out of Grayson's and screamed, "No." He could see she was dangerously close to complete hysteria. "It's not okay and we're not okay and it's gonna eat us all up if we don't run!"

Then she burst into tears.

The three adults exchanged a look.

Grayson got to his feet and spoke in a low voice to Carter. "She is going to go off like C4 if we try to take her home right now. I think the only thing we can do is humor her."

"You mean take her and go … up?"

"Yep. Take her up to the dam and show her it's fine, that there's no black monster lurking behind it. I don't think she'll ever calm down if we don't."

But that wasn't the only reason Grayson wanted to go take a look at that dam. It was the boogie man in his closet, too.

"Are you suggesting the four of us walk all the—?"

"No, I'm hoping we can hitch a ride." He held out his arms to Sadie. "I'll take her …" and felt his throat tighten when she leaned away from Carter, her arms outstretched toward him. "You try to calm Maggie while the angel child and I have a little talk with our new friend Edna in the pickup truck."

Carter went to Maggie and knelt beside her. Grayson explained to the old woman as simply as he could what their problem was, then asked if she could possibly give them a lift to the dam.

"Them pore little things been lost in the woods for a day and a night a'runnin' from that little girl's nightmare monster?" Edna shook her head. "Well, get yoreselves in this here truck and we'll give this young 'un a peek under the bed so she can see for herself there ain't no monster hidin' underneath of it!"

Grayson turned to Maggie. "Come on, Sugar. We're going *up!*"

~

Nelson Warren clambered easily down the back of the

dam to the pipe sticking like a straw out of a chocolate milkshake. He wasn't merely fit, he thought to himself with pride, he was agile. Not bad for a man in his late 50's. Not bad at all.

When he got to the pipe, he peered in, but could only see a few feet before the tube gave way to absolute darkness. A claustrophobic man wouldn't have been able to pull this off, he thought. There was no room in there to turn around. He would have to crawl down the pipe, set the dynamite, then back out the way he'd crawled in.

For just a moment, the yawning black hole stared balefully at him with malicious intent, beckoning him to come on in and stay for awhile. For a *long* while.

He didn't have to do this. He could get back in his car and—well, actually, he did have to do it now. To turn around at this point would not be a rational decision but a reaction to fear. Give in to fear even once and it would become your master. Nelson Warren was his own master.

He set the bag on the floor of the pipe, opened it and took out the miner's helmet with a light on the front. He switched it on, took a deep breath of fresh morning air, then crawled into the pipe and began to shove the bag ahead of him into the darkness beyond.

~

Piper sat on the side of Marian's bed, holding her hand. The old woman's breathing was labored, but she was resting better now that Piper had given her another too-early dose of pain medication. Her eyes were open but Piper wasn't sure she knew where she was or what was going on around her.

Then Marian's gaze shifted to Piper's face and the look was as tender as a caress. Piper's throat ached with unshed tears.

"I been having the strangest dreams," Marian said. "Not bad, strange. I can't remember much about 'em, 'cept there was light and the music was … everywhere. It wasn't like you could just hear it. You could feel it like a warm blanket and smell it, the smell of the air after a spring storm."

Piper didn't trust herself to speak so she squeezed the old woman's hand, the skin fragile as tissue paper. She felt tears stream down her cheeks and reached up with the other hand to wipe them away.

"Tears ain't a bad thing. They're the truth your heart speaks."

"You need anything? Can I get——?"

"You don't really b'lieve Grayson could do a thing like that, do you?"

This time, Piper didn't speak because this was a conversation she absolutely did *not* want to have right now.

"You honestly think he could *shoot* your little brother … *Grayson?*"

"You don't understand. There was red mud——"

"Piper, Honey, things on the outside'll deceive you, trick you and confuse you. You got to look inside, down deep in your soul where truth is, where you *know* the man you married. Could he a-done a thing like that?"

Piper was silent. What was the *truth?* Could Grayson have ambushed Zeke? Suddenly, it was as clear as spring water.

"No, he couldn't," she whispered softly, ashamed she'd ever even considered the possibility.

Marian made an approving "mmmm" sound. The matter was settled.

"They ain't found them girls or they'd be back by now."

It wasn't a question, but Piper couldn't stifle a little sob in reply.

"Bless yore heart. Pain comes off you in waves like heat off a pot-bellied stove."

"I'm so *scared.*"

"God don't much like scared. Scared says to him, 'You ain't big enough or strong enough to handle what's goin' on in my life.' And them words smell like sulfur 'cause they come direct from the pit of Hell."

"But what if—?"

"What-ifs will wear you plum out, child. Them little lost girls ain't escaped the notice of the Almighty."

"It's not just Maggie and Sadie. I'm afraid—"

"For Grayson and Carter? Cause of Riley?"

"How did you know?"

"I'm dyin', Sugar, I ain't deaf. You think I slept through them gunshots? Or Riley hollerin'? He ain't gonna hurt nobody. He's a little runt of a thing and my boys is big, strapping men. They's fine. If they wasn't, I'd know it." She let her breath out in a sigh and her gaze shifted to the window. "But I ain't never gonna see either one of 'em again, not in this life."

"Why, of course you will."

"Naw." She looked back full in Piper's face. "I'm gonna go on home direc'ly. Just in a little bit. The veil 'tween me and glory's so thin I can see the light comin' through."

It seemed to take great effort to lift her right hand off the sheet, but she placed it on top of Piper's and patted softly.

"You rest easy, Sweetie. Right now the sun's shining in both them little girls' faces, the wind's blowing they hair and Sadie's a'laughin'."

Chapter Thirty

Sadie leaned out the cab window of the old red pickup truck and giggled at the wind in her face. Maggie sat in the truck bed beside Carter, with strands of hair escaped from her braids dancing in the wind like a candle flame.

Grayson was glad Edna was a chatterbox, prattling on about everything and nothing and all things in between. Her babble saved him from having to make conversation, and he didn't feel up to chit-chat. He felt now that battle-weary exhaustion that had become everyday normal in 'Nam. Not only in his body, but in his mind and his soul. He wanted nothing so much as to sit in a dim room alone and think of absolutely nothing for a long, long time.

The wind in her eyes made Sadie squint and before Grayson knew it, she'd closed her eyes altogether and lay with her cheek on her arm that dangled out the window. The universal lullaby—going for a ride—had put her to sleep. He eased her over into his lap, then stretched her out on the seat between him and Edna. She stirred, popped her thumb in her mouth, sighed and was out again. He snuggled her dirty pink blanket around her, loving her so much at that moment it was almost as painful as grief.

When they reached the ugly brown strip-mine scab where the top of Chicken Gizzard Mountain used to be, Grayson gazed out over Sadler Hollow below. It looked like a bowl full of milk. Strawman Road followed the top of the ridge, then curved right and descended into Cricket Hollow on the other side of the mountain. Right before the curve, a no-name mining road angled off to the left and followed the edge of the ridge toward the top of Sadler Hollow, where the black slurry dam stretched between Chicken Gizzard Mountain and Naked Turtle Mountain, holding back an impoundment of coal mine waste water in a stagnant, black pool. The behemoth pile of coal debris that was Impoundment Dam #1 lay less than half a mile up the valley to the east, where it imprisoned a far bigger lake filled with equally black, equally dead water.

Edna turned down the mining road, which was even bumpier than the main road, traversed by huge coal trucks and massive pieces of equipment. The bumps didn't awaken Sadie and Grayson thought the child was probably so tired she might sleep the rest of the day.

The old woman stopped on the top of the flat ridge well back from the edge above the dam where a 30-foot strip of bare dirt sloped sharply down from the ridge to a lakeshore piled high with jagged rocks and boulders as big as cars, jammed together in a jumble where they'd landed when a bulldozer shoved them off the side of the ridge.

When Grayson started to lift Sadie into his arms, Edna whispered. "Ya'll go on down and have your look-see. I'll stay up here with the littl'un."

He nodded thanks, got out, locked his door and closed

it quietly behind him. Edna got out and eased her door shut, then leaned back against the warm hood of the truck, shading her eyes from the bright morning sun.

Carter and Maggie climbed down out of the back of the pickup. Maggie's eyes were wide and wondering. She looked out over the panorama of valley stretched out below as if the image were registering for the first time, then nodded her head slowly and uttered a single, awed word: "Fog."

Grayson took her hand.

"Let's go take a close-up look at a monster."

She said nothing, merely walked between him and Carter toward the black lake. Grayson was careful to keep Maggie away from the front edge of the ridge that curved back from the dam. It wasn't a drop off, a sheer cliff like the dam, but on the Chicken Gizzard side, at least, the slope was so steep you wouldn't survive a tumble down it. The incline on the Naked Turtle side wasn't nearly as severe, but you'd still have to be a mountain goat to make it down alive.

WARREN WAS surprised at how glad he was to feel empty air with his feet as he crawled backward out of the pipe. This job had been more difficult and—go on, admit it, scarier—than he'd anticipated and he wanted nothing in the world so much as to light the end of the fuse in his hand and get out of here!

He eased down out of the pipe into the sunshine and took great, heaving gulps of good air as he opened the now empty sack and dropped his helmet down into it. Then he dug into his pocket for a lighter, an old-fashioned flint lighter, gold-plated, had his initials on it. He'd used it to light his cigars back when he actually smoked them. He flipped open the cap, thumbed the little wheel and a flame instantly appeared. He hesitated for a moment, then touched the flame to the end of the fuse. Sparks flew. Then the sparking light began to rush down the fuse into the black hole of the pipe.

He didn't remember that fuses burned so fast! In seconds, it was just a flickering light in the darkness. Warren turned quickly to climb up to the top of the dam and then run like his life depended on it to the spot he'd determined was high enough up the hillside to be safe. That's when he saw people below, standing above Impoundment Dam #1! If they looked up, they'd *see* him. He had to get out of sight—*all the way over the hill* and down the other side. Then he did run like his life depended on it.

Carter, Maggie and Grayson edged carefully down the steep incline, watching where they placed each step, digging their feet sideways into the loose dirt so they wouldn't slip and slide the rest of the way down. Once they got to the bottom, they carefully picked their way across the tumble of giant rocks and mining debris piled on the lake shore. Water that looked like viscous tar or used motor oil rose to within about fifteen feet of the top of the dam on their left. The three climbed out across the tumble of rocks until they were standing on a large boulder at the water's edge, looking down at the lake six or seven feet below.

Since they now stood in the bottom of a shallow, three-sided bowl formed by the ridges and the dam, there was no breeze and the stagnant stink off the oily, black liquid was almost over-powering—dead water, a chemical odor like sulfur and something else, something un-nameable.

"Is this it?" Grayson asked gently. "Is this the monster in your dream?"

Maggie's face was pale.

When she spoke her voice was quiet, filled with fear and awe.

"Uh huh. But it's not awake. Not yet."

WARREN REACHED the end of the dam, sprinted across the flat area beside the lake and began to claw his way up the hillside. He was panting and wheezing, a stitch in his side jabbed a dagger under his ribcage, but he didn't slow down. Unless he made it all the way over the hill, when the charge blew, the people below would look up and see him. They couldn't identify him from that distance, of course … *could* they? His hair! They might very well be able to see Warren's white hair! And they'd at least be able to tell he was a tall, skinny man and Addington said the Campbell guy who'd attacked him at the hospital was short. He struggled to climb faster.

And now that he'd actually done it, now that he'd lit the fuse, he was frightened, too. Like a little kid running away from a cherry bomb in a coke bottle, he wanted to get far away from the blast that would erupt in that pipe any second. He was no longer concerned that he hadn't made the charge big enough, that it wouldn't do enough damage, that it'd make a little hole in the top of the dam a work crew could fill in with a backhoe.

When he finally staggered the final few feet to the top of the hillside, he stumbled blindly across it and dived off the back. Gravel and small rocks imbedded in his palms painfully as he slid. He skinned both knees and tore his right pants leg before he finally came to a stop.

He lay there for a few moments trying to get his breath back, gasping from the strain—and from relief! He rolled over, looked up at the bright blue sky and sighed out, "I made it!"

They were the last words Nelson Warren ever spoke.

A great, grumbling roar split open the morning silence with such force the whole mountain trembled, shook like it was having a seizure. Then the center of the massive mound of coal slag that was Impoundment Dam # 2 heaved upward and erupted like a black volcano.

Warren had woefully underestimated the explosive power of the dynamite charge he had shoved four hundred feet into the guts of the dam. The instant the sparking fuse ignited the sticks of dynamite, thousands of tons of coal slag, rocks and mining debris spewed skyward in an ugly black column a hundred and fifty feet tall. When the velocity of the force propelling it upward had expended itself, the column collapsed and the rocks rained back down to the earth like meteors, sprayed out in every direction. They splashed down into the lake, hammered in the top, trunk and hood of Warren's new Pontiac and buried the man himself under four feet of rubble. No one found his body until it started to stink.

❧

At the first cracking sound of the explosion, Grayson instinctively dropped into a crouch and covered his head protectively with his arms. Maggie staggered backward a step, then stared up the valley, her eyes the size of dinner plates. Carter gasped, then couldn't draw in another breath, could only gawk in stunned disbelief. Something had exploded—it looked like *inside* the dam. A geyser of coal debris shot into the sky, then plummeted back to the earth leaving a cloud of black dust suspended in the air that obscured the explosion site.

With their attention riveted on the erupting dam above them in the hollow, nobody noticed a small girl with honey-blonde hair running toward the lake as fast as her little legs would carry her.

The crashing, rumbling roar of the explosion had catapulted Sadie from sleep. She sat up in the truck cab, alone and so terrified she couldn't even cry. Her eyes wide, she looked out the driver's side window and could see Unka Cardur, Mabie and Daddy in the distance. She turned toward the door beside her. It was locked, but Sabie knew how to unlock it. Mabie had shown her. She pulled upward with all her strength on the button, used both hands, grunted from the effort. When it slid up with a click, she pushed down the door handle and the door swung open. Quick as a baby rabbit, Sadie climbed down to the ground and took out at a dead run toward the lake, her long blonde curls flying out behind her in the breeze.

Nobody saw her reach the dirt incline, where her feet slipped out from under her and she slid on her backside all the way to the bottom. She got up and began to climb onto the boulders, now too out of breath to call out. She crawled up on the lowest one, then the next and next until she reached the top of the pile, then she started across the jumble toward the lake.

That's when Edna spotted her and started to holler. She ran as fast as an old lady with arthritis could run across the ridge toward the incline, yelling at the three figures on the lake shore still staring in shock up the valley.

Maggie and Carter turned at her cry, but the explosion

had joined all the other explosions to form a jackhammer hum in Grayson's ears that all but blotted out sound altogether. He didn't hear Edna. But he heard Maggie.

"Saaaadie!" Maggie cried.

The word bounced around inside Grayson's skull like a pinball, setting off lights and whistles. He turned slowly toward her, his eyes wide, then saw the look of horror on her face and followed her gaze to the tiny child clambering across the rock pile toward them.

And then Sadie vanished.

Piper heard a rumble like nearby thunder, but recognized the sound for what it was—an explosion. Blasts set off at the strip mine far up the valley reverberated down to Sadler Hollow almost every day, making Piper grateful she hadn't lived here when Northfield Coal was ripping off the top of Chicken Gizzard Mountain. Marian said that two or three times a week, the cabinet doors flew open and plates, saucers or glasses leapt to the floor and shattered.

But today was Sunday. The mine didn't operate on Sundays. And this blast didn't sound like the others she'd been hearing for months. It was louder, like it was much bigger or much closer. It couldn't have been closer, of course, because there was nothing to blast on this end of Chicken Gizzard Mountain anymore.

"What was that sound?" Marian asked. Her breathing was labored again. It seemed to take so much effort for her to draw in a breath that Piper tensed every time she exhaled, waiting/hoping/praying that she'd have the strength to breathe back in. "Was it … trumpets? Could it be …?"

Her eyes grew bright. She looked up toward the ceiling and seemed to see something there Piper couldn't see.

The sound most certainly had not been trumpets. Something had blown up in the valley above the house. Something on the ridge behind the dam.

GRAYSON HAD no memory of crossing the rocks from where he stood beside the lake to where his daughter had disappeared. He was just instantly there, down on his knees, staring into the crack between the boulders that Sadie had fallen into.

Carter was less than a heartbeat behind, calling, "Sunshine!"

A little voice Grayson could barely hear in his rumbling ears replied clearly. "Unka Cardur. Sabie fall down!" And then she started to cry.

Grayson sucked in a great, heaving gasp of relief. She was unhurt! He could see her standing about eleven or twelve feet below, looking up at them. The gap she'd fallen through between two giant hunks of rock couldn't have been more than seven or eight inches wide. She must have scooted down the slanted side of the smaller rock like a slide into a space shaped more or less like a long-necked wine bottle—narrow at the top, wide at the bottom.

He began to look around for an opening where he could climb down to get her. As he looked, his gut began to synch into a knot. The boulders were jammed tight together. He couldn't see a space between any of them that was big enough for him to fit.

There was a rumble.

Carter said something Grayson's damaged hearing didn't quite catch, but the horror in his tone needed no translation.

Grayson turned to look up the valley toward the dam. What he saw clamped his heart in a steel vise. The dust had cleared, revealing a gash in the dam at the site of the explosion. The rip extended from the top of the structure half way to the bottom, a forty-foot slash where black water had begun to flow out in a deep-throated rumble. As they watched, spellbound, a hunk of the top of the dam beside the rip washed away, almost in slow motion. A waterfall of black water cascaded out behind it, down the back of the dam and began to flow down the valley toward them.

Even though Carter's voice was hushed, this time Grayson heard him clearly.

"That dam, it *can't*—it's not going to hold."

No, it wasn't.

The implications of that froze both men in place for maybe five full seconds. A flood was about to surge down this valley, water from a lake five times the size of the one below them. The smaller dam couldn't possibly hold the water back and the flood would gush down the mountainside into Sadler Hollow, which was swathed in an impenetrable veil of gauzy white fog.

They'd never see it coming! No one would have any warning at all.

There was another rumble as another hunk of the dam washed away. Now the water gushed out the crack where a twenty-foot section of the dam was gone.

The sight planted sudden terror in Grayson's gut to gnaw away at his insides like a lazy rat. What if … if that dam completely let go all at once, just *collapsed?* The whole lake behind it would roar down the valley, a wall of water thirty, forty feet tall! They had to get to safety on top of the ridge quick, go … *up.* Exactly where Maggie had kidnapped Sadie to take her.

But Sadie wasn't going anywhere. She was stuck down there between the rocks.

Chapter Thirty-One

PIPER GOT up from Marian's bedside and went to the window that looked out at the mountainside behind the house. Or would have if the puffy white fog hadn't obscured the view. For a brief, passing moment, she yearned to go racing out the back door and climb up above the fog. What a sight it must be to look back over the hollow at it, lying on the floor of the valley like cotton candy. A lake of white enclosed by the mountains. That sight would make a Kodak moment, she thought, if she'd had a camera, and the heart to care about beauty or art or anything except the family that life had chewed up and spit out bloody on the ground.

"Can you see it?" Marian's voice was soft, wistful.

"No, there's nothing to see," Piper said without turning. "The fog's still got everything socked in."

"It's so lovely it takes my breath right out of my chest."

Piper turned around and saw that the old woman was staring raptly out the window, but she knew the rheumy eyes weren't looking at what she could see there. There was an expression of such joy on Marian face, Piper knew. It was time.

~

Understanding passed between Grayson and Carter without the necessity of words.

"Maggie, get up to the top of the ridge!" Carter said. When she hesitated, he barked, "Now! *Go!*" and she turned and headed back across the rocks toward the dirt incline.

Grayson and Carter began frantically looking for some way to reach Sadie, who stood with her thumb corked in her mouth in a small open space between boulders far out of arm's reach.

"Maybe there's some way we could roll … move the smaller …" Grayson began but didn't bother to finish because it was a ridiculous suggestion. The "smaller" rock was roughly the size of a Volkswagen, jammed up against a larger one that was bigger than a Sherman tank. Even if the rocks had been lying out in the open, the two men couldn't have budged either one.

Grayson scrambled over the tops of the rocks, looking for anywhere he might squeeze through, somewhere he could move some other rocks, maybe, to enlarge a space —anything!

His glance passed over Carter, then yanked back to him like a fully extended rubber band. Carter's face had gone so white that blue veins showed at his temples. Grayson followed his gaze. The stream of water that had gushed out the hole in the Dam # 1 had reached the smaller lake and the water level in it was beginning to rise, like water in a bathtub with the spigot turned full blast.

The hammer blow of realization hit Grayson so hard it

knocked his knees out from under him and he dropped to the rock. The space where Sadie was trapped was only a foot or two above the lake. It would fill with water as the lake spread out of its banks and up the sides of the ridge. At the rate the water was rising—in three, maybe four minutes …

In a panic, he threw himself at the opening Sadie'd slipped through, jammed his arm down into it and tried to wedge his shoulder in, reach down to her. But Sadie would have to jump up more than twice her own height to grasp it.

His leg then, it would reach farther. He turned to shove his leg into the … it wouldn't reach far enough.

If she could swim, maybe she could just rise up with the water.

Sadie couldn't swim. In fact, he doubted she'd ever been in water deeper than a bathtub. When it began to swirl up around her, got into her face, she'd panic and…

Carter suddenly reached down, grabbed the front of Grayson's fatigue shirt and yanked it open, sending buttons pinging away like BBs. Grayson immediately understood what his brother meant to do.

"Hey, Sunshine," Carter called down to her as Grayson ripped open the buttoned cuffs and yanked his arms out of the long sleeves. "I need you to grab hold of your daddy's shirt sleeve and hold on tight and we'll get you out of there. Okay?"

The child stopped crying.

"Sabie want up wif you and Daddy."

Grayson turned to lower the shirt through the space between the rocks.

Carter dropped to his knees beside him. "My arms are longer!"

Grayson moved instantly aside and handed him the

shirt. Holding the end of one sleeve, Carter fed the shirt down into the hole. When he lay on his belly and stretched his arm out into the hole, the other sleeve dangled six or eight inches above Sadie's head.

Grayson saw something dark edging across the dirt toward Sadie. Black water. He nudged Carter and nodded toward it, rasping, "Hurry!"

"Okay, Sunshine, we're going to play a game," Carter said, his voice shaking with tension. "Get up on your tippy toes and grab Daddy's shirt. Then hold on tight, tight as you can. And don't let go! Can you do that?"

He jammed his shoulder into the crack between the rocks to lower the shirt another couple of inches. Sadie nodded, reached up and took hold of the sleeve. With one hand. The other held her thumb securely in her mouth.

"Both hands, Honey. Use both hands."

Sadie shook her head no and kept her thumb where it was.

"You can't hold on tight enough with only one hand. You have to use both."

Again she shook her head.

"Sadie," Grayson said, trying to keep the desperation out of his voice. "Remember when I pushed you in the swing?"

She nodded.

"You had to hold on tight with *both* hands so you wouldn't fall out, remember? You have to do that now. Please, Sweetheart, do that now."

Reluctantly, the little girl pulled her thumb out of her mouth, stretched up and grabbed the sleeve of Grayson's shirt with both hands.

"Hold tight," Carter said. "Tight as you can."

Then he began to pull slowly, steadily upward. The little girl began to rise.

Grayson flattened out on his belly and jammed his arm down into the crack. If Carter could just get her high enough so he could grab …

Sadie was still several feet beyond Grayson's extended fingers when she lost her grip and fell. She didn't slide down a smooth rock on her butt this time. She dropped three feet and landed on her knees, then flopped backwards and banged her head on the rock.

She lay there, still.

Neither Grayson nor Carter moved. Then she sucked in the air that had been knocked out of her and began to shriek. She sat up—in two inches of black water—and wailed.

Nothing the men said to her could calm her. She got to her feet and Grayson saw that both knees were bleeding. She was hurt and there was no way to get past that, to make a two-year-old understand that skinned knees didn't matter, she had to stop crying, grab the shirt and hang on.

The men couldn't even calm her down enough to get her to listen. Helplessly, they watched the black water rise up her calves. She didn't like that either. The water must have been cold. So she cried even harder.

Grayson shot a glance at the dam. More hunks had washed off the top.

When the water reached Sadie's knees it stung where she'd skinned them. She danced up and down and wailed louder. Then she looked up into the faces of her uncle and father and held up her chubby arms.

"Hold you!" she cried. "Unka Cardur! Daddy! Hold you!"

But they couldn't pick her up. They couldn't hold her. They couldn't do anything but watch her drown.

~

PIPER SUCKED in a little sob and crossed back to the chair by the bed. She took Marian's hand, but the old woman seemed not to notice. Just stared, with tears forming in her eyes.

Her breathing had eased completely now. No longer was she hauling in great heaving, rasping breaths and sighing them back out in exhaustion. She was, in fact, hardly breathing at all. Shallow little breaths that barely moved her bony chest.

Marian shifted her gaze to Piper's face.

"Yore a good girl, Piper." She took a little sip of a breath. "Grayson's lucky to have you." Another little breath, smaller. "Carter'll get over losing you one day and find himself a good girl, too. You'll see."

Piper could only nod. Tears streamed down her face but she didn't bother to wipe them away.

"You love yore family with a fiercesome strength, best as you can ever day...promise."

Somehow Piper found her voice to answer.

"I promise."

"Yes..." Marian sighed out the word and closed her eyes.

Piper waited. Held her own breath. Hoped. But the old woman didn't breathe back in again.

She was gone.

Piper brought Marian's hand to her lips, kissed it tenderly and then let herself break down in tears.

CARTER LOST IT. "No, NOOOO!" he screamed in horror and frustration. He banged his fists on the rock again and again, leaving behind bloody prints.

Grayson had felt this ripped-open, airy sensation in his

belly only one other time in his life—when he looked around the edge of a rug hanging over the limb of a tree and saw Becky in the creek. She had drowned with him only a few feet away, too.

He leaned his head back and cried out in anguish, "Saaadie!"

The world dissolved, grayed out. Color slid down reality like a painting splashed with water, leaving everything around him a black-and-white image. A photograph. Then another image began to form on top of it, an image in verdant, green jungle color.

But this flashback—if that's what it was—was different from the others. Grayson wasn't imprisoned in the scene, a participant in the madness; he was standing outside it, observing. He could see himself, like watching Charleston Heston come down the mountain holding the Ten Commandment tablets.

A way-too-thin man with hollow, vacant eyes, U.S. Army Chaplain Grayson Addington dropped to his knees and cried out, "Saaadie!"

And Grayson heard now what the dazed chaplain had heard, an echo in his head, another voice crying out at the same time.

A moment had followed then of such profound silence that surely the universe had been holding its breath. Something had happened in that moment. Something fearful and powerful. The chaplain/soldier had sensed it, but didn't have any idea what it was.

Grayson sensed that same power now.

"Gray!" Carter shook his shoulder.

Grayson opened his eyes and looked into the space between the rocks where his brother was pointing. At first, Grayson's mind wouldn't process what his eyes saw. Then the impossible image resolved into an equally impossible reality.

Sadie was still crying. But not as hard as before because *Maggie* was hugging her, soothing her.

On her knees in the narrow space with the bigger rock jutting out above her, Maggie held Sadie in her arms so the child's skinned knees were up out of the thick black water. Maggie's cheek below the pale shadow of a shiner was deeply scratched and bleeding. Her arms were scraped raw, her shirt torn. Somehow, she had wormed her way into the enclosure through spaces so small she had barely fit.

"Maggie?" Was all the stunned Carter could say.

"I have to put you down for a second," she told Sadie, set her down and struggled to her feet. She had to turn sideways in the narrow neck of the wine-bottle-shaped enclosure. Sadie wailed and clawed at Maggie because the cold black water now reached to her waist.

Standing, Maggie was in a space too small to turn and pick Sadie up with both hands, so she reached down and lifted her by the arm as high as she could with her right hand, grunting from the effort. "Up onto my shoulders," she gasped, "so the water won't sting. I'll help you."

Sadie reached out and grabbed Maggie's shirt, then one of her braids, wet and slimy with black goo. She pulled herself upward, struggling and wiggling until she was finally standing on Maggie's shoulders. Then Maggie took hold of Sadie's ankles, using both hands now, and began to lift her into the narrowing bottle-neck space above her head.

"Climb up the rock, Sadie," she said, breathless. "Climb!"

Sadie pawed at the rock. Carter lay on his left side, his arm stretched out and jammed his shoulder as far as he could down into the crack to reach farther.

"Push me!" he told Grayson, and his brother leaned with all his weight on Carter's other shoulder, bounced on it, surely tearing all the skin off Carter's upper arm.

"That's right, reach out, come to Uncle Carter..."

Grayson held his breath.

"Good girl! Just a little farther."

Grayson could barely hear Sadie whimpering through the roar in his ears.

Then Carter grunted, *"Gotcha!"* as his fingers closed around a little hand.

Now, Grayson pulled on Carter's right arm to drag him out of the crevice where he'd wedged his shoulder. As soon as Carter's shoulder was free, he flopped over on his chest, reached his other arm into the crack, took Sadie's other hand and began to pull her up. It was a tight squeeze. She started to cry again when she scraped her nose against the rock. Grayson reached down to her and turned her head sideways so the fit wasn't so snug. It helped that she was wet because once her head cleared, the rest of her quickly popped up out of the hole.

Grayson greedily gathered her up in his arms. He didn't notice that he was crying harder than she was.

There was a rumble as another hunk of the dam washed away. The crack widened, a huge wave of black water surged out of the hole behind it and rushed down the valley.

"Honey, you have to hurry!" Carter told Maggie, panic edging into his voice. "Turn around and squeeze back out the way—"

"The way I came in is under water now." she said.

In their single-minded effort to get Sadie to safety Grayson and Carter hadn't considered Maggie's plight. Now the reality of her situation slammed into them like a wrecking ball.

"Then take a big gulp of air and hold your breath," Carter said, desperate. "You can—"

"I don't know how I got here. I just wiggled and wormed through the cracks. I don't think I could find my way back even if there wasn't any water."

Grayson leaned over with Sadie in his arms still whimpering, and put his face near the crack.

"Maggie, you have to try! Turn around and—"

"No, Mr. Grayson." Her bottom lip trembled and tears formed in her eyes. He saw terror wash briefly over her face, then her lips curled in a tiny smile. "It's done now."

"Done?"

"The dark's all out of my head. It's bright, now, full of light."

Her smile faded.

"You have to go, Mr. Grayson."

"*Go?* And just *leave* you here?"

"Miss Piper and Nan Marian are down there in the fog. You got to get them before the monster eats them up." She shivered. "It's *coming.*"

"No!" he heard his voice yell at her, but didn't know what he was going to say next until he heard it come out his mouth. "I already left one little girl behind and I'm not going to leave another."

He felt his brother's hand on his shoulder.

"*I'm* the one who left a little girl behind." Carter's voice was a strangled croak. "Gray, that day at the creek … I pushed Becky, shoved her out of my way. I didn't mean … I … it was my fault, not yours."

Grayson could only gape at him.

"I'll stay here with Maggie," Carter said.

"No!" Maggie cried, every bit as adamant as Grayson had been when he'd shouted the same thing at her moments before.

Both men looked down through the crack at her upturned face, into the full force of her green eyes, the eyes with daisies in them. She offered a shaky half smile.

"Sadie," she called out, her voice determinedly cheery, and the toddler leaned out of her father's arms and looked down at her, sniffling and sucking her thumb.

"Bye, bye little pretty," Maggie said, and though the black water had risen only as high as her chest, she began to sink slowly down into it like easing herself into a bathtub.

"Bye, bye Mabie," Sadie said and gave her a slow gnat-snatcher wave.

"Maggie, no!" Carter was frantic, almost hysterical. "Don't—!"Then her head went under, her red hair swirled for a moment and she was gone. "Maaaaggie!"

Grayson gritted his teeth and swallowed hard. The cry forming on his own lips died there. Then he took a deep breath and got to his feet.

Doin' the necessary.

He turned and took a quick survey of Dam #1 to his left where the water level had risen 10 feet in … what? Three minutes … five? If he was going to cross it—and that was his only hope of getting to Piper and his mother in time—he had to go right now.

He turned and shoved Sadie into Carter's arms. "Get her up to the ridge," he barked, then turned and leapt from one rock to the next, hop-scotched his way to the coal slag dam. When he got there, he stepped gingerly out onto it and began to pick his way across the top, praying it wouldn't crumble away beneath his feet and dump him and a couple of million gallons of water forty feet to the rocky creek bed below—where the incline was so steep he'd probably roll another hundred yards.

CARTER STOOD TRANSFIXED, staring at the black water bubbling up toward the top of the crevice at his feet. The precious little red-haired child had vanished in a heartbeat—was just *gone!*

He couldn't … everything was happening so fast comprehension couldn't keep up. All at once, Sadie was in his arms, soaked and whimpering. He heard Grayson bark, "Get Sadie up to the ridge!" but the words were meaningless. He turned to ask Grayson what … but his brother was no longer standing beside him. He was headed as fast as he could go toward the dam.

He's going after Ma and Piper!

Grayson was doing what had to be done; Carter was doing nothing at all.

He found himself running, but had no memory of commanding his legs to do so. His long strides cleared the boulders in a series of leaps, then he bolted up the dirt incline, so steep he slipped and had to use his free hand in the dirt to crawl/climb the remaining few feet.

He didn't know when his mind formed the intent. It was tangled in firing synapses that kept producing the face of a red-haired child superimposed on a dark shadow in tall grass, a man-shaped lump. But he acted on the intent as if he'd thought it through rationally and had come to what he was about to do as the only reasonable course of action under the circumstances.

Edna Turpin stood well back from the edge of the ridge, both hands covering her mouth, staring at the disintegrating dam. Her wide eyes bugged out of their sockets like two hens' eggs with black dots painted on the ends with a Magic Marker.

Carter ran to her and shoved Sadie into her arms.

"Take her and give me your keys!" he said.

Sadie shrieked, held out her arms to him.

"Unka Cardur, hold you," she cried but he ignored her.

"What do you want my—?" Edna began.

Carter made a sweeping gesture that took in all of Sadler Hollow.

"Somebody's got to warm those people!"

"Keys is in it," she said. He turned, cleared the distance to the truck in seconds and leapt inside. Edna called after him, "I'll watch after this little angel, won't let nothing hap—"

Carter missed the rest of it as he cranked the rumbling engine and threw dirt and rocks out behind the back tires as he spun the truck around and headed back down Strawman Road with his foot on the accelerator mashed all the way to the floor.

Chapter Thirty-Two

As he reached the Naked Turtle Mountain side of the dam, Grayson chanced a backward glance at the big dam. The gush of water roaring out of the rip in the center was eating away at both sides, forcing the opening wider and wider. Another few feet and the rising water in the smaller lake below would start to flow over the dam he'd crossed and down the back side into the creek bed. He was astonished the dam still held. But it wouldn't hold for long.

His glance swept the flat ridge on the other side of the dam where he saw Carter shove Sadie into Edna's arms and turn toward the pickup truck. He didn't wait to see where Carter was going. He knew.

Then he leapt down off the end of the dam and began to run down the sharp incline into the woods below Naked Turtle Mountain. The slope was so steep he was almost airborne with every step, his forward momentum so fast that if he stumbled, tripped or lost his balance, he would sail through the air and crash into the ground, a tree, a stump or a rock outcrop so hard he'd break something. Likely something vital. Perhaps incapacitating. If that happened, he'd be lying injured below the dam he'd just crossed when it crumbled, in the path of the millions of the gallons of black water now held captive behind it. More important, he wouldn't get to his mother and wife in time.

Then he hit the fog. It was lifting and on the edges it was a white mist no thicker than steam in the bathroom after a shower. It quickly got thicker, though, and a thin sapling he hadn't even seen caught his shoulder, knocked him off balance and he came perilously close to falling. Perhaps, he should have run down the dry creek bed. He'd considered it, no trees in the way there. He'd opted instead to barrel down the mountainside through the woods to the road because he'd feared that in the fog he wouldn't be able to tell where to get out of the creek bed and turn toward the house. Afraid that he wouldn't recognize the sycamore tree with a clothesline limb where you could hang a rug.

Carter had said he shoved Becky! He was *there?* How—

Grayson never saw the vine. It grabbed his right foot as securely as a bear trap and sent him flying through a clump of bushes into the trunk of a huge birch tree.

He lay where he had fallen, face down, not moving. Blood trickled out of his nose and down his forehead from a cut high above his left eye. Then it dripped into a growing puddle in the dirt. The thick mist he had disturbed swirled briefly around him, then formed a solid milk-colored blanket again that settled over his body like a shroud.

~

Carter roared into the fog at fifty miles an hour, betting

his life on his childhood recollections of Strawman Road. The dirt track lead over Chicken Gizzard Mountain to Cricket Hollow where there was a little church that was one of the stops on his father's preaching circuit—third Sunday of every month. Cricket Hollow was where the Campbell clan lived and Carter hated to go there, had counted the bends in the road like mileposts on his way to the gallows. He counted those bends now as he roared around them, and if his memory served, he'd gone around the last one and from here it was a straight shot down the mountain to where Strawman crossed Northfield Road.

If his memory *didn't* serve, however, he would miss a curve and go flying out into the woods and down a steep incline until he hit something sturdy enough to stop him.

He concentrated on peering squint-eyed through the fog at a road that vanished in swirling mist a few feet in front of the truck. And tried to think how best to pull off this Paul Revere routine.

How did you rouse people inside their houses—likely still asleep—on Sunday morning in a fog and convince them they had minutes to live unless they ran for their lives?

He tested the truck horn. It made a great, coughing, braying sound, loud but not commanding. Well, it was all he had. That and screaming.

What he wouldn't allow himself to consider was the fact that when the black water came roaring down the hollow, he and his little truck and honking horn would be directly in its path.

A vehicle suddenly appeared out of the fog in front of him like an apparition in a dream. Not there, then there. Dark blue was all he saw, right in front of him on the narrow road. He veered hard to the right but understood even as he yanked the wheel, that he was still going to plow right into it.

~

Grayson's eyes blinked open. He came to full consciousness abruptly, didn't go through any of the inter-mediate stages—like the time he'd fallen asleep standing up and awoke to find a hole in Haystack's forehead.

He knew instantly where he was, though he wasn't clear what specifically had happened that'd knocked his feet out from under him and put him face down in the dirt. But he knew the result of whatever it was as soon as he tried to move. Agony ripped up his left arm, made a hairpin turn at his elbow and exploded into his shoulder. When he eased over onto his right side, he saw that his left hand was extended at an extremely odd angle from his arm, courtesy, he was sure, of a broken wrist.

He gritted his teeth against the pain, took his left arm in his right hand and held it to his body as he staggered drunkenly to his feet, fearing that each new movement would reveal another injury. An incapacitating one.

He stood unsteadily, the pain making him nauseas, feeling a heartbeat throbbing in his head that made him suspect he might have given himself a concussion on the front of his skull to match the crack in the back. When he started to run again, the jolting motion set all the agonies screeching, each one determined to be the one his reeling senses attended to first. But he ignored them all.

~

Carter had misjudged. He didn't plow into the side of the blue vehicle that had materialized out of the fog in front of him. Oh, he hit it all right, a screeching, scraping, side-swiping jolt that sent him flying head-first over the steering wheel into the windshield.

Sparklers exploded in front of his eyes, his forehead felt numb and thick and a thousand bees took up residence between his temples and conducted a buzzing concert.

Then he felt a hand on his shoulder, but it seemed to take a long time to turn his head. When the jumbled synapses began firing accurate information again, he actually managed a little smile.

"Sheriff Cliff! Am I glad I ran into you!"

~

Grayson was not in great danger of falling again now because he couldn't generate enough speed, off balance with his arms clutched to his body and dizzy from getting his bell rung. How long had he lain there? How much time did he have left? He swallowed the vomit rising with an acid taste in the back of his throat—did *not* want to revisit the half-cooked venison from last night—and staggered forward into the white nothingness.

How would he carry his mother with a broken wrist? And carry her he must; she couldn't walk. The simple act of picking her up and hauling her out of the house at a dead run would very likely kill her. But what would he do now?

~

SHERIFF CLIFF HAD COME to investigate reports from Cricket Hollow on the other side of Chicken Gizzard Mountain of an explosion up near the dam. It took less than 30 seconds for Carter to tell the big man everything he needed to know.

"Come on!" the sheriff ordered, tried to yank Carter's door open and couldn't. The wreck had smashed it stuck. Carter quickly slid across the seat. He grabbed the pink blankie Sadie had left lying there and used it to wipe off the blood on his upper lip—courtesy, he was sure, of another broken nose. Riley's face appeared and disappeared like the burp of a song when you spin the dial on the radio. The sheriff was already back in his cruiser, had whipped it around and barely slowed down for Carter to leap into the passenger seat before he tore out back down the road with lights flashing and siren waling, babbling into his radio to dispatch to sound the fire alarm.

Even before they made the turn down Northfield Road toward town center, the sheriff had keyed the loud speaker on the roof and was literally shouting into the mouthpiece.

"Dam's busted. Get to high ground. *Run!*"

As they raced down the road, Carter turned backward in the seat and saw people rushing out of their homes. Some, but not nearly enough. And the ones who were leaving seemed too dazed and unbelieving to be in the kind of life-and-death hurry needed to save themselves. The cruiser flew past the Carpenter's house where Melanie Carpenter had the whole brood out in the yard in their Sunday best—which wasn't much given that Rufus Carpenter was still laid up in the rehab center in Charleston with a crushed leg he got in a roof fall in the mine. She and the seven kids were standing by the road, apparently waiting for a ride to Sunday School.

Melanie gawked at the sheriff's car, the loud speaker

blaring, "Run. Get to high ground. The dam's busted!" And Carter was absolutely certain the woman wasn't capable of forming the intent to run or carrying it out in time to save her family.

"Stop the car!" he yelled.

Sheriff Cliff obeyed out of instinct.

"What are you—?" he began.

"You go on; I'm staying here!"

WHEN GRAYSON STUMBLED out of the woods onto the road, he almost tripped over his own feet. He could hardly see at all now. Blood from the cut on his forehead had flowed into his left eye, blinding it and he couldn't let go of his broken wrist to wipe the blood away.

He knew that with the roaring in his ears, he wouldn't likely hear the rumble of the impending black tidal wave until it was right on him, and he had been running for— how long? Ten minutes? Two? A week?—with the hair standing up on the back of his neck the way you cringe away from a blow you know is coming at you from behind. He had no idea how long he had, but figured it might only be measured in seconds. And he thought all these thoughts as he turned without so much as a pause and began to run down the road toward the house.

"Down" was a relative term. There wasn't much of an incline here—which meant he was very close to the house. The road climbed the mountain in switchbacks, but after the last one down from the house, it leveled out, passed in front of the house and stayed more or less level, parallel to the top of the ridge, until the final switchback that went steeply up to the church.

With nothing in front of him, he could actually run

now. At least as fast as his body would allow. He willed his legs to pump madly—jarring his screaming wrist, jolting his throbbing head, every contact with the road sending daggers of pain into so many places he couldn't even distinguish exactly where he hurt. It was an everywhere agony that didn't matter in the slightest and didn't slow him down in his mad dash to—

The house materialized out of the mist. Like a dream, the white of the fog took on form with shadows and outlines. The roof. The porch. The fence.

The question of how he would get the gate open with a broken wrist formed even as he saw that it wasn't latched. He heard himself begin to shout when he was sure no one could possibly hear him yet.

"Piper! Piper. Come on! We have to—"

And then she appeared on the porch. He watched an incredible wave of emotions wash over her tear-stained face.

"Oh, Gray. What happened to you? Did you find the girls?"

"No time!" he barked the words harshly, a verbal slap to shut her up. "We have to get Ma and—"

"Gray, your Ma's ... gone."

Don't react. Do the necessary!

"Come on!" he cried, ignoring the shock on her face. "The dam's blown! "

She sucked in a gasp.

"Where's Sadie?"

"Safe." Then he did let go of his left wrist, ignoring the vision-blurring pain. He grabbed her hand, turned and yanked her toward the road.

"*Run!*" he screamed.

And they ran.

~

Carter bolted down the road toward the frightened, confused family, told himself his decision didn't have anything at all to do with the fact that every last one of those kids had red hair.

He slid to a stop in front of the Carpenters, grabbed the two youngest children—about two and three—one under each arm.

Melanie was holding the baby, so he said to a teenager and a boy of about 12.

"Grab the little ones and come on or you got less than five minutes to live!"

At as close to a dead run as he could manage hauling two small children, Carter took out across the road, over the railroad track and started up the hillside on the other side. The valley curved. Safest place, if there was such a thing, was on the east side. How high up would depend on how much water came tearing down the valley at once. If the smaller dam let go in pieces, allowing only a portion of the water to escape at one time, then … He could barely see ten feet in front of him as he ran and the others were merely terrified voices behind him in the mist. Both children he was carrying were silent, had never let out so much as a peep when a total stranger yanked them up and hauled them away like he was stealing pigs.

Then he heard what could have been distant thunder. But he knew what it was and the sound knocked the breath out of him so he staggered a step, slowed just enough for the others to catch up.

Melanie was running, but looking over her shoulder, yelling, "Tommy! Tom—!" She literally stumbled into Carter.

"Tommy went back for his dog, for Buttons."

Carter grabbed a teenager as the boy surged past, dragging his little sister by the hand, and thrust the two-year-old at him.

He set the three-year-old on the ground and told the little boy to *"Run!"* and the kid took off up the hill faster than Carter had been carrying him.

Then Carter plunged back into the mist, yelling, "Tom! Tommy!"

Chapter Thirty-Three

EDNA TURPIN WAS the only person who actually saw the collapse of *both* dams that hurled a wall of black water down into Sadler Hollow on that foggy morning in August of 1969. She would say until her dying breath that it was the single most horrible sight her eyes ever beheld.

She stood on the top of the ridge trembling after the blonde man—which Addington brother was he?—shoved the pretty little girl, into her arms and went barreling down into the fog in her truck. The child was drenched, overalls and tee shirt was soaked in nasty black water. The ends of her long hair was wet, too, musta hung down in it, and she was missing a shoe.

But what had happened to the other little girl, the red-headed child? She'd been down there with the men and then the little girl fell down into the rocks and … Edna's eyes wasn't good as they once was and she'd had to strain to see what was going on. They'd got the little one out— but where was the other one? The one who had dreamed of a black monster, a demon that at this very moment was about to come out of her nightmare to gobble up the world!

Edna understood that she was in no danger, far as she was above the two dams in the valley. But it was so awful and scary she wanted to run and hide anyway. She couldn't have dragged herself away even if she'd tried, though, which she didn't. She was transfixed, nailed to the spot in horrid fascination.

The angelic little girl—her name was ... Sadie!—had stopped crying, just sucked her thumb and sniffled that hitching sound of younguns who've cried for so long their breath won't go in and out proper for awhile after. Even she, little as she was, stared at the spectacle in wonder— with eyes that was purple! Can you beat that! Watching what was happening was like sitting in your car at one of them drive-in movies she'd seen one time when they was in Charleston. Only wasn't no movie screen nowhere big enough to hold the size of this catastrophe and she and the child had the only seats in the house.

Edna wouldn't let herself think about them folks in the holler. She knew some of 'em, though she didn't have no kin there. She'd only come over from Burnt Stump Holler last night to stay with an old lady had the palsy. She was the granny of one of the ladies in Edna's church, the Burnt Stump Full Gospel Fire Baptized Holiness Church, and there'd been a sign-up sheet just inside the front door for folks to help out the family. She'd come, slept sittin' up in a chair and left soon's the lady from next door come to take her place.

Those ladies—the granny and the one from next door —they wasn't going to live to see another sunrise. But Edna wouldn't let her mind go there, just stared as the huge black coal dam with a rip in its side came completely apart before her eyes.

For a little bit after the young blond fella left, didn't nothing new happen to the dam. Water kept coming out the rip and over the top where them hunks had washed away. The water flowed down hill and filled up the lake they'd come to see and like a bathtub, soon's too much water come in one end, it started overflowing out the other.

Within minutes after water started pouring over the top of the dam directly below her, she could see where pieces of it was starting to wash away, too. It didn't have no crack blown in the middle like the other one, but it couldn't possibly hold out for very long. There was too much water pushing on it and more coming every minute.

The little girl's hitching breathing had calmed almost back to normal, and Edna was getting real tired of holding her. She was a little mite of a thing and Edna was strong as a woman half her age. But her back had commenced to ache and her arm where she held the little girl's weight was starting to cramp.

She'd about decided she had to sit down right there in the dirt and hold the child in her lap when she heard a rumble. It was the rumble of thunder, of a storm cloud the greenish-purple of a day-old bruise, full of lightening and hail. Only it wasn't thunder. The sound wasn't coming from the sky and real thunder didn't go on and on, neither, getting louder and louder. The little girl commenced to crying again, but not the wailing hysteria like when her uncle'd handed her off to a total stranger and run off in the truck. This cry was a whining, terrified cry. And Edna didn't realize at first that her own voice had joined the little girl's in a horrified wail.

The rumble came from the big dam, the sound of it … *buckling*. The black water finally had its way and smashed the whole rest of the dam backwards out of its path in a massive, roaring collapse. Set free all at once, a wave of churning black water and coal waste—thick, almost like tar—careened down the ever-narrowing valley toward the smaller dam. It roared up the north side of the valley, back down and up the south side, zigzagging its way, gathering speed. Edna hadn't never seen no real buffalo. Just pictures. But a million of them stampeding couldn't have made a sound loud as that.

A wall of water rushed out over the little lake and slammed down with a hammer blow on the dam at the end, exploding it out of the top of the hollow like the cork out of a bottle of champagne. Pieces of the smaller dam flew into the trees below like shards of a crystal glass dropped on a hardwood floor.

Then water roared through the opening between the two ridges with a mighty rumble, crashed into the valley beneath the ridge and thundered on down the hollow, wiping out everything in its path, dragging a flood of black water behind it like the tail of a kite. A black monster—that's what the little red-haired girl said, a Boogie Man that wouldn't fit in nobody's closet, a horror whose roar would fuel Edna's nightmares for the rest of her life. And then the monster disappeared in the mist. Edna could hear it rumbling on down below, eating trees and houses and only the Good Lord above knew what else. At first, water gushed over the empty space between the ridges that looked like the hole where a little kid's tooth had come out. But the water level dropped fast and soon there wasn't much of a flow at all.

In the silence that followed, Edna walked slowly and carefully forward a few steps, far enough that she could see what there was to see above the mist. A swath of bare black mud wide as a football field lay before her that only a few minutes ago had been forest. Even the uprooted trees were gone. The black monster had eaten it all, then vanished into the mist.

Chapter Thirty-Four

GRAYSON HAD that awful sensation of running in slow motion, of being stuck in quicksand, of every movement taking ten times longer than it ought to.

Piper had taken his left elbow, allowing him to use his right hand to immobilize his wrist again against his belly, and was dragging him along with her long strides. He wanted to tell her to run on ahead, not to wait for him, but he didn't have the air to say it and knew it wouldn't do any good if he did. They'd both make it out of this or they wouldn't. But whatever happened, they were in it to the end *together*.

He was grateful the road wasn't steep here, that the sharp incline didn't start for another half mile, because he was using up the very last vestiges of his strength. This final push would leave him totally spent. They had to make it far enough north on the mountainside to be beyond the path of the flood that would be released when the little dam at the top of the hollow could no longer hold back the ever-growing lake behind it.

Then they heard a rumble, a grumbling thunderous

roar. Reverberations shook the earth, went on and on, growled louder and louder. Grayson knew instantly what it was and comprehension momentarily staggered him. Not the *big* dam …

Oh, dear G…

Even with his damaged hearing he heard the roar. But he'd have heard even if he'd been deaf because it was the sound of death itself, and even the deaf can hear death coming.

The world got brighter as he and Piper neared the edge of the blanket of fog. Here the mist merely obscured, faded images. Somehow the blurring was worse. It stole colors, softened shapes and made the ordinary alien. And then it was gone altogether and they were out in the bright morning sunshine. As he ran, he looked back over his shoulder at the black smile between the ridges where water three feet deep gushed over the crumbling top of the dam and poured in a thick black waterfall down the forty-foot drop to the creek bed.

Then the black monster of his nightmare—of *Maggie's* nightmare—reared up behind the dam like an evil sea serpent. One heartbeat. Two. Then the wall of churning black water crashed down on it, shattered it, fired huge hunks of the dam out into the air like shrapnel.

The monster dived down the side of the mountain, then, leapt like an attacking leopard. Black and oily, more viscous solid that water, it ripped trees out of the ground as it roared through them. He and Piper were both looking back now as it loomed above them, the outside edge hurling at them like an avalanche of black snow.

They hadn't got far enough! The water from both lakes in one huge wave would slam down on them any second! Piper screamed. Grayson knocked her to the ground and threw himself on top of her in a futile effort to shield her.

They smelled the nameless evil stink of coal vomit. Piper's screams and Grayson's, too, were gobbled up by the wall of sound streaking toward them. The ground shook and the malevolent rumble grew until it drowned out all thought and reason and intent. Water hit them with the force of a fire hose, soaked them as they cringed in the dirt of the road. The beast, the behemoth of Black Death shrieked a cry wild and Jurassic …

…as it passed them by.

Grayson raised up on an elbow and looked through the splashing water, watched the hideous black freight train race past—the farthest edge not 20 feet away. Then it disappeared into the mist.

Piper rolled over and the two of them sat up, watched as an ever-diminishing rush of water rumbled by them and then was gone.

It was over in—how long? Two minutes? Five? Thirty seconds? Grayson marveled that it took no longer than that for millions of gallons of black water to race past them down the hillside. But the grade was steep. The big dam was at least five hundred feet higher than where they lay in the mud. And the top of Chicken Gizzard Mountain was two *thousand* feet above Sadlerton, seven miles away.

Where the ugly black smile had been, a small waterfall of stagnant water flowed down to the creek bed below. Grayson and Piper stared in shock at what lay below the waterfall. The tidal wave of coal waste and water had stripped down to bare rock everything it touched.

Like the only two survivors of a nuclear attack, Grayson and Piper rose slowly to their feet in wonder, staring at the fog that was rapidly clearing with the warmth of the sun. They could see now as far as the house. But, of course, the house *wasn't*. The butterfly meadow was gone, too. Where it should have been was a slimy smear of black mud.

Without speaking, they lifted their eyes in unison and stared at the mist still swaddling Sadler Hollow. When it lifted, what would be left of the little town of Sadlerton?

Chapter Thirty-Five

AFTER THE BLACK monster crashed through the dam at the top of Sadler Hollow and leapt down into the creek bed and forest below, it gathered steam as it surged downward through the mist, picking up trees and rocks to use as battering rams on its first victim.

Though delirious with pain and dizzy from shock, Riley Campbell heard it coming. The grinding, roaring sound instantly roused him and he stared wide-eyed and afraid into the fog as the sound grew louder and louder, wondering what could possibly make such a noise. He saw it, got a good look at the oily, black serpent taller than the trees, but his voice was gone so his shriek of terror made no sound.

The monster chewed Riley up in a heartbeat, then surged toward its next victim, the metal bridge on North-field Road. The carcass of the bridge was later found eleven miles downstream, a mangled mass of tangled blue beams that looked like a clump of dead blue spiders.

The black flood that in some places spread out three-hundred feet wide, swept up the railroad track, tangled the rails and cross ties with telephone poles and wires as it plowed through the first of the homes, businesses and other structures it would destroy along an eighteen-mile swath of devastation through Sadlerton and the coal-camp towns downstream, Akin, Bent Twig, Alice Springs, Barberville, Copperhead and into the county seat in Chandler. In all, 16 coal mining hamlets were visited by death that day.

But Sadlerton took the brunt of the monster's fury and served up most of its victims.

The Granger family lived at the intersection of Strawman Road and Northfield Road. Tom's father had stuck the scarecrow in his corn field that had given the road its name. They were all asleep in their beds and never knew what hit them. Tom and his wife, Sonia and three little girls died instantly when their house just past the bridge collapsed on top of them. They had never heard the fire alarm Sheriff Cliff called in. The fire station was at the other end of town.

Oh, the oldest girl, Becca, heard the whoop of a siren in the distance and somebody yelling through a loud speaker. She covered her head up with her pillow and went back to sleep.

Five trailer houses sat beside Strawman Road, up from the Grangers. In all, a dozen adults and 17 children lived in the mobile homes. Four trailer houses were swept away, the ten adults and 14 children in them were killed. The fifth trailer house was slightly higher on the ridge than the other four. The monster carried away the chicken house, the clapboard garage and the pickup truck next to the trailer house, but only shoved the trailer sideways on its foundation and left it be.

Bennett's Five and Dime on the west side of the road vanished at the same time the post office on the east side was enveloped in the grinding black tidal wave.

Five more houses, five more families. No one survived.

~

CARTER FOUND Tommy on the other side of the road, running toward his house, crying, "Buttons! Come here boy! Buttons!"

He caught up with the boy, maybe 8 or 9 years old, reached out a long arm and grabbed his shirt collar, effectively yanking him off his feet.

"Hey, mister. I gotta git my dog!" the boy sputtered.

Carter grabbed the boy by the upper arm, jerked him upright and turned to drag him back across the road toward where his mother and siblings had disappeared into the mist.

He heard it when he turned. Two steps later and he knew what the roar was, growing louder and louder. Another three steps and he understood that they weren't going to make it.

Hey, maybe it was better to be out in the open like this, not crushed in a building or a house. Maybe the water would just wash you along, if you could manage not to drown until—

Then Carter saw the black monster roaring toward them out of the mist to his left, a boiling, frothing, carnivorous beast forty feet tall. And he knew no living thing could survive contact with it. The rumbling, grinding roar drowned out every other sound; the sight drove out all thought, like looking into the gaping, black maw of hell itself.

Tommy looked up the street toward it and screamed. Carter gathered the boy in his arms and hugged him to his chest, then turned his back toward the monster so the boy wouldn't see.

"Shhhh, don't look," he said into the boy's hair but the beast ate his words. He felt a spray of cold water, tensed and thought of Piper's face the day they walked to the meadow and saw the butterflies. The way her eyes sparkled when she smi—

Then it was on him and Carter and the boy vanished into the bowels of the beast. The monster hammered them to the pavement and ground them up with trees and roofs and bricks and railroad ties and thick black water.

Three more houses beyond the Carpenters' house were destroyed. The families living in two of them had heard and heeded the sheriff's cry of warning and had run for higher ground. The father in the third house wandered to the refrigerator in his underwear after the siren awakened him and was staring into its interior when the monster gobbled up his home and family.

Other families on this end of town, closer to the fire siren which had already gotten their attention a few minutes before the sheriff's run-for-your-lives warning, made it to safety. Everything they own vanished in an instant, leaving them shaking in disbelief on the hillside. But alive.

Jesse McCullough's family was not among the survivors. The fire siren awakened him and he wondered idly what was burning before dozing off. When he heard the sheriff's warning, he tried to get his family together to run, but it took too long. Survival rested on leaping out of bed and running for high ground. Jesse couldn't get the kids to cooperate. Buster had gotten drunk as soon as he heard about Zeke Campbell and had stayed mostly drunk since. He grumbled that he wasn't going anywhere no matter how loud Jesse yelled. Angie Faye was too fat to move fast. She made it out to the porch with their five-year-old before the black monster washed them all away.

Sheriff Cliff had turned around at the edge of town and started back. He'd called dispatch in Chandler with orders for deputies to warn the people living in the coal-camp towns downstream from Sadlerton, but knew they wouldn't be able to muster much of a response before the monster was on them. When he saw the black beast hurling at him, he whipped his cruiser back around and tried to outrun it. He very nearly made it. But not quite.

It was all over before it was even time for kids to be in Sunday School. The eerie stillness that followed the monster's rampage was testimony to the absolute devastation it had wreaked. One hundred and twenty-eight people died within fifteen minutes; one thousand, two hundred and thirty-two more were injured. Five hundred seven houses, forty-four mobile homes and thirty-seven businesses were destroyed. Out of a population of five thousand people, four thousand were left homeless.

Piper and Grayson Addington did not know that at the time, of course. But when the fog lifted, cleared completely by eleven o'clock, they saw that nothing remained in Sadler Hollow but a swath of smeared black mud that stretched as far as they could see.

"Maggie knew," Piper whispered, her voice hushed and awed.

Grayson tried to speak, wanted to tell her that he had known, too, had seen a vision he hadn't understood or believed. But his throat had closed up so tight he couldn't make a sound. So he just nodded, tears in his eyes.

"Where is she?" Piper asked. "Is she with—?"

Grayson shook his head slowly from side to side and Piper's face went white. She couldn't speak, just mouthed, "No!" her brown eyes wide and pleading. He reached out and pulled her into his arms and held her as she sobbed.

Chapter Thirty-Six

If it hadn't been for Sadie, they'd never have seen it. Grayson and Piper were buying groceries and other supplies in Charleston to take back to the shelter. They'd driven down through the riot of fall foliage, gold, russet and copper, and soaked up the color. Beauty was soothing to the soul and there was nothing beautiful in Sadler Hollow anymore. Two months after the flood, it was still a wasteland of tangled debris, wrecked cars and black mud. Northfield Coal had, of course, refused responsibility for the disaster, claiming both dams had been sound. If a crazy man blew a hole in one of them, that certainly wasn't the company's fault, even if the crazy man happened to be the company president.

The federal inspections, boards of inquiry and USBM investigations would drag on for years. Lawsuits would litter court dockets for decades.

Meanwhile, the tattered, devastated remnant of the populations of the communities along the eighteen-mile route of devastation down Sadler Hollow struggled to put their lives back together.

Piper and Grayson had decided to stay and help. When the press got hold of Gray's story—combat veteran, chaplain of massacred unit comes home and a week later his hometown is wiped out, his mother, brother and brother-in-law killed, along with nine cousins and assorted second and third-kin—the governor of West Virginia requested and got for Grayson a hardship discharge from the Army.

When his National Guard unit returned to Kentucky from Vietnam in September, Sergeant Hotchner lead a group of volunteers who showed up in Sadler Hollow and spent a week renovating the old church building at the end of Turtle Road as a place for Grayson's family to live. A little Baptist Church on Bates Road had been a quarter mile above the tidal wave's path, but the pastor and his family had not been so fortunate. Gray took over that church and worked with the Red Cross to set up a shelter and soup kitchen there for the Sadlerton victims of the disaster who'd made it out alive. And he conducted funeral services there for those who had not and buried them in the little cemetery out behind the church. Seventy-one new white crosses.

Grayson bought stones, not crosses, to match the older stones already set in the Addington family cemetery next to the church at the end of Turtle Road. One of them read "Marian Irene McCullough Addington, Born July 25, 1909, Died August 24, 1969." Hers rested on the right side of Grayson's father, Everett. On the left side, next to the old stone where Becky's name had started to fade, was a newer one: "Everett Carter Addington, Jr. Born June 1, 1940, Died August 24, 1969."

And on the other side of Carter's was a small new stone. It read simply, "Maggie, Died August 24, 1969"

That's why it was so spine-tingling when Sadie cried, "Mabie! Look, Mommy, I see Mabie!"

Piper knelt on one knee beside the child and looked into her eyes.

"No, honey," she said. "We've talked about this. Maggie's gone. She's in Heaven with Nana and Uncle Carter and Jesus. Remember?"

"Mabie's wight dere." Sadie grabbed Piper's hand and dragged her to the magazine rack beside a shelf of novels, cookbooks and calendars. "See!"

On the rack at Sadie's eye level was a copy of *Time Magazine.* Piper saw it and couldn't seem to draw another breath.

Grayson appeared with the basket, took one look at her face and asked. "What's wrong?"

She had no air to speak. All she could do was point to the magazine.

As if in a dream, Grayson picked it up and the two of them stared at it in shock.

"Mabie," Sadie cried, tugging on her father's pants leg. "Wanna see Mabie, Daddy."

Grayson reached down and gathered Sadie into his arms without taking his eyes off the magazine—where Maggie's face stared at them from the cover.

"Where Is Andy Shelbourne?" shouted the headline above the picture.

With numb fingers, Grayson flipped through the magazine to the story, which showed Maggie's picture again alongside several pictures of the shattered elementary school in the Vale of Amberclewydd, Wales, that was destroyed by a coal slide down into a fog-filled valley on August 11, 1969.

Grayson pointed to the date and whispered. "That was the day my platoon marched away from Yan Ling." He'd told her the story of the little girl named Nguyen they'd left behind there. But not the whole story. He'd only told one person all of it. Carter. And that was enough.

He'd also told her about seeing the black monster, falling to his knees, and crying out "Sadie!" and how he'd heard the echo of another voice united with his that day.

August 11 was the day he'd uttered a prayer to a God he no longer believed in that was answered by the God who still believed in him—and by a little girl who had looked up out of the space beneath two boulders and said, "The dark's all out of my head. It's bright, now, full of light."

Grayson's eyes dragged from one word of the story to the next, reading it aloud quietly. It described the findings of the board of inquiry about the disaster, contained interviews with the parents of children who had died and with those who'd survived. No mention was made of the little red-haired girl on the cover until the final paragraph.

"The lone mystery left to be solved about that awful day in August is the mystery of Margaret-Andryea (Andy) Shelbourne. Andy was milking the family cow on a hillside above the mist and saw the coal begin to plunge down into the valley—toward the school where her little sister was sitting in class. Andy raced to the school and made it into the building just as it collapsed.

"The mystery is that Andy Shelbourne's body was never found. The body of every other child was recovered and placed on the pews in the village church. But not Andy's.

"The girls' only relative, their grandfather, committed suicide after the accident. Now, he lies buried in the church cemetery beside the grave of his younger granddaughter, marked with a small stone that chronicles her short life in a single line: 'Born June 18, 1963, Died August 11, 1969,' beneath her name: Sadie Shelbourne.

Piper gasped, *"Sadie!"*

"The grave next to it, marked 'Andy Shelbourne,' lies empty."

Grayson raised his eyes and looked into Piper's. Puddles of tears had formed there and she blinked them into streams down her cheeks. He couldn't seem to form the words to tell her that the first time he'd heard Maggie's voice it had seemed familiar. He'd recognized it then, but couldn't place it. Now he could. Before he met Maggie in his mother's parlor, he had heard her voice in his head.

Outside a village in Vietnam, an army chaplain had cried out for his Sadie *at the same time* a little Welsh girl named Andy had cried out for hers. And somehow …

Piper's voice was ragged. "Who was she?"

Of course, they both knew.

Maybe Sadie did, too. In fact, maybe Sadie'd always known.

The child reached out her chubby hand to the picture, stroked it tenderly with her little fingers.

"Mabie," she crooned wistfully. "Mabie loooves Sabie."

THE END

Loved reading *When Butterflies Cry* and want more Ninie Hammon right now? You're in luck! You can start reading Ninie's *Nowhere USA* series today. Get started today with *Jabberwock*.

Get Jabberwock Today!

A quick favor...

Thank you for reading *When Butterflies Cry.*

If you enjoyed this book would you please consider writing a review of it on your favorite bookselling site so other readers can enjoy it too. Just a couple of sentences would mean a lot to me.

Thank you!

Ninie Hammon

About the Author

Ninie Hammon (rhymes with shiny, not skinny) grew up in Muleshoe, Texas, got a BA in English and theatre from Texas Tech University and snagged a job as a newspaper reporter. She didn't know a thing about journalism, but her editor said if she could write he could teach her the rest of it and if she couldn't write the rest of it didn't matter. She hung in there for a 25-year career as a journalist. As soon as she figured out that making up the facts was a whole lot more fun than reporting them, she turned to fiction and never looked back.

Ninie now writes suspense--every flavor except pistachio: psychological suspense, inspirational suspense, suspense thrillers, paranormal suspense, suspense mysteries.

In every book she keeps this promise to her Loyal Reader: "I will tell you a story in a distinctive voice you'll always recognize, about people as ordinary as you are--people who have been slammed by something they didn't sign on for, and now they must fight for their lives. Then smack in the middle of their everyday worlds, those people encounter the unexplainable--and it's always the game-changer."

Also By Ninie Hammon

Cornbread Mafia

Fire In The Hole

Blown' Up A Storm

Ridin' For A Fall

Nowhere, USA

The Jabberwock

Mad Dog

Trapped

The Hanging Judge

The Witch of Gideon

Blown Away

Nowhere People

Through The Canvas Series

Black Water

Red Web

Gold Promise

Blue Tears

The Taken Saga

The Taken

The Changed

The Hidden

The Saved

The Unexplainable Collection

Five Days in May

Black Sunshine

The Based on True Stories Collection

Home Grown

Sudan

When Butterflies Cry

The Knowing Series

The Knowing

The Deceiving

The Reckoning

The Fault

Stand-alone Psychological Thrillers

The Memory Closet

The Last Safe Place